WHEN MY SHIP COMES IN

Essex, 1959. Flo earns her money as a scrubber, cleaning the cruise ships and dreaming of a day when she might sail away from her life in the Dwellings, the squalid tenements of Tilbury docks. The Blundell family is evicted from home and Fred, Flo's husband, finds work in a factory town set up to look after its workers. Suddenly, it seems like everything is on the up. But when Flo's abusive husband Fred starts drinking again, he jeopardises everything. Flo must decide if she should fight to keep her family together, or strive for the kind of life she could have when her ship comes in.

WHEN MY SHIP COMES IN

WHEN MY SHIP COMES IN

by

Sue Wilsher

Magna Large Print Books
Long Preston, North Yorkshire,
BD23 4ND, England.

British Library Cataloguing in Publication Data.

A catalogue record of this book is
available from the British Library

ISBN   978-0-7505-4520-4

First published in Great Britain in 2016 by Sphere

Published in Large Print 2018 by arrangement with
Little, Brown Book Group Limited

Magna Large Print is an imprint of Library Magna Books Ltd.

Printed and bound in Great Britain by
T.J. (International) Ltd., Cornwall, PL28 8RW

For Audrey and Sid

Acknowledgements

Thanks to: My wonderful agent, Laura Longrigg at MBA for making this happen; Maddie West, Deputy Publisher at Sphere for connecting with the book, signing me and making my dreams come true; Thalia Proctor, Mari Roberts and the expert team at Little, Brown for getting the book into shape; my writing group for their years of support, feedback and education, with special thanks to Alison Burnside and Tanya Gupta and our gin-fuelled writing retreats; beta readers Shapla Hodges, Lorraine Fitzgerald, Charlotte Haynes, Lele Gemma and Mark Wilsher; Joan Dawson, Brian Roe, Betty and Jeff Lee, Lucie and Mick Block and Doris Bailey for their inspirational memories; the East Tilbury Bata Conservation Area for providing the inspiration for the setting of the book's fictional factory town; May Rippingale and Rhys Jones from the Bata Heritage Centre and the Centre's fantastic archive and documented memories that helped inspire the sense of place and time; Annie O'Brien and the wonderful Tilbury and Chadwell Memories project; Lynda Viccars, Cruise Terminal and Community Liaison Manager, for the tour of Tilbury Docks; friends and family for their interest and encouragement; the Mumsnet Facebook writing group, with special shout-out to Fay Jessop; Abraham Maslow for his Theory of Human Motivation; the 1959 West Ham team for using the East Tilbury Bata pitch for pre-season practice and unwittingly appearing in my novel (with apologies for the fictional injuries – but you did thrash them in the end); the wealth of fine social history on the library bookshelves that enabled me to imagine what it might have been like to live in fifties Britain (with inevitable inaccuracies on my part); last but not least, Kevin for vital football input, support and invaluable feedback when forced to read rough first drafts and Mia and Molly for loving that I'm published. Finally, my thoughts go to the real working class women of fifties Britain, especially those for whom the times changed too slowly.

1

Tilbury Docks – January, 1959

Five black beetles scattered when Flo Blundell lifted a rusty Oxo tin from the larder. Their green iridescence flickered into a dark corner. Flo didn't flinch; the tenement flat was riddled with them. The tin was good and heavy. She added that week's shilling and frowned, put her hand to her throat. The thick smell of the cold chip pan hung in the damp air, congealed lard, brown and speckled from use. She re-shelved the tin and ran for the only bedroom in the cramped flat, fell on to her knees, pulled the chamber pot from under the bed and spewed a rod of bile, sharp and hot, into the slops from the night before.

The muted bass tone of a ship's horn rolled off the river. Flo swallowed away the acid in her throat, swiped at her wet mouth and tucked a clump of blonde hair back into her headscarf. She stood to think for a moment, bit her thumb-nail and spat out a fragment in the direction of the pot. The clock on the mantle ticked. She stared at it, reckoning how many times she had been on her knees at the pot recently. And how long she had left to consider her position.

Her knitting bag sagged on top of the two apple crates Fred had nailed together for a cupboard. Knitting needles poked out of a ball of red wool like two fingers up. Flo wiped her nose upwards with the palm of her hand and leant over to pull one out. The pale turquoise-painted steel was smooth and cold as she drew it through her fingers.

Flo closed her bedroom door and lay down on the lumpy horsehair mattress. The cotton sheets were cold on her bare legs. Outside a seagull screeched and she imagined its open mouth and bulging eyes. She reached overhead to grip the iron bedstead, her other hand held the needle between her thighs and she blinked to try to focus on the dirty green floral wallpaper. The edges were unstuck and curled away from the wall. Rusty brown bed bugs crawled in and out of the opening; the wallpaper moved with the energies of the nest behind it. Their musty almond scent mingled with the ashes in the empty grate. She fumbled with her knickers and the needle, her body clenched as its coldness touched her skin.

'Mum?' A voice called from the other room.

Flo jolted, pulled down her dress and slid her legs off the bed.

Eight-year-old Mikey opened the bedroom door, wheezing, his greasy brown hair hung in the shape of a pudding bowl over outgrown back and sides.

'What you doing home?'

'Mr Greenwood says I have to have a bath.'

'Oh for god's sake.' Flo gestured for him to come over, sniffed at his head and wrinkled her nose, looked at his legs and short grey school trousers filthy with a week's dirt. Thank goodness he hadn't come in ten minutes later. She was glad

14

he'd disturbed her, she knew of more failures than successes in that regard. And not just that it hadn't worked either – Maureen Palmer had been found in her back garden in a pool of blood. Mikey's eyes searched hers for an answer to his dilemma.

'Oh stay off then, it's your Friday wash tomorrow.'

Mikey jumped in the air and whooped, then frowned and pointed at the knitting needle in Flo's hand.

'What's that for?'

'What do you think it's for?' Flo pushed past him into the living room. 'I'm off to work. Don't answer the door in case it's the School Board man.'

Flo tugged on her coat and thought twice. 'No, you can go and sit with your nan for a bit.'

She ushered him into the flat next door, peered into the gloomy front room that was fogged with cigarette smoke.

'All right, Mum?'

Ella Walker sat bundled in blankets and chin-to-toe winceyette in her fireside chair. She shifted and grunted in response. From the threshold, her perpetually hair-netted rollers gave her head the appearance of a savoy cabbage on a gnarled stalk.

'Here's Mikey to sit with you. I'm off to work.' Flo nudged him inside and pulled the door shut on the flat she was born in thirty years ago. She liked to think of her fingerprints on that door over the years, starting low down and getting higher and higher.

Outside, the whistle of gulls and clang of steel

were amplified. Flo stood for a moment in the salty biting air, closed her eyes and took a deep breath. She hugged her coat around her and hurried along the fourth-floor landing of the long, stone building known as the Dwellings. Wet washing marked with soot smuts slapped in the cold wind along the communal balcony. She held a damp sheet back, leant against the wall for a view of the docks. The lattice booms of black cranes and blue gantries jutted upwards across the skyline, gesticulating in all angles, dangling nets, hooks and winches. Vast grain silos and grey corrugated storage sheds towered above the dock wall. And over by the landing stage sat the immense white and yellow Orient Line SS *Orion* cruise ship in dock. Flo tutted, she was late.

Quickly through the docks entrance and she darted into the gatehouse to clock on. Reg the gatekeeper, bundled in pea coat and wind-beaten skin, stood smoking with one foot up on his desk.

'Hello, beautiful. Heard your Fred's in a ditch again, love.' He smiled and shrugged.

Flo closed her eyes and sucked in a breath.

'Best get him up, the flour boat's in the lock, get him over to Western if he wants the work.'

'Thanks, love,' she said, glancing up at the gate clock. 'At Eastern, is he?' Reg nodded. She started to sprint to the Eastern quayside, knowing where he would be. The dockmaster's office loomed on the left. She veered around then picked up the pace and raced to the grassy outskirts of the dock.

The River Thames stretched out before her, washed around the pilework jetties and slopped up the mud banks, a grey expanse that lay between

Essex and Kent, the industries of those counties competing for air, their smoke and chimneys cluttering the sky.

There he was, asleep on his back on the dusty grass, three feet in from the sea wall, his blood ale-warmed. One good kick and he'd be over. She strode across to him, a big meat carcass, his flat cap drawn down over his eyes, his open mouth emitting phlegmy snores. She picked up a long stick and prodded his neck. He growled and sat up with a jolt, his cap dropped to his lap and his black fringe flopped into his eyes. He frowned at Flo and then grinned, scratched his neck, rubbed the stubble on his chin with a slow rasp. That smile, even when he'd slept rough, was a remnant of what he had once been, a souvenir.

'The boat's in.'

'Eh? Oh Christ. Help me up then, woman.'

He held a hand up to her. She took it and gave a half-hearted tug. He pulled her down and, reacting too slowly, she lost her footing and toppled over on to him. His big hands pressed her body against his crotch.

'No, Fred, get off.'

'Ah come on, there's no one about.' Up close his breath was a sick-sweet booze tang, the corners of his mouth clotted with curdled spit. He laughed and pinned her arms to her sides. As she squirmed and struggled to get free, her head butted his jaw. She heard his teeth knock together.

'Shit.' He pushed her off. She bumped against a disused mooring bollard and jumped up ready to run, rubbing her shoulder. 'Stupid cow,' he said under his breath, reaching for his tobacco tin.

Flo hesitated. 'It wasn't on purpose.' He eyed her, too hung-over to get up. 'See you at dinner time,' she said, uncertainly, and took her chance to walk away, heading for the landing stage. At a safe distance she turned back to see him stand up and pull his cap on. She was satisfied he'd go over to Western for the call to work.

The cruise-liner terminal loomed up before Flo, a long brown-brick building emblazoned with *Port of London Authority* and topped with a turquoise cupola. The behemoth that rose up behind it was the SS *Orion,* a vessel inconceivably immense. Her corn-coloured hull, white decks and terraces, her single funnel in the heavens, her mast pricking the hand of God. In all her years Flo had never ceased to be awed by the sheer scale of these structures. Dock workers scurried, readying her for the next voyage to Australia. She was a migrant ship, ferrying the ten-pound poms to a new life. The land of tomorrow: opportunity, good wages, sunshine, sport and a wonderful future for your children. And all for £10 with assisted passage. Children go free.

She ran along the quayside, spotted the weather-hardened foreman. The cold wind fussed with his dark work suit, wiped his stoical face.

'Sorry I'm late, Jerry, my Mikey's not well.' A little white lie to keep her out of trouble.

Narrowed eyes peered from the peak of his cloth cap, appraised Flo's bosom. 'Go on then, get your bucket. Starboard gallery.'

'Thanks, Jerry.' She ducked into the shed to grab a white tin bucket of cleaning materials and trotted up the gangway into the belly of the ship.

Flo was a 'Tilbury scrubber', cleaner of the cruise ships. The liner was luxury travel, first class, ferrying emigrants in the decks beneath those occupied by the top-notch passengers. Swimming pools and promenades and first-rate food in air-conditioned dining rooms. She hurried through the passageway of the lower deck, clanged up the stairway and stepped out on to the parquet floor-ing of the passengers' gallery that was set with curved sofas, large round woven rugs and a long chromium and glass bar. Flo often rehearsed how she would tell the kids her plan to join the ten-pound poms. It'd be like going on holiday, they'd have a cabin and eat in the dining room. Mikey would love it, and it would get him out of their damp tenement that aggravated his chest, away from the bed bugs that bit him and the rats that sometimes gnawed his toes in the night.

The girls she wasn't so sure about. Babs might go for it, if she could tear herself away from that ruinous Billy. Babs's twin sister Jeanie was the difficult one. Not that she was talking to Flo or Fred. She'd been in a five-year sulk for some reason and walked around like she was waiting for the next war. Flo polished the coffee tables and wiped the Bakelite ashtrays, slipped into her familiar dream. She'd tell the children at the last minute so as not to alert Fred. She'd tell them about the ship first, the swimming pools and food, the sports deck and lounge. Then Australia, the sunshine and the beaches, the better life. And she'd tell them Fred would come later when he had the money. Although she worried that he would.

But Fred had put paid to all of it without even knowing. She scrubbed the rug harder, biting her cheek. It had all gone to hell.

'Flo?'

Beryl came running through the ship's gallery with her tin bucket, her grey cardigan flapped away from her floral pinafore, her cat-eye spectacles bounced off her nose and dangled from a chain around her neck.

Beryl had started it. *Take the kids and your mum,* she said, *don't tell Fred.* Flo had laughed it off at first. Everyone had problems, it wasn't done to go around mouthing off about them. But Beryl knew – she'd pull her chin back and her eyebrows down, mumble things like *He's quick with his hands* – and Flo didn't openly admit it, but she let her guard down a bit. And she started to save her shilling a week, a lot when you're on the debtors' list at the butchers. On a list in the window, the tight bastard. Beryl mentioned that too, cheeky cow. *But you're all working, how come you're on the list?* Beer and bets don't come free, that's why. The dream of Australia kept her going, it got the spuds peeled for tea and gave her a reason to lie there while Fred took his husband's rights. She couldn't let the dream go, couldn't have another child with him, just didn't have it in her.

'Quick, love, something's up.' Beryl rushed past Flo, then rushed back, clattered Flo's polish and rags into her bucket and dragged Flo up by the arm.

'What is it?' Alarmed, Flo jogged along to keep up with her friend.

'A fire, over on Western, a fire on a ship, they're

sinking it.'

Flo tutted and slackened her pace, put her hand on Beryl's arm.

'What is it?' Beryl frowned and looked along the corridor.

'I'm expecting.'

Beryl's sweaty excitement faded. She replaced her glasses on to her nose and peered into Flo's face, glanced down at her stomach. 'You sure?'

Flo nodded. 'Been sick every day for two weeks.'

'But you can still come, can't you?'

'How can I, Bels? Would I even pass the medical if I wasn't going with him?'

Beryl reached for Flo's hand and held it against her. They had been friends long enough to make some assumptions, a friendship like that gives you certain rights, it lets you say things you wouldn't dream of saying to anyone else. And if you happened to be a woman, you were used to making unalterable decisions, you had to. 'Look, maybe it's best if, you know...'

'Get shot of it? Yeah I know but that's all my money, isn't it?' Flo snapped, looked helplessly at her friend. 'I've been saving that up for ages.'

'Look, it'll be all right, drink some gin, have a hot bath, I bet it'll be all right. Then, just think, when we're in Australia, you'll meet a nice fella, you'll be a posh housewife with a twin tub and all, a proper little homemaker who doesn't have to work, you'll cook nice dinners for him and look so pretty, just like in the magazines.'

'I'm married, Bels, did you forget?'

'I know, but when you're over there you can say you're a widow, no one'll know, will they?' Beryl gave her a conspiratorial elbow nudge as if she'd concocted a brilliant plan. Flo shook her head. It was pie in the sky. Four more of the charwomen rushed past them, their white tin buckets clanging.

'Come on, let's go and see.' Flo let Beryl pull her along by the hand. They made their way over to Western dock, where a cargo vessel was berthed to be unloaded. The boat had caught fire, the entire superstructure burning and doomed. Flames slid along the decking, thick smoke boiled upwards and whorled around the dock.

In the next berth a flour ship was being discharged of its cargo. The dusty white dockers ran about, the dock-master bellowing orders for them to help with the fire, his face flushed red against his grey moustache. Several hoses pumped water in to sink the burning ship. It looked like she'd go down any minute. The hold was already well under, the cargo flooded, pulling her down. One side dipped below the surface, the water pooled on to the upper deck and pushed the boat under, a rush of water flooded each side and met together with a clamorous slosh. The fire fizzed away, acrid smoke stung Flo's nose. Just the funnels and mast protruded from the water.

Beryl elbowed Flo. 'There's your Fred, look.'

He stood quayside peering down into the dock, dusted head to foot with flour. He took off his cap to smooth back his black hair and stared harder into the water. Flo followed his gaze, squinted her eyes at what looked like little black balls floating about in the dock.

'Oi, give us a sack,' Fred cried out. Another

22

docker passed him a flour sack and Fred stepped back, took a run up and jumped in.

'What the hell's he doing?' said Beryl. They ran to the dockside, leant over with the others, waiting. Fred popped up to the surface and raised his hand, with a big grin he held up two dead black eels, his hair pasted down over his eyes. Everyone pointed and laughed. 'It's the sugar,' someone shouted. 'The sugar cargo.' The dead eels bobbed head-first to the surface in their hundreds. Fred trod water to stuff them into sacks, passing them to men who hung off the dock-wall ladders.

The dockers were chuffed. They would all be having eel for dinner. Fred finally climbed out and sat down, dripping wet on the wooden boards. The men laughed and slapped him on the back.

Flo didn't laugh. Fred grinned over at her, held up an eel. She turned and walked away.

'What time do you call this?'

Babs waltzed in, late as usual and there was me making pasties in the stockroom.

'Yeah, all right, not short of words when it's just me, eh?'

She took off her Teddy girl jacket, which was really just Granddad's old suit taken in, and peered into her compact, fancying herself, while I stuffed minced meat and onions into folded circles of pastry.

You wouldn't know she was my twin. The pretty one. Everyone thought she was older than me but we were both fifteen. She set and curled her hair into that silly Teddy quiff and ponytail, wore eyeliner, made clothes. Long and lank, that's what

Nan always said *my* hair looked like. Mr Purvis liked having Babs front of house, I was usually stuck out the back doing the donkey work. He said about me: 'She don't talk much but she weighs and counts a blinder.' So what? Any idiot can weigh a bag of bloody flour.

'Billy been in yet?' said Babs, pinning Nan's cameo brooch over her top blouse button and pretending she didn't care whether he had.

Making sure she was watching, I pulled a hair out of my head and coiled it down on to the mince and onions. I folded the pastry over and pressed the edges with my thumb to seal the pie.

'Nope, but here's his pasty all ready.'

'Jeanie, you're bloody disgusting, you are.' Babs hissed into my face and pushed the side of my head. 'You jealous or something?'

I just smiled and cut another bit of pastry, happy I'd made a dent in her annoying cheeriness.

The bell over the shop door jangled. Babs smoothed back the sides of her hair and pulled her white pinny on.

'This might be him,' she squealed.

'I'm telling Dad you're going out with that Teddy boy.'

'You better not, you rotten cow.' She snapped at me but she knew I wouldn't tell, it weren't like I was even talking to Mum and Dad anyway. Then she looked sly like she knew something I didn't. 'I'm gonna move in with him.' She stuck two fingers up at me, swung round and disappeared into the front shop.

My guts turned over. She wouldn't do that, silly cow, get herself in trouble. Not even to get away from Dad.

Something in the corner of the stockroom caught my eye. A greyish lump in the mousetrap. I nudged the trap with the toe of my shoe into the middle of the floor beneath the dangling light bulb and squatted down to see. A little mouse. At least it was dead, poor thing. Better than being trapped and alive. Like me in that job. The trap had come down on its middle, its belly had split. It was gory but that didn't bother me. I knew from my medical book out the library that they were the intestines and that might have been the tiny liver.

The shop bell rang three times, so I had to go out the front to serve. Dodging the open sacks of flour and dried prunes on the floor, I ducked round the side of the curtain and stood behind the counter next to Babs who was serving Mrs Bent. Noting down a box of Lux in the book for Mrs Proctor was Mr Purvis. Spare pencil stub stuck to the side of his meaty head, white coverall buttoned up over the grey chalk-stripe demob suit he wore every day. His shop stood on the corner of Dock Road and The Broadway, opposite Tilbury Dock train station. You couldn't miss it.

An old bag called Mrs Juniper marched over to my counter, bashed her wicker basket down on the glass top. She was a piece of work that one.

'Two of flour,' she ordered, squinting at her shopping list and not even looking at me.

The doorbell rang. It rang twice, and I looked over when it rang a few more times like it had gone doolally. Babs did a stiff double take, packed up Mrs Bent's basket and leant against the counter.

Billy Moss stood by the open door in his Teddy boy get-up. High-necked white shirt with bootlace tie, long grey drape jacket, which he must have bought on the never-never. Pale blue drainpipe trousers showed his bright green socks sticking out of his stupid scuffed brothel-creeper shoes with the sole flapping off.

The swanky Ted with his big greasy quiff and duck's-arse hairdo smirked around at us all. He thought he was something else. And so did Babs. He swaggered over to our counter and fingered the watch chain strung across his waistcoat.

'How are my two beauties today?'

He had some nerve. Babs looked at the counter and giggled. I went bright red and stood on her toe.

Eyeing Billy, Mrs Juniper talked at me out the side of her mouth. 'Windolene and tin of peaches.'

The wooden stepladder made a right racket when I dragged it along the floor. I climbed up to the Windolene on the highest shelf.

'Hmph, no stockings in this weather?'

The old bitch. Everyone stared at my legs.

'Here, what's them two pipe cleaners sticking out the bottom of your skirt?'

Bloody Billy. Babs burst out laughing. I wished I could turn into a beetle, fly away and burrow into the flour sack. I tried to reach out for the Windolene, the ladder wobbled and I grabbed on to the nearest shelf, knocked a tin of evaporated milk off. It bounced outwards, landed on the stacked cans of stewed steak and gravy on the counter in front of Mrs Juniper. You'd have thought she'd been shot in the arse. She patted her chest and blew out her cheeks. Mr Purvis rushed forwards to apologise, giving me a dirty look. I grabbed the damned Windolene and creaked back down the steps. Billy and Babs were in stitches. Mr Purvis shot Babs a look and she soon straightened up.

'And what can I help you with, sir?' She bit her lip to stop herself from laughing.

'Five of your best Woodbines, if you don't mind, madam.' Billy bowed low, pretending to tip his hat.

Babs opened a pack of twenty, counted five cigarettes into a paper bag.

'Would you like a little something on the house, Mrs Juniper? For the shock?' Mr Purvis put his hand on a glass jar of sherbet lemons.

Her eyes shone, but she kept her mouth dragged down at the corners and gave a pathetic nod. The sweets clanged into the weighing pan, two ounces, Mrs Juniper coughed, three ounces. Her fingers wormed into the paper bag while it was still on the counter.

As Billy took his bag of cigs off Babs, he put his hand over hers.

'Fancy the pictures tonight?'

Babs tried to stop a big grin from spreading across her face. 'Yeah, go on then.'

'*Rock around the Clock* down the Bug Hutch. At seven. What you reckon?'

Babs nodded and gave me a sideways smile. She was mad going out with him. I tried to kick her ankle but missed. The doorbell rang.

'*Dad,*' I hissed to Babs. We both stood rigid. Babs pulled her hand out from under Billy's, who hadn't seen him yet. Dad came into the shop looking like he'd slept rough. He strode over to our counter and stopped to see the after-trace of Billy's hand on Babs's. The guilty look in her eye, the bombshell that went off in Billy's face when he turned to see Dad standing next to him. Billy fumbled in his trouser pocket for a shilling, clicked it on to the counter and turned on his crepe heel. Dad watched him go, a hand-rolled fag clamped between his lips.

'What can I get you, Dad?' Babs said it brightly like he was an idiot.

'Box of Swan.'

Mr Purvis had the matches on the counter before Babs could reach for them. Dad slid his penny across and kept his finger on it, fixed his eyes on Babs. My guts dropped, she was in the shitter for sure. Once he'd got his message home he took his finger off and left the shop without saying anything.

'Decent young ladies should be careful about the company they keep,' said Mrs Juniper, slurping the spit off her sweet. 'And *you'll* never meet a nice boy with that expression, young lady.'

She said it to me and Babs spluttered a spiteful laugh and pushed past me into the stock room. My face burned hot and I started stuffing the bags into Mrs Juniper's basket, didn't care when she tutted and fluffed herself up. All of a sudden Mrs Juniper gripped the edge of the counter and stared at me like her eyes would pop out. I covered my smile with my hand. Babs must have seen the mouse in the back room. Screamed her head off, didn't she.

A week later and Flo stood in the great Customs House baggage hall without her bucket and without her pinafore. Beneath the lofty arched ceiling people rushed around her, high excited voices shot through the air and ricocheted off the walls. A porter shouted *mind your backs* and wheeled a trolley of suitcases with Australian shipping labels out on to the quayside. Children ran about the brown brick pillars in games of tag, dodging away from mothers' hands snatching at their collars. Hems of best dresses peeked out from smart winter coats, necks were scrubbed clean and hands were gloved.

Outside, the SS *Orion* thundered a bass note reminiscent of the earnest Welshman in the Sally Army choir. A fresh wave of energy came over the passengers and officials, the scurrying increased and more feet headed out on to the landing stage. Flo followed them, stood out in the hard wind and looked up at the great yellow wall before her that obscured the river and the sky. The wall was punctured with a line of port holes, above which were upper and lower decks partitioned into promenades edged with white iron railings.

The first-class passengers were already ensconced in their luxury rooms, somewhere Flo went only to clean the lavs and ashtrays. Those who had bought assisted passage crowded along the lower deck prom. The children stood upon the railings, hanging over to wave and shout. Thick mooring ropes were strung across from the ship to the dock. The towering mast fluttered with bunting and the lifeboats hung above like fat yellow beetles threatening to descend upon Flo's head.

The remaining passengers boarded, their feet clattered up the metal gangway. Flo pulled her coat tighter around her, slipped one hand inside to settle on her belly. She searched the decks and strained her ears, shot up her arm when she saw Beryl waving at her from the lower deck. The two women imparted their goodbyes with silence and small smiles. Flo touched her bruised left eye, covered it with her fingers. She had told Fred about the baby several days before.

'Get the bath out,' he said.

They had pushed the tin bath close to the range and heated pans and kettles of water on the stove. Fred laughed while Flo's skin burned and he made her drink nearly a whole bottle of potcheen he'd got from a navvy down the Irish club. She was blind drunk and vaguely remembered him pulling her out and on to the bed, having his way with her before she passed out. As if that would have helped.

The bath and booze hadn't worked though and when nothing happened, they talked about it again. Fred had come in late from work, pissed off.

'Just have the damn thing and lay over it.' He said it as naturally as anything, as though it wouldn't be killing a tiny baby on purpose.

'Go and see the old missioner,' he said later. 'He does it for six guineas. Lend the money from your mother, I bet she's got a bob or two stashed in her mattress.'

Flo knew her mum had some savings, had hoped it was enough to fund her own passage to come with her and the children, but she'd never tell Fred that.

'But the missioner is a dirty old man who'd likely scrape me to death after he'd had his fun.'

'I'll come with you, won't I,' Fred had insisted.

Flo had pretended to borrow the money from her old mum, but instead had raided her precious Oxo tin. Her savings for a new life with the children, away from him. Fred arranged it and she waited for him to come home when it was time, but he didn't. She walked on her own in the dark to the run-down house on the corner of Calcutta Road and Dock Road, made her way through the piled rubbish and post-war scrap in the bombed-out back garden. She had brought the bottle of potcheen and downed the remaining few mouthfuls, remembered what Fred had said about laying over the baby, and rapped on the back door of the lean-to. The missioner, a moth-eaten green cardigan hanging from his skinny shoulders, let her in without a greeting. His greedy eyes roved her body as he ushered her into the back room with a wave of his fingerless gloves.

There was a wooden table in the middle of the room covered with a green army tarpaulin. No proper curtains but the nets were brown with dirt and obscured the window well enough. Flo pulled her coat tightly around her and shivered. Effigies of Jesus hung around the room stared down at her.

'Well?' said the missioner in a whispering voice. His scraggly grey hair hung to his shoulders, his watery eyes wide. Flo noticed his long fingernails and nicotine stains when he took a drag from his cigarette.

She stared back at him and with a jerk reached

31

into her pocket for the money, handed him a paper bag of change. The corners of his mouth twitched as he took the bag and set it down on a sideboard. He spoke in a laborious rasp.

'There is a strong likelihood you shall need to go to hospital after I have helped you with your little problem.' His mouth twitched again. 'You may need blood and medicine to prevent sepsis.' He watched for her reaction. Flo gritted her teeth and said nothing. 'If asked, you will say you think you have miscarried.'

He paused, his bloodshot eyes scrutinising her. 'I know plenty of people in this town who will come after your family if you reveal my name. And remember, God is watching you. Is this understood?'

Flo nodded and tried not to cry.

'The doctors will guess what has happened but will treat you without contacting the authorities, that is what usually happens. If you tell them the truth you will be sent to prison.'

Flo nodded again. The musty room made her lightheaded as if she was in a dream, her skull seemed to melt and her mind leaked out of her head and filled the space around her.

'Please disrobe and lie down,' he said, indicating the table with his cigarette. He removed his woollen gloves and tied on an oilcloth apron, similar to those worn in the butcher's shop. As she pulled off her dress she could feel his eyes on her, and hesitated, kept her slip on and removed her briefs with modesty. The table was high, she climbed up on to its hard surface and lay down, pulled her slip up over her thighs and cradled herself with cold arms.

'Shall I tie down your arms or will you stay put and keep quiet?'

The old missioner ruched the skirt of Flo's slip upwards to her waist and eyed the new subject on his kitchen table. She flinched when he gripped her ankles, pushed them apart and towards her body, making her knees bend.

'Stay put,' she whispered. She wasn't at liberty to ask him why he didn't wash his hands or wear surgical gloves and she turned her head away sharply when she saw that he held what looked like a long metal pickle spoon.

Back on the quayside a four-piece brass band started up. Flo shook her head to dislodge the image of the missioner and found Beryl's face along the crowded railing. She started to cry, she couldn't help it. Beryl gripped the rail and leant forward, pressed her hand over her mouth, and her face crumpled too.

The brass band played 'Rule, Britannia!' The image of the missioner sprang back, as it had done since, how he had prepared her for the procedure, getting inside, whilst his cigarette burned away in an ashtray on the instrument table. Her body clenched and she pushed her nails into her palms when he inserted his fingers and his implements. He whispered things to himself too low for her to hear. Then the pain, whatever he did, the scraping pain that she bore without any help. She held her breath and thought about Mikey. One day she'd get him out of that tenement and somewhere better, and she'd get away from Fred's fist, they all would.

When she opened her eyes she saw the top of the missioner's head, the balding pate with the scraggly grey hair hanging down on to her and she cried out with pain and bit down on her fist when he told her to shut up. She looked up at Jesus on his cross hanging there on the wall with his cheek on one shoulder and tried to find comfort in him.

Finally the missioner had straightened up. Wiping his fingers on his butcher's apron he told her to stand and keep hold of the rags stuffed between her legs. He draped her coat around her shoulders and told her to call an ambulance from Calcutta Road, guided her towards the door with his hand on her back and closed it silently behind her.

Flo stood on the lamp-lit pavement and let out one sob, ground her teeth against the pain and the cold. She felt dizzy but made herself walk. Holding the wet rags in place between her legs she shuffled along, glad it was dark. She stumbled and put out a hand into space, shook her head and blinked, took another step and went down on one knee.

She woke up beneath clean white sheets and the glare of electric lights in Orsett Hospital. They told her she had lost her baby and was lucky to be alive and, just as the missioner had said, they asked no questions about what had happened. The knowing looks on their faces were terrible. Flo asked them to try calling the telephone box at the end of their street, but they told her no one knew where Fred was and she was driven home in an ambulance. Gripping the rail, she made her way slowly up the tenement stairs and into bed, waved the girls and

Mikey away when they came in asking for their tea.

Fred came stumbling in that evening, his cloth cap askew.

'Where you been?' he towered above her as she lay in bed, the smell of fags and booze coming off him.

'Missioner.' She flinched and tried a small smile, hoped for a word of comfort or praise.

'You went without me? You wanted to be on your own with that letch?'

'What? Don't, Fred, I need to rest.'

'Did you enjoy it?'

She realised in an instant she should have waited for him, made another appointment when he hadn't come home. In his eyes she saw revulsion that the missioner had touched her. She saw the memory of Fred's mother with another man. She stuttered, started to say sorry. Fred leant over her, his breath foul, the light in his eyes gone out. He was a boy following his mother to the pub to see who she had gone to meet.

He didn't need to draw back his hand when he struck her, the weight of his arm ensured good enough purchase to her eye. Flo sagged back against the pillow and turned her face away, unable to protect herself.

On the quayside, Flo fingered her bruised eye and watched the excited passengers. She might have been there on board with them, laughing and waving, might have swapped her white tin bucket for a suitcase. She'd be getting her old mum into a deckchair perhaps, or tutting and fussing over Mikey's scuffed shoes and Jeanie's sour expression, or consoling Babs about leaving that Billy. It was all done with. Her Oxo tin had been gutted for the abortion money, not emptied for passage to Australia as a ten-pound pom.

A loudspeaker blared, *All passengers aboard, all visitors ashore,* and the brass band played 'A Life on the Ocean Wave'. The anchor chain emitted a deep rattling rumble as it was winched up, the sound startling a flock of gulls from the cupola on the terminal roof. The whistling and cheering from passengers and those dockside increased to a jarring blister of noise. Multicoloured streamers shot out from the promenade deck. Flo backed up and leant against the wall of the baggage hall. The waving hands and laughing faces blurred into one moving image, the din of excitement made her head ache. She couldn't bear to wipe her eyes and refocus on the ten-pounders flapping their handkerchiefs side to side, couldn't bear to think about the swimming pools and first-class food, how like a holiday it would be, and the new life waiting at the other end.

Dockers ran along the quayside slipping the mooring lines. There was a roar of pain as one of them trapped his hand in the rope, his fingers sliced off, and the terminal foreman and workers dashed over to crowd around him. The accident was lost within the occasion of departure. Flo took a breath as the hardworking little tugboat pulled the ship heavily away from the dockside. A great plume of black smoke puffed from the liner's enormous funnel and rose to the heavens. The ship's horn bellowed an impossibly low note and the ropes slipped into the water and trailed away.

2

'Here you go, Mum.'

Flo knelt at Ella Walker's feet, dipped a rag into a chipped enamel bowl of steaming water and dabbed at the red sores on her mother's ulcerated legs.

'Hot,' said Ella. She tutted and sucked her breath through a gap in her missing front teeth, her lips burnt brown from wedging a cigarette in there and falling asleep. She had the appearance of an aged hen. Her rollered head sat atop a scrawny neck, her large chest was wrapped in a patchwork blanket pulled tightly around her shoulders and her skinny ankles stuck out from the hem of her nightie. She had gammy legs and a cataract in one eye that caused her to squint, and she refused to believe you no longer had to pay for the doctor, so consequently never went.

'What's in the pie?' asked Ella.

'Mum, something's happened.'

Ella looked down at Flo, tightened her lips in anticipation.

'Babs, Barbara's gone.'

'Gone? Where?' Ella pushed her head forward and squinted. Flo kept her eyes down.

'To stay with her fella, that Billy.'

Ella shifted in her chair, lifted herself up several inches and sat down again with a groan.

'Well, you better go and get her then, hadn't

you? It's you all over again.'

Flo gave her a look but held her tongue. Her parents were used to the neighbours whispering, they had refused to bow to shame and lose their only daughter. Flo was grateful they hadn't kicked her out.

'I know, Mum, but Fred has to do it and he's why she left.'

The bedlam at home the night before. Flo sitting by the fire knitting a jumper for Mikey when Babs came home from the pictures.

'Where you been so late?'

'Just the pictures,' laughed Babs.

Jeanie poked her head through the box-bed curtain to see and they all turned as a coal ember spat out a jet of flame from the grate. A moment later the door flew open and Fred crashed into the room, drunk and out of breath. He took one stride over to Babs and grabbed her arm.

'You been out with that boy?'

Flo's knitting fell to the floor and Jeanie cowered back behind the curtain.

'No I haven't,' shouted Babs.

'Fred, please,' said Flo, out of her chair and pulling at his arm. 'Here, I'll make a cuppa.'

Fred dragged Babs through to the scullery. She slipped and tried to get to her feet.

'I saw you with that Moss boy,' he growled. 'What have I told you about him? You're fifteen, you little tart.'

'I didn't do anything, just went to the pictures.' Babs sobbed and shielded her face as Fred raised his fist and brought it down hard on her back, making a dull thud. She yelped and crumpled.

'Stop it,' Flo shouted. He let go of Babs's arm and turned on Flo, knocking Mikey's jar of sticklebacks off the shelf. It shattered on to the floor, tiny brown fish flapping in the water and shards of glass. Fred held Flo's head back by her hair, his arm high up behind him. Flo winced and tried to turn her face away but couldn't. The children waited, impotent and scared, and the long distinctive horn of a cargo ship carried on the wind from the docks.

'The boat's coming in,' said Flo, cringing. With a pause of realisation, Fred released his wife, let her down slowly to the floor and the broken glass. He straightened his cloth cap and strode out of the flat, slamming the door.

They all watched him go. Flo let Babs help her up, but avoided her daughter's eye and dusted the glass from her legs.

'He doesn't mean it, love.'

'How can you say that? He's a pig. I hate him.'

Flo's face twisted. 'It's the drink, that's all. Just remember he's your dad,' she said, blotting her bleeding leg with a rag. 'He's had a hard life, you know he has.'

'Well, I'm having a hard life – I'm gonna lodge with Billy and his mum.'

Flo winced at Babs's words. She reached out, gripped her daughter's arm. 'No, Babs. What, get in trouble like I did at your age? Over my dead body.'

Babs tried to pull away but Flo gripped harder.

'And what, marry him at sixteen? Or worse, get in trouble not married?'

Babs started crying.

'I'm no idiot, Babs, I bear it because I understand your father, I know what upsets him. Pro-
miscuous, know what that means?' Babs nodded.
'Infidelity? War? You know what happened to Nan
and Grandad. Your dad gets a rage he can't control.' *And the drink makes it worse,* she wanted to
add, *and he can't control that now either.* Mikey
called out from the bedroom and coughed.

'Mum? What is it?'

'It's all right, love.'

Flo released Babs's arm and pushed her away,
glaring. 'No more talk like that, do you hear?'

'Yes, Mum.'

In the bedroom Mikey lay on a mattress on the
floor next to his parents' bed.

'Go on, back to sleep now.' Flo closed the bedroom door and brought a bowl of cold water to
the armchair in the living room. Feeling for tiny
pieces of glass, she tended to her legs. She could
hear Babs crying in the box bed with Jeanie.
There was only just enough room for them both
to squeeze in there; they didn't mind in the winter
when it was too cold to sleep on the floor. They'd
always been close like that, since they were babies.
Flo stayed still, listening to their whispers.

'I hate him,' sobbed Babs.

'Me too,' said Jeanie. 'What was it like then?'

'Oh,' Babs sniffed and cheered up, 'there were
all these Teds and in one bit in the film they all
started going mad, jumping around and jiving in
the aisles, and Mr Richards was running along
with his torch shouting at them to sit down, and
they started pulling the seats out, it was a scream.'
She paused. 'And after, we went out the back and

he snogged me.' She giggled. 'And other stuff, you wouldn't know.'

Flo imagined a boy touching her baby and wanted to rip the curtain back and give Babs a clout around the ear. She'd have a talk about it with Babs tomorrow. She tried to remember what Ella had advised her at that age. Something about not leading boys on, not getting carried away, nothing about what boys actually want, those things are best not mentioned.

'You have to watch it, Babs, you'll get in trouble.'

'Oh, you're about as much fun as the bloody Bomb, you are,' said Babs, yawning.

When Flo came home the next day, Babs had gone, and so had her things.

'Do you know where he lives, I said?' Ella snapped her question.

Flo twitched and resumed bathing her mother's legs. She nodded.

'Is it that slattern Biddy Moss's boy? Get my coat, I'll go and get the little tart back.' She stood up and winced.

'Sit back down, you silly old bat, where do you think you're going with your legs?'

Ella fell back into her chair, adjusting the blanket around her shoulders.

'Well, what you gonna to do then? You can't leave her there. She'll get herself in trouble and then what?'

Flo shook her head and shrugged, put her head down and squeezed her eyes shut.

'Don't you start crying on me, my girl. You're made of stronger stuff than that. Always moaning, you don't know you're born.'

'It's not that, Mum. I did something terrible.' Tears slid down Flo's face.

'It's all coming out now, I know what you done.' Flo's eyebrows rose in alarm.

'And you're not the first nor the last woman to do it either,' she spat.

Flo wiped her face with her arm and looked gratefully at her mother.

'Fred hasn't been working much lately.'

Ella frowned. 'It's the drink, I bet. He'll never change, that's your lot, you chose it, you like it or lump it. But I tell you this for nothing, I'm not leaving my little palace if he gets laid off.'

Flo looked around the pokey flat her mother referred to. It stank of mildew and smoke. The walls and ceiling were dark brown from the fire and cigarettes, the pattern on the wallpaper could barely be made out. The only other arm-chair in the room was brought close to the fire, straight-backed with wooden arms, a cloth cap on the seat, no one allowed to sit there. A newspaper cutting of the Queen and Prince Philip on Coronation Day curled on the mantel next to a faded black and white photograph in an oval frame of Ella and her late husband.

Ella took on a defiant tone. She knew Flo had heard it before but she was going to say it anyway.

'Your dad brought us here when we got out the workhouse. My knight in shining armour. We had our own rooms and food on our table and we was grateful for it.' Ella banged the side of her fist down on the arm of the chair, just like her husband used to do. 'And we had you and we kissed you every night before you went to sleep, because we knew what it's like when you don't get them kisses.'

'I know, Mum,' said Flo softly.

'Oh you know, do you?' snapped Ella. 'When I was your Mikey's age, younger even, I was put to work at the mangle, folding sheets and getting beat with a splintered stick of wood if those sheets touched the floor. Six years old.'

'Yes, Mum.'

'Yes, and you go moaning about this and that, you should thank your lucky stars for what you got. Keep the family together, that's priority.'

'Fred won't get laid off anyway, he's a docker through and through,' said Flo, reaching for her mother's pack of cigarettes and lighting one for her. Ella took a puff and leant back into her chair. Flo wrapped clean dressings around her mother's thin legs and put her feet back into her slippers.

'What's in that pie then?' Ella gestured with her cigarette.

'Sparrow,' said Flo, her eyebrows raised.

'It'll have a crunch to it then,' said Ella with a chuckle.

'I reckon it will.'

Fred Blundell pulled up his jacket collar against the easterly wind and stopped walking. Something brushed against his face in the dark. He looked up into the yellow sphere of light around the gas lamp on Dock Road and saw it was shot through with fat white clumps falling slantways. He lit a cigarette in his cupped hand and resumed his walk to the docks.

He nodded to Reg on the gate, who stood

smoking with one foot up on his desk. There was no need to clock on as his wife Flo did. He didn't know if he had a job yet. The work for dock labourers like him was only as good as the tide and the number of men needed. When the tide was in, whatever time of day or night, he could turn up for the call. If he was chosen for work, then he worked. If he wasn't, he didn't.

Fred's great-grandfather, Walter Blundell, was one of the original navvies who built the docks in 1882. At sixteen years old Walter had watched when they were first flooded with river water. Fred was the fourth generation of dockers in the family since then. His grandfather and father had worked there before him, it was tradition. They had all lived in the Dwellings, too. A tenement flat came with the job. Fred was a Blundell, and the Blundells were dockers.

Taking a shortcut he vaulted over the low wall by the Customs office and jogged to the Eastern dock. By the floodlights he could make out the dark bulk of the cargo vessel moving through the main dock from the lock. He squinted at the markings on her black funnels and made out two stripes of indiscernible colour, but could see a white diamond on the house flag and knew which berth to head for. He picked up his pace when he heard the rumble of voices. Rounding on to the Clan Line quay, alongside the foreman's hut, there stood around fifty men shuffling their feet in the cold, the quayside gas lamp animating their flat silhouettes, cigarette smoke rising in warm breath from snow-white cloth caps.

The door of the hut opened. Stan Winsford,

foreman of Eastern dock, stood on the top step with his pipe in his mouth. He considered the looming cargo ship, glanced up at the falling snow, took out his pocket watch and checked the time. Without seeming to move his lips he projected his deep voice around his pipe and over the heads of the men.

'I need two dozen men.'

At this, there was a clamorous scuffle amongst the labourers. They raised their hands, called out the foreman's name, jumped in the air. Stan picked out man by man, by name or by pointing the stem of his pipe. Fred balanced with one foot on a mooring bollard and waved his hand in the air, calling out, 'Stan, over here.'

Fred knew he'd be all right. Stan Winsford had known his dad, Morris Blundell. When Stan was on duty the Blundells always got called for work. He'd been in the war with Morris and after had made sure Fred got work as a dock labourer.

Twenty-two. Fred shouted louder, and the re-maining men jumped higher and pushed them-selves up by other men's shoulders. Twenty-three. Fred bellowed, 'Oi, Stan, over here, mate,' and waved his cap in the air.

Stan Winsford took a puff of his pipe, ran his eye over the remaining men and turned to put his hand on the door handle of the hut. Without looking back, he called out, his booming voice resigned and sombre.

'Fred Blundell,' and let himself back inside.

'Cheers, Stan,' shouted Fred. He jumped down from the bollard and sauntered over to the sheds to join the others. The unlucky ones spat on the floor and shuffled off, their cigarettes bobbing away into the darkness.

The black prow of the SS *Clan Allen* moved towards the men in the gloom. Mooring lines were thrown down and caught up by the dockers, five or six men on each rope, pulling her in, securing her tight to the bollards. Audacious rats, black and arched, ran along the ropes off the ship and disappeared into the cargo sheds with quiet efficiency.

Fred hung back inside the door of number thirty-four shed until the ship's holds were opened and the cranes and winches were in operation. He lit a cigarette and kept an eye on Stan Winsford's hut while he stuffed handfuls of loose tea from an open crate into a large bespoke pocket inside his jacket that Flo had sewn in for him. Pulling a jemmy off the rack he wrenched open a banana crate and helped himself, sitting down for a late supper, soaking up the three pints he'd had earlier. A brown Brazilian wandering spider crawled over the crate's edge, as big as his hand and deadly poisonous. Fred watched its progress to the floor and squashed it with the heel of his boot.

John Shelton, known as Shelto, rolled the first of the hogshead barrels of tobacco ahead of him into the shed. Fred put out his foot to stop the barrel.

'Ah now, that will do nicely,' he said, grinning.

Shelto pushed harder on the hogshead but Fred put out his hand.

'I said, that will do nicely. Now you just roll that birdy over there and let's say accidentally bust the top open, eh?'

46

'Bust it yourself, you bleeding slacker. Sitting there stuffing your cakehole, letting us do all the work.'

'Now then,' said Fred, jumping up off the crate. 'You're feeling off colour tonight, I reckon. Now do as you're told and bust that barrel.'

'Bust it yourself,' hissed Shelto, setting the barrel against a flour sack to keep it steady. Several other men were in the shed now. They stopped work when they saw the row.

Fred took off his jacket, rolled up his shirt-sleeves and grinned at Shelto, who looked like he wanted to rip Fred's head off, despite Fred's head towering above his own. The two of them went at each other. Shelto's fist caught Fred in the gut under the ribs. Fred, winded, doubled over but straightened up and laughed, grabbed Shelto's head under his arm and rammed it into the tobacco barrel.

'You'll do as a box knocker,' he shouted as the wood splintered with the force and the onlookers cheered. Fred let go of Shelto, who dropped to the worn wooden boards in the dust.

'So you're knocking the shit out of each other already, eh?' Stan Winsford's voice boomed, parting the onlookers. He came into the clearing and saw Fred standing over Shelto. A line of blood ran down Shelto's face from his hairline. Stan prodded him with his boot; he groaned and rolled over.

'In the office, now,' he said to Fred. 'See to that,' he ordered one of the men, indicating Shelto.

'What?' laughed Fred, shrugging his shoulders and holding up his hands. As Stan strode away, Fred coughed loudly and punched through the split crate, grabbed a handful of dried tobacco leaves for his other inside pocket and jogged after Stan.

The foreman sat at a little wooden table in his office, looked up at Fred standing before him.

'Empty your pockets.'

'What?'

'You heard me.'

Fred shrugged, turned out his trouser pockets, produced a few shillings, half a crown and a dirty handkerchief.

'Not those ones,' rumbled Stan, and pointed his pipe stem at Fred's jacket.

The smile dropped from Fred's face. He emptied the contents of his hidden pockets on to the table.

'It's cold, ain't it, son?' said Stan looking at the piles of tea and tobacco.

Fred gave a sullen shrug of his shoulders.

'There's a bad winter coming, son, and you've just been laid off.'

Fred's head jerked up. He laughed. 'You're joking, ain't you?'

'No. You'll never work in these docks again.' Stan eyed him.

'You can't do that, I'm a Blundell.'

'Yes, you are, and a sorry sight for your old dad.' He paused and straightened his back. 'I've done what I can for you, son, but you're no good, and it's no good keeping you here.'

'What, the fighting? I'll stop it.' Fred said it with a scowl, as if the solution was obvious enough.

'And the thieving.'

Stan sighed. 'It's the drink, son, you know that.

I can smell it on you. You're a danger to yourself and to the men. There's enough accidents around here without asking for them. And there's plenty of other good men who need the work.'

'Now look,' said Fred, putting his hands on the table and leaning down to Stan's eye level. 'You can't do it, I don't know nothing else.' Fred's eyes flickered. 'And what about my Flo and the kids?'

'I can do it, Fred. And you should have thought about that.' Stan blinked but held his gaze. He paused and took a puff of his pipe. 'I might know somewhere you can try. It's Monday's Leather along the river, you've heard of it. You go along there, but watch your manners, mind, they don't like wrong 'uns there. If you toe the line there's good money and regular work, maybe even a house for the family.'

Fred brought his fists down hard on the table, the tea and tobacco leaves bounced.

Stan jumped up. 'Now get out of here, I've done you enough favours. It breaks my heart to let you go, I don't mind saying that, your old dad...' He turned away and took out a match to relight his pipe.

'For Christ's sake.' Fred turned and kicked the office door with the flat of his boot. The force splintered the jamb and the door swung outwards on its hinges. He flung it back on his way out.

3

The posh voice on the wireless told Flo it was the harshest winter since 1684. The Big Freeze. In Tilbury the snow drifts stood higher than a man. Icicles three feet long hung from the outstretched hands of Jesus on the Our Lady Star of the Sea church porch. The deep water of the Essex Thames froze over for a good two hundred yards out from the shore and no boats could get down the river and into the docks. No boats meant no work. The rent hadn't been paid. There was ice on the inside of the windows in the flat and the eggs in the larder had frozen in their shells.

'Mikey, love, come here.'

Eight-year-old Mikey barked a croupy cough and looked up from his comic. 'Still got your sparrow traps out?' said Flo. Mikey nodded and coughed again, wiped his red nose on his sleeve.

'Tell me where they are, I need something to put in a pie.'

'Down the fort, off the road by the moat.'

Flo pulled back the curtain that shielded the box bed in the alcove. Jeanie sat in there, bundled in blankets, reading a library book.

'Jeanie, we're in trouble, love,' she whispered, perching on the bed. 'I know you give me your housekeeping but I need to lend any money you got, and I need you to pinch a couple of bits from the shop if you can do it without getting caught, all right?'

Jeanie stared at her mother through narrowed eyes.

'Look, love, isn't it about time you talked to me about what's wrong?'

Jeanie reached under her pillow for her little purse, took out the one pound and six she had saved and gave it all to Flo without speaking. Flo looked at the money and bit her lip. Tears flooded her eyes, she smiled at Jeanie and gripped her hand.

'Thanks, love, I'll give it back, honest.'

Jeanie pulled her hand away and carried on reading.

'Love, you know your dad hasn't given me the housekeeping for a long while. Now there's no work for me since the river froze, so I don't know what...'

Jeanie didn't look up from her book. Flo watched her for a minute and let her be.

There was a thick navy pea coat Fred had pilfered from somewhere. Flo wrapped herself in it, tied on a headscarf and buttoned some rubber galoshes over her shoes.

'I'm off out.'

Outside it was freezing. Taking sips of air that bit into her lungs, Flo hurried down the stairs and tried to stay steady on the compacted snow that hid the roads and kerbs and sat high upon every flat and sloping surface. It had suffocated the life out of the place. There were no babes in prams outside front doors, no bicycles or delivery vans going by, even the children had stopped playing out in the road. Everything stood still.

51

The ships' horns, clang of steel and shouts of men loading cargo had ceased. The sky no longer screeched with gulls, there was only the distant howl of a woman giving birth in the Dock Road terrace.

Flo kept her head down and crossed the bridge out to open country where the northern wind had blasted the snow into deep drifts, leaving a smooth white expanse. She didn't need to go as far as the fort to look for the sparrow traps. There were dead birds strewn about on the ground, dropped cold out of the trees, lying on their backs, stiff matchstick legs sticking up. She scooped up their hard little bodies and stuffed them into her coat pockets.

Fred hadn't been home for a day and a night. Flo hoped he was hanging around the docks sniffing for a bit of work. She turned into the dock entrance to look for him, headed over to the Clan Line quay. Stan Winsford was in his office with his feet up on the desk, smoking his pipe and muffled in a thick woollen coat.

'All right, Stan?'

'Flo,' he said, with a nod of his head.

'Fred about?'

'Nope.'

'No work?'

'Nope, not for him.'

Flo gave him a nervous smile. 'There's a boat in the dry dock. Wondered if he's over there doing something?'

'No he ain't.'

'Well, where is he then?' Flo laughed.

'On a bender more than likely. Ain't he told

you?' Stan puffed on his pipe and eyed her. 'I sacked him.'

Flo laughed. 'Eh?'

'He don't work here no more, Flo, I'm sorry, love.'

Flo's smile faded. She searched Stan's face.

'But, he's always worked here, Stan.'

'I know, love, and you know what he's like, I had to do it, I'm sorry. I told him where there's work. Over at Monday's, they're hiring for the leather factory.'

'Fred, in a factory? At that Monday's place? You've got to be joking, Stan, please.'

Stan shook his head, his eyes lowered. Flo let out a sob and left the office, ran down the deserted quayside alongside the frozen dock and made for the Bomb Crater social club by the dock entrance. She climbed the stairs and hesitated at the door, it wasn't done for women to go in there during the week. In a large room, a dozen or so men sat around in a cigarette soup, recreating the miasmic gloom outside. They stopped talking and turned their heads.

'All right, Flo love?' said Ron Plannard, who sat closest.

'All right, Ron? Seen Fred?'

He shrugged his shoulders and turned down his mouth, his hand-rolled cigarette dangling from his lip. Her heart beat sped up, she ran back down the stairs and stood outside shivering. The light was fading, her toes were numb, a soundless snow started to fall. Fred sacked, out of the docks. Everyone knew you only got to work there if your father had and his father before him. It was un-

53

thinkable, Fred would be out of his mind. She trotted alongside the rail track and on to Fort Road. The World's End public house appeared in the distance, standing alone near the river, *Charrington's Ales* painted in large white lettering across the roof. The wind coming off the water pushed the falling snow slantways, made her progress difficult. She leant forward into it.

A pocket of warmth from the open fire and the stink of stale beer and fag-ends greeted her as she came into the public bar. A silence fell over the place as the punters turned to stare.

Fred was there, slumped against the bar, alone, chinful of stubble and limp fringe, one hand wrapped around a pint glass of mild, his other hand rolling a boggie. Flo edged towards him, the other men went back to their drinks and banter. He looked at her through half-closed eyes.

'Fred, where you been?'

'Don't question me, woman,' he slurred, eyeing her. 'Do you want a drink or not?'

She shrugged. 'I haven't got any money to pay for it, Fred, have you?'

'Pint of wallop and a stout, Arthur, on the tab, mate.'

The landlord gave him a dirty look and pulled at the pump, slopped Fred's pint down on the bar. 'That's your lot, Fred.'

Fred pulled on his smoke and lifted his chin at the landlord, squinting his disapproval.

Flo poured her bottle of stout into a glass and took a sip, glad of it, and pulled up a bar stool. She too rolled a cigarette and took a deep drag, letting the nicotine flood her system and soothe her nerves. They sat in silence until at last he said in a thick slur,

'Well, then?'

'Well, then, you tell me, Fred. I went looking for you, and saw Stan.'

Fred's jaw shifted. 'I suppose he told you, the bastard?'

'What happened? A fight?'

'It's over. I'm finished there. Went back today and he told me to get lost. Told me if I went back he'd shop me.'

'What for?' Flo frowned.

He leant in towards her, whispered thickly into her face. 'The call-up.'

Flo gave a small gasp. 'He wouldn't, what and risk his own neck too?'

Fred shrugged and gulped his beer.

'Well, that's that then.' Flo flicked her ash on the floor. It was out of the question to risk being reported, the very idea made her stomach turn.

Fred put a hand over his face and made a strangled snorting sound. Horrified, Flo turned to check the other men hadn't seen.

'Christ, Fred, pack it in.' She pulled his sleeve. 'Come on, let's get out of here.'

His foot slipped off the bar-stool rung and he jerked sideways, then regained his balance. She'd never seen a man cry. There was something unsettling about it, as well as gratifying. After all, she had shed plenty of tears herself. She pulled his arm again but he had taken root. He rubbed his hand over his face as though he'd rub away his tears but they kept coming.

'What am I gonna do?' His deep voice caught

in a low sob. He pressed his palms into his eye sockets, elbows on the bar. Flo looked around in alarm. The other punters had fallen silent, were half looking at Fred and half looking at each other.

'For Christ's sake, Fred, come on.' She pulled him again.

He slipped off the stool and landed on one foot, righted himself and let her push him towards the door with one hand on his back and one hand steadying his elbow. Flo struggled to keep balance with his weight against her.

The icy wind dashed falling snow into their faces. Flo turned right to head home but Fred pulled away and stumbled towards the river, two hundred yards of dark marsh between him and the bank. She lunged to pull his arm back but couldn't deter him. He leant into the weather, his bulk propelling him forwards.

'Come back, you bloody fool.' Her shout was caught up by a howl of wind. She watched Fred's hunched back lumber towards the water, wondered whether he'd stop and turn around. She jogged to catch up with him, grabbed for his hand. He snatched it away and continued on.

'Oh, go on then, jump in and kill yourself.' She shouted the words with spite, the tendons in her neck bunching and taut. 'Leave us, leave your kids just like your own dad left *you*.'

He faltered and swayed on the spot, seemed unable to change course and dropped to the ground instead, one hand out to break his fall. Half frozen, Flo stood over him, put her hands in her pockets and pulled them out quick when she felt the dead birds in there, greasy feathers soft against frozen bodies.

'I'm nothing.' He ground the words in his teeth, chewed on them with disgust.

A dim light from the pub barely stove off the darkness. The black marshes all around, the river falling away on one side, frozen hard for a good way, lethally cold and deep further out. Flo looked at Fred on the ground and they could have been thirteen years old again. Thirteen and Fred swiping away his tears after the night of the air raid. *She left me to go and see her fancy man.* Flo had been squashed in the damp tenement basement with the others, the mould spores growing up the wall. She'd seen Fred's mum leave him and go outside. When Fred got up to follow her, Flo leant forward and wanted to tell him not to go. Everyone in the basement froze when the bomb hit somewhere nearby, put their hands over their ears and waited.

I followed her, Fred told her, *she went into the Anchor, I just remember the back of her coat disappearing inside.* The pub took a direct hit right in front of him and he never saw her again.

The next time Flo saw Fred, his big sister was shouting at him to take his evacuation orders but he wouldn't go. He started coming next door to Flo's mum Ella for his tea and confided in Flo, said he couldn't talk to anyone else. He clung to an unshakeable hope that everything would be all right once his dad was home from service. Flo blinked and they were sixteen and Fred's dad was found hanging by his neck in number twelve shed. Something broke in Fred and he couldn't seem to do a thing about it. Flo blinked again and Fred had a job at the docks. He'd found a way to cope, with a pint or two after work. He had sealed the bargain, the non-negotiable exchange. The drink gives comfort but demands loyalty. Whatever he had put Flo through, he had been through worse. He drank to forget and when he was drunk he sloughed off his burden on to her shoulders. She bore it for him.

'It's all right,' she said. He looked up, wiped his nose on the back of his hand. She bit back a sob, thought how you persist in life, get by without even realising how bad things have become. You get used to living a life not normal. Over the years she had learned to keep her mouth shut, but now was the right time to say something – when he was on his knees.

'I'm not stupid, Fred. I know I don't say anything but I know it's the drink, I know how much you need it and what it makes you do.'

He got to his feet with some effort, the wind pushing him easily off his spot. 'You reckon?'

'Yes, I reckon, and I can't stand it any more. How can I keep things going the way you treat us?'

'Oh, you as well? You're gonna shaft me as well?' He put his hands on his head, talking to himself and suddenly looked at her in alarm. 'You wouldn't leave me, Flo?'

Clumps of her blonde hair escaped her headscarf and dragged across her wet face. It was madness being out in that weather. For a mad second she felt like laughing. What choice did she have? Her savings for Australia all gone, and if she had no escape route, then what? *Keep the family together*, that's what her old mum always said. *Put up and shut up.* And that's what everyone else did around there.

She took a gentle hold of his coat lapels, moved in close. 'You need to stop drinking and get another job, Fred.' His jaw clenched, she fixed her eyes on his and kept her resolve. 'You need to get over what happened to your mum and dad' – at this he stiffened and pulled back, wrapped his arms around himself – 'you need to get over it without the drink, then we'll be all right, I know it.'

It was eight in the morning. The sun forecast its shy arrival with a tentative blush across the grey clouds heavy with more snow. Fred, clean shaven and washed, in flat cap and work suit, shirt and tie, trudged across the frozen Tilbury marshes. He kept the river to his right and Tilbury Fort behind him, the Kent side of the river still hidden in the dawn. His trouser legs were wet to the knee, a boggie hung on his lip leaving a long plume behind him that hovered for a moment before dissipating into the silence.

'Back end of nowhere,' he mumbled. After six miles or so, Coalhouse Fort appeared up ahead on the top of the hill. Fred veered left inland, through dormant wheat fields. The smell of manure and the low of cattle announced a gated entrance signed *Monday Farm and Dairy.* The fort loomed in the clearing mist, its battlements grey and austere, and clinging to the brow of the hill was St Catherine's church, its forgotten headstones leaning in the little churchyard.

Fred headed down the steep hill, dense wooded areas on either side of the road, turning his head when a clump of snow slipped from a branch and thudded to the ground. The trees cleared, the land flattened. Before him lay Leather Town, spread out like a surveyor's map. His first time there, Fred stopped still in the growing light to consider the view of the small town set out below him.

The whole place was Monday's. To his diagonal right, at the edge of the woods, was a large lido area, three outdoor bathing pools partly enclosed by a two-storey glass-fronted building. The road on which he stood went straight ahead through the whole place towards the rail line. Halfway down, the road was crossed by another, from left to right, lined with tall poplar trees, with a quadrangle and statue in the middle. On the left, the factory complex, three enormous rectangular buildings, all glass and concrete. The middle one featured a *Monday* sign on the roof, standing five feet high, smoke churning skywards from a large chimney. The road on the right stopped at a large box-shaped mansion house, with a football pitch behind it, evident from the grandstands along two sides. Beyond the mansion stood a hotel and a grid of around five hundred workers' houses.

Every structure, big or small, was cuboid shaped, flat-roofed, painted white with a thick black band near the top, *Monday* lettering stamped across it in white.

'Looks like a load of bloody shoeboxes,' said Fred. At the bottom of the hill he passed a coffee bar that sat alongside the road. It was open and empty, the light shone through the glass door with long diagonal chromium handles like banisters. He walked past a long low row of shops, all Monday's, on the left of the road: a shoe shop, a leather goods shop, a hairdresser's next to a barber's, a post office and a long supermarket, the likes of which Fred had never seen. He peered through the window and saw open shelves and displays standing in the middle of the floor.

In the centre of the quadrangle he looked up at the statue of Mr Monday senior, who stood smoking a pipe with his hands in his pockets, surveying the estate, all so neat and tidy, no rubbish, grass verges close cropped, the trees evenly spaced. Starlings chirped in the bare poplars, darting in and out of the swaying branches in synchronised groups, choreographed by the cold breeze. Mesmerised, he watched them, took off his cloth cap, smoothed back his hair, replaced his cap and relit his cigarette. He turned left and headed towards the factory gates.

The churn and rattle of machinery in operation became louder as he approached. The white-painted iron gates stood eight feet high, a squat glass and concrete gatehouse stood sentry on the right, a large clock on its flat roof. Fred looked in at the window. A thin, hatless, wily-looking man sniffed at him.

'Morning,' said Fred, nodding. 'I'm looking for work.'

The gatekeeper regarded Fred for a moment and sniffed again, as though checking the air for trouble. He handed a clipboard and pencil through the hatch. 'Fill this in.' Fred wrote his

61

name and reason for visit – *work*. 'Come round,' said the sniffer man. He left the gatehouse to open a door set within the main gate.

'You want the office, over there,' he said, unsmiling, and pointed to a large building signed *Administration and Services*, situated behind the gatehouse.

Inside the main door Fred rang a bell by a hatch in the wall and waited, looked around, unsure, and rang the bell again. The hatch opened and a thick-set man with indifferent eyebrows asked, 'Yes?'

Fred shifted on his feet and took off his cap. 'I'm looking for work.'

The man looked Fred up and down. 'Name?'

'Fred Blundell.'

'Hands.'

'Eh?'

The man pointed. 'Show me your hands.'

Fred pocketed his cap and held out his hands. The man looked at Fred's calloused palms, indicated that Fred should turn them over, and frowned at Fred's dirty fingernails and yellow nicotine stains.

'Sit through there and wait to be called.' The man flicked his hand towards a door opposite and closed the hatch.

Fred stepped into an empty waiting room lined with wooden chairs and sat down. The clock on the wall gave a loud tick as each second passed. The distant hum of voices and machinery vibrated through the room. The walls were bare, there was nothing to look at. Just a small table and an ashtray. No one else came in.

One hour and four cigarettes later. Fred paced the room, glanced at the door every few seconds, took deep breaths through ever-tightening lips. He took two determined strides towards the door and, just as he reached for the handle, it turned and a man walked in, drawing up short to avoid stepping on Fred's boots.

'Watch yourself there,' said the man with an amiable smile. He was a foot shorter than Fred, very neat and slim, not a speck of lint on his dark woollen work suit and a tidy Brylcreemed quiff. He held out his hand.

'Sid Bucknall, how do you do?'

'Fred. Blundell.'

'Bucknall, Blundell, we'll have to watch else folks will mix us up proper,' said Sid, smiling, still shaking Fred's hand and looking him in the eye. Fred frowned and gave a small nod of his head, holding Sid's stare.

'Well, I'm sorry you've been waiting so long, it took a while before we could see to you, but here I am.' He let go of Fred's hand and held out his arms, keeping his eyes fixed on Fred's. 'I'm in a bit of a bind as it happens, one of the lines broke down and we're making up for lost time. I'd appreciate you giving us a hand if you've got nowhere to get to?'

Fred raised his eyebrows and smiled a little. 'Yeah, course, that's why I come, I'm looking for–'

'That's good of you,' said Sid. 'If you'll follow me.'

He led Fred out of the administration building, across the compound and into the first factory

63

building, nodding to the man on reception as they went through.

'This one here's bags, the next factory over's gloves, the last one's shoes.' Sid headed up a flight of stairs and stopped. 'I will say, there's no smoking in the factories. That's in stone. We keep hazardous chemicals on site for the manu-facturing process.' Fred nodded.

They came to the first floor, a vast space with grey concrete underfoot and smooth round con-crete pillars at intervals. The floor was split into three sections, each with a long conveyor belt sur-rounded by factory workers, some operating machinery. Looping cables and long electric lights hung low from the ceiling and the air throbbed with an abrasive whine, clunk and chug. Sid beck-oned Fred over to the farthest section, where the conveyor belt was motionless.

'This line's putting the straps together, see?' Sid's expression changed from amiable to serious; he continued in a harsh tone close to Fred's ear. 'We're a man down. I need you on this machine, punching holes in the strap, get it down the line quick-like so's the next one can thread it on. Quick as you like, these workers are on a target, see? If they don't reach it, they're going to be pretty brassed off. It's up to you to keep up. Bill here will show you the ropes, but get going when you know it. Over there's Harry, the foreman, the one who already looks brassed off, he'll be watching. That line there's coming close up to target,' he said, nodding to the next conveyor. 'If they reach it before this one, there'll be hell to pay from Harry.'

Sid slapped Fred on the back and left.

'You look like you've been caught in the head-lights, pal. I'm Bill.' They shook hands. 'But look lively, here.' He showed Fred how to stand at the punching machine, how to line up the strap and when to press the foot pedal at the right moment. He let Fred practise a few times, and gave the signal for the conveyor belt to be switched on. Fred glanced around at the other workers and took hold of a strap, placing it just so. The punched holes were out of line. He discarded it and started again. Harry the foreman started to walk over, the man working next to him stood straight, watching Fred, waiting for a strap to work with. Fred tried again and laid the strap down on the conveyor, watching it pass along and be swiped up by his colleague.

'This ain't no good, mate,' the man said, passing the strap back to Fred.

'What's wrong with it?' asked Fred, squinting at his work.

'Out of line, mate.'

'What's the hold-up here?' said Harry the fore-man, who appeared at Fred's side.

Fred sniffed. 'Just getting the hang of it, that's all.'

'Well, get the hang of it a bit sharpish,' said Harry. 'They ain't got all day waiting on your work.'

Beads of sweat dotted Fred's forehead, he bit his lip and tried again. This time the next man smiled at him and used the strap.

'That's a winner, mate.'

Fred took a deep breath and punched another, and another, and was soon in full flow, punching out good quality straps and keeping up with the other workers.

There was a loud grinding noise and Fred's counterpart on the next conveyor belt shouted out.

'It's jammed, the darn thing's jammed.'

The workers on Fred's line carried on as they were. Bill caught Fred's eye and shook his head, nodding at Fred to get on with his work.

'Aargh, I can't get the darn thing free.' No one offered to help the man in trouble. Fred looked over at him while punching his straps. The man caught Fred's eye and beckoned to him.

'Oi, pal, give us a hand, will you?'

Fred broke eye contact, looked down and carried on punching.

'Oi, pal, help me out with this bleeding thing, will you?' The man was pulling at a piece of leather strap, trying to dislodge it. His work was building up on the conveyor, his workmates called out for him to get a move on.

Bill shook his head at Fred again. Harry the foreman looked over and frowned. Fred glanced at the man in trouble.

'For Christ's sake.' He left his machine to help, strode over to the next conveyor and tugged at the stuck leather and managed to pull it free.

'Thanks, pal, you're a winner,' said the man, smiling at Fred.

'It's all right,' said Fred, going back to his station to resume his work. He kept his eyes down – he didn't want to see Bill or the foreman – and worked hard at the punching for another half hour.

Sid from Administration appeared at Fred's side.

'Well, thanks a bundle, Fred, you've done us a grand favour, come with me.'

Fred looked up surprised, glanced at his fellow workers, who watched as he was led away. Sid took him back over to the administration building without saying a word and into an office with a desk and two chairs.

'Sit down, Fred.'

Fred took a seat and pulled out his pouch of tobacco, holding it out to Sid.

'Not for me thanks, but you go ahead.' Sid pulled out a pack of Woodbines and lit one. He regarded Fred for a minute as they both smoked.

'Well, Fred, I'm afraid to say we've had you in a little test.'

Fred coughed on his smoke and leant forwards in his chair. 'What the...?'

'It's all right, it's just something we do here at the company. We like to weed out the bad ones early on if we can. Don't take offence, it's just the way we do things around here.' He chuckled. 'And as it happens you did all right.'

Fred sat back and let his arms drop down.

'You've got good standards, Fred, throwing out that first strap that weren't no good. And you took it on the chin and redid that second strap and, most important, you showed you can work for the good of the company when you helped that chap out on the next line. You proved you're patient and hard-working. You're our kind of man, Fred.'

'You was watching all that?'

'Let's just say it's a little test and I know you did good.' Sid smiled, stood up and held out his hand. 'Welcome to Monday's.'

4

The tenement door opened, freezing air rushed inside to pull smoke down from the chimney. Fred was home.

'I done it.' He smiled and fanned the smoke back with his cap.

A grey sock lay deflated in Flo's lap waiting to be darned. Mikey sat squashed in the fireside chair beside her, a blanket around his shoulders, reading a battered Eagle comic.

'Done what?' Flo was confused, what did they have to smile about? She braced herself, waited to see how drunk he was.

'I only went and got a job.'

'What?' Flo sat upright.

'I got a job. At Monday's. You would have been proud of me, Flo, love. Listen to this. They said,' he paused for effect, chuckling to himself, 'they said I was patient.' He laughed and Flo frowned at him. 'And hard-working.' He let out a big belly laugh, red in the face, his lips glistened with saliva.

'What?'

'Yep, you heard me right, and they said I got high standards, what do you think about that then?'

'High standards?' Flo mouthed the words. 'So,

68

what job is it then?'

Fred sloughed off his coat, put his shoes by the fire to dry. 'Don't know yet, in the factory I expect. And they said we can go to their winter do.' He eased into the other chair and rolled a cigarette.

'Winter do?'

'Winter festival or something, this Saturday coming.'

'What is it, Dad?' Mikey jumped up.

'Don't know, son, ice skating and food, your old dad did it, eh?'

'Ice skating?' Mikey's eyes widened. 'What kind of food, Dad?'

'Don't know, but you should see it, funny place, all these queer-looking houses, white and square like shoeboxes, and there's some swings and a swimming pool outside, it's proper good it is.'

'Mum, ice skating.'

Flo stared at her husband. For one, he wasn't drunk. For another, and she could hardly believe it, he had ventured beyond the docks. It was their birthplace, their birthright even. They knew the docks as well as they knew their own hands, it was where they belonged and never thought they'd leave. He'd marched straight into someone else's world. He'd done it for her and no amount of words in all the world would have struck her with more force.

Her head spun, she smoothed down her dress, watched him ruffle Mikey's hair. He may have been a new man sitting there. She caught Fred's eye and he looked away, he seemed humbled somehow, like he'd surprised himself. She immediately started to worry that he was numb from shock and would come out of it too late and kick against what he'd been forced to do.

A ripple of cold panic ran over her. Thoughts tumbled into her mind, as if she had opened a jar full of ants and they were running over her hands. His old dad would turn in his grave at the thought of them leaving Tilbury. And her old mum, they'd be breaking up the family. How could she leave her? It wouldn't be far away in miles, but it would be like separating rhizomes that grow beneath the soil's surface, prising them apart with a ripping sound.

And from that her mind slipped to Babs, and again that shiver of panic. Babs had run off and shacked up with that Teddy boy, doing just what everyone expected, bringing shame on them all. She would ruin herself, do what Flo had dreaded, follow in her own footsteps. Getting caught too young, feeling high and mighty and all special but too soon feeling the cold slap of it round your face and by then it's too late, and you look around and see that you're the same as everyone else and they aren't too happy about it either.

Flo stood up. 'Everyone get your coats on.'

Jeanie peered out of the box-bed curtain.

'Jeanie, coat,' said Flo.

'We going ice skating, Mum?' said Mikey.

'No, love. We're going to get Babs back, aren't we, Fred?'

Fred went rigid, his smile dropped.

'Yes, love, by God we are.' He stood up too, reached for his coat.

They all bundled out of the door, a buzz of excitement uniting them. Flo led the way down the tenement stairs, Mikey trotted along to keep pace with Fred, and Jeanie dragged behind. Flo knew Billy lived along the Calcutta Road terraces but didn't know which house. It was still bitterly cold out, crusted grey snow clung to every surface. In ten minutes they were there. Flo knocked at number seven. A middle-aged woman wearing a holey cardigan over a tatty floral dress opened the door.

'All right, Flo, love?'

'All right, Marge, love? You know where that Billy lives down here?' she said, indicating the street.

Marge wiped her hands on her dress and looked perky. 'Oh yes, love, number twenty-two he is.' She added, awkwardly, 'With your Babs, love.'

'Thanks, Marge,' said Flo and marched off down the road, the family following. Marge leant out of her door to watch them go.

Number twenty-two sat squashed between its neighbours, one window up and one down, both with torn grey nets. The sound of raised voices could be heard within. Flo banged on the door and looked down at the dirty step. Everyone waited in silence, their breath hitting the cold air in plumes. The voices inside hushed and the door opened.

'Biddy,' said Flo, unsmiling.

'Flo,' said Biddy, Billy's mother, her arms crossed over her large, apron-covered bosom, expansive nose and cheeks red from drink.

'We've come for Babs.'

'Well? What do you want me to do about it?'

Fred pushed forward through the door and into

the house. Everyone followed him in.

'Here, what the bloody hell do you think you're up to?' Biddy's voice was lost in the jostle.

'Babs?' Flo called out, following Fred into the back room. It smelled of damp and old grease. In a second Flo took in the state of the place. Biddy didn't do a lot of cleaning up, that much was clear. There was Babs, standing by the back window, her face swollen from crying. Billy sat on an armchair smoking, his Teddy boy quiff in disarray but still wearing his embroidered waistcoat and drainpipe trousers. Fred dragged him out of the chair by his arm.

Billy resisted. 'Get off me,' he spat, yanking his arm away, his face white and twisted.

'Dad, don't,' yelled Babs. 'It's all right.'

'What do you mean, it's all right, love?' said Flo, nudging up to her daughter. 'What you doing going off like that?'

She took the lit cigarette out of Bab's fingers and smoked it herself.

'Billy heard yesterday. He's been called up for National Service.'

Fred burst into laughter, coughing, and pushed Billy back down into his chair. 'Well, that's your lot then, ain't it?'

Flo leant into Babs, her voice low. 'You think you're in the family way, love?' Babs frowned and shook her head and Flo closed her eyes and let out a sigh through her nose. 'That will teach you then, eh?' she said to Billy, a sob catching in her throat. 'Teach you for taking our Babs away.'

'I didn't take her, you stupid cow, she came here off her own back.'

Fred lunged at him, grabbed him by the shoulder and raised his fist, then reconsidered and let him go.

'Mum, I wanna go home,' said Babs, wiping her nose on the back of her wrist.

'Yeah, go on then, don't worry about me, you selfish bitch,' said Billy.

'Come on, love, get your stuff.' Flo put her arm around Babs and led her out. Fred stood sentry as she ran upstairs for her bags.

They walked home reunited.

'How old is he then?' said Flo, working it out. 'He'd have to be at least twenty-one and bloody unlucky to be called up now.'

'Yeah, twenty-one,' said Babs quietly.

'Christ, what you playing at, Babs?'

'Can he get out of it, Mum?'

'What?' Babs had changed the subject, Flo hadn't known Billy was six years her senior.

'Can Billy get out of the call-up?'

'No, love, he can't. Not unless he wants to do time.'

Fred's head jerked. He stuffed his hands deep down into his pockets and trudged ahead.

'Well, it's not bloody fair, is it?'

'I dunno, love,' said Flo, out of Fred's earshot, 'it might do him good.'

The Blundells arrived by train on Saturday, dressed in their best. *Welcome to Leather Town*, said a sign on the platform.

Monday's Leather Goods, said another. Babs giggled and nudged Mikey's arm. Outside the station, the family huddled together. Mikey, in his frayed school blazer, looked back at the hiss and grind of the hard-worked steam engine as it dragged the carriages away, leaving the smell of soot in the air around them.

As they walked, the estate of employee housing appeared on their left. Long straight roads leading off the main road, each the same with identical white box houses stretching away as far as they could see. Families came walking along, chatting and laughing, turned on to the main road that headed into the centre of the town, past the enormous factory buildings that loomed on the right-hand side. The smoke of the train gave way to a faint smell of leather, glue and chemicals.

'One of them's for making shoes, one's for gloves and one's for bags,' informed Fred, nodding at the factories. Flo lit a new cigarette from the butt of the one she'd just finished, and noticed Fred doing the same as he walked stiff and straight.

'Them houses are bigger, bet they're for the bosses,' said Babs after the rows of smaller houses had passed. She was dressed up, hair set and scarlet lipstick, shivering in her hobble skirt and blouse tied in a knot at the waist, jacket open. 'And there's a village hall, do you reckon they have dances there?'

'Don't know yet, love,' said Flo, with a tight smile. Distant music strained towards them, drawing them into the festivities.

'Blimey, Mum, a big hotel,' said Mikey, hopping from one flagstone to the next to avoid the cracks. 'And who's this geezer?' he said, looking across the quadrangle at the statue of James Monday, senior.

'Dunno, love.'

They all looked left at the same time when their attention was caught by the mansion house at the end of a poplar-lined avenue. Fred whistled.

'Blimey,' said Flo. 'I reckon that's where the boss lives, eh?'

'Mum, look.' Mikey ran over the road to the quadrangle, lined with six-feet-high snow sculptures, intricate in design, works of art, an effigy of Winston Churchill, a soldier leaning on his gun, a moose, a man with a large moustache, a giant stiletto shoe. Flo shook her head in wonder, what was this place? She couldn't take it all in.

The Blundells followed the crowd and stopped to gape at the sight of the lido diagonally opposite. The main U-shaped lido building enclosed three outdoor pools, one with diving boards. The cafes and sun decks of the lido were draped with Union flag bunting. People milled around and queued up for food and drink, ate things out of paper napkins and sipped steaming drinks. A band played from under the lido awning, the old-time dance-hall music drifting across the estate. Children ran about shouting and chasing. The bathing pools were frozen over, the largest was being used as an ice rink. Skaters laughed and hung on to one another, adults held children's hands, everyone bundled up in warm coats, hats and gloves.

'Told you,' said Fred, looking down at Mikey with a wink. 'Food and ice skating.' Flo glanced at him, she could tell he was as overwhelmed as she was herself. All these people, they looked so happy, like they were on holiday or something, the music and everything going on, it was a big party, she hadn't expected it. They headed into the lido to watch the skating, unsure of where to stand.

'All right there, Fred?'

A shortish, neat-looking man wearing black leather gloves and a new hat approached them. He grabbed Fred's hand and shook it up and down, not letting go while he spoke.

'It's good to see you here, and this is your family?'

'All right, Sid? This here's Sid, he's the one who pulled a fast one on me, with that test, eh?'

'Well, come on, you know we had to do it, Fred, that's how things get done around here, and you passed it, didn't you?' Sid finally let go of Fred's hand and waited for an introduction to Fred's family. Flo threw a worried glance at her husband.

'Hello, I'm Florence, Flo, and this here's Barbara and Michael, and that there's Jean.' Flo held out her hand to Sid. He took it, holding just her fingers with his gloves.

'How do you do, Mrs Blundell, I'm very pleased to make your acquaintance. Well, what do you think of our little winter festival then? Ain't it gay? Wait until it gets dark and the lights come on in the cherry trees, they're pretty as anything.' Flo smiled at him and he let her hand go.

'It's lovely, it's proper lovely.'

'Right then, let's get you fixed up,' said Sid, waving them along to a kiosk. Flo raised her eyebrows at Fred, he shook his head and waited for Sid, who was chatting to the kiosk attendant. He handed them all a little stub of brown tickets.

'These'll get you a free drink. Fred and Mrs Blundell, I strongly suggest you try the caribou, it's a Canadian tradition, potent to the point of poison, you only need one. And, kids, there's a lovely bit of hot cocoa with whipped cream for you, and there's tickets for a bit of grub and for ice skating.'

Mikey's eyes were wide with wonder. He gave a loud gasp when Sid handed him his own set of tickets, and looked to Flo for confirmation that it was all right to take them. She nodded at him. Babs gave Sid a little curtsey and fluttered her eyelashes to say thank you, and Jeanie took the tickets without a smile. Sid gave her a second look and caught Flo's eye.

'Don't mind Jeanie, she's been in a five-year mood, she's all right, though, aren't you, Jeanie?' Jeanie scowled at her and Flo shrugged at Sid.

'Off you go then.' Sid gestured to Flo to take the children ice skating. 'There's open day in the factories, too, if you fancy a look around after.' He led Fred to the cafe where he procured two cups of caribou, then over to lean against the pool railing, both men putting one foot up on to the lower rail.

'Christ, what's this stuff?' said Fred, wincing at the hot drink.

'Ha ha, good, ain't it? It's whisky, sherry, port and a touch of maple syrup.'

'Maple syrup?'

'Yep, it's Canadian, this whole festival is Canadian, the boss is from Canada, he likes to keep the traditions going a bit.'

Fred nodded and sipped his drink. Flo, Babs and Mikey were strapping on their ice skates on the other side of the rink. Jeanie was standing nearby, sulking.

'So you're starting work Monday?' said Sid.

'Yep, if there's work for me.'

'What is it you've been doing?'

'Docker.'

Sid nodded and thought for a moment. 'So if I told you there's a job going in the loading bay, that might be along the lines of what you're used to and inclined to be good at?'

Fred blinked. 'I'd say that would be right on the money and I'd be glad of it.'

'Ha ha, I didn't think you looked at home on that conveyor. We won't put you in the factory, you're an outside kind of bloke, I reckon, and by the look of you, you can lift a good weight and put your back into some hard work.'

Fred reached for Sid's hand and shook it with gusto, banged his cup against Sid's and gulped down its contents.

'I tell you something, Fred.' Sid paused to offer Fred a cigarette, lighting it and his own. 'Monday's is a bit special, right? It's not your average place, granted it's a bit queer in some things, it has its own ways, but if you play your cards right, if you work hard and toe the line, there's good prospects, and regular money, and a lively spirit about the place with lots of benefits thrown in. We don't need the unions around here, everyone works hard and saves up and can afford to buy everything they want.'

Fred puffed on his cigarette and squinted at Sid through his smoke.

'How you fixed for a place to stay?'

'Well, the docks are frozen and there's no work so we have to move out the flat and I don't know where to.'

Sid regarded him for a moment. 'Well, that's your business but we can put you and the family up in the Monday's hotel for a bit if you're agreeable. After a bit, if things are going well there might be a house come up.' Sid watched Fred.

'That would be decent of you, Sid, we'd be much obliged. When can we move in?'

'Ha ha, right then, I've got my answer I reckon. You can move the family into the hotel on Monday and start work on Tuesday, how about that?'

'Much obliged, Sid,' said Fred, shaking Sid's hand again.

'The rent'll be taken out your wages. It's all right, the rate is very reasonable, you don't have to worry. Now then, how about the girls and the missus, will you want them to work?'

'Yes, I reckon. They're good girls. Jeanie don't talk much but she's a good worker and clever with it.'

'Leave it to me,' said Sid, winking at Fred. 'There's a school here too for Michael if you want to move him. Look, they're having a right good laugh there.'

They watched as Flo clung to the sides of the rink, laughing, her skates slid back and forth on the spot, Mikey trying to pull her hand to go faster. Babs had got the hang of it and glided along on her own, back straight, chest out, nose up.

Mum looked a right idiot falling over on the ice and holding on to Mikey, and Babs looked full of herself, she knew all the lads were looking at her. Fresh meat for the factory boys to slobber over, freezing in that stupid Teddy girl jacket. *I* was glad to be wearing my thick coat and galoshes, I wasn't about to freeze for no boys. I thought I might as well get the grub, so I wandered over to the lido cafe. They were serving something called beaver tails and poutine so I asked for poutine, and handed over my ticket. It was thin chips with gravy and cheese stuff, pretty good. I sneaked off eating it to have a look around the estate.

The factory buildings were open, so I walked into the bag factory, saw all the conveyor belts and sewing machines, the cutting machines and the piles of leather. The factory floors were massive but made me feel like I was choking, all crammed with machinery, metal and pipes and big lights hanging down from the ceiling. It must be hellish noisy during a work day. One of the workers handed out Monday keyrings and pencils. I took one of each and put them in the nearest bin. Dad had brought us there to be factory fodder, I bet he was telling Sid to put us to work. It was even worse than working at the grocer's. I felt sick at the thought of it.

It was a waste of time going in to look at the shoe or glove factories. It would have been more of the same thing. Instead I went back outside and walked over to a set of buildings behind a row of shops on the front road. The first one was a cinema, so I went in to have a look. A war film was showing. A few couples sat in the dark, arms around shoulders. I left and went to the next building. I wasn't even sure what it was until I was inside and saw the bookshelves. A library. My heart thumped. It was empty except for one young bloke on the far side sitting with his back to me. At least there was *something* for me in that place, looked like a newish set of encyclopaedias too. I picked up *The Adventures of Tom Sawyer* and sat down at one of the little reading tables. It made me jump when the young bloke's shadow moved over me and when he spoke the book fell on the floor.

'Hello.' He was sure of himself, cut a good figure, neat and tidy, dark auburn hair and a big grin on his freckled face. 'Haven't seen you around here before.' He bent to pick up my book.

'I haven't been here before, that's why.' I snatched the book up before he could get it.

'Oooh, sorry I asked,' he said. I frowned and looked at my lap.

'What are you reading? Oh, I love that one, even if it was written by a yank.' He grinned again. I kept my chin down but lifted my eyes.

'You been trying out the Canadian fare? The poutine's good, isn't it?' he said.

Cheeky bugger. I bet I had food round my mouth, I wiped it with the back of my hand. His accent wasn't local, it was a mixture of posh and something but I wasn't good with accents. I heard all sorts down the docks and could never tell where any of them were from.

'You go to school or college or what?' he said, still not going away.

'I work in a grocer's shop.' That'd shut him up.
'Oh, righto.'
'What about you then?'

'Oh, I go to Palmer's sixth form, doing the old A levels, then off to university.'

'That's what I wanna do.' I blurted it out before I knew what I was doing, it was the surprise of what he said, I didn't know anyone who was going to a university.

'It is? Well then, why don't you?'

'Can't.'

'Why not?'

'Nosy, aren't you.'

'Well, yes, maybe I am.'

I tutted. 'Because I didn't go to grammar so I haven't got any A levels.'

'What do you mean? You want to go to university but you didn't get into grammar?'

'I *did* get into grammar but I wasn't *allowed* to go.' God, he was nosy. I looked at the book cover.

'I don't get it, sorry,' he said, sitting down at the table across from me, a bit too friendly for my liking.

'My mum and dad made me go to sec mod with my sister.'

He laughed. 'What on earth for?'

'Because they wanted me to get a job when I left school.' I shrugged and looked him in the eye. 'We need the money.'

He screwed up his face all funny. 'But that makes no sense. You mean you passed the eleven plus?' I nodded. 'And they made you go to secondary modern where you've no chance of going on to sixth form?'

I nodded again. 'I went to the interview on the sly and got offered a place but it didn't make any difference.'

'Ludicrous,' he said. 'You must be furious.' Now that made me laugh, I couldn't help it, he was the first person to understand how I felt about it all.

'It sounds bloody stupid, doesn't it?'

'It does, yes,' he said, laughing too.

'But that's my life, isn't it?' I said, and I wasn't laughing any more.

'Yes, it is. But you could still get your A levels.'

I just stared at him.

'There's a college in Barking where you can do them, out of hours as it were. What do you want to study at university, as a matter of interest?'

'Medicine.' I took a deep breath and looked at the far wall. I didn't even know why I was telling him, I hadn't told that to a single soul because I'd be laughed at. 'But girls like me don't get to be doctors, they get to be shop girls or factory fodder, or, if your face is pretty enough, a copy typist in an office.'

'Well, I must say, that is very courageous. And that's not to say your face *isn't* pretty enough,' he added with a smile. 'Would you like me to help you find out? What are you doing here today?'

'Dad got a job here.'

'So you'll be living here?'

I shrugged, no one tells me anything.

'Well, if I see you again I'm going to help you find out. I'm sick of the way things are done in this country, the class divide especially, and if someone wants to be a doctor they should bloody well be able to.'

I just stared at him and got a funny feeling inside my guts and in my nose like I was going to cry. 'Really? Why would you go and do a thing like that?'

'I don't know why, I just think it's not fair, our parents decide everything for us like we're children. It's time to strike back.' He laughed at himself being all dramatic.

'Right, well, I'd best be off, I've got a ticket here for a beaver tail, whatever that may be.' I had to get out of there before I started crying and anyway I didn't really believe he would help me.

'See you around, hopefully,' he said, smiling. My stomach had that funny feeling again. My cheeks were hot. I left the book on the table and walked out into the cold air. The band was playing a dreamy song that washed over me, I drifted back over to the ice rink. What if he was right, that I could get my exams? I needed to find out where and how much it cost.

The rest of the family were standing in the lido having their food and drink. Mikey had gravy all round his face and was eating a huge waffle pancake-type thing with brown powder and runny stuff on it. 'Beaver tail,' he said, his mouth full of food. Urgh, I went to get a cocoa. It was made with hot milk and piled high with whipped cream. It was the most delicious thing I had ever tasted. The light was fading. Hundreds of little lights came on in the cherry trees and around every doorway of the lido. The crowd gasped, it was really something else. The ice skaters had all come off and a neat line of what looked like wooden beer barrels had been placed on the ice.

I sidled up to Babs, whispered into her ear. 'Someone just told me where I can do my A levels.'

She wrinkled her nose. 'What do you wanna do that for? It won't help you get married.' She tutted. 'You're such a square, Jeanie.'

The band stopped playing and a man made an announcement on a loudspeaker.

'Your attention, ladies and gentlemen, boys and girls. Presenting Mr Monday, champion barrel jumper.'

Sid appeared from somewhere and in a low voice said to us,

'Get ready for one of the loony bin Canadian traditions. This here is the big boss coming out, Mr Monday junior. His late dad built this place. Watch this, he's a force to be reckoned with.'

The band gave a long drum roll. A man wearing a tight-fitting skating suit over a muscular body came on to the ice. Arms raised, he swooshed along in long glides, he knew what he was doing all right. I caught Babs's eye and sniggered, his trousers were so tight you could see a big bulge between his legs. The crowd cheered. His hair was slicked back, he had a large bushy moustache, a cleft in his chin and looked really serious. He skated around the rink, leant forwards, got faster and faster, his straight arms pumped at his sides. Everyone held their breath, even I did. Mum and Dad looked at each other. Mr Monday was going really fast, his skates carved up the ice, shavings sprayed up. He went round one more time and raced up to the row of barrels, bent his knees and made a gigantic leap right over them, clearing them easily, and landed on his backside on the hard ice with a loud thump. The crowd cheered, shouted and whistled. It must have hurt like hell, landing on the ice like that. What an idiot. Sid shook his head and clapped.

'And that, kids, is Mr Monday. You wouldn't believe it, but you're supposed to land like that. Like I said, loony bin traditions.'

Ten minutes later a voice with an accent boomed from the loudspeaker.

'Friends.' Mr Monday was on a platform wearing a long camel hair coat and talking into a microphone. *'Bon Hiver!'* Everyone around us called out Bon Hiver, which I knew meant *Happy Winter.* 'I hope you are enjoying the fruits of your labour, and know that while this harshest of winters is a difficult time for many industries, here at Monday's Leather we thrive because we know the importance of integrity, loyalty and elbow grease, and we know that the customer is king.' Everyone cheered, but not quite as much as before. 'Here at Monday's Leather we provide prospects, regular high wages, housing, social activities, a community of workers like nowhere else. *You all* belong to the Monday's family.' He raised his arms again. What was he, some kind of god or something?

'Wait 'til you see the boss's wife and all.' Sid winked and blew a low whistle.

'Now then, announcements,' said Mr Monday. 'The winner of the snow sculpture competition is Mr L. Jarvis of twenty-five Monday Avenue.' The crowd cheered. Mr Jarvis came up to the podium to collect a small trophy. 'I will announce the Winter Festival Queen later at the masquerade dance, so keep looking beautiful, you lovely girls. Enjoy your day and keep up the hard work.' With that he walked away, the crowd parting to let him through.

'We'd better be off then, cheers, Sid,' said Fred.

'See you then,' said Sid, shaking hands. 'And just think,' he winked at Mikey, 'if you work for Monday's you can save up for a car.' Mikey gasped.

'Oh, the masquerade dance, Mum, please, please, please,' said Babs. She would, wouldn't she.

'Sorry, love, not this time.'

We set off for the station. I kept thinking about that boy in the library.

'Sid said we can move into the hotel on Monday,' Dad said to Mum.

'I want to live in a hotel,' said Babs.

'Can we, Mum? Will there be beaver tails, Mum?' said Mikey.

'Live in a hotel? What you up to, Fred? We're not living in a hotel. We can stay at the flat then sort something out when you start earning. I can't leave Mum, can I?'

'We'll see then. He also said there's work for you and the girls.'

I felt sick.

'Oh, did he now? Well, that's good, I reckon, give us a chance to get back on our feet,' said Mum, linking her arm through Dad's. I couldn't remember the last time they did that.

'So, kids, I'll be working here next week,' said Dad. 'And your mother will be working here, and the girls will be working here, and Mikey will go to the school here. What do you think about that, then?'

I was disgusted. Mum beamed around at us all

and squeezed Dad's arm. 'Oh, it's just wonderful, Fred, love, just wonderful, you really come up trumps.'

'Yeah, supersonic,' shouted Mikey, jumping up and down, his face smeared with gravy, cinnamon and whipped cream.

I caught up with Babs and whispered into her ear. 'Yeah, if you like being factory fodder until you die.'

Babs gave me such a dirty look. 'Oh you ungrateful little dog, didn't you see all the boys there looking at me? I can't wait.'

5

The Blundells trudged up the tenement stairs in the dark, Flo pulled Mikey along, almost asleep on his feet. Fred walked ahead along the balcony and stopped at their front door. It stood open.

'What the...'

Pushing Mikey back behind her, Flo came up short next to Fred. Against the wall in their living room, a gas lamp at his feet, leant Stan Winsford, the foreman from the docks, smoking his pipe. Their furniture had gone, all of their belongings had gone, the flat was empty.

'What the hell's going on?' Fred shouted, looking around the room in disbelief.

'Fred. Flo,' said Stan, nodding at each of them and stepping forwards.

'Stan?' said Flo. 'We been robbed?' Flo pressed

her hands over her mouth.

Stan took a puff from his pipe. 'No, you ain't been robbed, Flo, you've been evicted.'

'Mum?' said Mikey, his little face worried. 'Where's all our stuff?'

'Yeah, Stan, where's all our stuff and what the fuck's going on?'

'Well, Fred, it's like this. Someone reported you to the dock police. Said you been using your flat for a betting shop.'

'That ain't true,' cried Flo. 'Tell him, Fred.'

'No, it ain't true, Stan,' he said in a low menacing voice, taking a step towards the foreman. 'So what you gonna do about it, eh?'

'Well, Fred, if some illegal activity gets reported to the dock police they act on it, they have to. They got the dockmaster involved and he had to evict you.' He hesitated. 'What with you not working at the docks no more and all.' Stan looked at the floor.

'And whose fault is that, you bastard?' said Fred. He rushed towards Stan, grabbing his jacket lapels, pushed him against the wall. Stan was as big as Fred, he reacted fast, stood erect, brought his arms down on Fred's, freeing himself, and pushed Fred backwards.

'You calm down now, Fred,' hissed Stan, pointing his finger into Fred's face. 'I done a lot for you, you know that, now don't go throwing it back in my face. We both know whose fault it is you lost your bleeding job.'

The men glared at each other.

'Your dad was a good friend, Fred. I didn't have to hang around waiting for you to come back.

And there weren't no evidence of a betting shop here, so I told them they'd be wasting their time arresting you, that we'd just get you out the Dwellings.'

Fred stood at ease and lit a cigarette. 'Well, I ain't done nothing wrong,' he mumbled. 'Who was it? Who reported me?'

'I can't tell you that, Fred, you know that.'

Fred spat on the floor. 'That Billy's mother, I bet.'

'Flo, love,' said Stan. 'Your old mum was out her flat on the balcony, in a state, flapping at them, telling them to put your stuff back. They ended up putting it all in her flat next door. She was doing her nut, effing and blinding. I got her sat down in her chair, made her a cup of tea.'

Flo ran out, skidded around the doorframe, pushed into her mother's flat that was never locked. It was almost dark in there, the last flickers of fire in the grate casting the only light. Their furniture piled around the room was silhouetted in the gloom, an armchair on top of a table, wooden banana crates with their things stuffed in. Ella sat in her armchair by the fire, holding a cup of tea in her lap.

'Mum?' called Flo. 'What you doing in the dark?' She stopped short and looked at the cup of tea. The saucer was slanted and the cup half off it, Flo could see the dark brown tea had slopped over the top on to the patchwork blanket across her mother's lap. The daft old thing had fallen asleep with a fag in her teeth again, a column of ash curved downwards, threatening to break off, lucky it hadn't set the place on fire. She looked at

Ella's face and frowned, walked closer, squinted through the half-light. She could hear somebody crying but didn't know where. Flo's body felt heavy, her legs a dead weight all of a sudden, and her throat tight. She dropped to her knees, down hard on the wooden floor at her mother's feet. She had been there countless times, bathing Ella's legs, those wretched ulcers that plagued her.

'Mum?' A voice came from someone else, it was a harsh whispering voice that didn't sound like hers. She put out her hand, it trembled, everything was slow and numb and there was no sound, like her head was under a pillow.

Her hand settled on Ella's hand, it was cold. Her mum felt the cold, she was always moaning about her frozen hands and feet. Bad circulation, she said. Flo chuckled, relieved. She was just asleep.

'Mum?' Yes, that was her voice, loud and strong. She reached up and shook Ella's shoulder. The ash broke and fell. Her mother's body slid over to the opposite arm of the chair and slumped there, her hair-netted rollers rattled as her head lolled sideways, the cup and saucer clattered to the floor. Someone screamed. Flo stared at the cup spinning on the wooden boards, a Catherine wheel on Bonfire night, little flecks of tea flicking out around it in a circle of sparks. It spun and spun.

When Babs screamed in the flat next door I ran to see. Mum was on her knees by Nan's chair, her face in Nan's lap, crying and saying something I

91

couldn't make out. Nan looked dead. She was kind of sideways and her eyes and mouth were open. A jolt of fear went through me. Babs stood there, her hands on either side of her face, jiggling up and down, moaning and blubbering. I just stared at her, wondering how she knew what to do. Mikey came over and put his arms around my hips, buried his face into my skirt. I put my hand on his head and didn't know what to say.

There was a sound behind me. I turned to see Dad in the doorway, his eyes flicked from one of us to the other. Stan appeared behind Dad, he took off his hat and looked at the ground. I waited for Dad to say something, to tell us what to do. He looked so big in the doorway like he could scoop us all up and keep us safe. But he took a step backwards and walked away.

'Fred?' Stan tried calling him back. I heard Dad's boots tramp along the balcony. Stan put his hand on my arm and moved me aside so he could come into the flat. He knelt down beside Mum, she looked into his face, and then I saw what grief looked like, that was it, sure enough.

'Let me see,' whispered Stan. He lit Nan's gas lamp and checked Nan's pulse. He shook his head, put a hand on to Mum's shoulder. Mum sobbed and shook her head, squeezed her eyes tight shut. I moved closer to see. Nan's face was purple with blue around her eyes and nose. Stan pulled her to sit upright, pulled the fag butt out of her teeth and ran his big hand over her face. Her eyes were closed after that but her mouth was still open. Stan tried to lift her jaw but it didn't budge.

'Close her mouth,' sobbed Babs.

Stan shook his head.

'I'll go and telephone the authorities, Flo,' he said. 'Barbara, look after your mum for a minute, I won't be long.' He closed the curtains on the way out – that's what you do when someone dies.

Before long the room was full of strangers and I stood in the corner with Mikey trying to keep out of the way. Dr Langton came to check Nan was dead. He felt her neck and said she was. I leant in to hear him tell Mum it was a heart attack from the shock, he said her jugular was swollen, said it would have been very quick. He reckoned she weren't dead long... Mum put her hand over her mouth and screwed her eyes up. Dr Langton gave her his hankie.

The dockmaster and a dock copper came, and the undertaker to measure Nan up for her coffin. They carried Nan into her bedroom and laid her on the bed, someone said they should do it before she got stiff. An old woman came rushing in soon after that – she had a white line around her jaw like she'd washed off her cold cream in a hurry – and went into the bedroom with Mum. The doctor said they were 'laying her out', something about the 'last offices'. I went over to the door and put my hand on it.

'Jeanie, don't,' whispered Babs. When I opened the door, Mum and the old woman looked up. Mum gave me a small smile, anyway it was up to me if I wanted to go in or not. They had taken Nan's clothes off, a sheet was over her bottom half and they were washing her body. It didn't even look like Nan, her mouth was still open a bit, like she was asleep but different. She looked like she was made of grey bread dough, her chest looked weird, all flat and spread out over her body and hanging over the sides.

They finished washing Nan's body then the woman looked under the sheet and did something with Nan's privates, I don't know what, maybe she had to plug it up to stop it leaking or something. I looked at Nan's bare feet sticking out of the sheet, they looked like purple brawn.

Mum whimpered as she took off Nan's hairnet and started taking her rollers out.

'She wouldn't have wanted everyone seeing her in her rollers.' She brushed Nan's curls out, then started crying, quietly though, sort of through her nose. Nan looked different with hair.

Mum got out Nan's best nightie, a white frilly one, and they really had trouble getting that on, they sat her up a bit, then Mum asked me to help, said can I put Nan's arms in. It was weird touching her cold skin and she was a bit stiff so I think we did it just in time. Mum rummaged through Nan's chest of drawers and got out some cream rouge, which she rubbed into Nan's cheeks, and a bit of pink lipstick, then Nan looked really weird, like a lump of grey bread dough with lipstick on.

The woman took out some long white ribbons and we all tied Nan's arms to her body at the wrist then tied her ankles together. The old woman tried tying Nan's jaw shut but it was already too stiff. Mum pulled a sheet up to Nan's shoulders and we all stood back. Then Mum said she looked lovely and the woman said yes she did. I didn't say anything, anyway she didn't look lovely. Mum grabbed on to me and kissed me and said *well done, love* into my ear, then said I should go and wait with the others.

Babs and Mikey stared at me when I came out the bedroom.

'What happened?' Babs asked, her face all white. I shrugged and sat down. A vicar knocked on the door and went into the bedroom, then came out again. The old woman came out, Mum said to look in Nan's knitting bag for a crown to pay her with, which I found and gave her. She left and we pulled our mattresses off the pile and squeezed them on the floor to sleep. Everyone had left by then. Mum stayed in the room with Nan.

In the dead of night we all woke up when Dad crashed in.

'Where's your mother?' he said in a thick drunk voice. Babs pointed towards the bedroom. He staggered through there, stood quietly by the door looking in. He changed his mind and came back in the living room, looked around for somewhere to sit or lie down, looked at Nan's chair and then sat in Grandad's chair, sat right down on Grandad's hat. *Nan'll go mad,* I thought, then remembered that Nan wouldn't be going mad about anything any more. He fell asleep with his arms crossed and the sound of his snores was nice, made me feel safe.

The next morning Dad got up and put his hand on the bedroom door, stood there for a minute and went in. We heard Mum cry, it was proper awful that sound, low and pitiful, like she wanted to die herself.

There was a knock at the door. It was the undertaker with two men carrying a wooden coffin. We

95

pushed our mattresses against the wall so they could set it down in the front room. We were all asked to stand outside and when we came back in, Nan was in there. That was the worst bit and then I started to cry. Why couldn't they leave her on her bed? She just looked like any old dead thing in that hateful coffin, like all the other dead bodies I'd seen in other people's houses. They had brought nice-smelling flowers with them and sprigs of dried lavender, which they set around the room. Mikey asked what it was for and I wanted to tell him it was because dead bodies stink, but I didn't. When the men had gone he took one of the flowers and put it on Nan's chest. That made Mum cry again and she leant over and kissed Nan on her forehead.

We had nowhere to go that night so had to put our mattresses on the floor in Nan's bedroom. Dad said the day after we'd move to Monday's.

'Well, Mum, the ground's too hard for burying people so you're gonna have to go and wait it out at the undertaker's. I know, I know, it's not right but you went and popped your clogs in the worst winter in history now, didn't you?'

Flo's smile faded when she looked at Ella lying there in the open coffin. She turned back abruptly to her dusting, stood on tiptoes to reach up with Ella's ancient feather duster to get at the cobwebs in the corners.

'I told him, it ain't right, and he says yes I know, Mrs Blundell, blah de blah.' Flo felt herself slip into her mother's personality, she wore it readily, took on Ella's turns of phrase and mannerisms, it was a comfort to her. 'And let's be honest, Mum, you can't stay here for ever, you're getting a bit ripe, if you know what I mean.' Flo dusted around the doorframe and skirting board.

'And I tell you something for nothing, I'm not having anyone saying your flat weren't clean. I'm not having it.' The kettle bubbled on the range. Flo emptied it into the large enamel bowl and stoked up the fire again. She couldn't stand the idea that the kettle would be boiled for the last time, for the last cup of tea. She had grown up in that flat, an only child, that was unusual around there, everyone had loads of kids, that was one thing you could rely on around the docks. Her dad was a docker and her mum a char on the ships, that's why Flo had started doing that job. And she'd fallen in love with the boy next door, Fred Blundell. She tutted, for better or for worse.

'How many cups of tea have I seen made on that range with that kettle over all those years, Mum? I can't imagine how many, a bloody lot.'

She pinned up the corners of the wallpaper that had fallen away from the damp walls and rubbed at the dark brown dirt until there was a clean spot and you could see the little yellow primroses in the pattern.

'Now I've gone and done it, Mum, got to do the whole bloody lot, now.' And she did, in both rooms, and she was so engrossed in boiling water and scrubbing the walls and throwing the filthy water down the sink, that when she finished and stood back, it was a surprise. The whole place looked different and she didn't know then who she'd done it for, for Ella or for her own pride.

97

When the rooms were spotless Flo made herself a cup of tea, her eyes darting about the flat, settling on Ella in the coffin and darting away again. Her hands were red raw from the hot water and wringing out the rag.

There was a sense of promotion in all of it, a moving up a level. She was the elder of the family now, she wasn't anyone's little girl any more. There was a strength to be had, she wouldn't crumble, she would stand up and get on with it, that's what Ella would have done. What her Mum had gone through in life, the workhouse, losing two babies, that wouldn't be for nothing. Flo would think of the woman her mother had been and only hope she could be half as much.

Flo took a deep breath and started to strip the sheets and blankets off the bed. Ella wouldn't be sleeping there any more. The grief rolled around her insides and up into her throat but she pushed it down with her new resolve. Through a gap in the curtains, a thin panel of light reached across the room over the bed. As she pulled the sheets off, dust particles rose up and hung suspended in the light. It became a ribbon of glitter, moving and alive. Flo stopped to watch it, mesmerised. The glitter tumbled and spun in slow motion. If there had been no gap in the curtains she wouldn't have known it was there. A corner of paper stood out from the seam of the mattress on the left side. Flo frowned and pulled at it. A greasy pound note came out with a little swish. She bent down to look, there was a slit in the seam, she pushed her finger and thumb in there, pulled out another pound note. She got a bread knife to make the hole bigger and pulled out a few more. All one-pound notes. She couldn't resist the compulsion to count them. Eleven pounds. Flo let out an angry sob. She knew Ella must have stashed some savings away. She'd been right; it would have been enough for Ella's passage to Australia with her and the kids. So much for that.

'Well, Mum, we don't have to worry about paying for your funeral no more, do we?' She held the notes to her chest, tears rolled down her cheeks.

Stan had brought two wooden boxes. Flo filled them with Ella's clothes and belongings from the dresser and chest of drawers. There wasn't much really, not much to show for a life. Homemade clothes that had been worn out and repaired over the years.

'They're all over at Monday's now, Mum. Fred took them yesterday. They couldn't stay here any more, could they, and Fred's got a new job, we all have. And I reckon it might be all right, Mum. I reckon Fred'll turn over a new leaf. We'll see, eh?'

Flo hoped they were all right, and tried not to cry when she thought about leaving the Dwellings for the first time in her life. Fred had a new job and so did she. It was a big new start and if they worked hard they might even get a house. A house with a garden for Mikey.

Flo shook her head. It was too much to hope for. None of it seemed real. Even Ella being dead, even though she was lying there in her coffin. She was just glad she'd been there to sort her mum's things, being able to do anything for her at that point was precious.

Flo sat down in Ella's chair and took out the yellow cardigan her mother had been knitting for Babs. There was a row of stitches half finished. Flo sighed deeply and made the next stitch, held the yarn round her finger and pulled it around the needle, feeling herself slip into Ella, she felt so close to her at that moment. She made another stitch and another until there was a knock at the door and the undertaker and his men came into the room carrying a coffin lid. She heard what they said, she just nodded and they looked at each other and placed the lid over Ella and one of the men hammered nails in while the others held the lid in place. Tap, tap, bang, for each of the twenty-one iron nails. But Flo didn't look. For each nail she made another stitch in the cardigan. She felt the wool compact and strong, making something more than itself, and the men carried Ella away.

6

A rumble of thunder woke Flo. She kept still to stop the rustle of the sheets obscuring the sound. It was in the distance but getting closer. Not thunder, a bang. Flo sat up in bed, alarmed, turned to Fred, face squashed against his pillow, asleep. It was getting louder, it sounded very close, bang, bang, bang, then BANG on their door.

'Fred?' Flo hissed, shaking him awake.

'What?' he snarled.

'Someone's banging on the doors.'

'It's the knocker-upper,' he said, and turned over.

'What?' The sound receded along the corridor.

'No one gets a lie-in at Monday's,' he growled.

Flo shivered, it was cold in the hotel. Pulling on her dressing gown, she got up and peeked through the huge curtains. Still dark. The wall clock said six o'clock. They were expected at the induction when the factory opened at seven thirty. She had arrived late the night before on the train from the docks, had got a few words of sense out of Fred before he fell asleep. Padding over the carpeted floor to the door, she felt for the light switch and flicked it on, flinching at the brightness. Fred growled again and pulled the sheet over his face.

This was the first time Flo had woken up in a strange place, the first time away from the Tilbury tenements. Everything was unfamiliar, there was no fire to rake out, no kettle to fill, the lights were electric. It smelled different, of bleach and carpet, not chip fat, coal smoke and mildew. She thought about her mum, in her box at the undertaker's waiting to be buried. What would Ella have thought about this hotel? She'd never be able to show her. Flo pushed the thought away. There was a bathroom inside the room. Flo flicked another switch and the en suite flooded with light.

'Mum.' Mikey ran at Flo from the adjoining bedroom and collided with her leg, nearly knocking her over.

'Hello, love,' she said, holding him close. 'You all right then?'

'Mum, it's brilliant, go in there, they've got a

bog indoors and hot water in the tap.'

He pushed her into the bathroom and switched on the basin tap. Before long the hot water steamed into the sink.

'Good, isn't it, love?' she said, smiling. 'How's your cough?'

'I had a bath in there last night.' He pointed to the tub with an expression of rapture. 'Look how clean I am.' He turned round in circles so she could inspect him.

'Your hair don't half smell nice,' she said, sniffing his head. 'Let's go and get the girls up.'

They walked through into the adjoining room. Three single beds had been lined up for the children. Babs sat up in bed, hooking the sleep from her eyes. Jeanie pretended to be asleep.

'Well, what do you think about this then?' said Babs, gesturing to the three beds.

'Bit of all right I reckon, love,' said Flo, beaming at the plump pillows, white sheets and thick grey blankets. 'You sleep all right?'

'Like a little baby. Well, *I* am going to the bathroom,' she said, and flounced past Flo with her nose in the air.

'Jeanie, love, you getting up now?' Jeanie stayed silent. Flo sat on the edge of her bed and pulled the sheet back a little. Jeanie snatched it away and turned over. 'We need to get up for breakfast, Jean, our induction's at half seven.' Flo left her to it. 'And you, Fred, we don't wanna be late on our first day, do we?'

Fred roused himself and pulled on his clothes, rolled a cigarette.

'Need a piss,' he said, going to the bathroom.

Finding it locked he banged on the door.

'All right, all right,' shouted Babs from inside. 'This bathroom lark's all right but there's no piss pot under the bed when you're caught short.'

On the ground floor the noise and smell of mass catering hit them as they opened the doors to the canteen, a cloying wall of fried food held in a vapour. Flo shrank back. There were so many people, strangers, in there. She'd known everyone at the docks, it was like that, everyone knows everyone's business. But here. She let Fred go through, then the children, and she followed behind, her eyes flitting all over the place, at the long wooden tables crammed with people eating and talking, the food service along one side of the room, women in hairnets spooning portions on to people's plates, all under the glare of the electric lights. Fred and the kids had been there a day and a half and already knew the ropes.

'Come on, Mum,' said Mikey, giving her a wooden tray. Flo slid it along the service counter and looked at the food on offer. She leant around the children to pull at Fred's arm, whispered into his ear.

'How we gonna pay for all this then?'

'Comes out the wages, don't it,' he said, winking at her.

'But we haven't done any work yet.'

'It's all right, Sid said.'

'Sid said what?'

Fred sighed. 'Sid said they like to settle new workers in.'

Flo relaxed and went back to her tray. She asked for helpings of sausage, fried egg, tinned tomatoes and a slice of fried bread, and helped herself to a cup of strong dark tea from the large urn at the end of the counter. The crockery was white, edged with a black line, with *Monday* printed in the middle. Fred spoke to the woman at the till, who nodded and wrote something in a book. They took seats together at one of the long wooden tables and Mikey fell on to his food as though he hadn't eaten in a week. He talked and laughed with his mouth full.

'Brilliant, ain't it, Mum?'

'Yes, love,' she said, smiling and cutting some fried bread. It tasted different from hers, it hadn't been cooked in chip fat and didn't have as much flavour. With his fork, Fred stabbed his pat of butter embossed with *Monday* and held it up to show Flo.

'Here, what happens if it's Tuesday?' he said, laughing, open-mouthed, a piece of sausage falling off his lip on to his lap. Flo suppressed a smile and looked sideways to see if anyone had heard, and realised that some of the workers were leaving. The enormous wall clock showed five past seven.

'Quick then, we better get a move on,' she said, gulping her tea.

Back in the room Flo pulled on her coat. 'So, love, you're gonna be all right, are you? You know where the school is?'

'Yeah, a woman come yesterday and took me over there. It's in the middle of them houses,' said Mikey, standing tall.

'So what time you going?'

'Gonna leave the room at half eight and walk over there. It's all right, Mum.' Mikey threw himself on to the double bed and burped.

'Come straight back here after school, do you hear? You can go out to play another day when you know your way round a bit more.'

Mikey nodded and fiddled with the wireless. Flo yanked the curtains open and gasped. They were on the top floor. The huge, square, plate-glass window showed her a view past the factory, across the mud flats by the sea wall and right across the Thames estuary. The sun was coming up, it touched everything with a pale light and illuminated an Orient Line cruiser passing by along the grey river towards Tilbury Docks. She squinted. It was one of the cruise ships she'd cleaned for the ten-pounders, she was sure of it.

Beryl would be in Australia now, and Flo might have been with her, with the kids and her mum. Her mum would still be alive, they'd be away from Fred. It hadn't worked out like that. Turning her head she saw Babs reapply her lipstick in a compact mirror, Fred light a cigarette and pass wind, and Jeanie slouch by the door. They were all together, weren't they, the family, not broken up, that must be better, mustn't it? And who knows if it was just her mum's time, she'd never know that now.

'I reckon someone else'll be cleaning her today,' she said, still looking out the window. The family fell silent and came to see.

'Suppose the river has thawed then,' said Fred.

'I reckon,' Flo said, looking up into his face. He nodded at her and she willed him to try with all his might to make this good and not muck it all up, to make it worth not leaving for Australia.

You're standing so close I can smell you, she wanted to say to him, *I'm breathing you in. You're a part of me, Fred Blundell, and that means if you let me down, I've let myself down.*

'Right then,' she said, her stomach contracting with nerves. 'Everyone ready? Look at the face on that.' Flo laughed at Jeanie's sour expression.

'Yeah, buck your ideas up, look sharp today, right?' Fred said to Jeanie, who gave him a dirty look.

They all jumped as a loud air-raid siren sounded, it whined louder and louder, filling the air around them. Mikey put his hands on his ears. Flo froze, she had learned to fear that sound, it brought back memories of running to the tenement basement, crowding in there with hundreds of others, waiting for the roar of planes overhead, the sound of bombs hitting houses.

'It's all right, it's just the call to start work,' said Fred, laughing.

'Christ, is it? We'd better get a move on then.'

They said goodbye to Mikey, left the hotel and were engulfed by a swarm of workers, thousands of people streaming towards the factory gates. Smoking, calling out to friends, cloth caps and aprons, overalls and work boots. Marching music blared out from a loudspeaker on the factory gatehouse. Flo gripped Babs's arm and gave her a weak smile. They were jostled along and waited their turn to file through the open double gates. The sniffer man stood on a box next to his gatehouse office, watching the workers stream through. His eyes scrutinised the crowd and fell on the Blundells. He sniffed and glared at them

106

as they passed through.

After some confusion about where to go, Fred led them to the Administration building and they found themselves sitting in a room, the chairs facing a blackboard attached to the front wall. Fred looked too big for his seat. Flo elbowed him to take off his cap. Two others sat with them, a couple. Flo sat next to the woman, her amiable face framed by auburn hair frizzy from a home perm left on too long.

'What, we at school or something?' said the woman, breaking the ice.

Flo chuckled. 'I reckon,' she said. 'Your first day too, is it?'

'Yeah, Lilly, Lil,' said the woman, touching her chest. 'And this here's Ted, me husband.' Ted leant round to nod and smile at Flo and Fred. Fred extended his hand, Ted shook it across the two women sitting in between.

'These yours are they?' said Lil, looking at Babs and Jeanie sitting behind.

'Yeah, that's Barbara and that's Jean, Babs and Jeanie we call them,' said Flo, smiling. 'They're twins but not identical.' Lil smiled, as if she could see they weren't. 'You got any?'

'Nah, not yet anyhow, we'd like to,' said Lil, turning to smile at Ted. 'You staying at the hotel then?' asked Lil.

The door opened and Sid Bucknall came in, as neat and trim as ever. He stood by the blackboard and beamed at everyone for a full minute before speaking.

'Welcome to Monday's,' he said, his arms spread wide. 'A little birdy told me you all got through the gates by half seven.' He smiled. 'Now that is what I call a good start, and that is what we like to see every day. Timekeeping here at the factory is crucial to our working practices, see? You must be through those gates by seven thirty, a little earlier wouldn't go amiss, and in your workshop or department ready to start work on the dot. I'll leave it to you to find out what happens if you're late.' He smiled again. Everyone shuffled in their seat. Sid watched them, he seemed satisfied that he had got his message across. He chalked *1. No being late* at the top of the blackboard.

'Monday's Leather Goods can offer you good working conditions and good prospects if–' he put his hands behind his back like a policeman and leant forward '–if ... you have the right sort of go-ahead spirit and enthusiasm for working for the company.'

Flo dug Fred with her elbow and tried not to laugh.

'We had a chap who worked as a checker in the glove factory. After eight months he was promoted to foreman, then chief examiner, and within two years he was a floor manager.' Sid's wide-eyed gaze panned across their faces. 'See?'

Flo put her fist against her mouth to hide her smile.

'One of the sewing girls was even promoted to forewoman within two and a half years, see?'

The twins whispered behind Flo and Babs put up her hand.

'Yes, Barbara?' said Sid, distracted.

'When was the sewing girl promoted to floor manager?'

'Sorry, I don't follow,' said Sid.

'Well, you said the chap was promoted to manager. Was the sewing girl promoted to manager too?'

'Oh, ha ha, I see what you mean, ha ha.' Sid's face creased with laughter. 'Oh no, young lady, she weren't a manager, no, there aren't any women managers at Monday's.'

Babs leant in to Jeanie who whispered something into her ear.

'Why not?' asked Babs.

Flo spun round in her seat to glare at the girls, mouthing 'shut up'.

'Why not?' said Sid, puzzled. 'The Monday Girls ain't interested in that sort of thing, in high-level men's work.'

'Your Babs is a right one, isn't she?' said Lil, leaning in to Flo.

Flo frowned. 'Isn't she just, it's the other one telling her what to say though. Funny how she can't speak two words to me but she can cause trouble when it suits her.' Flo glared at Jeanie, mouthed *You watch it, my girl.* Jeanie blinked and looked sideways with a smile on her lips. Babs nudged her, angry at being used as a mouthpiece. Fred turned in his seat and gave both girls a warning stare.

'Workers at Monday's are a grand crowd of friends, they don't keep themselves to themselves,' continued Sid. 'There is a thriving social club here, and the management like the workers to keep themselves happy, entertained and fit. There's sports clubs, chess club, sewing club, young wives club, old-time dance club, table tennis club, photography club, music club, gardening club, there's snooker and darts competitions, there's swimming in the lido in the summer, there's a cinema, there's dances in the social club, there's Scouts and Girl Guides. As you can see, there's a friendly feeling at Monday's, and what does a friendly feeling make?'

Silence.

'Well, it makes happy workers. And what do happy workers do?' Again, no answer. 'They work hard, don't they?' Undeterred, Sid beamed around at them. 'The work is not at all difficult, and I will say that I could do my first job by dinnertime on my first day.' Flo and the others gave a murmur of approval and relief. 'And, ladies, I have it as reliable fact that part-time work at Monday's Leather is *not* too strenuous for a married woman with a small family.'

Flo had never known anything like this. Sid passed some merchandise around, a leather handbag, a pair of leather gloves and a pair of sky blue stiletto shoes.

'Here is a selection of products made here in the factory. One day soon you'll be making these wonderful articles to the same exact quality you see here. I will add that there's also a technical college for the young men who really want to do well for themselves.'

Lil passed the gloves to Flo and leant in to whisper. 'I heard the young wives club is invitation only.'

'Really?'

'Yeah, it's Maggie Monday who runs it, the boss's wife.'

Flo looked at the gloves and passed them on, they really were lovely things, the likes of which she'd never had for herself. The long gloves were made from the softest ivory leather. She saw Babs hug the stilettos to her chest. Sid saw her too.

'Monday's workers get a hefty thirty-five per cent discount in our shops, young Barbara, so one day soon if you work hard you'll be able to afford a pair of them shoes and maybe you'll go dancing in them at the Friday-night dance.' Sid broke into infectious laughter and everyone chuckled along with him, except Jeanie who remained stony-faced. 'Remember, with high wages, low rents and plenty of free entertainment, Monday's provide a lifestyle that allows you to save.'

'I'm saving up for them shoes,' Babs whispered to Flo. Flo gave her an enthusiastic nod. Sid's words were music to her ears. They had never even been comfortable, let alone able to save. She thought of her Oxo tin back at the tenement and what she'd been forced to spend her paltry secret savings on. If Fred carried on behaving himself they'd be living the high life. If he stayed off the drink they'd be all right.

'There are wonderful opportunities here at Monday's Leather for hard workers prepared to do a good day's work for a good day's pay, es-pecially young men who want to get on,' said Sid, looking at Ted and at Fred. 'And for families, there's a chance, once training has been signed off, that you will be allocated a Monday's house on the estate. A three-bedroom house with garden and central heating and indoor bathroom. Now there's something to aim for. Here's a form to fill in and we'll get you on the list.'

He passed the form to Fred. Flo couldn't breathe for a second, it was all she wanted, a proper house for the family.

'Houses are for families only, so one day we might be giving you a form too,' he said to Ted and Lil, laughing again at his own joke. 'On a serious note, though. Houses are for Monday's workers. It stands to reason that if you don't work for Monday's, you don't live on the estate, right? All the more reason to work hard and stick to the Monday way of doing things.'

That meant if your face didn't fit, you were kicked out of your job, and if you were sacked, you were kicked out of your house too. Flo had already been through that at the docks.

'Right, more forms.' He handed everyone a clipboard and pen.

'All right to smoke?' asked Fred, holding up his tobacco tin.

'By all means,' said Sid. 'Just never in the factories, for obvious reasons, like burning the place down.' He passed Fred an ashtray. Flo flinched when she came to the *Are you pregnant?* question. It brought back memories of the old missioner's back room and the pickle spoon she had tried to put out of her mind.

'Thank you, thank you,' said Sid, collecting the clipboards. 'Now a chap from the company newspaper *The Monday Week* is coming in to have a little word, he might print a little piece to let everyone know who's starting. The paper lets the workers know what's going on at the company, what's on the dinner menu, who is off sick and so on. After that I'll show you around the factories.'

Fred leant forwards, his elbows on his knees. 'What you reckon then?' he asked Flo.

'Well, it's all right, it sounds grand, don't it?'

'Yeah, I reckon,' said Fred and stared ahead into his cigarette smoke.

'I can't wait, I'm gonna work so hard and get some shoes and gloves, no, gloves first then shoes.' Babs was breathless by the time they got back over to the hotel. The induction had lasted most of the day. After the tour of the factory they had eaten in the workers' canteen.

'You got that house form then?' Flo asked Fred.

'Eh? No, I forgot it.'

'Oh, Fred, I'll have to ask them for another one now.'

Flo opened the hotel room door and called out.

'Mikey, love?' There was no answer. 'Where is he then? Mikey? Where is he? I told him to come straight home after school. He's lost, I bet, poor little sod, probably wandering around trying to find us.'

'He's all right, probably out playing with the other lads, he'll come back.'

'I'm going out to look for him, you stay here and rest yourself,' she said, giving Fred a dirty look.

'I will,' he said, lying back on the bed and closing his eyes.

'And you, young lady, if you make any more trouble for the family you're for it, do you hear me? Maybe you'll think about talking to your

113

own mother first before telling your sister what to say to strangers.'

Jeanie turned her back and walked through into the other bedroom. Grabbing her bag, Flo left the room and quickened her pace down the stairs and out into the quadrangle. Mikey said the school was near the workers' houses. She headed that way along the main station road and found it, closed. An elderly caretaker with a limp leg was sweeping the entrance foyer with a large broom.

'Excuse me, love, I'm looking for my boy, he's new, just wanted to check he's all right.'

The caretaker stopped sweeping and regarded Flo for a moment.

'There's no one here, missus,' he said in a sleepy voice. 'Your boy's probably gone out playing with the others. They go over the woods or the sea wall or the swings or the farm...'

'Oh, right, where's the woods? I'll look there.'

He pointed his arm straight south-easterly. 'Past the lido the woods are,' he said in a voice so slow it was like he was sleepwalking.

'Thanks, love.' Flo looked back at him as he resumed his sweeping, he really did look like he'd fall over any time. She headed to the lido, remembered seeing all the trees behind there at the winter festival. Something made her run, made her think Mikey was in trouble, he'd had an accident or was lost and crying. He wasn't well enough to go wandering around for hours, his cough was bad. Past the swimming pools that were covered now and into the woods. The tangy smell of conifers enveloped her, her feet bounced on the thick layer of brown pine needles, she could hear shouts further off, deeper into the trees, the shouts of boys, and then a great collective flapping of wings and caw of rooks and she saw several black birds rise into the air above the trees.

'Mikey?' she called out, wanting to get to him.

Further in she ran, catching her nylons on a bramble.

'Damn it,' she said, seeing a ladder run up her leg. 'Mikey?'

She came upon a small group of boys Mikey's age and stopped, out of breath.

'Have you seen Michael Blundell? He started school today.'

The boys stood still, staring, one of them pointed straight up. Flo followed the direction of his arm, craned her neck and saw Mikey in the top of a bare elm tree, way up high, in amongst a rookery, a cluster of large nests, with what looked like a small pale ball in his mouth. He was so high up she screamed when she saw him.

'MIKEY!'

It was a scream that came from the depths of her being, and when Mikey heard it he lost his balance, couldn't find his footing. Flo's body turned runny and cold; her arms shot up towards her son but of course she couldn't reach him. He fell backwards, just slipped off the branch, it must have been damp or mossy, and his arms flailed, his school shirt snagged and caught him for a second. Flo held her breath. There was a small ripping sound, he hung down from the shirt, it ripped right through and it let him down to the branch below. The boughs were small and dense and his bottom landed on one of the nests. He just sat down in it and there he was, sitting up in the tree a couple of feet from where he had started, quite safe.

He looked down at Flo. There was something yellow dripping off his chin. A bird's egg. Flo started laughing, out loud until her eyes watered, she couldn't stop, and the group of boys gawped at her.

'Come on, love, get down here,' she called. Mikey made his way down, spitting the egg out of his mouth, finally jumping five feet from the lowest branch, and Flo rushed to him, grabbed him against her, felt his eggy face wet through her dress.

He pulled away. 'Mum, what you doing?' he hissed, looking at the other boys.

'Sorry, love, I thought you were lost. I told you to come straight back today, didn't I?' She cuffed the side of his head. 'Come on, let's go.'

They headed back through to the estate.

'Mum, they're gonna think I'm a right pansy now.'

'Well, you should have thought of that before going out when I told you not to. I was worried sick, wasn't I?'

Mikey looked at the floor.

'Oi, get off the pitch.' A man shouted at them from the other side of the football pitch they were crossing. They swerved sideways to walk alongside it.

'What's all that about?' said Flo.

'It's the number-one pitch, you're not allowed to walk on it. West Ham play there.'

'West Ham?' Flo laughed.

'Yeah, they practise there and play the Monday's team every season, the boys said it's brilliant, the players signed their cards.'

'How'd your first day at school go?'

'Mum? Can we get some Typhoo tea?'

'What for, we haven't got a kettle at the moment, have we?'

'Just for the football cards, all the lads have got them, for when West Ham play.'

Flo looked at his little face, grubby and smeared with snot and egg yolk.

'Yeah, course we can, love, soon as I get paid, all right?'

7

'There are numerous varieties of leather: box-calf leather, sole leather, Russia leather, hogskin, enamelled leather, waxed leather, velvet leather, split leather...'

Christ alive, I was nearly asleep in my chair. The training bloke droned on for hours, leather this, committee that, targets, quality, blah de bloody blah. Then he sent us off for the actual training. Dad was shipped off to Dispatch, where he'd be lugging crates on to lorries, served him right. Ted was sent off to the clicker department, cutting out bits of leather all day; I couldn't think of anything more boring. Us girls were sent off to sewing, now wasn't that a surprise. I hated sewing. Mum used to try and show me, but I always dropped the stitches or stuck myself with the needles. Babs loved it, proper little housewife in the making she was. We were led over to the shoe factory, the whole place stank of leather and glue – the workers must have been high as kites, maybe that's what they came back for – and it was awful noisy, people shouting and so bright from all the electric lights.

We came on to the sewing floor, the din of a hundred chugging sewing machines. A woman came over, her arms crossed over her massive bosom that strained for life under a black pinny. She had a face like a smacked arse, hair up in a scarf, red lippy that leaked into the fag lines round her mouth.

'This is Doris Lightman. Doris, these are your new recruits,' said the trainer. He leant in to whisper into Doris's ear. She looked me up and down – bloody cheek – I did the same back to her but she was looking at Mum by then.

'This way,' she said, turning on her heel. She told us to sit at a sewing machine each in a little section in the corner.

'Ooh, look at this,' said Mum. 'It's on the electric.' She stroked the enormous Singer machine on her table like it was a cat.

'Gather round,' said Doris. Everyone shuffled in to see. 'Gather round,' she said and looked only at me. I gave *her* a dirty look and squeezed in next to Babs.

She had an open, flappy bit of black leather like a queer topless hat that she said was a little girl's shoe and showed us how to edge-stitch it, how to press the foot lever to make the wheel go round, how to change the needle if it broke. Then she waved us back to our machines and gave us a shoe each to stitch. I cocked mine up right away, the stupid needle got stuck and I had to ask Smacked-Arse for help. The way she looked at me, like I was some sort of cretin. The others were sewing theirs, hunched over their machines. Mum finished first and held it up, showing off. Smacked-Arse inspected it and even smiled. One of her front teeth was brown.

'Well done, what's your name?'

'Flo Blundell.' Mum beamed like the Queen had told her to come to tea.

My needle kept snapping and Smacked-Arse got all hot and bothered with me and said I wasn't doing very well. Mum looked like she felt sorry for me and leant across.

'Do your best, love, try a bit harder, you'll get it,' and she had a look on her face like it'd be my fault if we didn't pass the training. Well, why should I? This was all hers and Dad's fault anyhow. Did she expect me to try hard for *her* when she had ruined *my* whole life? Babs kept laughing, saying how I never was very good at sewing. The whole thing was a pain in the arse.

The next thing I knew the hooter went off. A loud babble of chat replaced the noise of the machines. We headed out the doors with the other factory fodder, swept along, down the stairs and out into the compound, a swarm of ants scurrying out the factory gates, lighting fags and planning their tea, getting ready to swarm back again the next morning.

'Where's Lil?' Flo sat down to join Ted, Lil's husband, at a little round table in the club bar.

'Feeling a bit off colour, having a lie-down,' said Ted, offering Flo a cigarette.

'Oh? Not too bad I hope?'

'Nothing serious. She'll be back at work on Monday I expect.'

Flo nodded and sipped her drink. Fred stood at the enormous snooker table in the middle of the room, chalking his cue. She saw him as a stranger might, a monolith of a man, erect and unsmiling, shirtsleeves rolled up on his veiny biceps, Vaselined quiff shining, a strand curved over one eyebrow. He looked like something out of Hollywood. He blew the cue tip with his Woodbine smoke, glanced at his opponent, Jack someone or other, and leant down to break.

'Your Fred'll fleece him,' said Ted, snorting. He looked like he'd been in there a while and, with a flutter of panic, Flo sat up to see what state Fred was in. 'How's the training going then?' Ted asked.

'All right. Only got another week then we're out on the floor proper.'

'Lil says you're the golden girl.' Ted winked and gulped his beer.

'I'm doing all right, yeah, they're training me up as a key worker.'

'What's that then, you'll make keys?' He snorted again and Flo noticed the line of condensed saliva that joined his upper and lower lip stretch and contract when he spoke.

'They'll train me up on different jobs so's I can help out in any department. They reckon I've got potential.' Flo tried to stop herself smiling. They had also said she'd be up for promotion if she kept it up, maybe a forewoman in a year or two. Inside she was jumping up and down.

'You must be blinking good at sewing, Flo.'

Flo shrugged. 'I love it, don't I.'

Jack someone or other missed his shot. Fred motioned with his chin to the target pocket and closed his eyes to slits as he leant his face down to peer the length of the cue. His right arm pulled back and jabbed forwards to kiss the black into middle left.

Ted belched wet laughter into his pint glass. 'Told you he'd thrash him, should of had a wager.'

Flo allowed herself a small smile at Fred's triumph. Jack someone or other bristled with bravado and threw his cue down on to the green baize. It bounced and quivered, the sound cracked loud through Doris Day's 'Everybody Loves a Lover' on the jukebox. Fred's lower lip disappeared.

'Pick that up.'

Jack laughed and took a step towards Fred. 'Make me.'

Flo's stomach dipped with anxiety. She grabbed her gin and bag and strode towards Fred, pushed past him and stopped to look back. He didn't register she was there, he stared ahead at his opponent, his body set. There was nothing Flo could do, she couldn't make a scene. She doubled back to her table, leant down to speak into Ted's ear.

'Don't let him do anything stupid, love, I know what he's like.' She hesitated, wanting to tell Ted

121

not to buy any more drink for Fred but it wasn't her place to say such things.

Ted looked up at her, distracted, wanting to watch the fight. He saw the look on her face and nodded, but she wasn't convinced his need to help her was stronger than his need to see someone's fist find purchase against someone's cheekbone.

Helpless, Flo walked out of the bar door into the little lobby. She nodded at old Bill in the cloakroom and pulled back the curtained doorway into the adjoining dance hall. The Friday-night dance was in full swing. Flo downed her gin and lit another cigarette; she stayed back against the darkest wall.

Monday's had a band in again, it was pretty decent of them. GEOFF HAYWARD AND HIS ORCHESTRA, it said on the A-board at the door. A cheap night out for the workers. Flo looked at the dresses and laughing mouths and felt a pang of fear. If Fred caused trouble, they'd be out of there.

'Have you a spare?'

Flo jumped and turned to see a woman smiling at her.

'Yeah, here,' she said, shaking out an Embassy. Flo stared at the woman's immaculate eyeliner and hairdo as she looked down to light the cigarette. Her scarlet lips made an o as she blew out the smoke.

'Thanks. I'm Maggie,' she smiled, holding out her hand.

Flo's clutch bag fell to the floor as she tried to free her right hand from her drink and cigarette. She snatched up the bag, stuffed it under her arm and shook Maggie's hand with a nervous smile. She pulled away from the woman's bemusement and hooked a loose strand of hair behind her ear.

'Having fun?'

Flo shrugged and wondered what to say. She couldn't stop her eyes flicking over Maggie's dress. It was sleeveless and straight and only just on the knee, made out of bottle green silk, really lovely stuff, not homemade. The shoes she wore were fancy too, very high spiked heels, pointed toes, matching green silk. Flo was pretty sure they weren't Monday shoes.

'All right, I suppose. You?'

'Well, it could be worse, we could be next door where things are getting a little heated.' Maggie laughed and gave a mock grimace.

Flo hugged her bag tighter. There was something about this Maggie, she seemed bigger than her size.

'You're new, aren't you?'

'Yeah, I started training a few weeks ago.'

'What do you think of it here?'

'I love it, it suits me down to the ground, I wanna go for promotion as soon as I can.' Flo blurted it out without thinking. She sounded like she was getting ahead of herself. What she really hoped was that Fred would be the one to do well.

'Really? A career woman? That's what I like to hear.'

Flo stared hard at the dancers. The partners clutched one another earnestly, the young ones savouring a legitimate reason to hold someone close.

'Can I get you a drink?' said Maggie, looking at

Flo's empty glass. 'I know the barman, come on, let's take advantage. Sorry, I didn't catch your name.'

'It's Flo. Flo Blundell. Yeah, why not, a drink would be lovely.'

Maggie strode over to the bar, Flo trotted behind her, noticed Maggie wore those new seamless nylons.

'What's your poison?'

'Gin and lemon please.'

Maggie smiled and held her gaze on Flo's face for an uncomfortable second. She held up her hand to attract the barman's attention. He saw her and rushed over.

'It's not often I get bought a drink by a girl.' Flo giggled.

Maggie took a drag of her cigarette. 'No? Well, like I said, I know the barman. My husband knows him too.'

'What is he, the owner or something?' Flo laughed.

'Yes, that's right.' Maggie smiled at her again.

'What, you're Maggie *Monday?*' Flo immediately tried to pull her face together.

'Uh huh. That's a pretty necklace, Flo,' she said, reaching to Flo's string of white plastic poppit beads she'd borrowed from Babs.

'Oh, thanks.' Flo gave an embarrassed laugh and took a long gulp of her drink.

'Have you joined any social clubs yet?' Flo shook her head. 'How'd you like to join the young wives club?'

'What's that then?'

'It's just a little group I run, a group of friends,

we get together once a week, have a little drink and a bit of fun. How'd you like to join us some time?'

'Me?' Flo wasn't sure it was the best of ideas, what with Fred causing trouble next door and Maggie being the owner's wife.

'Yes, why not?' Maggie laughed. 'It's just a bit of fun. I tell you what, one of the girls has organised a Tupperware party for tomorrow night. I know, it's all very *domestic*, but it will be a chance for you to meet everyone.'

'Tupperware, eh?' Flo had heard about it – the ladies in the magazines went to Tupperware parties – she wouldn't mind having a look, she'd been paid, could maybe buy something little for when they got a house.

Maggie chuckled. 'Yes, Tupperware. How'd you like to? Tomorrow night, at mine?'

Flo spat on to the little black block of make-up grease, mixed the saliva in with the applicator and brushed some more over her already thick eyelashes. The blue dress she had bought as a special treat from Grays market with her third Monday's pay packet fitted her well enough, the bodice curved over her bust, the full skirt spanned out from her waist. Gritting her teeth she crammed her feet into Babs's new sky blue stilettos, purchased from Monday's shoe shop with her first wages.

There was a knock at the door. Mikey ran to open it.

'Well, don't you look a picture,' said Lil from the doorway, seeing Flo all dressed up. 'I thought it was a ladies' club, not a dance.' Lil looked down at her own floral day dress.

'What, too much is it?' A flash of doubt.

'Nah, you'll do,' said Lil, linking her arm. 'Hope they've got something to drink over there, I'm a bit nervous.'

'Me too. Your hair don't half look good,' she said, admiring Lil's auburn backcombed perm. 'Bye then, be good.' She waved at Mikey and the girls who lounged around the room.

Flo and Lil walked arm in arm towards the Monday Mansion.

'Blimey, never thought I'd be going inside this place,' said Lil. 'You sure it's all right I'm coming?'

'Yeah, Maggie said.' Flo shivered, her old coat wasn't good enough for going out in and although the Big Freeze had thawed, there was a cool March breeze blowing off the river that her nylon dress didn't buffer.

The mansion loomed before them. The closer they got the bigger it grew.

'How many bleeding rooms you reckon?' said Lil, counting the numerous front windows. 'Go on, ring the bell then.'

Checking her hair, Flo pressed the doorbell. A maid answered wearing a little white apron. Flo stifled a giggle as they were led through the wide entrance hall into a sitting room. The conversation ceased when they entered the large room that looked very modern and very expensive. The wall-to-wall thick pile carpet, the walls different colours, one a deep salmon, the others beige, bookcases full of books, French windows like they had on the cruise liners, a walnut cocktail cabinet she had seen in a magazine, and a large closed cabinet that she guessed housed the television set. The lighting was low, the slow beat of jazz music came from an electric record player set into its own side cabinet. Eight women lounged on settees and chairs, smoking and holding glasses. Flo smoothed down the full skirt of her Grays market dress and squirmed as the eight pairs of eyes scrutinised her.

'Flo and Lil, come in, make yourselves at home, meet the other girls.' Flo gave Maggie a nervous smile and looked her hostess up and down. Black slacks, black polo neck jumper, some proper undies, her figure looked amazing. Hair done up in a French pleat, slingback high heels. Lil caught Flo's eye and raised her eyebrows.

Maggie pointed her scarlet-lacquered fingertip at each woman.

'That's Tabby, Doreen, Dot, Liz, Alice, Marge, Carol and Sue.' The women said hello in turn, some raised their glasses. 'Alice is our Tupperware hostess this evening. If she can tear herself away from her gimlet, that is.' Maggie winked at the newcomers and gestured for them to sit down. Flo felt all eyes on her as she perched on the edge of a lounge settee that was wooden with tie-on pads to sit on.

'Now, Flo, if I remember correctly, yours is a gin and lemon? Or would you like a Singapore sling?'

'A what? Yeah, go on then, I'll try one, and you, Lil,' she said, lighting a cigarette and pulling a thick-cut-glass ashtray towards her.

'Tabby will mix them for you. She used to drink them out in Malaya, didn't you, darling?'

127

'Yes, that's right,' said Tabby, in a husky voice, making a show of dragging herself off the sofa and swaying over to the cocktail cabinet, cigarette in hand. She wore her fair hair up in a lemon silk turban, and was tall and slim but hunched her shoulders a little, giving the effect of a long banana. The dress she wore had no waistband, as Flo had suspected when she first saw Tabby on the sofa. It hung straight down from the bust and looked very modern.

'It's gin, Benedictine, bitters, lemon and a dash of cherry brandy,' she said as she made the concoction, pouring the ingredients into the shaker. 'Shaken,' she said, with her cigarette between her thin lips, her long beads rattling as she shook the cocktail, 'and strained on to ice.' She handed the peach-coloured drinks to Flo and Lil. Flo sipped it.

'Sour?' said Tabby.

Flo nodded. Tabby smiled and went to make herself another. 'We lived on these in Malaya, it was so damned hot out there, all one could do was lounge and drink.'

Flo wasn't exactly sure where Malaya was but didn't want to ask and appear stupid.

'How come you were out there, then?'

'Husband ran the rubber plantation for the shoe factory.'

'Ex-husband, darling,' said Maggie.

'Indeed,' agreed Tabby, shaking her cocktail.

Maggie caught Flo and Lil exchanging a look. 'Tabby here escaped her fate. It can be done, you know, a girl can make her own fate nowadays.'

'The only downside is, the Mother's Union

128

won't let me in.' Tabby made a face and a couple of the others laughed.

'I'd love to go abroad. I've never been out of Essex even,' said Flo.

'Nor me,' concurred Lil.

'Oh well, you must,' said Maggie, perching on the edge of a chair. Flo noticed that the chairs and settees were all different and funny-looking, weird plastic and wooden shapes with thin metal legs. She wondered where the upholstered three-piece suite was. 'Travel is stimulating and gives a new perspective.'

'I fancy Australia,' said Flo.

'Bet it's full of Brits now, with all them ships going out,' said Alice.

'I used to clean the ships down the docks, lovely they were, top class,' said Flo. She gulped the rest of her drink, it went down like Tizer. She jumped when Tabby handed her another. 'Oh, thanks.'

'You must of seen all them coloured migrants come in then?' said Liz. 'They're coming here and we're going to Australia. Musical countries, isn't it?'

'Yeah, I suppose. We saw all sorts, saw an elephant being winched off a boat once.'

'I once rode an elephant in Burma, it was bloody uncomfortable,' said Tabby. Everyone laughed.

'Well, the closest I got is seeing one on the television,' said Liz.

'Oh, got a television set, have you?' said Lil.

Liz smiled. 'The best thing I've done. I can plonk the children down in front of it and, hey presto, quiet as mice. I've taken some part-time home work from the factory, it's very good, I can be there for the children and earn a bit too.'

'Ooh, that's good, isn't it?' said Lil, elbowing Flo in the arm.

'You got any kids then?' said Liz.

Lil blushed and twisted her hands in her lap. The women stared at her.

'Well, I wasn't gonna say anything yet.'

Flo coughed on her cigarette. 'Lil?'

'We haven't told anyone yet but I can't keep it in.' Lil gave Flo a sheepish grin. A murmur of expectation ran around the room.

'Yep, that's right, I'm expecting.'

'Oh, Lil, that's wonderful news, it really is,' said Flo, patting Lil on the leg and forcing a smile. It wasn't that long ago that she'd been expecting herself.

'Well, well, congratulations are in order I see,' said Maggie. 'Let me grab a bottle of something a little more appropriate.' She left the room and reappeared carrying a bottle of Champagne. The women oohed and aahed and squealed with laughter when Maggie popped the cork.

'You've done that before,' crooned Tabby.

'Well, Tabby, you know me,' said Maggie with a wry smile. 'So when's it due, Lil? I see my husband is going to lose one of his workers before she's hardly begun.'

'Oh, yeah, sorry about that,' said Lil, blushing again. 'I'm a few months gone, but I've had a lot of misses over the years so I never know, but this time the doctor says it looks promising, over the worst, well, fingers crossed, eh?'

'Oh absolutely, yes,' said Maggie, 'and I do

believe there's a wonder drug for that kind of thing now?'

'Oh yes, the doctor's put me on something new that'll do the trick he said.'

Flo forced a smile. She glanced at Lil's belly; she couldn't tell with that flared dress she had on. Flo's baby would have been due a bit before Lil's, then. She should have kept it, managed somehow.

'And don't forget the Black Beauties to keep the figure trim,' said Doreen, a plump woman wearing a fitted yellow dress and yellow court shoes. 'But don't take my word for it, mind. I've had four nippers and there's only so much science can do.'

'Doreen, the Black Beauties are the *reason* you had four nippers,' said Tabby.

'Well, they are rather good,' said Doreen, lifting her shoulders and squinting a smile, 'but I'm not sure about putting this working lark into Lil's head if she's having a family. My George says it's too modern here, that women belong in the home, keeping house and being useful.'

'Oh, Doreen, you know that's not the Monday way. We like mothers to work if they want to,' said Maggie, pouring the champagne.

'I never had much choice, we didn't have a pot to piss in so I always *had* to work,' said Flo, downing her second cocktail and accepting the champagne from Maggie, who raised her eyebrows.

'See? There you are, a modern woman straight from, where did you come from, Flo?'

'Tilbury Docks.' Flo hadn't had champagne before. She sipped it, feeling the bubbles wet her nose, it tasted sublime.

'Yes, Tilbury, there you are, a modern place just

like Monday Leather.'

'Well, I like being a housewife, actually I love it,' said Doreen. 'It suits me that George goes out to work, he's the man of the house, women shouldn't try to be the boss, they're not equal to men. You must come to see my new Mixidiser, Lil, have you seen one?' Lil shook her head. 'You fix it on to the tap and it does all your pulping and mixing, it really is quite a miracle, it saves me hours.' Doreen gave a big sigh and smiled like a contented cat.

'And *I* like working,' said Alice, standing up. 'Doing Tupperware parties has been the making of me, I'm happy as Larry.'

'Yes, Tupperware does liberate women in a queer sort of way,' said Maggie, taking the record off the turntable. 'It's not just about keeping your husband's food fresh,' she said, grinning. 'But it is very good for that too, of course. Over to you, Alice.'

'Yes, thank you very much, Maggie, for that *super* introduction.'

Flo's eyes flicked from Maggie to Alice, who exchanged a look like they had a private joke.

'Now for the reason we are here this evening. To start off we'll play a little game to get us in the mood. Guess the waist measurement, it's a bit of a laugh.'

'Oh not that one again, we did it last year,' groaned Doreen.

'You first, Flo,' said Maggie, calling her to the centre of the room.

Flo blanched, it was just as well she was half-cut. Maggie leant in close to pull the tape measure around Flo's back, she could smell Maggie's perfume, it made her feel even more lightheaded.

'Right,' said Maggie, drawing back. 'What are your guesses for Flo here? And don't you think she looks just like Doris Day, with her cute blonde curls and her full skirt? All you need to complete the look are some dainty white gloves.'

There was a general consensus that Flo did look like Doris Day tonight. Flo put her hands behind her back, she had forgotten the gloves.

'Twenty-five?' guessed Dot. Maggie shook her head and lit a cigarette that she'd pushed into a long black holder. 'Twenty-seven?' said Lil.

'Nope.'

'Twenty-six?' guessed Doreen.

'Yes. Doreen wins it, twenty-six it is.'

Flo gave silent credit to her corset.

'There you are, Doreen, now for your prize,' said Alice. Doreen clapped her hands together and shuffled forwards in her seat, showing her nylon slip. 'You can choose either this super Jel-N-Serve, a completely sealing jelly mould, or this sealed butter dish perfect for larder or fridge storage. You've got a fridge, haven't you, Dor?'

Doreen bristled. 'Yes, course I do, what would I do without my Frigidaire?' She looked around the room for agreement, Maggie rolled her eyes. 'I'll take the butter dish, thank you, Alice.'

'I wouldn't mind a bloody Frigidaire,' Flo whispered to Lil, glad to be back in her seat.

'What, to put in your invisible dream kitchen?' The women lit cigarettes to stop themselves laughing.

8

'Flo, our shining star, is now a key worker for this floor. Well done, girl, that's smashing.' Smacked-Arse gave a big brown-tooth smile. 'You'll start here in my sewing section and will be "on call" from now on. Barbara, well done on finishing the training, you'll start here too. You too, Lil, but I know you'll not be here long.'

They all giggled and patted each other's arms. Then they looked at me, realised they were being bloody selfish. Smacked-Arse's smile dropped off her face and slid down her pinny.

'Now then, Jean, you'll be working in the dispatch department.'

I frowned. What did she mean? That's where Dad worked.

'In the box-making section. I'm sure you'll be very happy there.' The woman smirked at me. In the box-making section?

'Ah, that's good then, love, you hate sewing, don't you?' said Mum, putting her arm around my shoulders. I shrugged her off; she was just relieved I hadn't mucked it up for her.

'Jean, you wait there while I show the others over.'

I stood like a mug in the corner watching the others take their walk of glory over to the sewing section. Not that I would want to be there either.

'Girls? I know you've all met Flo, Lil and

Barbara by now. You'll be pleased to hear they are joining you lot today as fully fledged sewing girls.'

The machinists stopped work for a millisecond to give a round of applause, and that was it, the new ones sat down and plugged themselves into the factory, human sewing machines, and who knew how much of their lives they would give over to it. Five years, fifteen, thirty? It made me shudder. They looked so pleased about it all too.

Smacked-Arse came stomping over to me and didn't even bother speaking, just waved her head at me like she was taking me for the slipper at the headmistress's office. All I could do was follow her to the boxes. The whole place was like one big box, falling down over me, blocking out the light. The stale sweat wafted off her body as I padded along after her. I could hear her stockings chafe together, I was surprised she didn't set the place on fire with all that static.

We walked downstairs, *underground*, and came into a grim-looking room in the factory cellar. No windows, the air was clogged with cardboard dust that made me choke. I couldn't see Dad anywhere. Smacked-Arse handed me over to a Mr Turtle, who didn't look at all like a turtle but more like a desert rat. He was small and pinched, God knew how old. The grease in his hair was caked with cardboard dust. His fingers made me sick, they were really long and spindly, like he had an extra knuckle or something, and when he talked they crept like spiders. It was almost a shame to see Smacked-Arse go back up, she didn't seem too bad compared to this one.

'This way please, Miss Jean.'

I scowled at him, wondered why he walked with a limp, then decided I didn't care. He sat me down on a dusty stool alongside a conveyor belt that hummed and rattled. There were eight other people stationed along it, at right angles, making boxes, their hands going ten to the dozen. They made a box on a little table at their side, put it on the conveyor and when the box came to the end, one of the last two workers took the box off and put it into a larger box. Hell on earth.

They all stared at me, not talking, their hands still working, the work so idiotic they didn't need their eyes. They looked like the future robots in Mikey's comics.

'Cut the string that holds the bundle of flat boxes together,' said the desert rat, and I jumped when I realised he was showing me the job, 'with the cutter,' he said, using a little metal cutting tool that hung off the side of the conveyor. 'Make sure you hold the stack together until you have placed the boxes safely on their end at the side of your table. If you do not place them safely on their end at the side of your table you will find they will slide down and be on the floor where they will be a danger to yourself and your fellow workers and, more importantly, you will not be able to reach them.'

I just stared at the cretin. How long had he worked there, in the dusty dungeon, caked in cardboard? He paused. I think he wanted me to say that I understood him. I wanted to scream into his ratty face that any two-year-old child would understand him easily enough. I nodded and gritted my teeth.

'Take one flat box from the stack, place it on your table, like so.' He stood the flat box up on its end. 'Open out the flat box, like so, turn in the flaps, like so, turn the formed box over and place it on the conveyor.'

His simple little eyes scanned my face for any sign of understanding, as if he expected to have to show me twice. I gave a loud sigh and picked up one of the flat boxes, made it into an actual box and drew in my breath when I cut my finger on the damn thing.

'A hazard of the job, I'm afraid. Your skin will toughen up in time. No blood on the boxes please.' With his hateful spindly fingers he wiped my blood off the box on to a bit of grey rag and gave me the rag, for future injuries I imagined. I sucked my finger, damned paper cut. I slammed the box on to the conveyor and watched it go down the line to be picked up by one of the robots at the end.

'*Place* the box on the line, do not smash it down, otherwise the corners will be damaged and it won't pass quality control.'

I stared at him, at the dust on his eyelashes. He waited there with no expression. I sighed again and took up another flat box, pushed the thing together and placed it, carefully, on the line and watched it go down.

An expectant April morning, winter behind and summer ahead, magnolia buds pouting heavy and ripe in the trees around the quadrangle. The Blundell family walked along in a gaggle, following Sid Bucknall and Housing Manager Bob Philips, whose stiff trilbies nodded and concurred. They turned off the main station road into Queen Elizabeth Avenue, one of the five roads that made up the workers' housing estate. Lined with poplar trees standing sentinel, the avenue of cube-shaped houses stretched away.

'The architecture of the entire estate and factory complex is built to a modernist design,' explained Sid, turning to the Blundells as he walked. 'Notice the square shapes and flat roofs, the buildings are simple, functional, unornamented.'

Flo looked at Fred, who frowned and lit a cigarette. The men in front slowed and stopped at the gate of number thirty-eight. Flo could hardly bear it.

'Here we are then,' said Bob Philips. 'A three-bedroom semi-detached with front and back gardens. While we are outside I will say that the company does expect tenants to keep their gardens to a good standard. You'll notice that the plots along the street are neat and tidy. There is an annual garden competition, with first prize keenly sought after. Mr Ductle, your next-door neighbour, has won it three times. By the look of that topiary I expect he's in the running this year, too.'

A topiary cockerel stood proudly in the garden next door. The garden of number thirty-eight looked a bit tatty in comparison. Flo's gaze lifted to look up at her new house. It was big and white with metal-framed windows. It looked enormous, she just couldn't believe it was theirs. Babs grabbed her arm and squealed.

'Mum?' said Mikey.

'Yes, love, this one's ours.' Mikey's jaw fell open. He sniffed to reclaim a wet line of snot and gaped at the house, nudged Jeanie who stood next to him, unimpressed.

Bob Philips unlocked the front door while Sid held the gate for the family. Flo walked in first and turned right from the hallway into the unfurnished front room with a modern beige-tiled fireplace. The floor was covered with a fitted brown carpet. She wandered around in a daze and pushed through an adjoining door into the kitchen at the back. She put her hands over her mouth. It had to be a dream. There were built-in cupboards to table height right around the kitchen, with an electric cooker in the left corner. She turned a knob and one of the rings on the hob glowed red. No more lugging coal for cooking on the range.

Doing the laundry would be a world easier, she'd be able to leave the clothes to soak overnight in that deep butler sink. She turned on a tap. Within a few seconds hot water came out of it. She gasped at the water heater on the wall and turned the tap off. Back in the tenement flat the sink was shallow and she had to boil a kettle on the range when she needed hot water. When she glanced around the door into the back corner her breath caught in her throat. There stood at shoulder height a tall white refrigerator. It said *Frigidaire* along the top of the door. Flo pulled at the long chrome handle, it opened with a hiss, there was an ice box at the top and two vegetable trays at the bottom. It smelled of stale milk but Flo didn't care.

'Oh yes, the previous tenants moved abroad so

they left the fridge. Lucky you, eh?' Bob Philips had poked his head into the kitchen. 'You'll be a proper little housewife now, won't you?'

Flo nodded, on the verge of tears. She wouldn't have to keep the milk in a bowl of cold water, she'd be able to buy meat and keep it cold, she'd be able to make ice and buy those new frozen fish fingers. She wouldn't have to go shopping every day, it was like a proper dream.

'MUM.' Babs's screech echoed through the house. Flo followed the scream out of the kitchen and right into a door at the end of the hallway. Standing with her arms held wide, Babs stood in a bathroom, an indoor downstairs bathroom with a bath and a toilet and a basin.

'Oh my god, I can't believe this is ours, love.' Flo couldn't help it, she burst into tears. Babs grabbed her and cried too.

'No more sharing a lav with five other families, Mum.'

'What's all this then?' It was Fred filling the bathroom doorway. He frowned with surprise and looked away quickly when Flo and Babs laughed and cried at him.

'Not bad, eh?' he said to the bathroom window.

'Babs, upstairs,' called Mikey. Babs ran off, her feet thumping up the stairs.

'Reckon we'd better get hold of some furniture pretty quick,' said Fred. Flo sat down on the edge of the bath tub and looked up at him.

'Is it real, love? Will it last?'

'Course it will, why not?'

'We haven't known anything like it, have we? We got to hold on to this, all right?' She looked up

140

into his face. He mustered a smile, patted her on the shoulder and unbuttoned his trousers to use the toilet.

'Here you are then,' said Sid in the front room, glancing around for Fred then handing the keys to Flo. He passed her a copy of the *Monday Week*. 'There's some ads in there for furniture folks are selling on the estate, might get you started. Bringing any over from Tilbury, are you?'

'Yeah we are, thanks, Sid, I don't know how to thank you enough, it's a right palace.'

'Pretty good, isn't it? Well, you're part of the Monday family now, and Monday's looks after its workers. We don't treat them like cogs in a machine like some companies, our workers are happy, we've never had a single strike at Monday's, and that says a lot considering what's going on in the country.'

'I can believe that, Sid.'

'A little bird told me you're doing pretty well in the factory. Keep up the good work.' He winked at her and walked away, chatting to Bob Philips.

'Mum.' Mikey called her upstairs. She found him in the front bedroom with Babs. 'Can this be mine, Mum, please?' he said, flicking the light switch on and off.

'Smashing, isn't it, love? Well, I dunno, let's have a look round.' Mikey ran ahead to show her the other rooms, all with shiny linoleum floors. 'Well, I reckon this one the girls can share and this one is yours, love.'

'Oh, the smallest one?' His face dropped.

'Mikey, love, you didn't even have any bedroom before, you slept in with me and your dad, have

141

you forgotten so quick? You've got your very own room now, love, isn't that special?'

'Yeah!' Mikey jumped in the air and ran around his room, touching his walls.

There was a knock at the front door. Doreen from the young wives club stood on the step, beaming at her.

'Oh,' she gasped, clapping her hands together. 'I thought it was you. I says to myself, that's Flo moving in across the street.'

'Well I never, you live over there?'

'Oh yes, just across the way, number thirty-nine. Welcome, neighbour.'

She thrust a wet wobbling pink blancmange into Flo's hands.

'It's strawberry, made it last night luckily, used my new Tupperware mould. Be lovely with a drop of Ideal. Let's have a look then.' She brushed past Flo into the house. 'Yes, it was the Singletons here before you, he was a manager in the bag factory and they asked him if he'd train to work abroad. They had three nippers, all at Monday's school. She did part-time work at home, mostly putting metal tags on shoelaces. Oh, you should get an electric fire in here' – she gestured at the fireplace in the front room – 'we have, we use the room at a moment's notice, very good. Yes, the Singletons, they had a television set, we came over to watch the Coronation on it, all the neighbours crowded round, imagine. We've got our own set now, of course. Had a street party right on this road too, really gay it was, didn't pay a penny, the company gave presents for the children, balloons, every-thing laid on. Ooh, they left the Frigidaire.'

Standing speechless, still holding the blancmange, Flo listened to Doreen's commentary.

'Ooh, you lucky thing, what a bonus, yes I suppose they couldn't take everything with them, only a six-foot crate to pack their belongings and off they went to Canada.'

'Canada?'

'Yes, the parent company is over there. I've heard it's wonderful, imagine all those mountains and lakes, but bears too, I wouldn't fancy that very much. Bit like Davy Crockett I should think.' She smiled at Flo, took the blancmange off her and placed it on the kitchen worktop. 'Right then, I'll get my cleaning things and we'll have a go at it, shall we?'

She bustled away and returned ten minutes later wearing her floral housecoat and carrying a bucket full of rags, brushes, soap and polish. 'I'll bring the Hoover over later, but first the kitchen.'

Flo followed suit and pulled on Doreen's spare apron and some fuchsia Marigolds and started scrubbing the kitchen cupboards. Babs and Mikey poked their heads around the door, saw the cleaning equipment and disappeared to charge around the house, their footsteps banging overhead.

'So, your girls courting yet?' asked Doreen, her head in the open oven.

'Oh, Babs has been going to them dances, says she's taken a fancy to a boy, a real cool cat, she says.'

'Oh, ha ha, the youngsters talk funny nowadays, and all that loud rocking roll music, that Elvis, oh my goodness, it's all *very* wicked,' she said, giggling. 'You seen him on the television?

143

How he shakes hisself, oh my word.'

Doreen's cheeks were bright red when she pulled out of the oven.

'I haven't really seen much television, but I saw a picture of him in a magazine at work, and heard him on the wireless, and Bill Haley, I like him, that music's a bit, well, dirty, isn't it?'

'Oh, I reckon it is too.' Doreen blushed again and chuckled, her portly body jerking up and down in time with her laugh. 'George won't have it on, says it's disgusting. We like the traditional music, you and your Fred must come to the old-time dance club with me and George.'

'Oh blimey, I don't think my Fred would go.' Doreen looked crestfallen. 'I'll see though, I'll ask him.'

'Mr Ductle next door goes with his Ethel. They're a right old sight, don't crack a smile they don't, take it really serious. Like his garden, he's proper serious about that too, keeps it spick and span for the competitions, you met him yet?'

Flo shook her head. She frowned at the sound of Babs and Mikey shouting upstairs, then relaxed when Mikey squealed with laughter.

'Keeps budgies he does, dozens of them, shows them he does, you heard them budgies?'

'No I haven't.'

'You will when the weather's warmer and he opens his windows. And mind, your garden needs some work. If your garden's not up to scratch you'll get a letter through the door from the company. Well, that's us done I reckon.' Doreen stood back to admire the clean kitchen. She put the blancmange in the fridge. 'That'll do nice for your

144

tea. You must get a washing machine, saved my life mine has, and you getting a television set?'

Flo flushed. She couldn't imagine getting rid of the old dolly tub let alone owning something as luxurious as a television.

'The wages are good here, what with you both working and the girls too, I bet you'll get one, good they are, especially when you've been married as long as we have and run out of things to say.' She chuckled. 'And good for keeping the nippers quiet. I'll bring the Hoover over tomorrow. I better get home and put the tea on for George, he'll have finished reading his paper by now. Staying at the hotel tonight, are you?'

'Yeah, Sid's getting us a van tomorrow to bring our things over from Tilbury.' Their things sitting in the damp tenement cellar, probably being gnawed at by the rats. 'Bye, Dor, thanks, love.'

With the door closed, Flo wandered back to the kitchen and sat down on the brown linoleum floor. It was really hers, a proper kitchen with hot water and a fridge and a cooker, she just couldn't believe it.

'Jeanie's out there.' Mikey called Flo upstairs to his bedroom window.

Jeanie sat in the back garden, on the grass with her back to the house, her legs pulled up to her chest. Flo sighed, she'll never meet a nice boy moping around like that. And it wasn't very good in the factory being all miserable. Flo didn't want to make a bad impression, it was important for the family to do well. Jeanie just didn't seem to understand how important it was.

'Ungrateful cow,' said Babs, looking over Flo's

145

shoulder. 'Just because her hands are all ripped up from the boxes.'

'She'll be all right. Where's your dad anyway?'

'He went out when you were doing the kitchen with that lady.'

Flo guessed where he'd gone, down the bloody club.

'Do you know Canasta?' Maggie gestured for Flo to join Tabby and Alice at the card table. The sitting room was heavy with smoke and perfume, just the two standard lamps by the table switched on.

'Can't say I do. Posh parlour game is it?' Flo gave Maggie a sidelong glance and grinned.

'It's like Rummy but with two packs of cards and jokers for wild cards,' said Alice.

'What would you suggest, Shove Ha'penny?' Maggie put on Flo's Tilbury accent and gave her a tipsy smile. 'Shall we partner up?'

'Yeah, go on then. Doreen not here?' Flo took a seat at the table and looked around Maggie's unusually empty room.

'We don't invite Doreen to these little soirées, she can be a bit of a drag, droning on about house-keeping rituals,' said Maggie from the cocktail cabinet, holding out a bottle of gin with her eye-brows raised.

Flo nodded yes to a drink. 'She's all right. She came round with a blancmange the other day and helped me clean the house.'

'Well, I had to put a stop to her jam-making malarkey, this isn't bloody *Woman's Own.*' Maggie laughed and took her seat next to Flo, passing her drink across.

'Oh stop being a bully, she's just a bit of a square, that's all,' said Alice, her hair up in a head-scarf and wearing a dress with an open collar that Flo liked the look of.

'What's wrong with being a housewife? I wouldn't mind,' said Flo.

'Be careful what you wish for.' Tabby shuffled the cards and smiled, offered the cut to Flo. 'It's the male conspiracy.'

'The what?'

'The male conspiracy, those government and advertising men idealise unpaid domestic drudgery.' Tabby glanced at her, then back to the cards as she dealt them out.

'Doreen wants to be a *Woman's Realm* advert,' said Maggie. She rolled her eyes and picked up a card from the stack, looked at her hand and placed three queens down on the table. 'The perfect doting housewife, waiting to greet George home from work with a smile and a dish of coronation chicken.' A pause to draw from her cigarette. 'He doesn't allow her a career, to work at all, or even to wear trousers.'

Flo was sure neither Maggie nor Tabby worked, but it seemed to be the principle of the thing, they could if they wanted to. Perhaps a career was something you chose to do, whereas work you didn't. She didn't know any women with a career, except Alice maybe.

'Her career is in the kitchen,' continued Maggie, 'and involves Brillo pads and cod liver oil. And do you know, even though her daughter went to grammar, Doreen told her she should be a homemaker, not a career girl, in case it should be off-putting to potential suitors. She maintains, as does her husband and half the country, a career for a girl is a waste of time because she'll only get married.' Maggie indicated the queens with her cigarette. 'You add to mine if you have any of the same rank, or any wild cards.'

Flo picked up a card, the two of clubs and put it back down on the stack. 'There's nothing wrong with making a nice home for the family,' said Alice, picking up a card and placing three aces down between herself and Tabby. 'And Doreen's all right, she goes to the WI, they're doing some really good work.'

'Doreen has her head firmly in the sand,' said Tabby, adding another two aces to Alice's. 'She likes the WI for the craft and cooking, she's not interested in anything else. She's bored silly at home really, though she'd never admit it.'

'Well, it's all right for you two, you can afford to think about other things, you've got the time and money to go to the theatre and go on marches and read fancy books while the rest of us have to work hard keeping house, looking after the kids *and* bringing money in,' said Alice, flicking her ash twice when it didn't need flicking. 'With the husbands expecting us to fetch their slippers for them.'

'Sorry, darling,' said Tabby, squinting a smile through her cigarette smoke, 'I sometimes forget how lucky I am to have ditched that swine of a husband of mine.'

Flo downed her drink, her eyes flicked from Tabby to Alice.

'Course I want to make a nice home. You should've seen how we lived down the docks, it wasn't anything like this' – she twitched her hand at the room – 'and having a bathroom indoors is a wonder to us, let alone a bloody fridge.'

The women fell silent.

'Yes, I get it,' said Tabby. 'Flo has been deprived of all the things she sees in the magazines, so be it. When she has all of that, let's see how she feels.'

'Tabby darling, you've hit the nail on the head,' said Maggie. 'It's Abraham Maslow, of course it is.'

'Never heard of him,' said Flo.

'Hierarchy of needs, dear. At the bottom are your basic physical needs in life: breath, food, warmth.' Maggie made a low sweep with her manicured hands, she was enjoying herself. 'These are the first things you must have, without these anything else is impossible, all right?'

Flo gave a noncommittal shrug, Maggie was always trying to teach her something. 'The next level up is safety, knowing you and your family are safe and away from violence, having a roof over your heads, and having your health.' Maggie put her hand of cards face-down on the table and picked up her glass. 'And on the next level is love, your husband, your children, having friends who care about you.'

'Sounds like common sense to me,' said Flo, wondering whether she had even got past the safety level, with Fred being the way he was.

'Yes, all right, Flo, dear.' Maggie wagged her head and smiled a reprimand. 'Now we get to the

149

interesting part. There are two levels left. The next one is all about self-esteem.' Maggie paused, Flo gave a small shake of her head and wished Maggie would pick up her cards.

'It means feeling good about yourself,' said Alice.

'Yes,' said Maggie, 'it means feeling that you are worth something more than your basic functions. It means having respect for yourself, and when you have that you have the confidence to achieve things in life.'

It was like someone invisible had taken Flo's shoulders and given her a little shake. She felt a tiny sting in her eyes. No tears fell, they pooled there and blurred her vision. The glass in her hand was empty but for the iced water at the bottom, diluted and weak. She stared at her cards, made sure she hadn't missed a queen. She had never thought of her life like that before. Why would she? Getting food on the table and keeping Fred out of trouble was her life.

'If you don't have all of these needs met, you will be anxious and unhappy,' declared Maggie with a satisfied smile. 'But once you have met these needs, you shall be ready for the next and ultimate level, which Maslow calls self-actualisation.' She said it with a flourish, spreading her hands apart in the air to imply an invisible floating sign. Self-actualisation might have been up in lights on Southend pier. 'It means being ready to fulfil your potential, to be everything you can be.'

Maggie leant back in her chair, smug and happy, her eyes still fixed on Flo's. She had imparted her knowledge, had enlightened Flo with the benefit of her wisdom.

'Blimey,' said Flo. She laughed, out of her depth.

'The point is, women at the kitchen sink may never get beyond their basic needs, they may never reach their full potential as individuals,' said Tabby. 'Men treat women as functional, as long as they fulfil their function of cooking, cleaning and having babies they should be happy. It's since the war, you know, things have gone backwards not forwards. Shall we blame Hitler?'

Tabby smiled, the women waited for Flo to say something.

'You know what, my old mum had a bloody hard life, she grew up in a workhouse, can you imagine?' Flo kept a check on herself, Maggie's expression had changed from charity to pity. 'She brought me up to be grateful for living in the tenements. Mags, you'd hate it there, no hot water, sharing a lav with five other families. Now I'm here with you ladies and that's something else again. You've lived abroad, Tabby, and you, Maggie, you've got all this, and you've got your own business, Alice, and you've all got nice homes. Well, it's a different world, isn't it.'

'Gosh, it's *just* like the "New Wave", isn't it? How thrilling,' said Tabby.

'Flo's life isn't a kitchen-sink drama, darling,' said Maggie, picking up her cards and putting them back down again.

'You two don't know the difference between hard graft – *work* that you have to do to make ends meet – and a *career* that's a luxury choice for a lot of people.' Alice shook her head at Maggie and Tabby. 'What do you think of Monday's so far, Flo?'

'I'm doing well, been trained up as key worker. It's good how everything's laid on, the dances and the clubs and all.'

'A happy worker is an efficient worker,' said Tabby, grinning.

'And the swimming and football and stuff.'

'A healthy worker is a productive worker.'

Maggie scowled at her. 'Monday Leather is one of the few employers interested in employee welfare. And we encourage married women to work. This is a mini garden city, a company town, with housing, school, entertainment, it's a business with a conscience.'

'Yes, it's a business all right,' said Tabby, 'and don't forget it. For a start women are paid less than men, aren't they? Forty per cent less, I think. So it makes money sense to encourage them to work. And company towns are a cheap way to keep and control the workforce. Here, darling, you have a little patch of communism on the Thames estuary.'

'Tabby, you are *such* a cynic,' laughed Maggie. 'This is *corporatopia,* everything is provided, the workers don't *need* to leave. Are you saying people aren't happy here?'

'Well, you've rather got them over a barrel, haven't you? Big Brother and all that jazz. The architecture *is* super though, I'll give you that.' Tabby smiled and took a long drag of her cigarette, peering at Maggie through her smoke.

'Ha, Big Brother indeed,' said Maggie. 'So, Flo, with Fred earning a good wage you could be just

152

a housewife if you wanted to, have you considered that?'

'I've always had to work, Mags, I'm used to it, and I want to help Fred make a nice home for us.' She paused. 'Anyway, I like the sound of going abroad, like you two.'

'You don't have to go abroad to be happy, I haven't been and I reckon I'm high up in Maslow's levels,' said Alice. 'Doing the Tupperware has given me a new lease of life.'

'Yes, but you could go abroad with the company if you wanted to, Flo,' said Maggie. 'We have factories in Canada and Australia and shops all over the world. Not that we'd want to lose you, of course.' Maggie cocked her head and smiled. 'When we're just getting to know you.'

'Where does your Fred work?' asked Alice.

'The loading bay in Dispatch.'

'Well, how about him getting promoted and doing a course at the company college, then he could get transferred somewhere? You fancy Australia, don't you?'

Flo's face fell. 'I don't know about that, Fred's probably all right where he is. He's not really the sort to get promoted.'

The other women seemed to consider this for a moment, reading between the lines.

'Well, what about you then, Flo?' said Alice. 'You're doing well, key worker already, I bet you'll be forewoman before long, they like promoting good workers here.'

'Yes, they like promoting *men* here, women get as far as forewoman, but never manager or director, and that college isn't for women, is it?' said Tabby.

153

'No, it's not,' said Maggie.

'So Flo wouldn't be able to train to work abroad because those courses and jobs are only for men?'

'That's right,' said Maggie.

There was another pause. Tabby stretched her long arms above her head, Maggie lit a cigarette. Tapping her foot and picking her nails, Flo sat there like her life was on the card table in front of them. It was exciting beyond words that they were even thinking of her that way.

'Well, don't you think that's rather behind the times, Maggie darling?' said Tabby.

'Yes, Mags, that's right, this place is stuck in the early fifties, isn't it?' said Alice, raising her eyebrows and grinning. Flo didn't know where to look.

'Well, what if we get Flo into that college and see how far she gets?' said Maggie, holding up her hands with a small shrug. 'I shouldn't wonder she'd be rather brilliant.'

Flo's eyes shot to Maggie, she held her breath.

'I'm the owner's wife, after all, and it's the end of the bloody brown fifties, things are starting to change. And if Flo's husband isn't ambitious, there's no need for that to be the end of it. There's full employment, the men don't have to worry about the women taking their jobs, the country's booming, *We've never had it so good.*' Maggie laughed, slurring her words.

'A social experiment, Maggie?' said Tabby, smiling and glancing at Alice. 'That's right up your street.'

'Well, it's high time some rules were broken,' said Maggie, sitting up straight. 'The new decade

154

holds great promise – aside from the dratted *Bomb,* of course.' She picked up her hand, plucked a card from the stack and slid it, a joker, amongst the queens on the table.

Flo shrugged, her eyes wide, how drunk were they? Get her into a men's college so she could work abroad? Do important men's work with decisions and authority? She gulped her drink but her glass was empty. Could they really think she could do a man's job? What on earth would Fred say?

'Whatever is the matter, Flo dear?' Tabby leant forwards in her chair.

Flo shook her head and looked down, she didn't want to cry in front of them. She had never been around people like this, she'd never had the luxury of thinking she could do well, be happy with herself. She wanted more, she did. It was like Maggie had told her to climb up a hundred-foot crane at the docks, to look down, dizzy and exhilarated, to see a view of something she hadn't been able to see before. A big picture of her life and its possibilities.

'Here, let me refresh that glass for you,' said Tabby. 'So what do you say then, Flo? Are you up to the challenge? If Maggie gets you in, are you game?'

9

The joint was in. The smell of roast beef gave the house a meaty wholesomeness. Mikey sat on the floor in front of the new television set watching Eamonn Andrews pile prizes and cabbages on to laughing children on the *Crackerjack* show. Jeanie was upstairs reading, Babs was in the bath and Fred sat in the armchair peeping over the top of his paper at the television.

Flo was exhausted, she'd been scrubbing clothes in the kitchen sink all morning, had pulled them through the wringer, hung them to dry indoors – it being a Sunday – she'd swept out all the rooms, taken out the rubbish, made the lunch, cleared up the lunch things, cleaned the hall, got Mikey bathed, swept out the grate in the front room and brought in some coal. While the spuds boiled on the hob in the kitchen, Flo stood at the ironing board by the front window pressing Mikey's school uniform and Fred's shirts.

She had never been happier.

Flo's mum was never far from her thoughts. What would Ella have said about her new yellow electric iron and television set? Flo hoped Fred might get out to do a bit of gardening after dinner. There were some nice iris growing in the back that Ella would like. Flo settled on taking some out to the churchyard. She swallowed and pushed the iron down hard on to Fred's work shirt. The

Tilbury churchyard where they put Ella away. The kids had looked so smart in their mourning clothes, poor things, all the neighbours staring. Even Fred in a new Burton's suit, £2/10s, that bit of Ella's money left over. It was a nice little service. But the one person Flo had wanted to talk to about it all was being buried.

Ella would have been happy to see Flo at Monday's. A right little homemaker, just like in the magazines. Babs already had three new pairs of shoes, and she'd got herself a little electric record player for dancing around in the bedroom. Flo didn't have anything like that at her age, no money of her own to spend, like the new 'teenagers'. Fred was at home after work waiting for his tea. He wasn't out drinking half as much and hadn't raised his hand to any of them since moving away from the docks. She'd been proved right, it was the drink that made him bad.

'I was talking to Maggie the other day,' she began tentatively.

'Who, your posh pal?'

'Maggie Monday. She said there's a good college here for the workers who want to get on.' She daren't say it was for men only. Fred gave no reply. 'You're doing all right in Dispatch, aren't you?'

'What's that got to do with anything? You been talking about me?'

'No, course not. It's just, if you do well you'll get promoted then you could see about getting in that college and training up for something really good. Abroad maybe.'

Fred lowered his paper to look at her. Flo

157

glanced his way then back to her ironing.

'Abroad? My job not good enough then?'

'I'm not saying that, am I? Don't you want to get on here?'

'Can you see me in a bloody college? I'm a labourer, not a suit. Don't go getting ideas above your station, Flo, you'll soon get burnt.'

He disappeared behind his paper. Flo let it be for a minute.

'Maggie said she might be able to get *me* into that college. What do you think about that?'

Fred cracked his paper down on to his lap. *'You?* In a college? She's having you on, you daft bird.'

Flo stiffened, it was as much as she had expected.

'But what if she can get me in, don't you think it's worth it? It'll be more money when I'm trained up. Still not as much as you're on though,' she added quickly.

Fred feigned a bored sigh and resumed reading. 'Just don't come crawling when you see you're showing yourself up.'

Resisting a smile, Flo started on Mikey's school uniform.

Fred peered over the top of his paper out through the front window. Next door Mr Ductle was doing his garden in the fading sunshine, in shirt sleeves and trousers. Watching him through the nets, Flo smiled. He was a queer fellow, very serious and short, balanced atop a three-stepped ladder to trim his topiary cockerel with tiny brass secateurs. For the garden competition that summer, Flo guessed. Between each snip Mr Ductle rubbed the top of his balding head with the back of his gloved hand as if considering his next cut.

Folding his paper and slapping it down on his chair, Fred stood up and went out to the front garden. Flo watched him through the nets; maybe he was going to do a bit of weeding. Their grass was long and growing into the beds, a rusty upturned wheelbarrow on the lawn. Dead leaves and stems from the previous autumn hadn't been cut back and swept up. A few daffodils had come up in the early spring but they hung down, gone to seed.

In the garden, Fred put a foot up on the wheelbarrow and leant on his knee, rolled a cigarette and watched Mr Ductle over the low boundary wall. Flo eased open the metal casement window to eavesdrop. The smell of next door's freshly cut grass wafted in with the twittering of a dozen budgies from Mr Ductle's front window.

'How are you and your lovely wife settling into number thirty-eight?' Mr Ductle called over.

'Well enough,' said Fred.

'The missus was saying only this morning how your Flo is the spit of Grace Kelly, had a right little laugh we did about a film star living next door.'

Flo flushed, people were always saying she looked like Grace Kelly, or Doris Day, or some other film star. She just had that kind of face. Fred stared back at Mr Ductle's crinkled smile.

'A friendly word of caution, the garden competition will be coming up before you know it. You've still a couple of months to do a bit of planting.'

Fred shrugged, stood straight and toed something in the grass.

'Well, you wouldn't want to get a letter from the company, they like the estate to be tidy. You know, you could join the gardening club, we meet monthly in the village hall, have flower shows there and outside the company. I've shown my chrysanthemums in Kent and Sussex.'

Flo could only see the side of Fred's face, his jaw was clenched.

'I've brought them indoors before now to save them from the weather. Mrs Ductle isn't too impressed when I roll the carpet back for them. You know, if you were to trim your edges and dig over your borders, yours wouldn't look too bad.'

'Turn that off now, Mikey, and go and wash for dinner,' said Flo.

'Oh, Mum, it's nearly finished.'

'Go on now, and set the table.'

Mikey slouched off, Flo strained her ears to hear the men.

'There's a cash prize, you know, for the best garden in each avenue and a winner's cup for the whole estate. It's normally between Mr Bottomly on Monday Avenue and myself.' He bristled. 'He took it last year because my topiary wasn't established, that's what I reckon, but this year me and the missus have high hopes.'

'Let's have a go,' said Fred, walking towards his neighbour as if to jump the low wall.

'Oh, no, no.' Mr Ductle gave a nervous laugh and held on to the stepladder. 'Better not.'

'Yeah, I'll help.' Fred grinned. He stepped over the wall and headed for the cockerel, his head at the same height as Mr Ductle and the stepladder combined. Flo set the iron down and leant in closer to the window.

'Oh, er, oh no, not really, Mr Blundell.' In his alarm the stepladder wobbled close to the cockerel and Mr Ductle compensated by leaning backwards. Flo gasped, pressed her hand on the glass. The ladder toppled, he flapped his arms to steady it but it fell and Fred reached out and caught him by the wrist just in time. The ladder clattered to the grass, Mr Ductle dangling from Fred's grasp.

'Bloody hell,' Flo hissed.

'Steady on, what you up to then, eh?' said Fred, laughing around his cigarette and placing his neighbour back on two feet.

Mr Ductle took a step back, his eyes popping up at Fred. He held the secateurs out in front of him.

'All right, all right, I won't touch your flippin' chicken. I might borrow your mower though, if you don't mind?'

Mr Ductle lowered the secateurs and took a breath, glanced sideways at his lawn mower. There was a Jerry can of petrol on the ground nearby.

'I was about to service it actually, so perhaps you could ask Mrs Rutland on your other side.' Mr Ductle wiped his head and stood his ground, glaring. Fred eyed him. A kettle whistled from Mr Ductle's house. His eyes flitted from Fred to the house and back again. The kettle screamed.

'Excuse me, the wife's out,' he said and trotted indoors.

Flo tensed as Fred watched Mr Ductle go. He took a long drag from his cigarette, walked over to the jerry can and unscrewed the lid. Before Flo had time to realise what he was doing and shout out of the window, Fred had sloshed petrol over the topiary, vaulted back over the garden wall and flicked his cigarette. The cockerel went up with a whoosh, the flames making an impressive torch. Flo's hands flew to her face, her body rushed with dread.

She jumped when Fred came crashing back into the house. He stood there in the front room and tried to speak but doubled over, convulsed with laughter and coughing like he'd just seen the funniest thing in his life.

'What the hell are you doing?' screeched Flo, pulling the window shut and peering out at the burning bush.

He didn't seem to notice her astonishment but got himself to a chair and sat down, still laughing, his face bright red and tears on his cheeks.

'He won't be showing us up in the bloody garden competition *now*, will he?'

Flo could only stare at him. She ducked back behind the curtain when Mr Ductle came running out to his front garden, his arms flailing.

'Aarrgghh no!'

Fred's laugh calmed to a chuckle, his took out his tin to roll a fag, shaking his head at his prank. He sat there like he was waiting for his tea while Mr Ductle ran for his garden hose. Flo was dumbfounded, she didn't know what to say, he wasn't even drunk.

'Mrs Monday is expecting you.'

The maid turned to climb the curved staircase

162

that led directly off the large hall. Flo faltered, then followed, clutching the note that had been passed to her at work that morning. *Come to the house at 12:30 when you break for lunch, Mr M wants to see you, Mags x.* She licked her dry lips, this was it, her chance to get into the college. Maggie must have had a word with him, maybe he had an office upstairs at the house.

The maid led her into a lavish bedroom, gestured that she should sit down in a chair at the far end by the window and left the room. It was luxurious and modern, there was even a vase of fresh white dahlias on the little table where she sat. As naturally as anything, Maggie strode out of her en suite into the bedroom wearing nothing but her makeup and undies. Flo jumped and turned her head to stare at the wall.

'Blimey, sorry, Maggie, the maid brought me up.'

'Oh, Flo, don't be such a prude, I'll be ready in a minute.'

She sat down on the chair opposite Flo and leant forwards to pull her stockings on.

'I've had the *busiest* morning, mentioned to my husband your wish to join the college, you should have seen his reaction.'

Maggie rolled her eyes as she buttoned on a white blouse, gave Flo a look as if to say *Don't worry, it's as much as I expected.* A beige skirt suit with navy trim was laid out on the bed, the jacket had three-quarter sleeves and no collar.

'It's lovely, where's it from?'

'Chanel, darling. Paris.' Maggie smiled and stepped into the skirt. 'We must go one day.'

'Blimey,' said Flo under her breath.

Maggie put on the jacket and smoothed her skirt down in the mirror with a satisfied nod.

'Now then, let's have a look at you. Take off that overall, darling, and that headscarf. Let me do your hair a little.'

Maggie stood behind Flo to twist her hair into a French pleat.

'You really are lucky, you have the loveliest hair, I shouldn't think you even need to set it. I'm in the salon every few days otherwise I look an absolute fright. Now here, put this on.' She handed Flo a nasturtium heart-shaped lipstick and turned to place a beige feather pillbox hat on to her immaculate wash and set.

'You'll need something for those,' she said, indicating the scarf and overall in Flo's hand. 'Here.' She pulled a black leather handbag with a large metal H on the front out of a cupboard. 'No, not Hermés, too much, here, perfect.' She gave Flo a tan leather Monday's handbag.

'Right, onward and upward.' Maggie strode ahead in her spike heels, pulling on some beige leather gloves. Trotting after her down the staircase, out of the mansion and across the quadrangle into the factory complex, Flo's lipstick and bag only served to make her work clothes more obvious.

They came into Mr Monday's office on the top floor. Two men stood at the far window, looking out intently at something.

'Whoa, see that? Crikey, he's good.' Flo recognised Bob Philips, the housing manager, and froze. She had seen him two days before when

164

Fred burned Mr Ductle's cockerel. He turned up on their doorstep having a right go, telling Fred he'd be up before the committee. And he'd given them a letter about the state of their own garden. What was this? Not about the college after all. Helpless, she looked around at Maggie, who smiled and gave a reassuring nod, coughed to announce them. The men turned and Flo caught her breath, she hadn't seen Mr Monday close up before and thought she would have picked him out in a crowd of a thousand. He stood tall, broad, in crisp white shirtsleeves rolled up to his biceps. His trousers did nothing to conceal his thighs thick with muscle, his hair slicked back, he was the image of Clark Gable, but with a bushy moustache.

'Well, well.' He looked Flo up and down. 'You really outdid yourself, Mags,' he said in a strong Canadian accent. 'So this is...'

Flo realised she was still holding her breath. 'Flo, Blundell,' she blurted.

'Yeeesss, indeed,' he said, coming towards her, his eyes scrutinising her face and figure, making her squirm. 'So I hear you want to join my college for Monday-men, eh?'

Flo nodded, trying to smile without grimacing. She hoped he wouldn't shake her hand, it was as sweaty as anything.

'Now why would a pretty thing like you want to do a thing like that, eh?' he said, booming a loud laugh, looking round at Bob.

'I want to do well and work for Monday's abroad.' Her voice sounded strained and meek.

'Oh, you do, eh?' he said, standing over her. She

could smell his cologne and his fresh sweat. 'But you know my college trains up young men, those jobs overseas are managerial, high level, with lots of responsibility. That's men's work, little lady,' he said, giving her a broad toothy grin. 'So why don't you run along back to the factory sewing machines.' He turned away.

'No, hang on,' she blurted, not knowing what she'd say. 'I *can* do that work, I know I can. I want to.'

'Yes, that's right,' Maggie said. 'Flo is quite the star in the factory, she's only been there a few months, they earmarked her for a key worker right away.'

Mr Monday lit a cigarette and turned back to face them. 'Yes, Mags, I know this is your little – project – shall we say? But I'm running a business here. You do realise the implications?' Maggie ignored him. He paused, looking at Flo. 'So what qualifications did you get from school, Flo?'

Flo stared at him, unable to say anything worthwhile. Her name sounded strange in a Canadian accent.

'I did a bit of typing.'

'Typing? The men in those positions have someone else doing their typing, and they have to make big decisions, have you thought about that? And what happens if you have more children?' Mr Monday frowned. 'Hang on, *Blundell,* you say?' He snatched the cigarette from his lips. 'Bob, isn't that guy with the fire Blundell?'

'Yes, that's right, sir, Fred Blundell.'

'Riiight.' He nodded at Flo. 'Was it your husband by any chance who took it upon himself to set fire to your next-door neighbour's garden?'

Flo nodded. A fast chill slid from her scalp to her groin.

'Not exactly in keeping with our company philosophy of community spirit now is it, Flo?' he said, chuckling. 'You know, when one of our workers doesn't toe the line, doesn't fit in, we tend to cut our losses. And of course, when a worker no longer has a job here, they no longer live here either.'

Flo glanced at Maggie, who glared back at her.

'Come over here, would you?' Mr Monday beckoned Flo to the window.

She walked over, wondering what on earth would happen. Looking down, she saw a football pitch laid out, several of the factory workers, including her Fred, kicking a ball around. She made a mental check that it was dinnertime, he wasn't in trouble for skiving off work.

'I can't imagine how Fred Blundell slipped through the net.' Mr Monday looked out of the window. 'Sid is usually very good at weeding out the trouble-makers during the interview stage. I must have a word with him about it. Now, would you say your husband is down there on his lunch break playing soccer right now?'

'Yes, that's him there, with the ball,' she said, pointing, wishing the window was open so she could spit at him.

'I thought so. Bob and I were just watching him. You know he's quite a player, I mean, he's damned good.'

They watched Fred. He knew what he was doing. Someone passed the ball to him, he dodged around one player, and another, the ball seemingly attached to his foot, and dribbled past the other players until he was right beside the goalkeeper, who tried to tackle him, and Fred nudged the ball into goal without even looking at it.

'That's a hat trick, sir,' said Bob Philips, shaking his head and chuckling. 'He's in a league of his own.'

A little surge of pride lifted the corner of Flo's mouth. She'd grown up watching Fred play football in their street. The way he held up his arms in defence while he let his feet take the ball. Eyes down and focused, his face animated, his mouth slightly open, hair flying. All the girls had watched Fred, nudging and whispering. Flo had a secret ownership, he lived next door to her after all, she had some kind of status in his life. She was chuffed when Fred really started to notice her for the first time, after his mum died in that horrible bombing. When he came round for tea he would confide in her, he couldn't talk to anyone else he said. And of course Flo comforted him. For Christ's sake, she hadn't meant to fall pregnant at fifteen.

'I might be in the mood to make a little deal with you, Flo,' said Mr Monday, turning to perch on the edge of his desk. He was about her height now, she felt a little more at ease.

'I suppose you've heard that we have a first-class pitch, and West Ham United practise here pre-season?'

Flo nodded. So what Mikey had said was true.

'And that they play a friendly charity match with our first team once a season as a return favour?'

'Yes, I think I heard that.'

'Well,' he laughed, 'the Monday team have, shall

we say, a less than ideal record in that respect, isn't that right, Bob?'

'That's right, Mr Monday.'

'How I would dearly love to give them a good thrashing this time. I think we might have a chance with a player like your Fred on the team, and with me as captain as usual, of course.'

Maggie and Flo exchanged glances. Maggie shrugged her shoulders and nodded, lighting a cigarette.

'You know, Bob here was about ready to lynch Fred for what he did to that fellow's garden, but I'd say even Bob has changed his tune.' Bob Philips nodded in agreement. 'I understand Fred declined a place on the team when he first came here, I can't fathom why. What say Fred joins the team, helps us to beat West Ham, I put a halt to disciplinary action for the garden fiasco and let you into the college? I'd say that's a bloody fair deal. In fact, I'd say you owe me one there.'

Flo's eyes widened involuntarily. 'Thanks very much, Mr Monday, I'm sure Fred would want to join the team. I can go and get him and send him up now if you like?'

Mr Monday looked at his wristwatch. 'Hmm, no, I'll see him later, I have my rounds to do in the factory after lunch.'

'All right then, thanks again, Mr Monday, me and Fred won't let you down.'

'Yes, well, I think Fred will be of more use to me than you in that college.' Mr Monday laughed at Bob Philips. 'You'll soon see what you're letting yourself in for, but no hard feelings when you decide to bow out.'

Maggie sidled up to Flo, linked arms and ushered her out of the room. As they left Flo noticed a teenage boy sitting in the back corner of the room.

Once outside, Flo put her hands on top of her head and blew out her cheeks.

'Crikey, sorry, Maggie, but he's a piece of work.'

'Yes, well, I did mention that he's a pig, but who cares now, you're *in*, my darling, you are *in*.'

'I know.' Flo grabbed Maggie's arm and squealed with delight. 'I can't believe it.'

'Congratulations, darling, you were magnificent, although I was shocked to hear about Fred's arson attack on that poor fellow's garden, you should have told me about it.'

Maggie frowned at her.

'I know, sorry, I'm so cross with him for doing it, he just loses his temper sometimes, he's all right really.' Flo fumbled in her bag for a cigarette, changed the subject. 'Who was that boy at the back of the room?'

'James? Our son. Handsome, isn't he? His father likes to take him around the factory sometimes to show him the ropes.'

'Oh, look at the time, I'd better be getting back. Look, Maggie, thanks so much for sorting this out for me, I don't know what to say.'

'You're welcome, darling. You're in my little club and we help each other out, don't we?'

'Here, look, take this, thanks.' Flo took her overall and scarf out of the tan handbag and handed it back to Maggie.

'Oh, you keep it, I have dozens of the things.' Maggie strode away back to her mansion and Flo ran to the canteen to get a quick dinner before break was over.

Swinging her new bag, she pushed through the doors of the canteen and a great rush of noise and fog of food engulfed her. More than a thousand workers were having their midday dinner there. Flo grabbed a plate, whizzed along the service hatch and asked for the luncheon meat fritter, greens and mash, which were dumped on her plate by the serving woman. She paid her shilling and looked around. Lil sat at a table by herself with her arms folded.

'Where you been then?'

'Sorry, love, you won't believe it when I tell you.' She forked in a mouthful of fried luncheon meat. 'Maggie said I should do a training course at the college so's I can work abroad for the company, but the college only takes men, so she said she'd talk to Mr Monday, and she did, and we just now went to see him in his office.' She swallowed and inserted a forkful of greens. 'God, he's big and fearsome and looks like Clark Gable, and he wasn't gonna let me in the college, saying it's men's work and that, then he realised I'm Fred's wife and he was being done for setting fire to next door's bush and made a deal that Fred would join the football team to beat West Ham and I could get in the college.' Flo stopped for breath and licked some mashed potato off her dinner knife.

Lil stared, her teacup hovering below her chin.

'You wanna work abroad? But you only just got here.'

'I know. I've always wanted to go abroad, Lil, since I've been cleaning the cruise liners. This is my chance, the whole family could go, but not yet, I wanna do the training and then see. Smashing, eh? I'm really gonna do it.'

The other workers were getting up to leave. Flo looked at the wall clock and shovelled in some mash and greens to chew as they walked along.

'I dunno, Flo, what do you wanna do it for? Won't Fred be put off by it?'

Flo wiped her mouth with the back of her hand, glanced at Lil walking beside her. *Yes, Fred would be put off by it,* she wanted to say, *he's already set fire to someone's garden because of it.* She wanted to tell Lil the things Maggie, Tabby and Alice were saying the other day. They had left Flo with a sense of what they meant, a general feeling about women and people's lives and how things were changing, but she wasn't sure how to put it without it coming out wrong. But instead of all of that, how about this: *sod him for once.*

'Nah, he'll be all right. Imagine, Lil, I'm the first woman to go to that college. I'm so scared I could shit myself.'

Lil shrugged, her mouth pulled down, and let Flo hold the door open for her.

My hands were ripped to shreds on the damn boxes. If I held them still it wasn't too bad but soon as I bent my fingers to put a box together it hurt like hell. The other workers on the box line were idiots. The four girls talked about dresses and boys and giggled a lot. The three older women went on about their ailments, the royal family and their kids. I could feel my brain rotting in there so I started to put little notes in the boxes, hidden under the bottom flap, *Help, I'm a prisoner in a box factory,* things like that. There was one fella who worked opposite me, really tall and skinny he was, they called him Skylon, he was the only one who was all right, I suppose. At least he didn't jabber all day. They were all quick though, their hands like lightning, putting the boxes together, hundreds a day they did. Mr Turtle tried to crack the whip when we didn't reach target but no one listened to him.

'You get to the pictures much?' said Skylon.

He was talking to me, my face got really hot all of a sudden.

'Oooh, Skylon's sweet on Jeanie,' called Carol, one of the box girls. Nosy cow.

I shook my head and Skylon looked down at his box.

'Here, look sharp.' Mr Turtle limped round to the conveyor, looking like he'd seen a ghost. A loud voice boomed through the workshop.

'TURTLE? TARGETS.'

The big boss Mr Monday came in with a group of people trailing after him. He stood at the head of the conveyor, hands on hips and legs apart, staring at us all. We gawped at him like fish in a bowl. Mr Turtle shuffled over holding a clipboard.

'Estimate?' shouted Mr Monday.

'Ninety-seven per cent, Mr Monday, sir.' It looked to me like Turtle clicked his heels together.

'Result?'

'Ninety-five per cent, Mr Monday, sir.' I could have sworn Turtle nearly raised his hand in salute.

'Ninety-five per cent, eh?' Mr Monday pierced

Turtle with his glare and stroked his moustache. Everyone held their breath, even me, the bloke was scary enough. The group of people behind him shuffled their feet, waiting for the verdict. I did a double-take. One of them was that boy from the library, the one who told me about the exams. I stared at him and his face sort of jolted and lit up when he realised it was me.

'NOT GOOD ENOUGH, TURTLE,' boomed Mr Monday. Everyone jumped. 'If you don't reach estimate next month there'll be hell to pay, understood?'

Mr Turtle gulped like he was gonna be sick.

'Yes, sir!' His flat hand came halfway up to his head before he realised what he was doing and dropped it back down again.

'WELL?' Mr Monday shouted like a lunatic. We all jumped to attention and started making boxes like our lives depended on it. Skylon dropped his on the floor then banged his head on the conveyor when he bent to pick it up. Mr Monday gave him the dirtiest look then stormed off, his group running after him. The boy from the library hung back and sidled over to me.

'Hello, fancy seeing you here,' he said.

'Well, I told you I worked here, didn't I?' I tried to brush some of the cardboard dust off my hair without him seeing.

'Look, meet me after work, in the library, I've got something for you.'

I went dead cold. Skylon gawped at us.

'I've got to go, will you meet me?'

I nodded and he ran off to catch up with the others.

174

'What's he want then?' said Skylon, with a sulk on.

I shrugged.

'You know who that is, don't you?'

'What you on about?'

'It's James Monday, the boss's son.'

'So what?'

Skylon got on with his boxes and so did I. So the boy was the boss's son, well blimey.

At clock-off I brushed the hateful dust off me and went over to the library. When I walked in James looked up from his newspaper and smiled and my legs felt weak like in the silly magazine stories. I frowned for fortitude and sat at the table across from him.

'I'm James, by the way.'

'I know,' I said. 'You're the boss's son.'

'Yes, that's right,' he said, looking like his dog had died.

'So?'

'Yes, I thought you might want the details of that college I was telling you about. It's a post-secondary college, it's in Barking, like I said, here's the address.' He gave me a bit of paper. 'Good Lord, your hands.'

I showed my palm. 'Yeah, that's what happens when you make boxes all day in the dungeon,' I said. 'That's why I've got to get out of here.'

He reached for my hand, I don't know why I let him take it, he held it and looked at all the red slices across my fingers and palms.

'Ouch,' he said. 'Poor you.'

I pulled my hand away, my bloody face burned again.

'So if you're the boss's son, how come you're helping me get out of here?'

He laughed. 'Yes, you might be on to something there. But it's a big secret so I can't tell you.'

'Well, *you* know *my* secret, I haven't told a soul I want to go to a university.' He looked bemused. 'My mum and dad think you need to know enough to go and get a job, and that's it. They don't want me getting above my station. I don't even talk to them any more, they ruined my life.'

'All right then, you seem like a girl a boy can trust.' He tapped his finger on the wooden table top. 'My father drags me on the factory rounds to give a show that he's teaching me the ropes, and they send me to a local school, but they also send me for extra coaching to that college in Barking because what they really want is for me to study law.'

Blimey.

'They had me cleaning out the stinking chicken sheds on the company farm during the holidays to make a show that Monday Leather is a classless community, but it's all a front. Like I said, I'm to be a barrister. They're practically forcing me to do it. So I understand your situation in some ways, lack of freedom, et cetera.'

'Oh, right.' I didn't know what to say. I wouldn't have minded his problems instead of mine, but he was being nice to me so I let it go. 'I better get off. When's that college open then?'

'It's open during the day and evenings and Saturdays. You just take the steam express to Barking on the Tilbury line and then a bus to the college. I can take you there if you like?'

'Oh, no, it's all right, I'll find it. Look, thanks a lot.' I got up to go, and looked back at him. He smiled and made my guts feel funny.

I ran home to find Babs. She was in the bathroom as usual, getting ready for going out. She wouldn't let me in when I banged on the door and Mum was looking at me so I waited upstairs.

'Come with me to find a college,' I said to her when she came up.

'What you talking about?'

She started backcombing her hair like a maniac.

'I need to get my A levels, so come with me just to find it then I'll be all right after that.'

She ignored me and giggled, pinned her hair so it sat in a big bouffant on top. 'Guess what? I've got a boy, I mean, we're going steady.' She clapped her hands and squealed like a pig then sprayed her head with a can of hairspray until I thought I'd choke.

'What? Who is he?' I coughed.

She clutched her hair lacquer to her chest and danced around the bedroom.

'Jim, his name is Jim,' she sang. 'And he is dreamy, takes me to the pictures *all* the time, and says we'll go to a dance together, but we haven't yet.' She stopped twirling to squeeze into the tightest dress I'd ever seen. And it was just over the knee.

'He's a real cool cat, wears those Italian bum-freezer suits and winkle-pickers.'

'I thought you liked Teddy boys.'

'Oh, Jeanie, you're such an old maid. I'm a *modernist* now.'

I tutted. 'Never mind that, will you come or not?'

'Can't, sorry, you big square, I'm meeting Jim after tea at the pictures. We saw *Sleeping Beauty* last week, I told Jim he's my prince. But we don't even care what's on, we just talk and get close, and–' she gave me a coy smile '–after, when it's dark, we go out the back and have a little snog.' She giggled and covered her mouth. Dirty tart.

'Oh suit yourself, you always do,' I said.

Mum called us for tea. I scoffed mine down and walked to the station. I'd find that bloody college by myself.

10

By the time Flo found the right training room in the college building, everyone else had arrived. The other students, all men of course, sat at desks, one arm draped over the back of the chair, buffed shoes crossed over smart trouser legs, smoking and chatting. Flo stood in the doorway and coughed. The trainer looked up from his desk, smoothed back his hair and pulled down the hem of his suit jacket.

'Yes?' His small eyes were blank but for a flutter of irritation.

'Flo Blundell, it's my first day.'

'First day doing what, sweetheart? You've taken a wrong turn.' One of the students nudged his neighbour and laughed.

The trainer looked her up and down with a critical eye, and spoke to her bust.

'Come in, won't you, and find a seat.'

Flo kept her head down and walked in her flat pumps to the only free desk, in the middle of the room. Folding her hands on her lap, she lifted her eyes and waited, every muscle in her body clenched, a drop of sweat sliding down her back beneath her blouse. She moved her eyes sideways to the large metal casement windows. The training room was up on the fourth floor, there was a good view over to the grey Thames, she could see a cargo ship heading inland towards the docks, pulling forwards imperceptibly. It was just for a second before she slid her eyes back, but enough to remind her of why she was there.

'Right, shoe manufacture, we've covered clicking and closing, who can tell me what's next?'

The trainer approached Flo and without saying a word dropped a large thick book on to her desk with a thump. She flinched. *Overseas Induction Course Manual*, it said on the front, *From Tannery to Retail*.

'Um, finishing?' she said. The trainer ignored her.

'Lasting?' said the man next to her, another one with a Canadian accent.

'Yes, Mr Anderson, correct.'

Mr Anderson grinned at Flo. She frowned at him.

'The finished upper comes from the closing room to the lasting section, where the shoe is given its shape and style with the help of a wooden *last* that simulates the foot's shape. Please pass this example around. After morning break you will all go to the lasting section to observe these techniques and acquire some hands-on experience of these processes.'

Flo put her hands on the manual and tried not to smile.

At ten o'clock sharp they stopped for tea break.

'Ten minutes's not much, is it?' It was the Canadian, Mr Anderson, who'd been sitting next to her. He was at her side walking down the corridor.

'No it's not, but I'm used to it, it's the same as in the factory.'

'Oh?'

'Ten minutes to get to the canteen, chuck a tea and biscuit down your neck, have a quick smoke and get back up. There's a knack to it.'

'Yes, I tend to stick a cigarette up my nose, that way I can smoke and eat at the same time.'

Flo looked at him for a second then burst into laughter.

'Where you going?' she said. 'Canteen's this way.'

'Ah, not any more, we students are privileged, we have our own break room.'

Flo followed him into a room in the college building where a woman served drinks and snacks from a little trolley in the corner. There were tables and chairs, a pool table and a gramophone.

'Blimey, this is nice.'

The other students gave Flo wary looks but Mr Anderson got her a coffee and they sat down at a table together. 'Flo,' she said, extending her hand.

'Carl. Nice to make your acquaintance, Flo.' He shook her hand properly, not just the ends of her fingers. 'So what brings you into this lion's den? You're the first girl to do it, I hear. Quite the pioneer, eh?'

'I dunno about that. I've always wanted to work abroad, me and the family, you know.' Flo glanced down at his wedding ring, and at her own bare hand; she'd pawned her ring several times, needed to get it back now she was earning. 'I've got my work cut out, doing this course and working in the factory.'

'Oh, not doing the course full-time?'

'No, that was part of the deal, I have to work *and* study.'

From the look on his face Carl thought that was a tall order but he didn't say as much.

'You know it started in January? What are we now, April? You've missed a few months but you can swot up before the exams.'

'Exams?'

'Yes, at the end of the year.' He smiled. 'The course runs from January to December, then the graduates go off to do Monday jobs, usually abroad.'

'The trainer didn't mention exams to me.'

'Well, do you think our factories abroad are any more accepting of female management than this country's culture?' he said, draining his coffee cup and getting up to leave.

'Dunno,' said Flo, as he held the door for her.

'I'm not sure they are, but good on you for giving it a go.'

The students headed over to the shoe factory and up to the lasting section. The machines and lines were already back in operation after morning tea break, the noise invasive and edible, forcing itself into Flo's ears and down her throat. As the students filed through, the workers' eyes were on Flo, watching her walk with the men in suits. She kept her chin up and gripped the handles of her handbag so tightly they made marks in her palm.

The trainer was waiting for them in the lasting room, standing by one of the many machines, big hunks of riveted steel, menacing and lawless.

'This is Ken, he will demonstrate toe lasting, whereby once the shoe upper is pulled over the toe of the last it is secured into place with tacks and thread,' announced the trainer.

Flo watched as Ken pulled a half-made shoe off a rack and placed it upside down in a metal vice, which he pushed forward into the machine. With deft movements he pulled a lever and used a little tool to guide the leather as it was pulled under the toe. He took a tiny, funny-shaped hammer and banged in little tacks around the sole, then used the pincers on the back of the hammer to wind thread around each tack, linking one to the next. He snipped off the thread and pushed the lever to release the shoe from the vice. The whole process took less than a minute.

'Mr Anderson, why don't you go first?' Carl stepped forwards to put on the leather apron Ken handed to him. He stood at the machine, took a shoe and last from the rack and placed it into the vice. Placing a tack at the edge and aiming the hammer, he tapped the tack but it slid out and fell to the floor. He tried again but the tack buckled and fell out. The trainer gestured for Carl to stand aside and waved Flo forward.

'Mrs Blundell?'

Flo's heart banged in her chest. She pushed a curl behind her ear and stepped forwards to put on the leather apron and take the hammer from Carl. She steadied her hand and placed the tack, took a breath and tapped it in. On the next one she banged her thumb but carried on and tapped in tacks all around the shoe.

'Good girl,' said the trainer with raised eyebrows and a curt nod. Flo did her best to keep a straight face. 'On to heel lasting next,' he said to the group.

As they continued on, Carl sidled up to her and gave her a nudge.

'That's the spirit.'

Flo smiled but looked ahead and kept walking. She was a married woman, after all.

'Well, are you coming or not?'

Outside Barking station James Monday waited for me to catch up. I needed to make sure I knew what to do on my own next time, so he had to bloody well hang on while I got my bearings. Not that I wasn't grateful for him showing me where the college was, I'd already tried to find it on my own once and bottled it, jumping out at Tilbury station and going back.

My guts squirmed, I hadn't been so far from home before. Already Barking looked bigger than Tilbury, and it smelt different too, the air wasn't salty, more greasy and grimy, closer to London, that's why.

Teddy boys hung around the Odeon. I kept my head down and trotted over to stand with James at the bus stop.

'It won't be long.' James looked up at the trolleybus wires that rippled overhead. A double-decker came silently round the bend. James walked up the stairs while the bus was moving, I hung on the rail for dear life. We sat up the top at the front where the floor was covered with fag butts and bus tickets. It was brilliant looking out from high up like that.

'This is Longbridge Road,' said James, me next to the window and his leg nearly touching mine. 'The college is on this road so you don't need to go far and it's just the one bus.'

'I might walk it next time if it's not far then, to save on the bus fare.' I stared dead ahead, not wanting to face him up close. I didn't want him to smell my fried-egg breath.

'What? Oh yes, I suppose you could, although it is quite a long road, you'd have to get an earlier train and so on.' He took out a pack of cigarettes and offered me one, smiling when I shook my head, making me wish I'd taken one. He lit his fag and put his arm on the back of the seat behind me. I tried to lick the sweat off my upper lip without him seeing.

'So you told them I'm coming?'

'Yes.' He laughed because I'd already asked him that loads of times. 'They just need you to register and pay then you can start your classes today.'

'All right.' I needed a drink of water. I couldn't believe I was doing it, and it was James helping me, I'd never forget that. Trying not to let him see, I opened my bag and checked inside my purse.

'Not dropped it yet then?' he said, chuckling.

184

I turned away so he couldn't see me bright red, looked out at the shops and pubs with flats above that lined the wide road, women carrying shopping baskets and pushing prams. More motor cars than I'd seen before whizzed past the cyclists. The air was hazy with the spring sun shining through the grot. The bus trundled on, the shops gave way to little terraced houses, rows of teeth, here and there one shattered or missing completely, thick with weeds and children playing in the rubble. I wondered how much thicker the weeds would grow, the war had ended fourteen years ago.

James nudged me and stood up. I followed him down the stairs and out towards a huge mansion-like building with wide lawns out the front and a sign that said SOUTH EAST ESSEX TECHNICAL COLLEGE.

'Blimey, this it then?'

My heart was going nineteen to the dozen. When I got to the office a po-faced woman said it wouldn't cost anything because I was still a minor and hadn't done A levels before.

'Nothing? It's free?'

'Yes, that's correct. Make your way to room two-five-one on the second floor. You shall be in Mr Jenson's class for both biological sciences and chemistry.'

I think I said thank you, I was all in a blur, she sent me off to do my A levels, it was really happening.

The end of the day at five o'clock I left the classroom and ran for the toilet. I got in there and burst into tears. It was exhausting and hard and I had taken so many notes and it was so interesting and everything I wanted to learn and I ate it up, I swallowed it down and wanted more.

James was waiting for me out the front. 'Well, don't you look super, you're absolutely glowing.'

My face got hot when he said that but I just laughed and I don't know what made me do it but I put my arms around him and gave him a big hug.

'Thank you, James, it was brilliant.' I'd never hugged a boy before. I stood back and looked at my feet, but still couldn't get that big grin off my face.

'Well, I'm pleased to be of assistance.'

'I didn't have to use my savings from work neither.'

'Really? No, of course.' He clicked his fingers like he'd had a good idea. 'Mine is supplementary tuition, but yours is just schooling. Well, that's a bonus.'

'I wish I could do English too, but I think it'd take too long and I want to pass my exams and try to get into a university.'

'Well, why don't you leave the factory and study full-time?'

My smile dropped away then. 'You know why – my mum and dad wouldn't let me – they just want me to work.'

'Well, I think you should *try* asking your parents, it wouldn't hurt, and isn't your mother in the company college now?'

He didn't know, it was no use asking them. Mum might be in that stupid technical college but it was just learning factory stuff, nothing like what I wanted to do.

'It's all right for *you* saying that, you and your money and your grammar school.'

'Whoa. Remember who's helping you and who isn't. You know how I feel about all of that.' He looked a bit hurt.

'Well, I don't know, I just wanna be a doctor, that's all.'

The light came back into his face, he was so handsome and jolly and I was sorry to snap at him.

'Sorry,' I mumbled.

'I don't want your apologies, you funny little monkey. Look, I'm supposed to be meeting someone later, but how about you and me going for a bite to eat before we head home? You can spend some of that money you saved on the classes, we can celebrate.'

'Yeah, all right, go on then.' I could have died on the spot. We went off to the eel and pie shop where James talked about the 'Establishment' and his 'sympathy for the working classes' and choked on a jellied eel and I had a meat pie with mash. After that we went to Woolworths where James looked at the Miles Davis records and then we sat in the cafe at the back on bar stools and had milk and big cream buns.

I'd never been happier in my life. The journey home went by in a flash because I was with James, who talked like no one else I knew, and because I'd started my A levels. To think that Mum and Dad denied me all that.

We said goodbye on the main road back at Monday's. What a day. I pulled the key string out of our letterbox and ran upstairs before Mum saw me.

Babs was up there with a right face on her.

'Where you been?' she said, all sulky, looking through her records.

'Nowhere.'

'Tell me. I'm telling Mum you're up to something.'

'You little bitch, you wouldn't.'

'Oh, wouldn't I?'

'All right, but you mustn't tell or they'll go barmy.'

'What?' She smiled and came to sit on my bed.

'I'm going college to get my exams, A levels.'

'Oh.' She looked bored.

'And guess who I went with?'

'Who?' She was interested then.

'James Monday, the boss's son, but you mustn't tell, it's top secret.'

'James Monday? Why you going with him? What's he like?'

I shrugged my shoulders and looked at my feet.

'You're sweet on him.' Babs bounced up and down on the bed, laughing. 'Jeanie's got a boy-oy, Jeanie's got a boy-oy.'

'Shut up, you idiot.'

Babs squeaked with excitement. 'Now we've both got boys. And *you've* got a *rich* one. I just love it here, don't you?'

Flo's laughter was lost in the hiss of steam and scream of whistles as she gave her gloved hand to Carl and stepped off the train on to the grimy St Pancras station platform. She had on her new mid-brown Marks and Spencer suit, smart jacket nipped right in at the waist with pleats fanning out around the back, and a pencil skirt that skimmed her hips. She held on to her matching pillbox hat to look up at the advertising hoardings on the soot-smattered walls, hugged her new tan handbag in the crook of her arm and felt like a million dollars.

'I've always wanted to come to London, I feel like I'm in one of them films or something,' she said.

'Yep, I reckon you've mentioned that once or twice,' said Carl, laughing. As she stepped down, he brought her in close to him.

'Right then, where to?' said Flo, breaking away and dodging an ancient-looking man bent over pushing a wooden luggage trolley.

'Oh boy, shop service, I just can't wait.'

'I don't care, it can't be that bad,' she said, coming out of the station into the bright April sunshine that highlighted the King's Cross grime. 'Blimey, all these motor cars.' The noise and smell of the traffic was overwhelming.

'Well, the one good thing, it's Saturday so the shop will be shut for the afternoon, but the assistants hate you because not only do you lessen their commission, they have to keep showing you where the stock is kept,' said Carl. 'We need to catch the bus to Oxford Street,' he said, looking up and down the road.

Flo craned her neck to look up at the station's curved façade. It was like a grand cathedral. She spun slowly on her toe to look at the London skyline.

'That one over there is a block of flats,' said Carl, pointing westwards to a tower fifteen stories high.

'God, can't imagine living up there, what about neighbours and family?'

'Well, that's your uncle Mac for you, sweep up a slum and tip it into a tower block, let the community ties drift to the heavens like dust.'

'That's a bit poetical. Anyway what do you mean, *my* uncle Mac?'

'Oh sorry, I suppose you'll vote for the socialists then?' He grinned and lit his pipe. 'All the strikes are maddening, aren't they?'

Flo lit up too, puffed on her smoke and shrugged, looking up again at the skyline.

'I've never really thought much about it.'

She stepped out into the road and Carl pulled her back as a black Morris Minor whizzed past, nearly knocking her over.

'Hey watch it, country girl,' he said. 'Come on.' He pulled her, running, to the other side of the road to board a red double-decker trolleybus, climbing the stairs to the top deck.

The bus trundled silently down the Euston Road and turned on to Oxford Street from Tottenham Court Road. They watched the crowds of people strolling around in their holiday best clutching shopping bags. Flo was transfixed. The women were elegant in hats, high heels and posh coats, children all done up too. And so many shops, the whole street was shops. The big one that looked like a palace, Selfridges, with the Rolls-Royces parked outside, uniformed chauffeurs waiting. Flo pointed up to the roof of the magnificent store where steeplejacks on bosun's chairs cleaned the grime off the many flagpoles.

'It's a long way from Tilbury, this is,' she breathed.

'Tilbury, that's where you come from?'

Flo nodded. 'Yeah, it's one of those slums you was talking about. Likely they'll knock all that down too and put some tower blocks up.'

'Rather different from Leather Town then, eh?'

'Yeah, just a bit. I dunno, down the docks it never changes, the same families all know each other and each other's business,' she said with a nostalgic smile. 'But there's no way out of it, if you know what I mean. It's kind of its own little world where everything stays the same. If you're hard up you stay hard up, and don't think anything of it.'

'And at Monday's?'

'It's just lucky we ended up there.' Flo didn't want to share why they had to leave the docks. 'And that's its own little world too, as far as I can tell, but it's different, people can get on and do well, make life a bit easier.'

'Well, that's the case in general now I would say. It sounds like the docks are a little behind the times.'

'Yeah, maybe that's it.'

'Old Mr Monday, senior, was a philanthropist with a vision. He built a utopian garden town and wanted to look after his workers. His son, however, doesn't share that vision and the original idea is going to get lost in increased rent and decreased social funding.'

'That's a shame, it's a marvellous place.'

'So what about your kids, how old?'

191

'Twin girls, fifteen, and Mikey, he's eight.'

'And what do your girls want to do with themselves?'

Flo was surprised at the question. 'Well, they both work in the factory. Babs had a notion about being an air hostess but she's all right, she's happy to earn decent money in the factory. And Jeanie, well, she doesn't say anything about it. She's never happy. Working to help the family is what's important.'

'They must be inspired by you doing this?'

'This? I haven't done anything yet, have I?'

A West Indian bus conductor came swaying down the aisle and stopped by a young couple to collect their fares. As he clipped their tickets they asked him if they could touch his hair for good luck. He obliged by tipping his head forwards, his face expressionless, his leather moneybag hanging down. They stroked the top of his short curly hair, giggling; he barely blinked. Carl and Flo exchanged glances.

'What about you then?' she asked. 'How long you been over here?'

'Oh, only since January. I was with Monday Leather in Canada, Toronto, but needed a change of scene, man.'

Flo laughed at him mimicking the youngsters. How old was he? He looked about her age.

'You married?' she blurted, and felt her face get hot.

'Me? Oh, you know, well, I *was* married, but she, my wife, died.'

'Oh, god, sorry, I didn't mean ... I saw your ring and...'

'Oh it's all right, she was having a baby, but there were complications, she died in childbirth, and so did the baby.' Carl looked at his ring and smiled. 'Can't seem to take it off just yet.'

Flo covered her mouth with her hand, tears in her eyes.

'You poor thing, I'm really sorry.'

'Oh well, you know, I wouldn't have gotten to see the wonderful Essex if that hadn't happened, every cloud has a silver lining.' He laughed, and so did Flo. She couldn't take her eyes off him. He wasn't handsome like Fred, but there was something about him, a kindness and an easy elegance. And he really talked to her. That was a novelty.

'You like it over here?'

'Oh yeah, it's fine, except for all that scratchy toilet paper,' he said, leaning in. 'And the meat. God, how I crave a big juicy steak when I'm faced with the sausages and faggots in the canteen. Won't be for ever though. I'll be going off to pastures new once I've finished the course. You too, I guess?'

'Well blimey, yeah, that's the idea, the family too, it's all a dream at the moment.'

'This one's us,' said Carl, standing up to let Flo go first. They clattered down the bus stairs and out on to the pavement.

'Ooh, look,' said Flo, pointing at the large double-fronted shoe shop in front of them. 'Monday's.'

Behind the enormous plate-glass windows stood a life-sized mannequin leaning in an elegant curve, hand on hip with a lemon leather handbag in the crook of her arm, fitted grey suit and lemon stilettos, matching gloves held in the other hand, and a grey pillbox hat pinned to a brunette wig with set curls. Hundreds of shoes littered the floor around her and hung from the ceiling, leather bags studded the walls. For a second, if it weren't for the glassy-eyed stare and waxen shine, she looked just like Maggie.

The bell rang as they opened the door. In the centre of the shop was a long row of back-to-back Formica-covered chromium chairs. Along each side of the shop, more shoes on free-standing display trolleys and glass cases with fans of leather gloves in all colours. Ambient Muzak played. Bright lights glared down at all angles from the ceiling. A slim sales assistant padded across to them wearing a Burton's Italian-style suit.

'Good morning, how may I help?'

'Hey there, we're here from Monday's for shop-service experience,' said Carl.

The assistant looked like his milk had turned sour.

'I'll get the manager.' He swung away and disappeared into a back room. The manager appeared, extending his hand. He was shorter than Flo in her heels, the grease in his hair seeming to ooze also from the pores on his face.

'Hello. Mr Peabody. How do you do? From Monday's then?'

'That's right, Carl Anderson.' Carl smiled and shook his hand.

'Sorry, I didn't realise the trainees were bringing wives along these days.' Mr Peabody laughed through his wide-spaced teeth and looked around at the assistant who shook his head, smiling.

'What? Oh, no, this is Flo Blundell, another trainee.'

Mr Peabody stood stock still and forced a smile.

'I see, well I never, *well* I never. A career girl eh? How do you do?' He took Flo's hand; his was so oily it slipped away of its own accord. 'It is a pleasure, it really is,' he said, and stood back so as to gain a top-to-toe view of her. She reddened and wiped her hand surreptitiously on her hip.

'Well, where do you want us then?' she said.

'Oh, ha ha, that's good, where do we want you?' Mr Peabody looked around at the assistant again. 'I wouldn't like to say, Miss Blundell, I really wouldn't, ha ha.'

'It's missus.' Flo stared back at him, trying not to blink.

'Oh yes, a working wife eh? Righteo then, let's get you both started. Have either of you had retail experience before?'

'I have, once, it was really delightful, in Fulham,' said Carl.

'Oh, yes, Fulham, I see, well, we run the flag-ship store here in Oxford Street, so you may find things a *tad* different from the Fulham store, Mr Anderson. Jerry here should be pleased to show you the ropes, if you take them out to the storeroom first, Jerry. Just shoes, Jerry, leave bags and gloves for now.'

'Here's all the stock, then,' said Jerry without enthusiasm. 'Men's there, ladies there. Alphabetical by style name. Look on the box for the size. Come here and I'll show you how to measure.'

'Oh, Jerry, let me do that, there's a customer needs serving,' said Mr Peabody, shoving Jerry aside. 'Mrs Blundell, if you wouldn't mind placing your foot into this measure?'

Flo grimaced and slipped off her court shoe.

'Ah, I see you're wearing style number five-ninety-two, the Eleganza.'

Mr Peabody knelt down on the floor and guided her foot into the measure, holding the back of her calf, slipping his hand higher until it was behind her knee, beneath the hem of her pencil skirt.

'It's quite straightforward. Making sure the customer's heel is well back against the heel rest, whichever gradation is first beyond the customer's longest toe is the size,' he said, running his finger over her toes to demonstrate. 'Left and right usually differ somewhat, and in that case, use the bigger sizing.' He gave them a sickly grin, looking up at Flo from the floor. She smoothed down the front of her skirt and pulled her foot back.

'Thanks, I think we got it,' said Carl.

'Any problems, give one of the lads a shout. I shall be in my office.' He smiled at Flo and slunk away.

'What a creep,' said Carl, once he had gone.

Flo laughed, embarrassed. 'Come on then, let's sell some shoes.'

11

'Give you a ride if you like?' Carl mounted his NSU Quickly moped when they arrived back at Monday station from doing their London shop service.

'I dunno,' said Flo. 'It looks like a death trap.'

'She's seen better days but she's all right. It's up to you, it's only down the road and she only does twenty, tops.'

'Oh, go on then.' Flo lifted her leg over the seat behind Carl.

'Or side-saddle?' he grinned.

'Course.' Flo blushed and perched with her legs on one side. 'Lah-di-dah.'

Carl stood up on the pedals, pedalled them round to start the motor.

'Bombs away,' he shouted. They chugged down the main road, the houses passing by. Flo's face was alight, the side of her hair came free of its pins, she held on to the basket rack over the back wheel for dear life and felt as joyous as she had ever done before.

'Where do you live?'

'Just stop along here,' shouted Flo, reluctantly. She didn't want Fred seeing her with Carl, even though there was nothing going on.

'Thanks, that was really good. Bye then.'

'So long, Flo, I enjoyed it.'

He sat on the Quickly watching her go, and

pulled away into the road. It was a lovely day, the sun was low but still bright and warm. Flo swung her arms as she walked. She'd been so nervous about going up to London but she had survived it. And Carl, he was a gem.

As she turned into her garden gate she saw Babs's worried face disappear from the top window and her stomach dropped into her bowels.

'Mikey's had an accident.' Babs pulled the front door open before Flo could reach for the key.

'What? Oh my god, is he all right? Where is he?'

'Upstairs in bed, he broke his arm.'

Flo clambered up the stairs on all fours and ran into Mikey's room. He was lying on his bed reading comics and sucking a lollipop, his arm in plaster in a sling. He looked up, worried.

'What the hell you been doing?' snapped Flo, sitting on his bed to look at his arm.

'Fell off the gun bunker down the fort.'

'Well, that was bloody stupid, wasn't it?' Flo examined his sling. 'Where's your dad?'

Mikey shrugged and popped his lolly back in. Flo raised her eyebrows at Babs.

'Don't know, *I* made the tea.'

'Well, who got him to hospital then?'

'Jeanie ran for the Monday's doctor, he came and took Mikey in his car, Jeanie went with him.'

'I'll bloody kill him. Sorry I wasn't here, love, you all right?' She softened and stroked Mikey's hair. 'If it's not one thing with you it's another. Always worrying me, aren't you, eh?'

'Yeah. Look. Jeanie got it for me.' He showed her his new comic. 'And this.' He held his orange lolly out on a string of spit for Flo to see.

'What happened though, who was you with?'

'Just the boys, mucking around on the bunker, that's all, Mum. I didn't mean to, Mum.'

'Did it hurt?'

'Yeah, I puked up all over my shoes. One of the boys ran to find you but you weren't anywhere so Jeanie came.'

'Did she now?' said Flo softly. 'And where's Jeanie now?'

'Went out somewhere, don't know where,' said Babs. 'Can I go out now you're back?'

'Yeah, course you can. Oh no, hang on, I've got a do tonight, supposed to be going with your dad. I need you to sit in with Mikey, sorry, love.'

'Oh god. That's not fair. I told Jim I'd go to the pictures.'

'Sorry, love, I can't get out of it, it's a posh dinner and dance, all the trainees are going, it's work, and Mikey can't be on his own like this.'

'Well, is it work or a dance? Make your mind up.'

'Less of the lip, young lady, you're not too big for a good hiding you know.'

Fred didn't come home in time for the dance. Flo had to go alone. Wearing her new dress and heels, her hair done up in a French pleat, she walked into the ballroom on the ground floor of the hotel. Around the dance floor large round tables were laid out with white tablecloths, candles and flower centrepieces. At the back was a raised podium with a microphone and lectern. The room churned with voices, laughter and the smooth music of the Andrew Mead orchestra crammed into the far corner.

'Name?' A falsely jolly woman who stank of lavender sat at a little table by the door and consulted her floor plan.

'Florence Blundell.'

'Table twelve, over there.'

Flo held herself erect, tried to walk gracefully over to her table. Lil and Ted were there and Flo smiled with relief.

'Sit yourself down here, love, where's that husband of yours?' Ted held out a chair for her.

'He's got a sore head, you know Fred.' Flo wondered why she thought Fred would ever have come.

'Sorry, love, ain't it a shame,' said Lil, scrunching up her face in sympathy. 'Here, have some of this, it's all laid on.'

Lil poured Flo a glass of white wine from a carafe. It tasted sour but Flo drank it anyway, she needed something to get her in the mood.

'How you getting on, Lil, love? I haven't seen you for a while.' Flo glanced down at Lil's stomach; she was starting to show.

'Yeah, smashing, those Black Beauties are working a treat, high as a kite I am.' She whispered the last part and downed her glass of wine, gesturing to Ted to pour her another. 'How you doing then? How's that fancy college of yours, we don't see you much now, do we?'

'Yeah, Miss Fancy Pants, eh?' said Ted, laughing round at the others at the table, two other couples Flo recognised from the factory. 'Swanning round with all them college boys now, eh?'

Flo ignored his copious winks. 'It's all right, yeah, I was up London today.'

'Eh? Up London was you? Did you hear that, Ted?'

'Well, I'm sitting right here, aren't I?' Ted erupted into loud spluttering snorts, his large front teeth pulling on his bottom lip. 'What you do up London, Flo, love?'

'Shop service, worked in a Monday's shoe shop for retail experience.'

'Oooh, retail experience, hear that, Ted?'

Ted lifted his palms upwards to demonstrate to the table that, yes, he had heard.

'So, how's it down the factory then? Any gossip?' asked Flo.

Flo frowned when Lil gestured that there was someone behind her.

'Well, if it isn't my protégée.'

Flo jumped and spun around in her seat. Mr Monday, a large cigar in his mouth, smiled down at her.

'Oh,' said Flo, half standing, not sure what to do.

'Sit down, honey, relax. I came over to see how you're doing in my Monday-men college,' he boomed. Everyone at the table assumed fixed smiles and rigid shoulders.

'Very well, thank you. I was up London today doing shop service.'

'Where's that no-good husband of yours?'

'Oh, he's feeling a bit off colour.'

'Off colour is it? Is that why he hasn't been to half my soccer practices?' He laughed. 'By god, when he does come he makes up for it. You men seen him play?' The men all shook their heads. 'Well, look lively and get out there to watch them practise, take an interest in your factory's glory, because with a player like him we're gonna beat West Ham, you mark my words.'

The men mumbled 'Yes, sir' and gulped down their drinks.

'And *you,*' he said, turning his attention back to Flo. 'I saw you come in and thought hey, I did not know I had invited *Grace Kelly* to my little dinner dance. Then I thought, gee, that's my college girl.'

Flo blushed and looked down at her gloves. Lil elbowed her.

'I'll give *you* a nine out of ten,' he boomed. 'If you were younger you'd be a ten for sure, and it's not often I say that.'

He waited, as if for Flo to express her gratitude, but all she could manage was a weak smile.

'Anyhow, I've been thinking how I need a new personal secretary, and only high scorers are in the running for *that* privileged position, and guess what, little lady? You're it.'

A collective shuffle and gasp went around the table. Flo looked up at him and her heart sank. Sweaty and hungry, his eyes everywhere. She'd done so well to get into the college, with Maggie's help. Mr Monday was trouble, she knew it.

'Start Monday, seven thirty sharp, go off for college when you need to, but be back prompt. My office, college girl.' There was something sinister in his smile. 'Think of it as good experience for your college studies,' he said, leaning down to her level, his cigar breath repugnant.

'Yes, Mr Monday,' she mumbled.

Away he swaggered, back to his table, sat down

next to his immaculate wife with a big grin on his face, leant back and puffed his cigar through his teeth. Flo's eyes met Maggie's. Flo smiled and Maggie didn't smile back.

'Jeanie.'

Babs made me jump, ran up behind me along our road, done up to the nines in her silly tight dress and no coat.

'Where you going, Jeanie?'

'Getting chips, why?'

'Nothing. I'll walk along with you. I'm off to meet my Jim.'

She put her arm through mine and clung on to me with a weird smile. I knew something was coming but I wanted to stay in my head for a bit longer. I was on cloud nine. All I could think about was college and James. For the past five years I'd been stuck in that stupid school, then stuck weighing butter in the grocer's shop. All of a sudden I had two amazing things in my life and I could hardly believe my luck. I realised I felt closer to Babs because of it, like we had something in common for once. Not the college, but boys. I would never have said it to her but she always had something over me. Now she didn't, we were equal in that.

As we turned into the main road and headed past the hotel towards the quadrangle I squeezed her arm. She looked at me and smiled with surprise when I grinned at her.

'God, Jeanie, I'm so glad you're cheering up a bit.'

I couldn't help but laugh. 'I know, me too.'

'Quick, in here.'

She pulled me roughly round the back of the hotel by the stinking bins.

'What you doing, you bloody idiot?'

'Jeanie, I got to tell you but you mustn't, you really mustn't tell a soul, especially not Mum and especially not Dad, promise?' She held both my arms, whispered into my face like a maniac.

'What?'

'It's Jim.' She paused to swallow. 'We want to get married.'

'What? What the hell are you talking about?'

'We're in love. Isn't it brilliant? Jeanie? It's all right, I just had to tell you, but I can't tell Mum yet, can I?' She did a fake laugh. 'Mum'll go mad, she's always telling me not to get into trouble.'

'You're up the duff.' My happy feeling drained away, I felt sick.

'What? Don't look like that, we love each other, Jeanie.'

'You're fifteen, Babs.'

'Yeah, I know that don't I?'

'Mum was fifteen when she had us.'

'I know, that's why I can't tell her yet.' She hugged herself, smiling like an idiot. My sister, in the family way, Jesus Christ almighty, what would happen to her?

'What you gonna do, Babs?'

'I'm so happy, Jeanie, you wouldn't believe it.' She started to cry then and rummaged in her bag. 'I haven't got a hankie.'

I gave her mine, she wiped her snot and mascara on it.

'Who's this Jim then and what's he gonna do

204

about it?'

'It's all right, he's a diamond, and, Jeanie?'

'What?'

'I love him, I really do.'

Well, I could understand that now. 'If he runs off at least we've got Dad to set on him.' That made her laugh. She wiped her face and lit a cig, started to look a bit more normal apart from the red blotches all over her face.

'Do I look all right? Got any powder?'

I shook my head.

'I'm meeting him now, at the pictures. Why don't you come and see him, Jeanie? He's really nice, you'll like him, he's clever like you, he's a grammar school swot.'

'Why do you only meet him at the pictures then? Doesn't he wanna be seen with you or something? And where's he work?' I felt protective over my sister, silly cow. She should be with someone nice like my James, not some idiot who only wanted to use her.

She tried to laugh but let out a nervy simper instead.

'He works in the offices, accounts or something, and don't say that, Jeanie, that's bloody mean that is, we like the pictures, it's private, isn't it?'

'Yeah, a bit too private I reckon. All right, I'll come, but don't think I won't give him a piece of my mind.'

'Oh don't, Jeanie, oh you won't really? Be happy for me, will you?'

I nodded and went with her. Christ alive, what would Mum say? I didn't much fancy that bloke's chances if he didn't step up and do the right thing.

Dad would rip his bloody head off. Everyone knows there's only one reason why you'd say you're getting married that young.

We came up to the pictures and I started walking up the steps to the entrance, but Babs called me round the side, where a boy stood on his own, smoking, one hand in his pocket. He looked up and saw Babs and smiled. And that's when my heart stopped beating. Babs ran to his side and nudged up against him. He saw me and the smile slid right off his face. He took the smallest step away from Babs.

'Jim?' she said. It was like someone had poured icy water over my head, it trickled down my neck and back and froze me to the spot. It was James, *my* James.

'Hello, Jeanie,' he said, and smiled. Babs looked from him to me.

'Jeanie?' she said, all worried. I gulped hard and wanted to run off right there and then. Babs and *James?* I couldn't believe it. Babs loved *James.* James was *Jim?*

'Jim, is it?' I managed to say. 'Work in the offices, do you, Jim?' My voice cracked and sounded weird.

'Jeanie, you're scaring me,' cried Babs.

'Have you even asked him who his mum and dad are, Babs, you stupid cow?'

'What? Who are they then?' she turned to him.

He gave her a twitchy smile. 'Look, I didn't want to make you feel awkward just because they own the company. I didn't want to scare you off, did I?'

Her face showed her brain working it all out.

'But you said you live on the estate with your folks.'

'He does, you idiot, he lives there.' I pointed across to the Monday Mansion. I could feel myself starting to cry but held it back.

'But, have you been going to college with Jeanie, then, you didn't say? I thought Jeanie was sweet on the boy she was going to college with.'

Her stupid face was scrunched up, confused. It was embarrassing and terrible. I thought he liked me, I liked *him* anyway. My head felt like it was floating.

He put his arm around her and pulled her in. 'Because I'm not supposed to tell anyone that, and I wanted to help your sister, she's really bright and doesn't want to be stuck in a factory.'

'Oh.' She brightened up. 'So you were doing it for me in a way? Helping my sister out?' She gave me a made-up smile, wanted me to agree with him. Well she could get lost, it was always her getting what she wanted, pretty Babs, popular Babs, well she was in trouble now and that was her tough luck.

'And I don't know what you mean about Jeanie being sweet on me. Sorry, Jeanie, if I gave you the wrong idea.' He made what he must have thought was a comical grimace. 'I really admire you for wanting an education, I wanted to help you. I had no idea ... if I thought...'

Oh my god. He shrugged with a stupid pitying smile and wouldn't stop.

'I thought I'd explained, I wanted to help because I'm against Britain's elitist class structure...'

'Ask him why he only ever takes you to the

pictures then,' I said to shut him up.

He frowned at me. 'Look, sorry, Jeanie, I didn't mean … this really is very difficult.' He looked at Babs. 'I don't know if you'll understand, but my parents are snobs really, they have forbidden me to see girls from the estate, I know, it's rubbish, but I like you so much I don't care what they think, and now we're getting engaged they'll just have to get used to the idea, won't they?'

'Oh, so you're slumming it with me, are you?' Babs laughed and put her arms around him.

'Yes I am, my little factory girl.' They almost kissed right in front of me, their noses touched.

'Hang on, don't tell me you two think this will all be all right?'

'Oh, Jeanie, you're always doom and gloom, course it'll be all right, we love each other, don't we?'

They stared at each other, and I really think he was sweet on her too, they looked like they were in some sort of a bubble. I couldn't take it any more. I shook my head and cleared off.

'Jeanie,' Babs called out. 'You won't tell Mum and Dad, will you?'

I didn't answer. Babs knew I wouldn't tell, it wasn't like I was even talking to them anyway, was it?

So much for bloody James, the bastard, leading a girl on like that, and what an idiot I was, the pig was just busy getting into Babs's knickers, the cheap little tart. I thought he was like me, we were both kicking against the shit, he understood me, no one else did. I reached for my hankie and then I remembered Babs had it, she had it and I had nothing. I was a mug and Babs was causing trouble for everyone, getting all the attention as usual. Spreading her legs and getting what she wanted. God, I wished I was already out of there. Whatever happened I had to get my exams, the rest of them could just get lost.

I blundered along the main road, wiped my nose on my sleeve like Mikey would do. Someone ran up behind me and put their hands over my eyes. I yelped and jerked away. Swinging around I saw it was just Skylon from work.

'You bloody idiot, what you playing at?'

He stood there like I'd slapped him. 'Sorry, Jeanie, I didn't mean to scare you. Where you going?'

'What's it got to do with you where I'm going?' I swiped the tears away from my face. He shrugged, the idiot. Factory idiot, just like Babs.

'I'm going to the dance.'

'So?' I realised then he was done up in his smart suit.

'Wanna come?' He went bright red and looked at his feet.

'Do I look like I wanna go to a dance?'

'Dunno, you look nice, like always.'

I just stared at him. He gave me a little smile and walked off, looking back over his shoulder. Me and Babs were twins, weren't we? Someone wanted *me* just like someone wanted *her.* She wasn't the only one who could get a boy's attention.

'Skylon, hang on.' He trotted back over with his hands in his pockets. 'Where's this dance then?'

'In the hotel ballroom, I've got free tickets, won

them in a raffle.' He held out the tickets and waited for his answer.

'Go on then but only if you get me a drink.'

His face lit up. 'Really? You're coming?'

'I said, didn't I? And you got to get me a drink, a real one.'

'Yeah, I can do that, come on then.' He offered me his arm and I took it. He was so tall and gangly but after what just happened I was glad. I was wearing a day dress and a tatty coat, but tough, they weren't gonna throw me out for not being dressed right.

We came up to the ballroom, the music jumped out through the doors and sort of folded around me. I hadn't been to a dance before, it was loud and gay, twinkling ball on the ceiling, band on the stage, everyone smiling like goons. All the couples, I didn't know how to dance like that. Skylon said to wait there. He disappeared for a minute and came up trumps, gave me a gin and lemon. I didn't ask where he got it from, just downed it in one before someone saw. Blimey, it hit me, it really did.

We sort of stood there a bit awkwardly in the corner.

'Get me another one.'

Skylon grinned at me and nodded, he seemed up for it anyway, maybe he wasn't so bad after all. I watched him. He sidled through the tables around the dance floor. I didn't see him pick anything up but when he came back he had a glass in his hand.

'Cor, how'd you do that?' He gave it to me. I didn't even know what that one was but I got it down my neck before anyone saw and cringed at the taste of it. A man with a face on him strode over in our direction. I nudged Skylon.

'I think you took my girl's drink?'

'What you on about, course I didn't.' Ha ha, Skylon looked really aggro, it was brilliant.

'You're Ron's boy, aren't you?' said the man, looking Skylon up and down.

Skylon grabbed my arm and pulled me away, leaving the man standing there staring at us. We ran out the ballroom laughing our heads off. The cool quiet air outside made me giddy. I missed my step and fell off the curb, Skylon caught my arm.

'Come on.' I pulled his hand and ran down the road towards the park. The little gate was locked when I tried it. Skylon just vaulted over the fence. I couldn't stop laughing. He put his arms around me and lifted me over, my body was pressed against his and when he didn't let go I was glad. I looked up at him, it was getting dark. My coat was open, the warmth from his body radiated through my dress on to my chest.

'I've liked you for ages, you know that?'

I just nodded and laughed like a drunken idiot. His face was quite nice actually. I'd never really noticed it before.

He leant down and put his mouth on mine, jelly-soft and wet. I squashed my lips against his, it was weird and nice, like my body was suddenly a magnet to his, I pushed up against him and he pulled back.

'What's wrong?'

He shook his head. 'Nothing,' he mumbled, and put his hands in his pockets. There was a little shed in the park where they must have kept the lawn mower and stuff. I grabbed Skylon's hand and pulled him round the back of it and put my arms around him. He just looked down at me, his eyes sort of glazed over.

'I've never done this before,' I said.

'Nor have I, and I don't think we should.'

'What's wrong? You chicken?' I don't know what got into me, I was like a mad thing, those drinks, I was upset, wasn't I? Why should Babs get all the attention?

'No, I'm not chicken,' he said, his voice all thick. He flattened his lips on mine, put his hands on my body and pushed me against the wall. I gasped and kissed him back.

'Sorry I'm late.'

Flo walked into Maggie's sitting room. The members of the young wives club smiled and murmured hello. Alice and Dot sat at a green baize card table at the far end of the room, peering at their fanned hands. Elvis Presley's 'King Creole' tumbled out of the record player and bounced around the room. But Maggie looked different, the happy notes skirted around her. She stood, her black cigarette holder aloft.

'What's your poison then, Flo?' Tabby did her usual bartending duty. 'There's a martini on the go?'

'Go on then, I'll try one. Is there anything on for tonight?'

'Well, yes there is.' Doreen was excited. 'We're going to learn the jive.' She clapped her hands and giggled.

'Who's teaching you lot the jive then? I won't be doing it,' said Lil, rubbing her belly.

'I am, I think.' It was Dot, one of the sewing girls from the factory. 'I'm no expert but I know a bit.'

'Perhaps a couple more of these first?' said Tabby, handing around glasses. 'And, Flo, I don't think I've seen you since your big news. I hear you have started at the college?'

'That's right, I'm in.'

'Gosh, well done, Mags, for pulling it off.' Tabby raised her glass to Maggie, who gave a small smile. 'Quite the victory I'd say. The implications are endless.'

'What do you mean, for other women?' asked Lil. 'Well, *I* wouldn't want to do it, going abroad and managing a factory, there's no way I could do something like that.'

'Nor me,' said Doreen, shuddering. 'The very thought, and my George would never want me to, I know that much, it's like being a man.'

'Oi,' Alice snapped. 'Maggie's done brilliantly to get Flo in the college and Flo's working really hard to get a decent job in her own right, and why shouldn't she if she wants to? It's not for everyone, no one said it was.'

'Well said, Alice, it's the principle of the thing,' said Tabby. 'If Maggie here weren't feeling off colour she'd tell you about Maslow, again.' She rolled her eyes and smiled at Maggie, who pulled on her cigarette and kept a straight face. 'And how Flo is on her way to fulfilling her potential, and why not indeed.'

'I wouldn't mind,' said Liz, who worked at the

factory part time and lived on the estate. 'When the little ones are at school though. I couldn't do it before that. They say it's not good for the children to leave them, don't they?'

Flo frowned. Maggie wouldn't look at her.

'There's been a bit of a hiccup though,' said Flo, testing the water. 'Mr Monday wants me to be his personal secretary, so I'm gonna have to do a full-time job and a full-time college course somehow. Not that I'm not grateful, of course.' She waited for Maggie's reaction.

'*Mr Monday?* Blimey, you never said.' Alice stared from Flo to Maggie, they all did.

'He only asked me the other night, at the dance, didn't he, Lil?' Lil nodded. 'I couldn't exactly say no, could I?'

'And why would you want to say no?' At last Maggie spoke, her tone slow and deliberate, commanding the attention of the room.

'I dunno, Maggie, I just get the idea that you're not too happy about it, and I wouldn't want to offend you or anything.'

'Why on earth wouldn't I be happy about it?' Maggie gave a tinkling laugh. 'My husband needs a reliable secretary, he sees a good committed worker in you, it's a job many women would be happy to have. Are you saying you don't want the job?'

'No, course not.' Flo looked down at her drink. There was a prolonged silence, just the tail-end of the Elvis song, which finished with a click of the stylus arm slotting back into place.

Doreen cast about, wanting to break the awkwardness.

214

'How's about this jive lesson then, eh, Dot?' she said.

'Good thinking, Doreen, what'll we play?' Tabby strode over to the record-player cabinet.

'Got any Bill Haley or something lively?' said Dot. 'Or stick that Elvis one on again.' She gulped her drink and jumped up. 'Right, who wants to be my partner?'

'Ooh, I will, I'll learn from the expert,' said Doreen, giggling.

Dot demonstrated the basic steps with Doreen.

'Get into partners then, everyone else, and have a go.'

Tabby grabbed Alice, Flo looked at Lil and raised her eyebrows.

'You haven't got a chance in hell of getting me up, Flo love, you dance with Maggie.'

Flo laughed nervously and looked up at Maggie, who stood by the wall.

'Oh, come on then, let's get it over with.' Maggie held out her hand. '*I'll* lead,' she said, putting her hand on Flo's waist. She seemed to soften then and Flo relaxed a little.

They danced a few steps, Maggie laughed when she stood on Flo's toe.

'Look, I feel funny about all this, are you all right with it?' Flo whispered into Maggie's ear.

'What, that scoundrel husband of mine, do you mean?'

Flo shrugged. 'I suppose.'

'Well, it's not your fault you're so beautiful, is it?' Flo flushed. 'Let me just caution you though, I know what he's like, you can probably guess, so just be on your guard.'

'I will, I promise, and the most important things to me are the college course and your friendship, you know that, don't you?'

With a smile, Maggie pushed Flo away at arm's length, spun her around and pulled her back in. 'Blimey, you've done this before, Mags.'

'I've missed you, Flo, you're so busy with all of this college work. I want you to come to see me. Don't forget who helped you to get started.'

'I won't forget, Mags, you know I'm grateful.'

'Arrggghhhh.' Doreen screamed as Dot tried to pick her up in a lift and slide her down between her legs. They fell in a heap, laughing hysterically. Maggie rolled her eyes at Flo and went to help them up.

The hooter went off and Flo hurried down the stairs of the Administration building and out into the swarm of workers in the factory compound. Fred wanted his midday dinner at home today. Mikey stood by the factory gates with a pile of papers on an upturned crate – he had a job selling *The Monday Week*. Flo smiled and threaded her way through to him.

Monday's was a funny kind of place. Shirley on the sewing team described it as a cross between Butlins and Holloway. It could be suffocating, everyone living on top of each other, bosses next door to workers, nowhere to hide. Fred was getting on with it and he had stuck to his promise. Yes, he had a drink at the club after work, but he wasn't drinking properly. It can't have been easy for him. He'd even got Mikey a little job.

Flo frowned and strained to look through the

crowd, one of the workers handed a piece of paper to Mikey. There was something about the way Mikey's eyes darted about and the way the man spoke with his chin down. It was only a second and then the man had gone.

'What you doing?'

Mikey jumped when he saw Flo standing there. He smiled at her, guilt flashing across his eyes.

'Nothing, selling papers, I gotta get back to school now.'

'What was that bloke giving you then?'

'What bloke? Nothing, honest. I gotta go, Mum, seeya.'

He dumped the pile of papers in the gatehouse and ran off to school. Flo watched him go. She had seen it often enough at the docks. Gambling was rife over there, and big business for those with the balls to do it. Men used their children as runners, gathering bets from punters in time for races.

She ran home to get there first, put the spuds she'd peeled and cut that morning into the chip pan and some sausages under the grill. The little bin under the sink was full with potato peelings, she took it out to their inherited compost pile in the back garden. As she shook the peelings out on to the pile she turned her face up to the sun. It'd all be all right, she'd talk to Fred about it. If she hadn't glanced down just at the right moment she might not have seen the sun reflect off a piece of glass in the compost. She frowned and pulled out an empty bottle of rum. Two cold hands cupped her heart. The front door banged, she pushed the bottle back down and rushed inside to turn over the sausages.

Fred came out of the bathroom drying his hands. He left the towel on the back of a dining chair and took a seat at the table.

'Hello, darling, all right?'

'Mm,' he mumbled and picked up his paper.

The sharp tang of malt vinegar and the tickle of white pepper irritated Flo's nose. As they ate, she counted down. When she'd finished her second sausage she'd say something.

'Fred, have you got Mikey running bets for you?'

He stiffened and lifted his eyes to meet hers. Lowered them and forked a chip into his mouth.

'So, what?'

'My god, Fred, for a start it's illegal, you know what they're like around here. What if he gets caught? We'll all be out.'

'You reckon?' He said it with a smirk, not taking her seriously.

'Well, are you gonna stop it?'

He shrugged his shoulders.

She swallowed and took her chance. 'And what about the drink?'

'What you on about?'

'You know.'

He chewed slowly, avoiding her eye.

'You said you'd stop, Fred. When you lost your job at the docks.'

'Christ, I came home for my dinner, not a nag matinee. You're the one swanning around doing this and that, not here for the family.'

'What, the dinner dance? You were supposed to come with me, it was important for work, it was compulsory.'

218

Fred smirked again. 'That's a big fancy word. You're getting big for your boots I reckon.'

Flo gripped her knife and fork for fortitude. 'Well, it's your fault I have to work for Mr Monday now. If you'd been there I bet he wouldn't have asked me.'

'Oh shut up moaning, woman, it's a job, isn't it? Just get on with it.'

'Well, don't burn people's bloody gardens down then.'

He stared at her while he sucked a piece of sausage slowly out of his teeth. 'Shut your noise and get the kettle on,' he said, dismissing her and going back to his food.

Flo stopped herself saying anything more. Self-preservation had trained her to know when to be quiet and it was suddenly as if the past few months hadn't happened. With a subdued flash of insight Flo realised they would slip back into doing what they'd practised over and again, living but not living, that's what they were good at. Flo was used to existing inside her head, finding a way to get through the days on her own. She wondered how long it would be before he started raising his hand again.

She took a deep breath and watched him eat, his eyes down to his plate. He might have been on his own for all the notice he took of her. *We've been here before, Fred, you and me,* she wanted to say to him, *and it's lonely. You're in there somewhere but you're so far away I think I'll never see you again. I'd give you a shove to make sure but you're on bloody elastic, or I am. Do you even think about what you're doing? Do you care? Are we just props on your stage?*

Flo did what she did best. She shut her noise and put the kettle on.

12

I had four pennies in my hand and a slip of paper with the *Thurrock Gazette's* telephone number. I glanced left and right and heaved open the door of the public telephone box. With the greasy black receiver to my ear I dialled the number and pushed two of the pennies in when the pips went.

'Hello? *Thurrock Gazette?*' A woman's voice.

'I'd like to report something.'

She put me through to a man.

'Yes? Who is this?'

'Something awful is happening at Monday's Leather factory.'

A pause. 'Go on.'

'They are using slaves in the factory.'

No answer.

'And ... they're not given water.'

'I see. And what are these slaves made to do?'

'You'd better come and see!'

I panicked and hung up, my heart pounding. It had sounded better in my head that morning. But they might investigate, cause trouble for the factory. It might get closed down and I wouldn't have to work there any more. Get back at Mum and Dad and get back at Babs.

I pressed button B, wiped my finger around the

change chute and grabbed my slip of paper, pushed open the door and ran for it. I could see other people jogging towards the factory gates. It was almost half past seven, the stupid marching music blared out like we were going to war. They didn't like it if you were late.

As I ran over to the gate the siren sounded, a long irritating whine. If you looked up the hill past the woods you could just make out the top of the fort that stood sentry over the estuary. I wished I was up there, looking down at them all, the ants scurrying around. Then I thought of Skylon, and what I'd done with him in the park the other night, how I'd liked it and how it had disgusted me at the same time. His slobbering mouth, his big tongue.

Through the gates past that sniffy man who stood there lording it over the workers, reporting them if they were late, living off the factory's hand-me-down glory like a football fan saying 'We won the cup'. The factory workers were always going on about the West Ham game, it was all anyone talked about around there.

In the dingy workshop I put on my apron and plonked down on the stool next to the non-stop whirring conveyor. It went round and round and round. That's what I felt like. Box after box after box. I was just part of the machinery. I looked at them all. How did they find the will to get out of bed in the morning with no end in sight? Except death. I started on my first box, I was really fast at it by then, I couldn't help it, I competed secretly with all the others, trying to be the one to get the most done in a day. It wasn't that I enjoyed it, just

221

anything to take away the brain-melting boredom.

Skylon looked like an eager puppy when I turned up, a stupid smile on his face like I'd be pleased to see him.

'Morning,' he said.

'Hm,' I grunted.

'You all right then?'

'Why wouldn't I be?'

He looked taken aback. 'Dunno,' he shrugged.

Mr Turtle was looking but I couldn't be bothered. I wished Skylon would stop staring at me. He was so tall and lanky. His long, skinny arms around me the other night, his trousers around his ankles. I didn't know why Babs was so desperate for all that stuff, if that's what you had to do to get someone. I still couldn't believe she was having a baby, even though she wouldn't admit it.

I didn't feel any better about things, even after the other night, when I was drunk and not thinking straight. It didn't make any difference that Skylon wanted me, he was just a caveman like the rest of them. Men like him couldn't be trusted, not if Dad was anything to go by. Men who smile and joke around with their pals at work, then they get home and plant their fists into their wife and kids. James was different, he was like *me*, we both needed *something else* that this lot didn't need, that Babs didn't need, so why would he choose her over me? She was pretty and confident, is that all it was? It serves them right, they could have each other. Stuff them both, trapped so young, that was her life over, wasn't it.

'Fancy the pictures tonight, do ya?'

'Not really.'

'What's wrong with you then?'

'Nothing.'

What did he want anyway? What more would he want from me than I gave him the other night? The stupid girls at the end were chattering away like sparrows, excited that the Queen was having another baby. I felt in my pocket for some more messages to cheer myself up. I held one down under the conveyor so no one could see. *Help I'm chained up in the leather factory and they won't give me water.* That was a good one. I put a box together and slipped the paper just under the bottom flap inside so it wouldn't be seen by Quality. Skylon looked over to see what I was up to but I scowled at him to get lost and he turned away back to his boxes. I wondered what the *Gazette* would do, whether they'd come sniffing around for a story. That would shut everyone up.

The factory siren whined its loud lament, calling the workers. It was 7:25 a.m. Fred strode out of the newsagent folding his *Daily Mirror* back at the sports pages and ran his finger along the horserace meetings for that day. A man in a cloth cap sidled up to him, passed him two half-crowns and a piece of torn-off newspaper. Scribbled in pencil it said *Bob #2 Derby 2/6 e/w Shantung.* Fred pocketed it without comment and the man trotted off towards the factory gates. Marching music blared from a loudspeaker on top of the factory gatehouse as the last of the workers swarmed through. Fred stopped to check his paper as the late-rising stragglers ran past him.

He ambled along, head down reading, and

stopped short when he came to the closed factory gates. The sniffing gatekeeper sat with his arms folded on the ledge of his hatch, looking out with a sneering smile.

'Open up, mate,' said Fred.

'You're late.'

'No I'm not,' said Fred looking up at the clock on top of the gatehouse. 'It's only just gone seven thirty, now let me in.'

'Tardy workers have to go through the staff office to get a late mark.'

'Late mark? For Christ's sake, just let me in, you twit.'

The gatekeeper came round to unlock the door set into the large factory gates.

'Over there, staff office. I'll report you if you don't go.' He pointed to the Administration building.

Fred stood in front of him, unblinking. The gatekeeper shrank back from Fred's glare and crept into his gatehouse.

'Yeah, crawl back under your stone,' mumbled Fred, and headed over to the building. He found the staff office, gave his name and was told to wait for the manager to come. There was nowhere to sit so he stood with his back against the wall until a man in a suit approached him.

'Fred Blundell?'

'That's right.'

The manager raised his eyebrows at Fred's tone.

'This is the first time you have been late. When *you* are late, *everyone* is late. You work in Dispatch?' Fred nodded. 'Your fellow workers are waiting for you right now, things are being held up because you didn't turn up on time. Production is being affected.'

'Let me get to work then.'

The manager's eyes deadened. He made a note in Fred's records.

'Don't let it happen again.'

Fred strode away, rolling a cigarette.

'Lot of bloody fuss over nothing,' he muttered. He smoked as he strolled over to the factory and made his way to the dispatch department. Putting out his fag with his fingers and slotting it behind his ear, he went in the back way through the loading bay door, into the hangar strewn with crates and boxes.

'Blundell? Where you been?' asked his foreman Ray Little.

'Nowhere. They closed the gates when I weren't even late.'

Ray Little shook his head. 'Well, don't do it again or they'll have you for it. Now get to work, your boxes are holding everyone up.'

Fred rolled up his shirtsleeves and started heaving the boxes stacked in the loading bay into the back of a lorry.

'Oi, Blundell.' One of the dispatch workers, George Berry, called over to Fred. 'You better not be late for the West Ham game.'

The men laughed, even Fred smiled.

'I won't be late, I mean to see them off good and proper.'

'Oh, you reckon? You haven't even turned up for half the practices, the boss is none too pleased, I can tell you.'

'The difference between you and me, Berry, is that I don't need to practise as much. I have what is known as a natural talent.'

At this the men roared with laughter. Fred chuckled to himself.

'It's about team work, pal, hasn't anyone told you about that?'

'I'll be at the next practice, don't you worry, and I'll show *you* a trick or two.'

'Yeah, yeah, you got any tricks up your sleeve for the Derby?'

'Keep your voice down,' Fred shot back, glaring at Berry. 'I don't give tips, you know that by now.'

Berry came over, glancing round to make sure the foreman wasn't in earshot.

'Here, I fancy Shantung, what odds you got?'

Fred thought for a moment, shifted a couple more boxes. 'Eleven to two.'

'Here, ten bob to win,' said Berry. Fred put the brown ten-shilling note in his trouser pocket, took out a little notebook, licked the lead of a pencil stub and noted the bet.

When three o'clock came around and Mrs Hinton wheeled the tea trolley in, the men took their cups outside the loading bay to smoke and listen to the wireless. By then most of them had placed bets on the Epsom Derby with Fred. The clipped voice of the BBC commentator described the Queen being escorted to the paddock by the Duke of Norfolk to wish good luck to Doug Smith, the jockey riding her own horse Above Suspicion. Shantung was favourite to win.

They were off, Rousseau's Dream in the lead around Tattenham Corner, but Fidalgo pulled ahead into the straight with Parthia on his heels, Parthia streaked ahead into the lead, with St Crespin and Shantung neck and neck behind.

'Come on, Shantung,' shouted Berry.

Into the final furlong, Parthia still ahead, closely followed by Fidalgo and Shantung. Parthia took it, Fidalgo second, Shantung third.

Berry shouted 'yes' and punched the air. All but one of the other men kicked the ground, the lucky backer of Parthia coming to Fred for his pay-out.

Fred told one of the men to keep a look out. He paid the winner off. Berry came over, grinning.

'What do you want?' said Fred.

George Berry's smile dropped. 'What you think I want, me bloody winnings.'

'You bet to win, you blinking clown,' said Fred.

Berry threw his cigarette to the ground. 'You what? I bet ten bob each way, what you trying to pull?'

Fred took out his notebook, showed the page. 'Ten bob to win on Shantung. I'm not a fucking thief, now clear off.'

Berry was almost as big as Fred. He pushed Fred's chest with both hands. 'Give me my dough or see what happens.'

Fred was knocked backwards, his cloth cap fell off. He took two steps towards Berry, pulled the man's head downwards to meet his lifted knee. His nose split open, his lips and chin painted red. He roared and charged into Fred, the two men falling into the dust, rolling around trying to find purchase with their fists.

The jeering of the onlookers brought Ray Little

the foreman running round to see. He split up the fight and Fred found himself sitting in the office, the red-faced foreman screaming into his face.

'You have been warned, Blundell.'

'FLO.'

Mr Monday's voice bellowed from his office into the anteroom where Flo sat at a little desk. She took a breath to steel herself, grabbed her notepad and trotted in. His feet were up on his desk, the room hung with the smell of cigar smoke and leather.

'Get Mrs Monday something nice, it's her birthday.' He didn't look up from his paper.

'Yes, Mr Monday, what sort of thing?'

He looked up, his tone curt. 'Something nice, like I said.'

'I just need to get off to class, I'll sort that out a bit later on. When's her birthday?'

'You can sort it out now then go off to your little class.' He shook his paper out in front of his face and withdrew from view.

Flo looked at the wall clock as she walked back to her desk. It was nearly one, the hooter would go off soon to signal the end of dinner break and she hadn't eaten yet. There was a class at one and now she'd miss it. Damn him for being so bloody awkward.

'FLO.'

'Yes, Mr Monday?'

'Where are those papers, they need posting.'

'Oh yes, just a minute.'

'Now, Flo.'

The document sat rolled into her typewriter

half-finished. She typed the rest and took it in for signing, pulling on her jacket as she did so.

'Where are your gloves, Flo?'

'Sorry, Mr Monday?'

He gestured to her hands. 'You are my personal assistant, you should be an emblem of Monday's. Wear the merchandise, Flo, it's not difficult.'

'Yes, sir. I haven't got any with me though.'

He looked at her the way she would look at Mikey when he left his school books in the woods. As he stood, Flo detected a whiff of sweat and expensive cologne that made her lightheaded. The sheer bulk of the man, the muscles in his arms strained against his rolled-up white shirtsleeves. He rummaged through some boxes of leather sample goods that sat against his office wall and pulled out a pair of beautiful ivory leather gloves, beckoning Flo to him. They were similar to the pair that Sid handed around at the induction, the gloves she had wished were hers. She gulped and stepped forwards, holding out her hand when he gestured her to do so. He pulled the glove on, careful not to bend her fingers, sliding the softest leather and satin lining on to her hand. The physical contact with him standing so close made her dizzy. The animal in her wanted to reach out and touch him. He watched her, gave a small smile that made her heart bounce a little.

'They're lovely,' she breathed.

'There are advantages to working for me, Flo. The college for one thing...'

Her eyes flicked up to his, she blushed and looked down.

'Keep them, they are made to be worn by a

beautiful woman. They suit you.' He handed her the other glove to put on herself.

Flo took a deep breath and made to leave, then turned back to place the document on his desk. Dipping his gold pen in black ink, he signed it with a looping flourish and handed it back to her. She felt his eyes on her as she walked away.

There was just time to nip across to the shoe shop for Maggie's present. She knew Maggie's size, there was a pair of tan suede slingbacks that looked expensive, she told the assistant they were for the boss and ran them up to the office.

'Well?' Mr Monday looked up at her when she stood before his desk holding the shoebox open. 'What's that?'

'For Mrs Monday, you asked me to get a birthday present.'

He frowned, looked from the shoes to Flo's face, then broke into a smile, his face creased with mirth, he emitted a booming laugh that threw him back in his chair. He couldn't stop laughing, he clutched his sides and laughed until his eyes watered. Flo stared at him, horrified.

'FOR MAGS? OH. HAHAHAHAHA. OH, NO.'

Flo backed out of the room, she sensed an explosion was coming. She grabbed her college bag and ran to class.

'Sorry I'm late, Mr Monday wanted me for something,' said Flo, out of breath and almost colliding with the trainer who was coming down the stairs of the college building. She waited for Carl and fell into step beside him. 'What did I miss?'

'Oh, nothing earth-shattering. We're off to spend more time *observing the factory processes and acquiring hands-on experience.*' He said it with a mock English accent. 'Has the boss got you running around?'

Flo nodded and said in a low voice, 'He wants me to get Mrs Monday a birthday present but I don't know what to get.'

Carl sucked his teeth, thought for a moment. 'That's a tricky one, but I'll bet it needs to be something special, expensive.'

Flo nodded her encouragement.

'Remember that large store we saw in London, Selfridges?'

'Yes.'

'Call them on the telephone and order something. A designer fur coat or stole perhaps, they'll send it by delivery with an invoice.'

Flo gasped. 'Really? They'd do that, for so much money?'

'Sure, I think so. Monday Leather is the largest shoe and accessories manufacturer in the country, they supply Selfridges, at least with gloves as far as I'm aware.'

'Carl, you're a lifesaver. I'll try phoning them from the office later.'

'We shall make our way to the clicking section,' said the trainer. 'I'll take you via the sewing department where you'll have a quick look for now.'

They came to Flo's old sewing section. Lil wasn't there; she must have been feeling iffy again.

Flo mouthed *Hello, love* and waved to Babs.

'Here she comes, Miss High-and-Mighty,' said one of the women, Betty Fairlight. 'Oh, I mean

231

Flo Blundell, sorry, love, just joking around with you.' Betty grinned at the other women. 'How's Mr Monday treating you then, love?'

'All right thanks.'

'Yeah, I bet.'

'Here is where the shoes are top-stitched,' said the trainer. 'Using the latest electronic Singer sewing machines. If you'll demonstrate?' He directed his question at Betty, who ran the shaped leather through her machine, snipped off the thread and held it up to show the students. 'Now, on to the clicking department, where you'll see a *skilled* machine operator at work, and you'll try your hand at the clicking process.'

'Bye bye, hoity toity,' Flo heard Betty say. She didn't give her the pleasure of turning around. Babs came running up behind Flo.

'You all right, Mum?'

'Yeah, course, love, you go off back to work now.'

Babs walked around the front of Flo and back to her sewing table. Flo took a few steps forward and faltered, felt something snag against her tights. A piece of nylon thread was wrapped around her legs. She turned to see it winding across the floor back to a huge cotton reel on one of the sewing desks. The women laughed at her, even Babs. It must have been Babs who did it.

'Very funny, you silly bitches,' she called out. She wanted to laugh and make a joke of it, they all called each other names at work, it was part of how things were. But she couldn't muster a smile and it came out seriously. They looked like their faces had been slapped.

Flo pulled at the thread, got out of it and caught up with the group who were walking into the clicking room. There were twelve clicker machines that each looked like a huge cast-iron anvil with a vice at the top. Men wearing thick leather aprons bent over, deep in concentration. Each operation emitted a heavy thump and crack, the combined sound deafening. The trainer stopped at the closest machine. The operator finished his cut and stood up. It was Ted, Lil's husband. He nodded to Flo, his face covered in dust.

'This here is Ted, he's a newly trained clicker. This is a highly skilled job, the elite skill of the trade, you might say. It's the job of the clicker to cut out the shoe uppers from the skins of leather with minimal waste. This takes intense concentration as several layers of skin are cut at the same time, and if you make a faulty cut you cost the company a lot of money.'

The trainer indicated that Ted should demonstrate. He placed a stack of skins on to the board and with his face twelve inches away from the press, carefully placed a shaped cutting knife on top of the leather. He pulled down a lever on either side to bring the press down and engaged the pressure plate with his right foot, leaning in all the while. The heavy press came down on to the knives, which stamped through the leather with a loud *thwump*. When the levers were pulled back up, Ted changed the position of the knives and brought the plate down again. Flo thought it looked quite straightforward and jumped when the trainer indicated she should go first.

'If you would, Mrs Blundell.'

Looking around at the expectant faces, Flo approached the machine, took a breath and positioned the cutting knives next to the hole just made. Wanting to get it over with as soon as possible, she quickly pulled down the levers and prepared to press the foot plate.

'No, wait,' shouted Ted, who lunged forwards and thrust his hand into the press just as Flo pulled the levers down. She didn't have time to stop. Ted screamed. The trainer jumped in by her side, pushed her away and pulled up the levers. Ted cried out and grabbed his hand, red with blood. Flo regained her balance and turned away sharply when she saw Ted's thumb hanging off by a thread of skin.

'Get the first-aider, get an ambulance,' the trainer shouted. The other men stopped working and ran to get help. Ted clutched his hand to his chest and moaned. The trainer took off his suit jacket and wrapped a sleeve around Ted's arm, trying to cradle his hand in the body of the jacket at the same time.

'You should have waited, you bloody idiot,' the trainer shouted at Flo. She jumped back from the force of his anger, turned and ran out of the clicking room, across the factory floor and down the stairs.

'Flo, wait.' It was Carl, running after her. She stopped on the stairs and sank down, sobbing.

'Look what I've done to poor Ted, oh my god.' She covered her face with her hands, shook her head.

'Ted will be all right, they'll stitch him up, don't you worry.' Carl put his hand on Flo's shoulder and peered down at her with concern.

'Oh god, he'll lose his thumb, what have I done? They'll sack me, they'll kick me out the college, I've messed it up just like Mr Monday said I would.'

'Hang on, they won't sack you, accidents happen all the time in the factory.'

Flo took the handkerchief that Carl offered her, sniffed into it.

'Really? Do you think so?'

'Yes, of course, there was a bad accident only last week. And I don't know what Mr Monday said to you about messing things up, but just remember during the war when the women stepped in to do the men's factory jobs perfectly well.' He smiled and patted her arm. 'Now cheer up a bit, the British don't cry, remember. And we're gonna beat West Ham next week,' he added, trying to distract her.

She shook her head at him. As if she was bothered about the bloody football.

Footsteps clattered up the stairs, the first-aiders pushed past, running to help Ted. Flo got up to follow them but backed against the wall. After a while a group of men bustled through, Ted amongst them, clutching his bandaged hand to his chest, the blood showing through already. He saw her and faltered.

She put out a hand – 'Ted, I'm so sorry' – and pulled it back when she saw the hatred in his face.

13

Fred was shifting boxes at work when the siren went off early. Everyone stopped what they were doing, stood up straight, eyes turned skywards. Rabbits in the field when the lookout thumps his back foot on the ground. The sound that was so familiar at seven thirty in the morning and five in the afternoon that it evoked an unconscious reflex either to walk faster towards the factory gates or to down tools and prepare to go home for tea. But at three in the afternoon the sound evoked a different reflex, learned from the terror of war, it was a sound that inspired panic, disruption, gathering the family. At best it meant the inconvenience of running to the shelter. At worst it meant trouble and fear and death.

A young lad burst into the hold, shouted at them and ran out.

'Bomb's been found up the pits, evacuate the factory.'

'Bloody hell,' said Fred. 'Come on, lads, let's clear out.' He checked his pocket for his tobacco tin and headed for the door, then paused and walked back through the dispatch hold.

'Blundell, evacuation point, now.'

'Yeah, I'm just getting my girl.' He gave the foreman a warning look.

'Oh, suit yourself, do us all a favour and get blown up.'

Fred waved the comment away. The box-makers, or stitchers as they were known, were coming through anyway. Jeanie didn't conceal her surprise to see him waiting for her, she softened, her younger self for an instant. He rolled a cigarette and they shuffled sombrely to the far football field with the other workers, a ring of laughter heard once or twice over the general murmur of curiosity. In the field they were told to sit in their section groups. Fred nodded to Jeanie as she sloped off with the other box-makers. He stayed standing, looked through the workers, five thousand of them gathered there. Others did the same, placing their family members, just to be sure. Foremen and forewomen marched about with pursed lips and official-looking clipboards, ticking off names, doing their drill duties.

'Sit down, Blundell, you're giving me a crick in the neck.'

'Well, stop looking at my arse then,' said Fred, grinning at John Blake as he sat down next to the old-timer.

'I tell you something, this don't half remind me of something, but I can't think what.'

The men laughed at John's joke. Most of them had vivid memories of the war, of being bundled into shelters, or out in active service, or helping the war effort at home. There was a silence as they cast their eyes down and sifted through their personal files, remembering, reliving, wanting to talk but wishing someone would say something light.

'You might not realise it, Blundell, as you haven't been with us long, but there's a war hero in our midst.'

'Oh yeah?' said Fred, pulling a strand of tobacco off his lip.

'Old Turtle over there.' John nodded towards Mr Turtle, Jeanie's foreman. 'Got a tin leg he has. A grenade was thrown into his tank in Italy. He put his foot on it to save the rest of the crew. Got a medal for it.'

Fred peered through his smoke at Mr Turtle, who chatted to another foreman. Jeanie sat nearby, scowling. Fred's face clouded over, he smoked and looked at the ground.

'Not impressed by that, eh?' laughed John.

Fred didn't answer. The other men exchanged glances.

'He was an officer in the first war too,' said John. 'I was there with him in the trenches, lied about my age to get signed up. Bloody decent chap he was, always the first one over the top. "Come on lads," he'd say, "let's be back in time for tea, the rats'll have the kettle on." We dug holes for plenty of good friends...' John's eyes glazed, his voice caught in his throat. 'The rats'll have the kettle on.'

A tinny voice blared from a loud speaker.

'Your attention please. An unexploded World War Two bomb has been found in the sand quarry on the hill. Please do not be alarmed. The authorities are dealing with the situation. The factory has been evacuated as a matter of precaution. You are to remain here until further notice. Thank you for your patience.'

'Who remembers digging the trench round the factory?' said George Berry.

'Oh god, yeah, who could forget that?' said Ray

Little, the foreman. 'Six foot deep and three foot wide, inside the factory gates. I was in engineering making gun parts for the war effort and when the siren went off we all had to run for it and stand in the trench. Remember watching that dogfight with the German planes? Right overhead it was,' he said, shaking his head. 'Here, Blundell, when was you called to the colours then, eh?'

Fred jerked up his head. 'Eh? I was fifteen in forty-four, that's the year we had our girls.'

'When you was fifteen? Christ, that weren't easy.'

Fred shrugged. 'It was all right, got a job down the docks.' His face twitched, he shifted position and rolled another cigarette, looking away across the field.

'Yeah, but when did you do National Service?'

A shadow passed across Fred's face, he chewed on the inside of his lip.

'Didn't.'

All the men looked.

'Why not?'

'Bit fucking nosy, aren't you?' Fred snapped, warning him off.

'Just asking, what's the problem?' said Ray, with a smirk.

'I was in the merchant navy, that's why.'

There was a murmur of approval amongst the men.

'My brother was in the merchant during the war, running munitions over to France,' said Ray, the smirk dropping away from his face. 'Got torpedoed and went down. Only twenty-two he was.' There was a quiet jumble of sympathy from the men. 'When did you join, round about forty-nine was it? What ship was you on?'

Fred stared at Ray and nodded his head, not in assent, but with a rage that reassembled his features. The men readied themselves, braced for trouble. Fred jumped up, took a long stride over to Ray and stood over him. For a second he seemed undecided about what to do, his lips drawn tight together. Ray shaded his eyes with his hand and looked up at the huge man towering over him. There was a moment when Fred could have kicked Ray in the side of the head and split his ear open, or dropped down on to him, pushed his face down into the grass and put his boot on the back of his neck.

'Need a piss,' he said, and walked off. The men stared after him.

'Something's up there,' said John Blake. 'Best leave him be.'

The perimeter of the sports field fluttered with strings of bunting and Union flags on poles. Crates of Double Diamond lager and cream soda had been carted into voluminous white marquee tents. New track lines were painted on the grass. Red-striped tombola and white elephant stalls were out of storage and in position, dusted off and wiped down. Hundreds of individual cardboard picnic boxes for the children had been packed by the women, a sandwich and carton of drink, tickets for a free ice cream and goes at the fair.

The July sunshine lit up the field and the workers' faces as they drifted in from the estate, the little girls in their best summer dresses and ribbons in their bobbed hair, the boys scrubbed clean and squeezed into their Sunday suits. The company management took their positions in deckchairs next to the table laden with trophies and rosettes, and the parents milled about; men threw balls at coconuts and women held on to their hats in the summer breeze.

Flo walked on to the field and was taken aback at the sight of her first Monday's sports day. The wind caught the skirt of her blue summer dress. She smoothed it down with a gloved hand and peered through her new sunglasses across to the Monday's brass band playing Glenn Miller, and over to Mr Monday who stood by the trophy table. Maggie sat on a deckchair, sipped a drink and nodded at Tabby who was saying something with a disdainful expression. Flo pulled Mikey's hand to steer him away from the Mondays, she didn't want to be put to work on the ice-cream stall or told to lend a hand with the children's races.

She was distracted. Fred hadn't come home the night before after all the fuss over the evacuation. He was terrified of anything to do with war, and that was no surprise. The trauma of what had happened had stayed with him all these years. Flo remembered the whispers about Fred's mum running around with one of the merchant seamen, and Flo had gone to see the Anchor pub after the bombing, charred and ruined. If Fred caught other kids playing on it he'd go berserk.

Flo was already pregnant with twins by the time Fred's dad, Morris, was discharged from duty in 1944 with half his face blown off by a landmine.

He killed himself a year later. It was a story that went round the docks for years, how Morris Blundell was found swinging in number twelve shed. Fred told Flo, just once and never again, how he'd been so happy when Morris came home, he'd never expected him to be traumatised, telling Fred horrific stories about the war. No matter how gently Flo tempted the subject into the light, Fred would just never talk about it again. Not when he was awake anyway, he had nightmares often enough.

The back of the beer tent looked like a good diversion to avoid Mr Monday. Flo led Mikey behind the white marquee and stopped abruptly. A young couple were necking behind there. Flo half turned to go when she realised it was Babs. The young man whose arms hung about her daughter started when he saw Flo there, the two of them broke apart. It looked like Maggie's son, James Monday. He pulled down the hem of his suit jacket, studied his winkle-picker shoes for a moment before deciding to speak. Just as he opened his mouth to address Flo, Babs pulled his arm.

'All right, Mum? I'm in the relay now, bye.' Babs giggled and pulled James away. He shot an apologetic look back her way and disappeared.

Flo came out the other side looking for them. She saw Babs running over to the race track but there was no sign of James. She pulled Mikey along to get away from the trophy table.

'FLO.'

Too late, Mr Monday had already seen her. She turned with a smile and walked towards the boss.

Mikey pulled away and ran off to play with his friends.

Mr Monday took off his jacket and handed it to her, rolled up his shirtsleeves and bellowed.

'Tug o' war, come and start us off, will you?'

Maggie stared across at them. Flo waved and trotted behind Mr Monday to the middle of the field. A rope was held up by nine men on one side, ten on the other, all in suit trousers, shirts and ties, and red or blue bibs. Mr Monday joined his side, took his position as anchorman at the back, wrapped the thick rope round his body and nodded at Flo. Unsure what to do, Flo stood by the middle of the rope, gave her biggest smile, put her hand in the air and brought it down with a loud 'Go!'

She jumped back when the men took the strain, grunting with little steps back and forth.

'COME ON, HEAVE,' shouted Mr Monday to his team. He pulled with such might and seriousness that the veins stood out on his neck. He gave a big roar and floored the other team and his own single-handed, their knees buckling as they tumbled on to the grass. Mr Monday reclaimed his jacket from Flo and wiped the sweat from his face with his handkerchief.

'Where's that husband of yours? Could have done with him on the tug o' war, although we didn't do too badly, eh?' He grinned at her and smacked her backside.

Flo cringed. 'Well, if that's all, I'll just run and get Mikey into his race.'

'Yes, yes, but stay close, I might need you.'

Flo got away, spotted Lil and Ted watching the

long jump.

'All right, Lil? Ted? How's the thumb, Ted?'

Ted forked some peppered cockles into his mouth with his good hand. 'How do you think?' he said, holding up his bandage.

'Still off work for a while yet,' said Lil, holding a little paper bowl of whelks, popping a large one into her mouth. 'Although it might not be a bad thing as Ted'll be around when the baby comes.' She stroked her large belly and pushed the whelk into her cheek with her tongue. 'He's not happy about having to leave the clickers though, or his darts team.'

Flo had apologised to them both numerous times, and felt the compulsion to say sorry again, but stopped herself.

'Look, Lil, you haven't seen Fred, have you?'

'Ted saw him in the club last night, didn't you, Ted?'

'Yes and a right state he was in, I can tell you. Nearly got into a fight if old John hadn't stopped it. Where is he?'

'Oh it's all right, he'll be around somewhere.'

'Yeah, well, he'd better sort himself out, it's the West Ham game on Wednesday and we're all counting on him. I've even had a little wager on it, between you and me.'

Flo gave them a weak smile and went to find Mikey. He ran around the field playing war games with his friends. They all had their old Tommy guns from the war, shooting one another and falling over with great drama. Flo stood for a minute to watch them. Mikey ran about with the rest of them, his eyes shone, his little face brown from the sun, he looked fit and well, a far cry from the damp Tilbury tenement where he coughed and wheezed and had skinny little legs. She caught him by the shoulder of his jacket as he tumbled by.

'It's your sack race in a minute, love.'

'Oi, lads, sack race.'

His friends ran over with him, yelping and whooping, shooting one another all the while. Flo helped him into his sack and cheered him along. His eyes popped with the effort, he clung on to his sack and bounded along, the sun seemed to shine down on him alone and Flo was glad of her sunglasses, she could blink away her tears unseen.

'Mum, I come second, will I get a trophy, Mum?'

'I dunno, love, well done. Maybe you'll get a rosette or something. Go on and get your picnic box.'

Flo sighed when she saw Jeanie sitting on the sidelines on the shaded grass with no sense of occasion about her.

'Seen your dad, love?'

Jeanie shook her head.

'You all right, love?' Jeanie's face twitched as though she wanted to say something but she held it back and stood up. Watching her walk away, Flo shook her head. Jeanie had looked off colour the past couple of weeks. If she didn't have Fred to worry about, she'd be fretting about Jeanie. If it wasn't one thing it was another.

The MC instructed everyone to make their way over to the lido for the swimming gala. There was a general gathering of cardigans and children. Flo joined the lazy stroll across with Mikey, looking around vaguely for Babs and Jeanie.

'What race you in then, love?'

'Back stroke,' he said, licking his ice cream. 'In the deep end, Mum!'

'Where'd you learn that then?'

'Down here.'

'You've only just had your cast off, will you be all right?'

Mikey ran off to the changing rooms in the lido building, a large modern U-shape that encased the main bathing pool.

'Flo, dear?' It was Joan, one of the school teachers organising the races. 'Give me a hand, will you? Get this lot ready and lined up, they're in first for the front crawl, then it's back stroke.'

Flo mustered a smile and set about ushering the group of school children along to the head of the pool, making sure they were spaced out. Joan blew a whistle and the kids jumped in and thrashed their way to the end, with Joan making a note of the winner and runners-up.

Mikey came out in his knitted swimming trunks with a bunch of others. Flo pulled them along the side of the pool. Flo whispered 'Good luck' into Mikey's ear.

'Thanks, dear. Now get the next lot ready, will you, it's butterfly stroke.'

Flo turned to ready the butterfly group, keeping half an eye on Mikey's race. Joan blew the whistle and the children jumped in.

'I need the toilet, miss,' said one of the boys in the butterfly group.

'Yes, go on then, hurry up,' said Flo, trying to look for Mikey in the general splashing in the pool. It was hard to see, and some of the crowd stood up for a better look. A loud murmur ran through the onlookers, people leant forward, squinted in the sun, pointing, calling out.

'There. He didn't come up. There.'

Flo looked from the crowd to the water to the children who had finished the length and were standing up at the end of the pool. In a second, she had searched their faces, realised Mikey wasn't there and ran forward to the poolside. Her arms shot out when she saw Mikey under the water, his arms flailing in slow motion against the water's resistance, his blue swimming trunks blurred and sinking. She wanted to shout out and jump in but a shroud of panic slipped down over her – the scream caught in her throat and her legs gave way, just folded up. She dropped to the ground and felt the smooth blue ceramic tiles bang against her cheekbone. There was a loud splash and fat bullets of water slugged into Flo's dress as someone jumped into the pool.

The crowd cried out, ran forwards. The person who jumped in went under, got hold of him and pulled him out. Others yanked his limp body over the side and on to the tiles next to Flo. She couldn't breathe, tried to reach out but couldn't move. The person who had jumped in was a girl, Flo could see her bare legs and wet skirt. The girl bent over Mikey, pulled his chin down, put her own mouth over his and breathed into him. Her long wet hair hung over her face. She sat Mikey up, banged him on the back and he coughed. Water spewed out of his mouth and he coughed some more and started to cry.

Flo heard his cry and wept herself; she crawled

247

to Mikey and pulled him into her chest, his wet hair soaking through her dress. Through a blur of tears she saw the girl who had saved him. It was Jeanie. The last person on earth Flo would have thought of. Flo sobbed and reached out an arm, pulled her in and kissed her head. She held them, said *Sorry, sorry, I panicked, sorry.*

A first-aider was there asking to see Mikey. Flo let him go, be checked over. Someone helped Flo and Jeanie to their feet. Jeanie doubled over and vomited on the tiled pool surround, it must have been the shock. Flo put her arm around Jeanie's shoulder. With her white glove she wiped the strands of wet hair away from Jeanie's eyes and the wet from her mouth.

'You all right, love? My god, you were brilliant, how did you do that?'

Jeanie was shaken up and teary, her eyes met Flo's for a second and flitted away but Flo saw it, her Jeanie at the surface again just for a moment.

'Thanks, love.' Flo squeezed her shoulder. 'You saved his life.'

By the time they had rested a bit and trudged home, Flo was exhausted, they all were. There was still the ironing to do and tea to make. Jeanie and Mikey were wet through. They bundled in through the front door and saw Fred slumped in his armchair, asleep with the television on and the pools coupons on his lap ready for checking. He woke with a growl, sat up and wiped his mouth, looked at them with bloodshot eyes.

Flo muttered *Thank God* when she saw him there, wondered where he had slept all night. The possibility that he'd been out with another woman was overshadowed by the stronger likelihood that he'd been on a drinking bender.

'Hello, love, where you been then? We missed you at sports day.' She forced a smile.

'Look, Dad, I won this.' Mikey waved his rosette at Fred, who nodded and rolled a cigarette. 'And I nearly drowned in the lido, I thought I could do back stroke but I couldn't, and Jeanie saved me.'

Fred looked up, surprised, seemed to satisfy himself that there was nothing to be concerned about, and went back to his roll-up.

'And don't forget who the *winner* is,' said Babs, standing on one hip and holding up a trophy by her little finger, letting it swing there. 'First prize for the girls' relay.'

'Very good,' said Fred, wiping his fringe back from his face. 'Get out the way now, the scores are coming on.'

'I'm just making a quick tea today, I'm knackered,' Flo called out as she walked through into the kitchen. He was back, and no harm done, that was the main thing. She was shaken up from Mikey's accident, she didn't want a row with Fred too.

'Jeanie, Mikey, go and get dry, tea's in a minute.' She clanged a frying pan on to the hob and scraped some lard into it.

In twenty minutes she called them for their tea. Fred was the last one to sit at the table. As he pulled out his chair he looked down at his plate of fried eggs and buttered bread. He sat down and picked up his cutlery, held the knife and fork in his fists, still looking at his plate. His face twitched and turned red, his lips tight.

'What's this SHIT?' he shouted, thumping the table with both hands, so hard that everyone's crockery clattered and they all jumped.

Flo's nerves, already jangled, clenched her body tight. 'What? What is it?'

'THIS,' he roared, gesturing to his plate with his knife. 'I get given this shit for my tea when I didn't have any dinner.'

His face twisted into something between anger and physical pain. Flo watched in alarm as his big hand swiped his plate off the table. It smashed against the sideboard and fell on to the floor in pieces. They all froze and stared at the yellow egg yolk smeared over the broken shards of china.

'Now make me a *proper* meal, woman.' He said it with quiet menace, a tone Flo knew so well, and went back through to his armchair in the sitting room. They heard the rustle and snap of his newspaper.

The children turned their heads from him to Flo. She felt her chin wobble a tiny bit but concentrated on keeping it still.

'Eat your tea then, loves. I'll clear this up, don't worry.'

Babs and Jeanie looked at each other, and Flo saw the look, she knew what it meant, they didn't have to say a word.

14

The giggling girls were twittering about where they were going on holiday during the shutdown when Mr Turtle was called into the floor manager's office. Then they started on about the West Ham game again, which was happening after work that day.

'You're Dad's gonna win it for us, isn't he, Jeanie?'

I didn't answer. If they thought Dad was a sure bet they were wrong, the state he'd been in the past few days since the evacuation. Drinking again. It had hit a nerve with him, because of Nan and Granddad. Mum never talked about it but we used to hear things in Tilbury about how Nan was blown up and Granddad hanged himself from one of the storage sheds down the docks when he came back from the war. Dad didn't do National Service, he got out of it somehow, I didn't exactly know how, but he got out of it because of Nan and Granddad and he'd be in big trouble if anyone found out. He deserved to get his collar felt, the way he treated all of us.

'Where *you* going, Pat?' asked Carol, her hands flying through the boxes.

'Skegness, can't wait, my John says he'll do the knobbly knees this time. You're going Southend, aren't you? Brilliant lights, aren't there?'

Everyone shut up so we could listen to the floor

manager shouting in his office at Mr Turtle. Something was up. Turtle limped back over to us, his face was white and his lips drawn in. He looked around at us all, one by one, and when he looked at me, he stopped.

'Jeanie, over here for a moment?'

I slammed my box down and tutted, dragged myself over to the window.

'Jeanie, something has come to my attention, do you know what that might be?' He spoke in a low voice so the others couldn't hear. There wasn't much work going on over there by the sounds of it. I shrugged and tried not to look at his wiggling spider fingers.

'No? Well, someone has been putting messages in the boxes. Did you hear the floor manager shouting at me just now?'

I shrugged again and looked at the paper cuts on my hands.

'Well, I sincerely hope the messages will stop as they have caused the company a lot of trouble and my job is on the line if they don't stop immediately.'

'What you telling *me* for? You better talk to the others as well, don't you think?'

He looked sad. I could have kicked that stupid tin leg of his, knocked him over.

'Go back to work please,' he said, and ran his spider fingers through his thin grey hair. 'Send Carol over.'

By the time he'd spoken to everyone about it, that's all they talked about, all day long, even stopped talking about the football and their boring holidays. They all looked at me, like they thought

252

I did it.

'James Monday has been hanging around here a lot,' I said. 'Maybe it was him, who knows, maybe he's got a grudge against his dad?'

'Oooh, do you think so, Jeanie?' said Carol, her eyes all wide.

'Yeah, well, they make him do extra lessons so he can go to university to be a lawyer, and he hates it, so he might wanna get back at them.'

'Oooh, yes, you might be right.' They nodded at each other, all intrigued by the mystery of it, like when they come in on a Monday talking about the sensation stories in the *News of the World*.

'Where you going, Jeanie?'

That Carol was a nosy cow. I was going to the lav, and I wasn't gonna ask Turtle any more. I didn't care if it held up the production line, they could stick it. I felt as sick as a dog. I'd been feeling off colour for over a week, no, longer, it must be a few weeks, I was losing track and getting worried that I was dying of something. From my medical book, I was fairly sure I had polio or TB, what with the sickness and tiredness. Sick and tired of this place probably. I was doing my best to ignore it and not let it show, I didn't want anyone to stop me going to college. I walked up the stairs to go to the lav on the top floor so I could throw up the quiet. The taste of the yellow bile that came out was bitter and disgusting, it made me gag again. Being sick was exhausting. I had a fluttery feeling of panic that something was really wrong.

To get some air I sneaked out onto the fire escape. It was a breezy day, the wind coming off the river washed over me, I could smell the salt and the mud, it was like taking a tonic, it was a smell I'd grown up on. Leaning right I could see the Thames and the boats going both ways, it reminded me of the docks, and Mr Purvis's shop. At least I wasn't there any more, but the factory was worse. Thank God for the college, every Tuesday I went, I wished I could be there every day, it just filled me up, my brain soaked it all up like it was medicine.

Pushing back through the factory door I saw Mum, and darted against the wall to hide. More training for her stupid factory course probably. I watched her and strained my ears. She looked flustered. I remembered her telling Babs she was doing experience as a forewoman. Well, it didn't look like she was very good at it. The women on the line were giving her the run-around. They were the old bags who had been there for years. I went back down the stairs and into the basement. Mr Turtle was there with his arms folded. He took me to one side again.

'Jeanie, this behaviour will not be tolerated. You must tell me if you need the lavatory, otherwise production is affected, and that affects everyone.' He paused, looked at the far wall. 'I can't avoid reporting you to the floor manager much longer, Jeanie. And what would your parents think then?'

I shrugged. He was such a wet fish. I went back to the line and made a box, sneaked a message out of my pocket.

My name is James Monday, I am being held here against my will.

Flo had had a pig of a day. Still reeling from Fred's outburst over dinner, she had done her fore-woman experience up in clutch bags, and the workers had given her hell for it. The women had sent a plastic tiara down the line. When it rumbled its way towards her, she had picked it up and frowned. That's when they all started laughing, called her the Queen of Sheba. Mr Monday had been a nightmare that morning, charging about, getting the football match organised, getting his team ready, shouting instructions to his staff about the dinner and dance to be held afterwards. She had been glad to get to the factory to get away from him. Maybe the match would put Fred back on track, cheer him up a bit. Maybe he'd stop the drinking. He had seemed on edge that morning before work, he was bound to be a bit nervous, it wasn't every day you got to play against West Ham United. Mikey was excited too, had his football cards all ready to be signed by the players. He couldn't wait to see his dad play, he had told all his friends about it. It would be a good day for all the family.

'What do you want for tea, love?' she asked Fred when he came in from work. She didn't want to get it wrong again.

'Nothing,' he said.

'*Nothing?*'

'You heard me, now leave me be, I'm off out for the match.'

'Oh right, good luck, love, do us proud.'

He gave her a dirty look, Flo thought it must be the nerves. He never, ever refused his tea. As he put his hand on the door handle, someone knocked. A nervous-looking James Monday stood there on the door step.

'Mr Blundell, is it?'

'That's right, what do you want?'

'May I have a word please, sir, it's about your daughter, Babs, Barbara.'

'What about her?'

'Do you mind if I come in? It's a little personal.'

'You haven't been messing around with her, have you?'

'What? No, no, I just wanted to ask your permission about something, but it can wait if you're busy.'

'Course I'm busy, it's the big match, haven't you heard?'

Fred pushed past the boy and strode off down the street, leaving him on the doorstep.

'Come in, love, what's the matter?' said Flo.

'Oh, thanks, Mrs Blundell?'

'That's right, love.' Flo smiled and led him through into the sitting room. He stood there shuffling on his feet, peering intently at the set of china Alsatians on the mantelpiece. 'Anything the matter? Barbara isn't here, she went straight over to the field to get a good seat for the football. Jeanie's upstairs though...'

'Oh no, yes, I just needed to have a talk with Mr Blundell about Barbara.'

'Oh yes, what's she been up to then?'

'Nothing, it's just that, we've been seeing a bit of each other, and we're very fond of one another, and I'd like to, I'd like to ask Mr Blundell's permission to...'

'Oh, I see. Oh.' Flo sat down with a plonk on

the settee. She stared straight ahead, speechless for a moment. 'You do know that Babs is fifteen, don't you, love? It's a bit young really, don't you think? What's the rush?'

'Oh, yes, of course, no, we wouldn't get married yet, but we'd like to get engaged, to show people we are serious.'

'Oh right, I see.' Flo's heart sank. She desperately hoped Babs wasn't in the family way.

'James Monday, sorry, I should have introduced myself sooner.'

Flo shook his hand. 'Oh yes. Yes, I thought I recognised you, you're Maggie's son, aren't you?'

'Yes, that's right.'

'I know your mum, she didn't say anything about this. I know your dad too, I work for him as a matter of fact.'

'No, well, we haven't told anyone yet, my parents are a little, how shall I say, a little reluctant about my seeing the girls here on the estate.'

'Oh, is that a fact?'

'I mean, they want me to finish my schooling first before settling down, so I wasn't sure when to tell them about Barbara. Perhaps Mr Blundell could, once I've spoke to him...'

'Oh, right, I see, I wouldn't know, dear, I'm sure I wouldn't.' Flo's face creased into a frown. Her armpits dampened. As soon as she could she'd have a talk with Babs. If she was up the duff there'd be hell to pay.

'Well, I'd best be off, my father wants me at the match, he's very serious about these things. Of course you'd know all about that, working for him now.'

'Yes, that's right, I would. Well, it was nice to meet you properly, James, and I'm sure we'll be talking again soon.'

James left Flo with an uneasy feeling in her gut. Why hadn't Babs said anything about it?

'Jeanie? Get down here.'

Flo waited at the bottom of the stairs until Jeanie showed her sulky face at the top.

'What's all this about Babs and James Monday? Did *you* know about it? Is she in trouble or what?'

Jeanie snorted and turned to go.

'So you *do* know, get here and talk to me, isn't it about time you talked to me?' Flo's voice grew louder.

Nothing. Jeanie disappeared into her room and slammed the door.

'Well, get yourself over to the grandstand,' Flo shouted up the stairs. 'Your father's in the football and you better be there to cheer him on.'

The July days were long and hot, one melting into the next. The day of the match was no exception. In a floral cotton dress, hat and gloves, and her new string of graded white plastic beads, Flo half walked, half jogged over to the number-one pitch behind the Monday Mansion. The sound of the crowd rumbled in the air before she turned the corner. What a sight. The two large grandstands along each side of the pitch were full to capacity. Union flags draped off the roof and hung limply against the red, white and blue bunting strewn around the field from one flagpole to the next. The workers who hadn't made it in time to get a seat stood twenty deep right around the pitch.

The whole factory must have turned out for it. The collective talking and laughter sounded like a throaty chuckle. Flo had been one of the few to go home to get changed. Cloth caps and grubby shirtsleeves, pinnies and headscarves were still on.

Flo wasn't sure where to sit. She scanned the crowd for Mikey and saw him on the grass with his friends a few yards back from the touchline. The grandstands were half full of people she didn't recognise. The visitors' supporters, she guessed. There in the directors' box in the nearest stand, Flo could see Maggie sitting between Tabby and Sid from the induction. There were some other management types up there. She recognised the housing manager and the sports and social club president. Maggie saw her and beckoned her over. It was a job climbing through the seats to get there. Maggie told Sid to make room, and Flo took a seat between them, wiping her upper lip with the side of her gloved forefinger.

'Thanks. Busy, isn't it?'

'Where have you been, darling? It's quite the event, you know.'

'I didn't realise you were all that interested in football, Maggie.'

'In short, I'm not, but this is an important event for the company, darling, and also we have the treat of watching the rather lovely West Ham boys running around in their shorts.'

Flo raised her eyebrows. She wondered whether to tell Maggie about Babs and James. Something stopped her. It should come from James, surely? Flo hadn't talked to Babs about it yet anyway. She would wait for the right moment when Fred wasn't around. But what if Babs was pregnant? She was too young, all Flo could feel was an intense fear for her. She laughed to herself and shook her head. Babs wouldn't be so stupid.

'Now, Sid, we are absolutely relying on you for commentary. I don't know about Tabby and Flo here, but I always forget the rules of the game from one year to the next.'

'Oh yeah, me too. Fred's the one who fills out the Pools coupon.'

'Of course, your Fred is the star player, I hear?'

'Is he? Well, I dunno, I think he's quite good.'

'Oh yes, he's good all right,' said Sid, leaning round to face them. 'I've seen him play, I make it my business to stay on top of these things. And mark my words, he's got it in him all right. Don't forget it's me who hired him, see?' Sid winked at them all, then turned to the pitch when the crowd cheered.

Flo jumped when a worker nearby whirled his rattle. It was louder than all the clicking presses at work going at once. The teams were filing out on to the pitch. The hosts first, led by Mr Monday, who jogged on to the field with his chest pumped out, chin up, large moustache and hair coiffed and splendid. The Monday team trailed after him in long-sleeved, black V-neck tops and white shorts, looking very serious. Flo saw Carl there, he hadn't said he was in the first team. And there was Fred. Flo suppressed a snort of laughter. He looked funny in his kit, all cleaned up like the others, and he didn't look too happy about it either. 'Look at the face on it,' Flo leant in to Maggie, who gave a polite smile.

The crowd gave a massive roar, the West Ham team ran on to the pitch sporting their round-neck claret and blue long-sleeve tops with white shorts and socks.

'Here come the Hammers,' said Sid, leaning forwards in his seat. 'Who we got then? Musgrove and Woosnam, and Dick too, that's not good for us, and Cantwell and Bond defending, that's not good, but he's playing a couple of newer fellows, see? Moore, that is, and I'm not sure who that is, Lyall maybe, and that's Ernie Gregory in goal. Here's Fenton.' The West Ham supporters in the stand behind Flo started singing 'I'm Forever Blowing Bubbles', and everyone cheered along, even the Monday workers, loving the atmosphere of the event. 'Ted Fenton' – Sid raised his voice to be heard – 'the manager.' He nodded to show the ladies who he meant.

Flo smiled, excited by all the electric noise and anticipation in the air. She watched as Mr Monday, self-appointed coach and captain, in his long black and white striped socks, started doing high-knee sprints along the Monday dugout. He stopped to shout orders at his team, some of whom launched into some lively warming-up. Flo was alarmed to see Fred sit down on the bench and take out his tobacco tin from his shorts pocket. He rolled a cigarette and smoked, looking at the floor with his elbows on his knees. Mr Monday sent needle-sharp glances his way, but didn't approach Fred, he left him to smoke, and Flo was relieved to see that there was an understanding between them. At least, Mr Monday seemed to understand that Fred would do things

Fred's way.

The crowd settled down a little to watch the players warm up. Flo couldn't believe such a famous team were right there in East Tilbury, on the Monday's pitch. She swatted a gnat against her ankle and tutted when she saw blood on her nylons and the palm of her white glove.

'Right, look, they're a first division team now, see?' explained Sid, 'but it's a friendly, a charity match, right? So they'll be larking about a bit, there'll be a happy, friendly spirit, it'll be a kick-about, a pre-season warm-up. They won't wanna push their players, they won't go in for any rough challenges, they don't want to risk any injuries for the season, see?' Sid had Flo and Maggie's attention, even Tabby leant over to hear.

'They usually let us get a couple in but they always thrash us in the end. This year Mr Monday fancies his chances, he can taste a win and *he's* not gonna have a happy friendly spirit, I can tell you that.' Maggie sniggered, and Flo felt herself caught up in the conspiracy.

'We haven't got a bad team this year,' continued Sid. 'We got Owen Jones, he's an ex-pro, didn't quite make it with the Arsenal, he's got some good moves and a bit of experience, and we got the boss, he's a lively thrustful player, and we got the Canadians in defence and in goal, Anderson, Ravensdale, Wilson, and Tremblay in goal, that's a good strong defence that is. And Mrs Blundell, we got your old man, your Fred. Now he's our secret weapon, West Ham aren't expecting him.'

The women made eyes at each other and lit cigarettes.

The Monday's brass band marched on to the pitch and started to play the National Anthem. The crowd rose to its feet, the players stopped warming up and with their hands over their hearts, gave a rousing chorus of 'God Save the Queen'. Mr Monday's voice roared above all others. There followed a loud cheer and rustling of feet and chip papers as everyone sat back down. Flo was quite enjoying herself by then. The vicar from St Margaret's in the village came out and said a prayer, then everyone stood up again to sing 'Abide with Me' and sat down again.

There was a prolonged hush as the referee, a chap from Southend according to Sid, called West Ham's captain Noel Cantwell and Mr Monday to the centre circle for the coin toss. The other players took their positions on the pitch.

'Oh shit.' Sid lunged forwards in his seat. He gaped at the players' positions in formation. 'Andy Malcolm is marking your old man. That's trouble that is. Excuse my language, ladies.' He leant back, studying the field. Maggie and Flo stared at one another, shrugging their shoulders.

'Who is Andy Malcolm, Sid, dear?' asked Maggie.

'He's a pretty stern tackler, that's who. Argh, why didn't he put Fred on inside right with that Robert Moore, he'd have an easier time there. Both teams are playing a WM formation, Mr Monday's got lucky, who is their centre back? Yes, I think it's Lyall, they're giving his legs a stretch today, and he's got Bond and Cantwell at the back so, yes, they'll mark the boss and the wingers I reckon...'

263

Flo was about to ask what all of that meant, when the ref blew the whistle and a cheer rose up from the crowd. Jones nudged the ball to Mr Monday, who booted it long, ran forwards and shouted at his team. Moore intercepted him almost straight away and cleared the ball, Woosnam picked it up on inside right, turned and shot past Tremblay into the back of the net before Monday's even knew what was happening. The crowd, half standing, emitted a long groan, with the exception of the West Ham group in the stand behind Flo.

'That was bloody quick,' said Sid, blowing out his cigarette smoke with great force.

After securing their first goal, the Hammers larked about a bit, showboating. Noel Cantwell at left back kicked the ball straight through Mr Monday's legs. The boss was furious. Musgrove, the left-winger, did some fancy footwork around Monday's right half Roy Callaghan, whose brother Sean got involved, but Musgrove was enjoying himself too much and gave the brother the treatment too. The Hammers cruised, doing tricks to please the crowd.

The 1-0 scoreline shook up the Monday team and, aided by the constant shouts and hand signals from Mr Monday, they took the ball and charged forward. Greenfield on outside left dribbled down the touchline and made a long arcing pass to Mr Monday at centre forward, who made a looping kick with all his might that glanced off the crossbar. The Hammers got it away and thundered down the pitch towards Tremblay in the Monday goal. Carl Anderson made a magnificent crunching tackle, which surprised Flo as he always seemed like such a gentleman. Monday's closed ranks and the visitors lost their chance. Flo shuffled forward in her seat to see Carl in action, he really was smashing, he cut a fine figure in his kit.

'What's Blundell up to?' said Sid, gritting his teeth. 'We need to go all out every minute, not slacken up.' Fred had stopped to cough and spit. He didn't look half as fit as the rest of the team.

'Your Fred train much?' smiled Maggie. Flo gave a nervous laugh. Fred had hardly touched the ball, he couldn't get past his marker, Andy Malcolm. Flo noticed the two of them shoving each other when the ball came their way, then Fred stopped trying and trotted along half-heartedly, pausing to cough again. By contrast the rest of the Monday team charged up and down, made battering tackles and gave a strong and steady display.

The Hammers were slick and measured in form-ation, they communicated without shouts or signals, knew where to go and looked like a dangerous machine. But they couldn't get another past the Canadian defence. They missed two chances and were tackled out of another. Jones took the ball close to the West Ham goal but no one was with him. The Hammers drove it back, Woosnam made a splendid cross and Dick headed it right to the goalmouth when Tremblay made a brilliant save. The Monday crowd roared their delight and wound their rattles. Flo was getting a headache from all the noise, but she knew that when the ref blew the half-time whistle it was good news for Monday's.

'By god,' shouted Sid, jumping up. 'The devils. They're bright and lively, they're playing a good tight game, only one–nil down; that's damn good.' He shot an apologetic look to the ladies and crashed back into his seat, puffed out his cheeks and wiped his forehead with his white hand-kerchief. 'And Blundell, he's not done a sausage. He's got Andy Malcolm hard on him though, not letting him *move*, is he?'

The teams jogged over to their dugouts. The crowd watched the pep talks with delight. West Ham's manager Ted Fenton had some quiet, sharp words for his team. Flo reckoned their tactics might change from a happy friendly spirit to something that got them more goals. Mr Monday on the other hand was shouting into his players' faces. Fred stood to one side smoking and snapped something back to Mr Monday when addressed.

After the change-round the second half started fast with some good play. Both teams wanted goals and attacked well. Tremblay, the host keeper, drove a long goal kick that sailed towards Fred, who jumped with Andy Malcolm for a header. Malcolm bounded with his arms up and elbowed Fred in the face. When they came down, Fred's nose burst with blood. Flo tensed when Fred confronted Malcolm, who shrugged and laughed. Wiping the blood across his cheek, Fred looked furious. The ref blew his whistle and awarded a free kick to Monday's.

Mr Monday took it from near the touchline and kicked it to Carl. The ball was lost to West Ham's Woodley on outside right, who took it down the field. Out of nowhere, Fred charged down the pitch, thunderous and seething, tackled the ball away from Woodley, beat Bond for pace and dribbled around Andy Malcolm, losing him for the first time. It was a magnificent run. The Monday crowd were on their feet screaming. Robert Moore ran in, couldn't get a touch but stayed with Fred, and they both went around Lyall at centre back. The Hammers keeper Ernie Gregory ran out to meet them, Fred charged as if no one was there, just as Moore made a sliding tackle into his side at speed. The momentum of the collision forced Fred and Moore forwards into Gregory, Fred fell into a skid and got his toe on the ball through the keeper's legs before the three of them collapsed in a pile in front of the goal line.

The crowd thought it was a goal and roared their glee, then quietened as the ref ran over. The ball had stopped right on the line. The three men on the ground scrambled up together, grappled for a foothold towards the ball. Fred barged ahead, bent over, and shoulder-charged them both forwards with him. He got his foot on the ball, just pushing it over the line. There was a gasp of breath from the crowd and a massive cheer. Fred and Gregory tripped over Moore's leg and fell on to him in a heap behind the goal line. The ref gave the goal.

'OH MY GOD, WHAT THE HELL WAS THAT?' screamed Sid, pulling his hair out. 'WE SCORED, BLUNDELL SCORED.' He jumped up and down. The crowd went wild, the rattles went wild, and the West Ham manager shouted with rage.

'I think things have taken a different turn, don't you?' said Maggie.

'Well, it doesn't look so friendly any more,' said Flo. She watched Fred, worried that he had gone too far. When the crowd stopped roaring, a scream of pain could be heard from the West Ham goal. The medics were called on to the pitch and forced their way through the players with a stretcher. Once the way was cleared there was a collective intake of breath and Flo gasped when young, blond-haired Robert Moore was carried off, half sitting up, clawing at his leg, crying out. Ted Fenton, his manager, bellowed into the referee's face and rushed towards Fred, whose team-mates closed in around him. Mr Monday bellowed back. The crowd shushed and listened. An accident, Flo heard him say. It was an accident. The Hammers' chairman groped his way from the stand behind Flo down to the pitch. There was a lot of arm-waving and raised voices. Mr Monday calmed things down somehow, and the referee indicated that play would resume.

Fred, cosseted in the group, freed himself. His team-mates gave him wary slaps on the back and returned to their positions.

'Bloody hell, is this a game or what?' Sid was back in his seat. 'How he got away with *that,* I do not know. The poor kid, he'll be out for the season now, I reckon his leg's broken, it's a damn rotten shame, it really is.' The ladies nodded in agreement with looks of concern. 'But that's football, isn't it? He'll be all right. Right, thirty minutes left, who we got coming on now? Another new one, not sure, I think it's Geoff Hurst, he's new out the academy this season, he was in the paper.'

Flo shifted in her seat and kept a close eye on Fred. 'It's one–all, ladies.' Sid relished saying it and rubbed his hands together with glee.

The whistle blew, West Ham snatched the ball and surged forwards with speed and vigour, attacking without reservation. The change in tension rippled around the field. The Hammers wanted a goal, they were no longer skylarking, they were pissed off. Dick on inside left found a path through the Canadians but shot hurriedly and the ball hit the bar. Carl recovered it, passed to Sean Callaghan, who kicked it down the field where it was caught in a scuffle and kicked off by Cantwell. Monday's Tyler on the right wing took the corner and swung it in front of the goalmouth.

'MR MONDAY'S THERE,' shrieked Sid. The boss lunged forward and headed the ball into the net. The Monday workers roared and jumped up and down. Sid did the same.

Mr Monday was magnificent. He stood on the pitch with his hands on his hips, his team congratulating him with pats on the back.

'It's two–one, it's two–one,' Sid screeched. 'Mr Monday is the hero of the day, he's done it, we're in the bloody lead.'

Maggie composed herself by lighting a cigarette. She half shrugged when Flo patted her arm, but Flo could tell she was pleased. Mr Monday had put them ahead of Division One West Ham United. It was impossibly brilliant and took some of the taint of the injured boy away.

West Ham's captain Noel Cantwell shouted commands at his troops.

'They'll come in hard now, they'll want to get back quickly. Our boys need to stay vigilant and go all out, clamp down the defence, don't give their forwards any chances.' Sid nodded at Flo, not really seeing her. 'Twenty minutes to go.'

Flo watched Fred, he was fired up, and so was Mr Monday. They put their heads together, nodded and pulled away. Play resumed. Fred dominated the field, came out of position and hunted down the ball, took it, skilfully, the ball attached to his foot, dribbled around Hurst but didn't shake off Malcolm, who followed Fred into the West Ham box and brought Fred down with an illegal tackle. Fred jumped straight up, happy, held his arm up to the ref for a penalty.

'Go on, son,' shouted Sid, up in his seat, his face alight with expectation. 'Penalty,' he shouted, with the rest of the Monday crowd. They all screamed 'Penalty!'

Malcolm caught the ref's eye with a wave of his hand and shook his head. The referee hesitated with his whistle at his lips, then indicated for play to resume. The crowd jeered in disagreement. Sid howled. The ball was kicked back down the field. Flo watched from the edge of her seat as Fred approached Malcolm with his hands up in question, his mouth angry and asking something. Malcolm laughed at Fred, pushed Fred's shoulder and ran off after the ball.

'No, no,' whispered Flo. 'No, don't...'

The ball was passed twice amongst the Hammers and ended back with Malcolm in Monday's area. Horrified, Flo's hands fluttered to her mouth as she watched Fred run down the field, his sights set on one thing. He slid with the force of speed at a forty-five degree angle into the back of Malcolm, kicking his legs away from him. The right half went down, and both sides of the crowd roared with anguish as Fred fell on to Malcolm with a vicious punch to the face.

The players nearest got Fred off before he could do more damage. He snorted and spat, the referee held up a red card and that was that. The Monday workers shook their fists at their own man. Mr Monday grabbed the back of Fred's shirt, furious. Fred turned and, in front of everyone, pushed Mr Monday away with brute force. It caught the boss off balance, he landed on his backside on the turf. The crowd fell into a stunned silence. Mr Monday sprang up, outraged and lunged for Fred. Carl stepped in to separate them and managed to get Fred well away off the field. Flo watched Fred stamp off. Everyone was looking at her, at least that's what it felt like. She wanted to crawl under the seat. The medics came to assist Malcolm, who lay writhing on the turf, clutching his broken nose.

The referee seemed confused as to what to do next. What had started as a friendly kick-about for charity had turned into a bloodbath. Ted Fenton the Hammers' manager was on the pitch again. Sid was on his feet, his hands on his head. Flo felt utterly sick, her stomach twisted with anxiety. Maggie had pulled her cigarette away from her lips to stare open-mouthed at Flo.

'Now, even *I* know that *that* isn't supposed to happen. What kind of creature *is* he?'

At that, Flo burst into tears and covered her face with her white gloves. What the hell had he done? What had he done to them now?

The crowd gasped with disbelief when the ref blew his whistle to start play. Eddie Bovington came on to replace Malcolm, and Monday's were a man down. West Ham were awarded a penalty kick for the foul on Malcolm. Woosnam stepped forward to take it and shot it past Tremblay without difficulty. Sid stayed in his seat. It was two–all, and Monday's had lost their lead.

'Well, that's it. We won't come back now with ten men. What the hell was your old man thinking about? The boss is gonna go off his head, you know that, don't you?'

Flo looked at Sid through a film of tears.

In the last ten minutes of play, West Ham scored another three times. They had two injured players just before the new season and they were furious. The crowd was silent and resigned but the man sitting near Flo kept whirling his rattle, seemed compelled to do it as though he'd just bought the thing and wanted to get his money's worth. It made a grinding racket that jangled Flo's nerves.

When the final whistle blew, the West Ham team walked off the field. Mikey waited with the workers' children in an excited gaggle for the team to sign their football cards. They strained forwards, holding their cards out but the players ignored them and walked away. The boys were distraught, stamped their feet and pushed Mikey away, spitting at his shoes.

Sid shook his head at the ground. 'This is the humiliating defeat the boss dreaded, and worse, it was out-of-order violence. Gentlemen don't behave like that on the football field.'

Maggie and Tabby got up to leave without saying a word to Flo. They shuffled past her along the row of seats.

Flo couldn't move. She watched the dismayed crowd leave. They would all blame her too, she was Fred's wife. He was truly an animal and now everyone knew what he was like. There was no hiding and no pretending any more, no hoping that Fred would fit in and play along for the family's sake. She dreaded to think what would happen, what Mr Monday would do.

Sid stood up to go, waited for Mr Monday to stride off the pitch with his fists clenched at his side.

'Your Fred is in trouble for this, and I'm gonna get it in the neck too, for hiring the bastard.'

'What's gonna happen, Sid?' Flo tried to say it without crying.

Sid looked sick and pale. 'I dunno, Flo, I'm gonna have to talk to him tonight at the dinner when he's had a few drinks, see if I can't smooth it over.'

She gave him a small smile, desperate for him to smooth it over for her and Fred too but unable to ask him to help them. He walked away with his head down and his hands deep in his pockets.

Flo climbed shakily down from the stand and walked across the turf to get Mikey who sat on his own by the touchline.

'What did he have to go and do that for, Mum? I hate him.' He swiped the tears away from his face.

'I know, love, I'm sorry, your dad just loses his temper sometimes.'

273

'But everyone saw and I'm really gonna get it from the boys, and I didn't get any autographs on my football cards.'

Flo swallowed, her throat tight, choking. 'Look, tell you what, love, on Saturday we can go and get one of them Airfix models from Woolies, if you like?'

Mikey screwed up his face, trying to keep his tears back.

'Come on now, buck up, boys don't cry.'

15

The ballroom was gay with multi-coloured streamers. A mirror ball rained happy light upon the dancers doing the cha-cha to Brian Walker's band. Even the older folk were on their feet, impatient for the waltz. Flo slipped in, glanced around the room and saw Ted and Lil sitting at a table on the far side. She tried to side-step around the dancers unnoticed. But they saw her as if the mirror ball had coalesced into a searchlight to pick her out. Doris Lightman, the forewoman from Flo's old sewing team, tarted up to the nines, stopped mid-step.

'Where's that no-good husband of yourn? He's wants stringing up, he does.'

Flo pushed ahead. Another of the women barred her way.

'It's a dirty shame. Fancy going on like that, he wants a good flogging, the rotten bastard spoiling it for everyone.'

Others turned from their cha-cha to give her dirty looks. She almost ran out, but clutched her bag to her chest and remembered Mikey's football cards inside.

'Thank God you're here,' she said, pulling out a chair next to Lil and hunching over with her back to the dance floor.

'Christ, Flo, what you doing here?' said Lil, rubbing her large pregnant bump as though the baby inside was upset at Flo's appearance.

'I've got to see Sid.'

Flo was horrified to see Ted stand up, shake his head at her and walk away.

'Oh my god, not Ted as well.' Flo put a hand to her cheek, her face creased with tears.

'Oh, he's just pissed off about losing his bet, don't worry about him.'

Flo took Lil's handkerchief with a grateful smile. 'It's not my fault, Lil.'

'Yeah I know it's not, but people don't see it like that, do they?'

Flo stared back at Lil, glad to have a friend.

'What the hell was he playing at, Flo?'

Flo's face crumpled again. She shook her head. 'I dunno, Lil, he loses his temper and can't control it, he just sees red, he can't help it in a way.'

Lil tutted and shook her head. 'It's a rotten shame. I'm surprised you came to the dance though, love.'

'I know, I just thought I could have a quick word with Sid, see if he could talk to Mr Monday for me, smooth things out.'

'I dunno, love.' Lil took a large gulp of her wine.

The music stopped and the dancers made their way back to their tables. Flo sniffed and straightened up as Ted took his seat with a puff of disdain.

'What, you didn't bring Sugar Ray with you then?'

A murmur of scorn went round the table.

'Who does he think he is, Willie bleeding Woodburn?' said a man Flo didn't recognise but who clearly knew who she was. 'We was in with a chance until he broke that kid's bloody leg. Where is he? I'd like a word or two.'

'Oh just leave her alone, it's not her fault, is it?' Lil snapped at them.

The MC made an announcement.

'Ladies and gentlemen, this super dinner dance is held in honour of West Ham United, who played a fine and fair game today.' There was a loud cheer of appreciation. 'Carl Anderson, vice-captain of the Monday team and college captain, will say a few words.'

Flo sat up as Carl took the microphone.

'Good evening, ladies, gentlemen, and West Ham United.' Everyone cheered and clapped. 'What an honour it has been to play against a first division team, and what a team of gentlemen they are.' He paused for applause. 'We had high hopes. We thought, in the year that a monkey returns from being launched into space, perhaps we can beat West Ham.' The crowd laughed. 'But their display of skill was fine, their play was thrustful and their goal attempts, unfortunately, hit the back of the net. Yet again, West Ham are the victors, and rightly so.'

Everyone clapped. Flo couldn't take her eyes off Carl, couldn't help but smile when he made a joke, as if it was just the two of them in the room. 'And now, I have the pleasure of introducing Mr Monday.' The crowd clapped politely.

Mr Monday took the microphone. He stood in his well-cut suit, washed, shaved and gleaming. His large eyebrows were drawn together in a frown as he looked at his audience for a few seconds before speaking.

'It was a sad day today.' A silence fell on the room, Flo shuffled uncomfortably. 'We had in our midst a man who was not one of us. He was not one of the team. He was not a member of the Monday family. He behaved in an unforgivable way towards our guests.' Flo went rigid in her chair. Mr Monday paused for several seconds for the effect of his words to be felt. Everyone looked from him to the West Ham team sitting at the top table. Everyone on Flo's table looked at Flo. In an instant the frown smoothed away from Mr Monday's brow, a large grin spread across his face, he touched his right eye, which Flo now noticed looked swollen. 'And I am happy to say that that little problem has been dealt with once and for all.' A lead ball dropped into Flo's guts. The audience roared and clapped, gave him a standing ovation. He settled them down with a wave of his arms.

'What's he done, Lil? What's happened?'

Lil clutched her hand and patted it. 'I dunno, where's Sid? Ask Sid, he'll know. Just wait until the speeches are finished.'

Flo thought Mr Monday would never stop

talking – she groped in her bag for a cigarette and gulped down the glass of wine that Lil pushed towards her.

'Man of the match goes to Robert Moore, and here's wishing him a speedy recovery.' Everyone clapped. Mr Monday waited for silence. 'Two more days of work and the factory shuts down for two weeks. You all go and enjoy yourselves. You work hard, you deserve a good rest. But make sure to come back revived and ready for more hard work. The company is doing well, and that's because of you. Monday Leather is as buoyant and optimistic as the country as a whole. And that's because of Supermac. Don't forget the election's coming up and we want him in for a second term. Anyhow, I think he won you over with the budget.' He grinned. 'Income tax cut and twopence off a pint of beer.' The workers laughed and cheered. Mr Monday sat back down and Flo scanned the top of the room for Sid.

'I'm gonna try and find him,' she said to Lil. With her head down she skirted along the ballroom's edge, heading for the top table. Hanging back against the dark wall she looked for Sid but couldn't see him anywhere. Carl saw her and came over.

'Hello, beautiful, this might not be the best time, you know.'

She didn't want him to be kind to her, it would only make her cry.

'Carl, look, can you get these signed for my Mikey?' Her hands shook as she felt in her bag for Mikey's football cards. 'You seen Sid, Carl? I need to find out what's happening.'

The smile dropped from Carl's face.

'Sid got fired, the boss sacked him, Flo.' Carl shook his head at the injustice of it.

'What?'

Flo jumped as Mr Monday suddenly loomed over her.

'You got some nerve showing up here, little lady.' He was drunk, his lips were spit-wet and stained red with wine. His right eye was swollen, a cut high on the cheekbone.

'Look, I'm sorry about Fred, Mr Monday,' she said, glancing across at Carl for moral support. 'He didn't mean it, he just loses his temper, he's really sorry.'

'OH, HA HA HA.' Mr Monday bellowed laughter at the ceiling, then just as easily a cruel smirk settled upon his face.

'I found your husband cradling his pint of beer in the social club. We had a few words as a matter of fact.' He smiled and touched his sore eye. 'But I was ready for the bastard this time.'

Flo stared up at him, horrified.

'I sacked him, of course. He doesn't belong here. And that means you too, and the rest of the *Blundells*. I'm only sorry you and I didn't get to know each other a little better.' His lips stretched away from his teeth in a sickening smile. She stood rigid, his eyelids drooped as he scanned her face and body.

As he turned away, he said something else, loud enough to make sure she heard.

'And that means you leave the house, of course, *and* your precious college, not that *that* would have amounted to anything.' He roared with laughter and loped off back to his table. 'Be gone by the weekend,' he called over his shoulder.

Flo couldn't move. The room blurred as the band started playing. They were out, it was all over, the promise of college suddenly beyond her reach, the house, everything.

'Flo?' it was Carl, concern in his voice. The football cards fell from Flo's hands, scattered on to the parquet floor. The light from the mirror ball played over them as she staggered from the room.

'Fred?' Flo opened the front door of the house and slipped into the hall. Peering around the doorway into the kitchen she saw him at the table, a bottle of Scotch in his hand, his hair dishevelled, his head hung down on to the red Formica. She tiptoed back to the front door, left it open on the latch, just in case.

'Fred, love?'

'What?' he growled, not looking up, his voice thick with alcohol and rage.

Flo glanced back at the door.

'Maybe you better go and have a lie down.'

'I don't wanna lie down, I wanna drink,' he snapped, turning his head to glare at her. He looked like a wild man, bloodshot eyes, hair all over the place, a fat lip and dried blood caked around the side of his mouth. He took a swig from the bottle, banged it back down on the table. Flo stayed where she was. It was no use trying to talk to him. It would be better if he went to bed to sleep it off.

'Don't stand there staring at me, woman, this

isn't a fucking circus.'

Flo turned away.

'Not a circus like that soccer game. Everyone thinks it's *my* fault, but that geezer, that *Malcolm,* he was winding me up, no one's blaming *him,* are they?'

Flo hung back in the doorway. For a second he looked helpless, he knew what he'd done and grasped for some way to justify it.

'He *fouled* me, didn't anyone *see* that?' He was ranting, it was a bad sign. Flo braced herself.

'And that Mr Monday, who the hell does he think he is, for Chrissake? Coming and telling me I'm fired. I don't want his fucking job in his poxy factory anyway, it can burn down for all I care.'

He rolled in his chair, waved his heavy arms around like a pathetic drunk, but Flo knew he was dangerous and stayed alert.

'Monday this and Monday that, Monday fucking everywhere like nothing else exists. Well, I'll burn it down myself, then they'll see it's not the only fucking thing in the world worth bothering about.'

The metal legs of his chair ground along the lino floor as he staggered to get up.

'Where you going, Fred? Don't do anything stupid.' Flo danced out of his way, but the back of his rough hand caught the side of her face as he swiped at her.

'Don't you tell me what to do, woman, or I'll give you some too.'

Flo fell back against the corner of the door-frame, banged her shoulder when he pushed past her out of the front door.

Out on the dark doorstep Flo stood and watched him walk away, his hunched figure lumbering along beneath the street lights. She jumped at the sound of a man's voice close by.

'Flo?'

'Carl? What you doing?' He came out of the shadows to meet Flo at the garden gate.

'I was concerned, are you all right? What's going on, where's Fred going?'

'I dunno.' Flo chewed her thumbnail. 'He said something about burning the factory down.'

'What? For Christ's sake.' Carl put his hands on his head and left them there while he thought.

'Police?'

'Oh, no, please don't, Carl, not unless we have to, eh?'

'What then? Come on.'

Carl started to walk and Flo fell into step beside him. When they turned the corner on to the main road they could see Fred up ahead, clumping towards the factory. There was no one around, the dinner dance was in full swing in the ballroom. They saw Fred go through the door set into the main factory gates and followed him around to the loading bay, watched as he pulled up the shutters with a loud rattle. They crept in after him, feeling their way down the dark stairwell to the basement. Fred switched on a light further through, which helped them pick their way through the engineering store room where old gun parts left over from the war effort were piled against the wall. Fred went through a door into the chemical store.

'Oh my god.'

'You think he would?' Carl whispered.

They stopped by the door. Fred stumbled about the room looking at drums and boxes, pulling things about. Flo found a heavy metal gun casing in one of the boxes and handed it to Carl, who looked horrified.

'I don't want to bloody kill him.'

Flo shrugged, what else could they do but hurt him?

They both jumped at a loud metallic banging sound. Fred was knocking the cap off one of the drums with a block of wood.

'Fred, don't.' Flo stepped into the storeroom, held her hands out in front of her. Fred stumbled, but went back to the cap and Carl rushed at him, grabbed his arms behind his back. Fred roared and fell backwards, rammed Carl into a work-bench and staggered back to the chemical drum. He got the cap off and kicked the drum over on to its side, a dark liquid pulsed out of the hole in the top and sloshed across the floor. Fred reached for his matches and Flo ran, covering her head with her arms. She got into the stairwell just as the drum exploded. Fred pushed past her up the stairs as a resounding metallic boom fired into her ears. It sounded far away as though locked in a little room. And then nothing. Only a terrible chemical stench.

A movement flashed by her.

'It's all right, look.' It was Carl, who held up a fire extinguisher to show her then disappeared into the gloom.

'Fire!' She groped her way up the stairs and outside, shrieked at the workers running over from the dance. 'Call the fire brigade.'

The factory fire team were there in minutes, they bundled into the dispatch hold and disappeared. Carl lunged out, coughing for breath, joined Flo and managed a tight smile.

'It's all right, it's not too bad,' he said into her ear. They stood facing a crowd of people waiting expectantly, half of them without a coat.

Mr Monday pushed through to the front, his tuxedo flapped open in the evening breeze. 'What's going on?'

Flo and Carl glanced at each other.

'What happened?' Mr Monday glared at them, ordered two of his men to investigate. 'Harry and Bill, get down there and see.'

'We were passing and heard an explosion,' said Carl. 'One of the drums in the chemical store must have exploded but we managed to keep the fire under control, the fire team are dealing with it now. It could have been a lot worse.'

Mr Monday considered the story and thumped Carl on the back. 'Well done, Anderson, you've done the factory a great service today. He put his arm around Carl's shoulders and led him towards the loading bay to wait for news – Carl shot an apologetic look back at Flo. She stood there alone, relieved that it hadn't been worse, looked around for Fred and guessed that he had scarpered. She was lightheaded from the chemical fumes and needed to sit down.

'Why don't you come to the house to sit down for a while?' It was Maggie. Flo wanted to laugh, but started to cry instead. Maggie held her hand and led her across the quadrangle to the Monday Mansion without saying a word. Her heels clicked on the concrete, her perfume nudged aside the foul chemical smell in Flo's nose.

'Here, this will help.' Once inside, Maggie handed her a drink. Flo flinched, it was strong, whisky or something. 'Do you think you'd like a doctor to come?'

'I'll be all right, just need to sit down for a bit.'

'Gosh, what happened with the fire?'

'We was, Carl and me was walking by and heard an explosion. We went in and saw the fire and tried to put it out.'

'That was very courageous of you. I wonder what started the explosion.' Maggie frowned.

Flo shrugged and sipped her drink, feeling better.

'Well, it was a good job you both happened to be walking by. I hope they manage to put it out.'

Maggie eyed her and lit a cigarette.

'Look, Mags,' Flo thought quickly, took a breath and a slug of her drink for courage, sensing a possible chance to put things right. 'I reckon I really helped the company out just now, maybe I can get my job back eh?'

'Your job back?' Maggie seemed startled.

'Yeah, didn't you hear? Fred got sacked about the football, and I got sacked because he got sacked. But maybe I can get my job back. Fred can work somewhere else. We can live somewhere else, not on the estate, and I can work here still and do my college course?'

'Oh, Flo, you *are* a funny one. Of course I heard about you losing your job. I don't think it's such a bad thing after all. I mean, you're much better suited to being a charwoman at the docks. My husband has explained that the boys in the college are being primed for the most responsible jobs overseas – I really shouldn't think you were up to it, old thing, would you? This is for the best, it really is.'

It was like Maggie had spat in her face. She said it all with her usual smile, her usual crossed legs and cigarette held aloft.

'Oh, is that right?' Flo said, half thinking that Maggie was joking.

'And as for that husband of yours, perhaps you should have him house-trained, my dear, I mean, *really*.' She gave a tinkling laugh, as though they were discussing something else altogether.

Flo put her drink down, her arm was weak as though the blood in her limbs had receded into her torso, it sloshed and pulsated in her chest, her heart working harder and harder to churn it round until she would drown in her own blood.

'And what about my Barbara and your James?' A flash of hope, it was something to keep them there, if Babs was in the family way and they got married.

'Excuse me?'

'What about Babs and James, they wanna get engaged, didn't you know?'

'Don't be ridiculous.' Maggie came the closest Flo had seen to losing her composure.

'Well, that's another reason for me keeping my job, isn't it? Seeing as our families will be joining.'

'Joining?' Maggie chewed up the word, her voice high pitched. 'I don't know where you get your information from Flo, but...'

'Your son. That's where I got the information

from, he came to see us, to ask Fred his permission to marry Babs.'

Maggie's lips drew in. 'If you think *my* James would marry a common factory girl like *her,* you are gravely mistaken.'

'What?' Flo rocked in her seat. Her head felt funny like it had stretched up to the ceiling. 'What do you mean? They're in love. They wanna get married, I thought Babs could join the young wives club.'

'Oh, you Blundells, did you have your sights set on us from the start? It certainly seems conspiratorial to me. All of you, causing trouble here, my god, it's an affront.'

Flo didn't hear her, Maggie's expression was enough. The cruelty of a friend's betrayal.

'They'll have a few nippers I expect, maybe live on the estate.' She could hear herself say it but the words were far away. It was different at Monday's, wasn't it? That's what Maggie was always saying, classless, where everyone mucked in together. Maggie had pushed Flo forwards and upwards, hadn't she? Made her think other things were possible, made her believe in that.

'Nippers? Good grief, could you imagine? Your Barbara with her hair in rollers, shouting at the children to come in for their *tea,* the children playing outside in the road, screaming, rolling around in the dirt. Good *grief. Never.*'

'What the hell's going on here?' Mr Monday was home.

'Oh my goodness, get her out of here, will you, darling, she's giving me a headache.' Maggie sagged back on to the chaise, fanning her face with her hand.

Mr Monday stood with his legs apart, glaring at Flo. It was enough, Flo stood up unsteadily and scuttled out of the room. As she came into the hallway, she heard Maggie call out to her.

'Just because you have a television set and a refrigerator, Flo, it doesn't change who you are, or where you're from.'

And as she opened the front door and a rush of cold air blew over her, she heard:

'Darling, mix me a gin and tonic would you? I've had a frightful time.'

'What's wrong with *you?*' Babs walked into our gloomy bedroom and looked at me like I had shit on my chin.

'Nothing.' I curled up on my bed and turned my back to her. I was sick again and didn't feel like talking.

'You been in here all day?'

It wasn't the usual bored question she'd ask while brushing her hair or smearing her face with make-up the way you grease a cake tin.

'Yeah, so what?'

'So what? So Dad's mucked up the football, that's what. He broke a West Ham player's leg and made Monday's lose. Everyone *hates* him. He pushed the big boss over on the pitch in front of *everyone,* you should of *seen,* I couldn't believe it, I mean, everyone looked at me like I did it.'

I turned over on the bed to look at her.

'What you on about, you...' I felt the sick coming up again and slid off the bed hunched over, ran downstairs to throw up in the bog. I was on my knees on the bathroom floor, the acid in the sick was awful, like I had a hot poker down my throat. I heaved for breath like I'd run a mile and tried not to cry. I managed to get up and stagger back to the bedroom.

Babs looked at me funny. 'What's wrong with you then, you eat something off?'

I sat on the bed and shrugged, wiped my mouth on my cuff.

Babs suddenly bounced on her bed. 'You're not up the duff, are you?' She clapped her hand over her mouth and burst into giggles. 'Nah, you're not, you've never been with a boy, have you?'

I looked at her and my head went dizzy.

'Nah, you haven't been with anyone, you'd tell me, wouldn't you?'

I thought I might be sick again.

'Well, if your tits feel sore you're up the duff, and if your whatsits have stopped you're up the duff, and if everything smells funny you're up the duff.' She gave me this sly, sideways look and smiled. *'So they say.'*

Jesus Christ. Was she right? Was I up the duff like her? The room started to move, the walls dipped and swayed. I put my hand out and felt the rag mat as I slipped off the bed.

'Jeanie? Jeanie. You look funny, shall I go and find Mum?'

I managed to get up on all fours. Babs crouched down in front of me, her face in my face, my twin reflecting back, my sister in the family way, and me in the family way. I hadn't even thought it might be that, but the symptoms weren't right for polio or TB, there was no fever yet, or weak muscles, no cough, it wasn't hard to breathe. My chest was sore, yes it was, had been for days, really tender so I flinched if anyone brushed past me. My whatsits had stopped, I hadn't realised it but they had. I hadn't had one in quite a while but didn't think of it because of the sickness and I never usually miss one, never. And I couldn't go in the kitchen because it stank like old cooking fat, like really bad old fat. And the fridge, I couldn't even open it, the smells were worse than anything, coming out towards me all together, like a punch in the throat. I ran past the canteen yesterday, didn't I, it stank so much.

The sick was coming again. Somehow I got to my feet and lurched ahead, bumped out of the room and crashed downstairs. I retched into the bath but nothing came out, just some foul-tasting bile, bitter and acidic that made me want to throw up again straight away.

'Oh my god, Jeanie, you must have got food poisoning. What you been eating? Here, I'll get you some water, hang on.'

I fell back on to the cold lino, my head against the sink pedestal, and this big, horrible groan came out of my mouth. It was like it wasn't me, like I was standing next to myself. A horrible groan, and then long gasping sobs that shook my whole body, with silences between each one when my face stayed all twisted up. Like Mum when Nan died.

'God, Jeanie, you sound like you're in a right state,' said Babs. 'Here, drink this.' She held out a glass of water and took a step into the bathroom. I put out my foot and kicked the door shut with such force that it knocked her backwards. I heard her fall on her arse in the hallway, the water splashing out of the glass.

'Jeanie, you cow. You can just look after yourself.'

Her footsteps went upstairs and soon she came back down and I heard the front door slam. There was no one in the house. Just me. Just me and the *thing* inside me. It must be that, it must be, I knew it as soon as Babs said it, I must have known already. The tears and sobs wouldn't stop. *Hysterical*, I knew what that meant now. I could hear myself crying, could feel myself shaking but couldn't control it. *Once!* I didn't know it could happen when you've only done it once. Just when I had got into college this had happened. Everything was ruined. I couldn't have a baby, it was the same thing as dying, it would be the end of my life anyway. A baby at fifteen? They'd make me marry Skylon. Oh god.

It's the shock, that's what people say when something really bad happens. This was a shock, it came out of nowhere and smashed me in the face. I sat there on the bathroom floor, my face swollen with pressure and drained of tears and after a while, I don't know how long, a cold calm came over me. It occurred to me that this might be something I could sort out myself. No one would have to know. I called out the textbook reproductive-system pages from the compartment in my brain. The uterus is the shape of an upside-down pear, I'd need something long to get up into it, with a flat scraping tool at the end, maybe I could tie a teaspoon on to a pencil. The main problem would be getting through the cervix. That's when I realised that one way or another I would die soon. Either I tried to do it myself, like Terry Palmer's mum, who did it with a crochet hook and bled to death in her back garden, or I got someone to scrape my guts out and kill me that way, like Linda Fitzpatrick's mum, who got a dodgy abortion from some woman and died from an infection.

I took a deep breath and got up, pulled a towel off the rack to wipe my nose on. Saw my deathly face in the mirror and, in the reflection, Dad's razor in the dish on the windowsill. I turned around to look at it, it was like I'd never really seen it properly before. My fingertips reached out to touch the smooth white china of the dish and then the razor handle, cold heavy metal. There was one other way, I realised, almost with a sense of relief, something quicker, more effective. Something that would take it all away, the thing inside me, the struggle to get an education, the humiliation about James. My other hand hovered nearby, the finger and thumb pinched the razor-blade, pulled to get it out.

Someone thumped on the bathroom door, over and again, I felt the aftershock of each bang – it made me jump, the razor cut my finger. I just stared at the blood seep from the line in little dots, something wicked oozing out of me.

'Jeanie? Open the door.'

I jolted, it was Mum, I didn't remember locking the door. The razor clattered into the sink and left a tiny spray of red on the white ceramic. I came to. Sucked my finger, turned on the tap to swill the water around. Put the razor back into the dish. When I opened the door Mum and Babs stood there looking all worried.

I brushed past them.

'You all right, love?' said Mum, looking into the bathroom to see what I'd been doing. 'Go and lie down. Do you want some water or something?'

My whole body felt so heavy, I pretended I was normal when really I felt like I was dragging a sack of spuds up the stairs. I fell on to my bed and squeezed my eyes shut. Babs came in. How could she be so happy and normal about it all? It was bound to go to shit for her too.

16

'I don't wanna go.'

Mikey spoke to his shoes with his arms folded.

'I know, love,' said Flo. They stood with Babs and Jeanie on the pavement outside number thirty-eight looking at the house that was no longer theirs. A pile of bags and packages sat at their feet. 'But it's the school holidays so you'll just go back to your old school after.'

'Bloody Dad. I could kill him.' Babs stamped her marigold cha-cha flats, her fifth new pair of Monday Leather shoes. 'I'm not having it.'

Flo turned, saw the net curtain drop at Doreen's window on the other side of the road. She waited for a second for the front door to open, for Doreen to run over with a look of concern on her friendly face. But she didn't. Flo realised Doreen would be glad to see them go, because they never fitted in anyway. Maggie was right. Flo was better off cleaning down the docks. They were probably all having a right laugh at her at the young wives club. Thinking she could do that college course and work abroad. The very idea seemed stupid, of course she couldn't do it. It was for men for a reason.

She turned back to the house for one last look. It was all a dream. The kitchen and bathroom, the garden, the Frigidaire.

'Come on then.' She picked up a wooden apple box, their pots and pans shifted and clanked inside. The children got the other stuff, all of them reluctant, only Jeanie not voicing her anger. It wasn't fair on them, showing them what they couldn't have. They shouldn't have come to Monday's, they didn't belong there.

It was the start of the two-week factory shut-down and looked like the whole of Monday's walked along the station road carrying their suit-cases. Off on holiday. Flo had listened to the workers talk about going away, to Skegness, Southend, Bournemouth. She thought it sounded so nice, packing a suitcase for the family, going to sit on deckchairs and eat ice creams. They had taken the girls on a day trip to Southend when they were little, had eaten chips on the beach and played on the penny arcade.

Fred hadn't come home since the fire, she didn't know where he was. He could have been dead in a ditch somewhere. The thought filled Flo with horror, to think of his dead body, white face, alone in the rain, animals sniffing around him.

She needed him there now, to help carry all their things, to throw back the stares and dirty looks, to smooth his fringe and take a puff of his cigarette. But it was just her and the kids, for the first time ever. It was a heavy weight on her shoulders. What would people down the docks think? No husband, three kids. She would be one of *those* women. But where else would they go but back home? It was the only place she could think of. She had been born at the docks, it was her blood.

They walked along in silence, carried their pots and pans while everyone else carried their sun hats and beach towels. On the station platform, they stood alone on the Tilbury side. Opposite, the platform heaved with holidaymakers going to Southend. Talking, excited, they showed no shame in nodding their heads towards the Blundells. Flo shuffled the children along to the waiting room.

'I've never been so embarrassed. It's shameful, really it is.' Babs cried into her handkerchief. 'I want Jim, I want him. He was going to take me to a skiffle club next weekend at Chislehurst caves, there's so much we want to do together, so many plans.'

Jeanie jumped off her seat and stamped out of the waiting room to stand outside on the platform. Flo ignored her, she was a pain in the arse lately. 'You can still see him, love.' But Flo knew Maggie would put a stop to that. She used to talk about sending him out to the Young Conservative balls, to meet like-minded girls, Flo realised now.

Babs wasn't good enough for his type, she'd learn that soon enough. The Southend train came puffing along, picked up the jolly passengers and took them off to the seaside. The Tilbury train screeched into the station, spat soot and smoke into Flo's eyes, blew its harsh whistle at her.

Mikey started to cry.

'I don't wanna go.'

'I know, Mikey, but get your backside on that train before the stationmaster gives me an earful.'

Flo dragged him on by his arm, the girls followed, and Flo jumped off to pass up the boxes and bags. Jeanie was already in the compartment sitting on the far side of the carriage refusing to help.

'Thanks a lot, Jean, you horrible brat,' said Flo, struggling with the packages.

The stationmaster shut the door for them and the train pulled away. Mikey looked out the window at the Monday Leather factories going by, his hands flat on the glass, his breath clouding the view.

'But what about the lido and the swings, and my mates and sports day and all that?'

He looked at Flo for the answer. She swallowed hard and bit the inside of her lip, his little face looked so sad and disappointed. What had he had in life? Not much before this, and now that was taken away from him. They shouldn't have come. It was Fred, all Fred's fault.

'You'll be able to see all your old pals at Tilbury school, won't you? And you can play down the fort again.'

'I don't wanna go back there, I want to live at

Monday's, it's brilliant, I want to live at Monday's.'
He started to bounce on his knees on the seat, his
voice loud.

'*Shut up.* Just shut up and sit down, you'll do as
you're told and be happy about it, you hear?'

Flo heard herself snap at him, her tone harsh, a
rush of anger in her chest.

'I won't. I won't. I don't wanna go back to the
docks.'

Flo leant forwards and slapped Mikey's face.
The sound stayed in the air and clung to them all.
Mikey fell back against his seat, held his cheek
and stared at her. Flo looked out of the window
and watched the leather factory disappear from
view. How quickly life could change.

When the train pulled into Tilbury Docks
station they bundled off and Flo led them along
the streets to Calcutta Road. She had been to see
Stan, the docks foreman, the day after the match.
He couldn't let them live in the Dwellings and
couldn't get Flo any work in the docks because of
Fred's form, but he found some digs for her that
Mary Niblett had for rent.

'What? Calcutta Road? Oh, that's bloody smashing that is,' said Babs, stopping to put her bags
down.

'Sorry, love, it's all I could get.'

'The last time I was down here you lot pulled
me out of Biddy Moss's house, or did you forget
that? I'm not living here, what if Billy comes back
home?'

'I know, now shut your noise, it's all I could get,
I just told you that. Billy won't be coming home
yet, he'll be away for a good while, he's probably

297

still crying for his mum in some godforsaken foreign hell-hole.'

'Urgh, and I don't wanna see his cow of a mother either, she'll still be here.'

Flo gave Babs a sideways glance. Yes, Biddy Moss would still be there.

'Come on,' said Flo. They picked up their bags and trudged along. Women sat on their doorsteps chatting while their children played runouts in the dirt road and tiddlywinks on the kerb. It was a hot August morning, already the sun burned into Flo's eyes. The smell of the docks made her dizzy, it was like walking through time, nothing had changed. The sea salt, smoke, grease and tobacco hung in the air. She wondered if they smelled of leather and glue, coming from Monday's. As they walked, the women stopped talking to watch them. Marge Wilson at number seven called out.

'All right, Flo? What's all this then?'

'Coming back, aren't we?' said Flo, forcing a smile.

'How come?'

'Ah, missed the old place, didn't we?'

Marge stared and nodded, her mouth pulled down. Flo carried on.

'No we never,' hissed Mikey.

Flo kept on until they came to number nineteen. It was only three doors down from Biddy Moss's house but on the other side and thankfully the woman wasn't on her step.

After a while Mary Niblett opened the door. A war widow in her eighties, Mary was tiny and pinched, just like her house. She hadn't put her teeth in so her cheeks billowed out and drew in like bellows as she spoke. Her cotton summer dress was buttoned up to her chin, her grey hair in a severe side parting, little pin curls covered her ears.

'Come on then.' She gave them a look of disdain and turned back into her dark hallway. 'You can use the scullery and the lav, but don't leave no rubbish nowhere or you'll be out. I can't abide rubbish or tat lying about.'

She showed them the sink in the scullery and gestured to the outhouse in the back garden, then pushed past them to lead the way up the stairs.

'Here's your bedsitter, two rooms, you can use the range for cooking but clean out the ashes regular or you'll be out, I can't abide a dirty fire.'

'Yes, Mrs Niblett, thank you, you got a key?' said Flo. Mary looked up at her as though she'd said something outrageous.

'Here's your key, look after it or you'll be paying for another one. It's on the electric, meter's in the hall, two shilling pieces.' She left them there and went back downstairs, still talking at the same volume, her voice gradually petering out.

'No noise, don't leave my step dirty or you'll be cleaning it, flush the lav, put your rubbish out, pay your rent on time, no wireless, I can't abide music, 'specially not that modern nonsense...'

The Blundells looked at each other and looked around their new home. A dark sitting room with a range, a settee and a large armchair.

'Well, it looks clean enough,' said Flo, trying the light switch then pulling back the curtain to let some sunlight in.

'It's a shit hole just like the Dwellings. We might as well have gone back there,' said Babs, throwing her bags on to the floor.

'I wanna go back to the house, Mum, can we?' Mikey looked up at Flo.

'Now pipe down all of you, this is where we live now, so make the best of it.'

'Where's the bog?' said Mikey.

'Outside, like she said, idiot.' Babs shoved Mikey, who toppled back into the fireplace and knocked the coal shovel into the hearth with a metallic clang. There was a thump on the floor from downstairs and they all froze.

'Keep the noise down, idiot, she can't abide noise,' said Babs, giggling for the first time that day. 'Where we all sleeping then?' she said, disappearing into the one other room. 'There's only a double bed in here,' she called.

They all followed her through into the bedroom. A large bed made up with a patchwork eiderdown dominated the room.

'You kids can sleep in the bed, I'll go on the settee.'

'What, us two and Mikey? Oh god.' Babs stamped her foot.

Mikey let out a loud, sloppy-sounding fart with a big grin on his face.

'Oh, god.' Babs looked at Jeanie for help, but Jeanie sat on the settee with her chin in her hand.

'Come on then, let's get our bits and pieces sorted out,' said Flo, opening one of the boxes.

'I'm going out,' Mikey called and clattered down the stairs, slamming the front door as he went. Flo went to the front window, saw him in the road, he ran up to a group of boys kicking a ball around, who crowded around him. Flo tensed, but Mikey looked happy, no doubt telling wild stories about this and that. She opened the window to air the stuffy room. It was small, yes it was, but it was clean, they would manage.

Flo and the girls unpacked some of their belongings. There was a chest of drawers in the bedroom, a wash stand, and a small sideboard in the sitting room, nowhere else to store things, so they shoved the rest of the boxes against the bedroom wall for the time being.

'What's gonna happen then, Mum?' said Babs.

'What do you mean, love?' Flo sagged on to the settee and lit a cigarette.

Babs shrugged. 'I dunno, what about Dad, and getting a job and all that?'

'Your dad's gone, I don't know where he is. We need to get jobs, I know that much. I've got a bit saved from Monday's but we need work. We'll go down the Labour Exchange tomorrow, see what they've got, all right?'

Babs nodded. Jeanie started to cry.

'What's wrong, love?' Flo tried to put her arm around her but Jeanie shrugged it away and went into the bedroom. Babs rolled her eyes at Flo.

The dulled sound of shouting came up from the street. Running to the front window, Flo and Babs saw Mikey on his back in the road, brawling with another boy. They rolled in the dirt, trying to land punches on each other.

'No noise,' shouted Mrs Niblett as Flo clattered down the stairs and out the front door. She grabbed Mikey's shirt and pulled him up, put a hand out to stop the other boy.

'What's going on?'

'He said we never had a fridge and a television,' said Mikey, puffing for breath and pointing at the other boy.

'Yeah, a likely story, I'd say.' It was Biddy Moss. She came forward from her front step, her arms folded over her chest. Flo's stomach turned over. She didn't have Fred with her this time.

'All right, Biddy, how's you then?'

'Well, we're all right, Flo, but it looks like you're down on your luck, eh? And your boy telling lies about fridges and televisions.' Biddy Moss smirked, her wide nose and cheeks still red from drink.

'My boy don't tell lies, Biddy.'

'What? You telling me you got a fridge and a television up there?'

'No, I'm not, but we did have where we were before.'

'Oh, so the mother tells lies as well, that's where he gets it from.' Biddy Moss took a step towards Flo and looked her in the eye. The boys in the street gathered around the women, waiting. 'What are you, stuck-up now, eh? A jumped-up snob now, eh?'

'No, Biddy, I'm not, and I don't want no trouble.'

'What, think you're too classy for the likes of us, do you?' Biddy took another step forwards, scuffed dirt on to Flo's shoes, her arms still crossed.

'You didn't go grassing on my Fred, making up stories to get us thrown out the Dwellings now did you, Biddy?'

'What? Bloody cheek.' But Flo saw a flicker in the woman's face. 'You're a liar. That's your problem.'

Flo looked at the woman, her twisted face ugly with spite. She felt Mikey's eyes on them. Knew the girls were watching from the window and didn't want to let them down. She wouldn't let them see her being pushed around, and she wouldn't have Mikey called a liar. Not by this filthy bint who stank of drink and old sweat.

'How's your Billy doing then, eh, Biddy? Crying for his mummy while he polishes his belt buckle?' Flo said it with a smile and Biddy went for her.

'You were brilliant, Mum. Really showed that old bag.'

That was the tenth time Mikey had told Mum how brilliant she was for knocking Biddy Moss for six. Mum didn't look so brilliant though, had a cut lip and a bruised eye, and she limped when she walked. That Biddy Moss was a size, I wasn't surprised Mum was in a bad way. Just like the docks it was, fighting in the road, back to the same old shit, I almost missed Monday's. And that horrible tiny bedsitter. Crammed in we were, on top of each other, I couldn't get away from them all, it was stifling.

Babs helped Mum wash her cuts, and told Mum she could sleep in the bed. That left me on the settee probably. There wasn't a tap upstairs, we had to bring water from Mrs No-Teeth's scullery. I needed a wash, had to boil a kettle on the range like the old days at the Dwellings, and pour some hot water into the enamel basin on the wash stand in the bedroom. Mum was asleep in the bed by then, and the other two were in the sitting room eating chips. I stripped off down to my drawers, started having a wash. The hot water and soap felt nice on my skin. I'd been sick that morning at the house. In the bedsitter I'd have to go to the outhouse to throw up so no one would see. I tried to push it all out of my head so I could think about my A levels. I wanted to keep up with it through the summer so when I went back in the new term I'd be really ready for it. It was the best thing I'd ever done in my life. Going to that college was like a second chance and nothing could get in the way of that.

'Jeanie!'

I jumped. Mum was sat up in the bed, gawping at me. I looked down, and looked back at her. I knew what she'd seen. I was so skinny from the sickness that my belly was showing already and I had a dark line from my belly button downwards. I grabbed my nightdress, put it on with my back to her, then sneaked a glance at her face. She sat there, her mouth hanging open, she'd gone all white.

'Jeanie?' She put her hand over her mouth and then there were tears in her eyes. Then I felt tears in my own bloody eyes and my chin quivered and I couldn't stop it. I put my head down, stuck my chin to my chest so I didn't have to look at her. That just made it worse.

'OH MY GOD,' Mum shouted.

Babs and Mikey rushed in.

'What?' said Babs.

'What is it?' said Mikey, his mouth stuffed with chips.

'Get out, Mikey,' said Mum. 'NOW.'

Mikey left, he didn't care, there would be more chips for him. All I could think of was what was I gonna say, I didn't even wanna talk to Mum, I still hated her for everything.

'Well?'

I looked up. Mum was staring at me, she looked a right state with her cut lip and purple eye.

'Can someone tell me what's going on?' said Babs, her hands on her hips.

'She's in the family way,' said Mum, her fingers over her mouth like she didn't want the words to come out.

'What, Jeanie? Ha ha, you must be joking.' Then Babs's face changed. I knew she was thinking about when I was sick before.

They both stared at me. I looked at the wall.

'Jeanie?' said Babs, coming close to me. She looked down at my stomach, put her hand out and drew it down over the hard bump that was growing there, pulled back with a gasp, looked at Mum.

'Well, *she* is too,' I shouted. It was the first time I'd spoken to Mum in a long time but she didn't show it, the news was bad enough to hide anything.

'WHAT?' screamed Mum, staring at Babs.

'What? Don't be stupid, course I'm not,' shouted Babs.

'Yes, you are, you bloody liar.' I rushed at her, pulled her dress down tight over her stomach, looked at it, pulled it down tighter, looked again.

She shoved me away with this awful frown like I'd gone mad.

'What are you talking about, Jeanie? You thought I was expecting? What the hell are you talking about?'

I shook my head, tried to shake up my brain so I could think. Babs's stomach was as flat as a pancake. She'd gotten pregnant before me, she should be showing more than me by now, I don't know why I hadn't noticed.

'You've got rid of it,' I said to her.

'No, Jeanie, *I* haven't done anything.'

Mum got up out of bed, came over to me. She put her hands on my arms. I was shaking.

'Jeanie? When did this happen?' She looked right in my face and pulled up my nightdress. 'You look about three or four months gone. Why didn't you say something? Have your whatsits stopped?'

She shook her head, she knew my monthlies must have stopped by the sight of me. I bit my lip but tears just came tumbling out anyway. They were both looking at me like I was some kind of animal.

'Who was it, Jeanie?' said Babs. 'How, I mean' – she looked embarrassed – 'how did, did you go *all the way?*' I stared at her, as if she didn't know how a girl got pregnant. 'I didn't even know she had a boy, she didn't tell me,' she said to Mum. She went all white then, and stepped backwards like she was gonna fall over. 'It wasn't. It wasn't *Jim*, was it, Jeanie?' She looked like she was gonna throw up. I shook my head, and she sort of laughed as though she hadn't really thought it would be. 'Who then? Tell me.'

I didn't say anything, I couldn't, it was too much. We all just stood there. It was getting dark outside. The curtains needed closing. Mikey came in yawning and climbed into the bed, too tired to realise something was up.

There was a loud bang on the street door downstairs, a thumping over and over again. We all jumped. Mum's eyes looked wild.

'If it's that Biddy Moss back for more, I'll have her, I bloody will.'

We all stood still to listen. Mrs No-Teeth took ages to get to the door, she must have been in bed already. We heard her raised voice, she wasn't happy. Then footsteps on the stairs. Heavy footsteps. And someone barged into the bedsitter, we heard them in the hall. The door of the bedroom swung open.

Dad. He stood there with his hand on the doorknob, pissed out of his head and hadn't shaved for days. He wiped his mouth with the back of his hand and looked at us all.

'What's this shit hole then?' he growled.

'What's this, Mum? It's got bones in it.'

Flo could feel herself sinking. Coming back to Tilbury made Monday's seem unreal. She'd been kidding herself: she thought she could do well, have a better life, whatever that meant. *Maslow's hierarchy of needs*, that was a laugh. It was something that posh, rich women talked about over their Singapore slings, not the likes of her struggling to keep a family going. She didn't have the luxury of aiming high, she had enough trouble keeping things together at Maslow's lowest level, down near the dirt on the floor.

Fred was back. In a way it was a relief. She didn't have to bear the shame of being on her own with the kids any more. With her career at Monday's down the khazi, she had given a fleeting thought to her old dream about going to Australia on the migrant ship with the ten-pound poms. But with Jeanie having a baby, for god's sake, that meant Australia was definitely off the cards. If Flo was honest with herself, it never really was on the cards. She hadn't filled in the migration application before. Even if they had let her go without Fred, would she really have had the guts to leave him? Go it alone, with all the stares and whispers that go with the territory of a mother separated from her husband. She realised now that it had all been a fantasy, putting her shilling away every week in her secret Oxo tin, it was like doing the pools, it had given her hope of change even though the chances of it happening were a thousand to one. Now they were stuck in the tiny bedsitter for God knew how long and their priorities had changed. Fred had to get work, Flo and Babs did too. They'd only be able to get somewhere better to live if they were all working.

'It's scrag-end stew, love, just eat it, will you?'

She was scrimping already, afraid to run out of money. She smirked ruefully to herself when she thought that just a couple of weeks before she'd been hoping for that Electromatic washing machine and spin dryer she'd seen on the back of the *Mirror*. Forty-nine guineas it was, and no more deposit needed on the never-never. Chance would be a fine thing. They'd given the television back to the shop. They were back where they'd started. She was being punished for getting above herself, punished for getting rid of the baby, she should have kept it, managed somehow. It would be due about now. There wouldn't be much to give it, but she'd have loved it.

Maybe Fred was right. They were where they belonged. He sat there with them, picked a shard of bone off his tongue and looked at it with interest. He was still in his post-bender sorry state. In a couple of days he'd be back to all-out drinking and belly-aching. Flo silently wished a bone would lodge in his throat and do them all a favour.

'Going down the Labour Exchange today then, love?' she asked him.

His body twitched with irritation.

'Well, I dunno, do you think they've got a job for me then?'

'You've gotta try, haven't you, love?'

'So have you then.'

'Yeah, I know that, don't I?'

'Oh, you know that, do ya?' He looked at her like she was a piece of shit on his shoe. She hadn't done a thing to deserve that.

'Another bone, Mum,' said Mikey.

'Yes, Michael,' she snapped. 'There's bones in the stew all right, I'm trying to save money, aren't I? We haven't got any work, have we?'

'I suppose you'd rather we was still at Monday's? With those stuck-up toffs, eh?' said Fred, with a sneer.

'What do you mean, who's stuck-up?'

'All of them, think they're something special.'

'Why, because they're trying to better themselves, have nice things?'

'You said it.'

'They're not toffs, Fred, they're all reaching up together, everyone wants those things if they can.'

'Well, I'm glad we're back here, this is where we belong.'

'Yeah, the docks is like an island, it's behind the times, at least Monday's is moving on.'

'You want banging up in Runwell, you do, you need some electric in the head, woman. We've *always* lived here, I dunno what I was thinking, getting a job over there.' He picked up his bowl, drank up the last few spoonfuls of stew and belched. 'I'm off out.'

'Yeah, that's right, go and spend our little bit of money on drink.'

She knew she'd gone too far, she was lucky he wasn't already drunk. He stared at her, a warning, before he stomped out and down the stairs.

'Here, Mum, look, get a candle.'

Mikey had finished his stew and was calling from the bedroom. He held the bed mattress up by the corner, peered down underneath. Where the headboard slotted into the iron-sprung base there was a nest of bed bugs, squirming.

'Get us a candle, Mum, I'll kill them,' Mikey said with glee.

'Babs? Light a candle and bring it here,' Flo called through to the other room.

Mikey dripped hot wax on to the bugs, enjoyed watching them struggle for life, his eyes wide when they stopped struggling and went still, just floated along in the molten wax.

Flo, Babs and Mikey trudged out to the Labour

310

Exchange. No one spoke. When any of the neighbours passed them there were small nods of the head but no smiles. The Blundells knew they were under scrutiny. A large advert was pasted up on the billboard next to the Ritz cinema. *Life's better with the Conservatives, don't let Labour ruin it,* with a picture of a smiling family washing their new car. It made Flo think of Carl, who'd probably talk about Macmillan and the election. He seemed so far away now, like she hadn't even met him. She had her own problems to think about, never mind voting.

Jeanie was having a baby, and wouldn't even talk about it. Fifteen, sixteen she'd be. Fred hadn't realised yet, when he did, there'd be hell to pay. Jeanie was just a child herself, an angry toddler, kicking out at everything. And no husband. It gave Flo the chills. She thought again of Maggie and it made her feel sick the way she'd been sent packing like that, as though Maggie had flicked away an annoying insect. At least if they were still at Monday's they'd have a better chance of coping, she might not have a churning ball of dread in her stomach. She'd never tell Fred what happened – Maggie's betrayal – give him the satisfaction. It was all pie in the sky, she wished she'd never met Maggie. She wished the factory had burned down.

17

The kids in the street played conkers, I watched them from the window. We'd been back at the docks for three months. It was early November and the weather had really turned, there was a chill in the air and a dampness that came off the river and clung to my shoulders. I was getting bigger, my belly felt so tight and my chest really sore but at least I had stopped being sick. I craved food now, any food, especially chips, hot and greasy with lots of salt. Mum and Babs had cleaning jobs in the Tilbury hotel on the river. They went off early every day. Babs always moaned about cleaning up people's shit but Mum didn't say anything, even though I knew she hated it.

I wasn't allowed out, in case people saw I was expecting. I was mad about that, the new term had started and I was missing my lessons. But at least I had my college books so I could study at home. I thought about buying a cheap wedding ring from Woolworths and sneaking out to the college, but Mum was always checking up on me. Dad didn't know about it yet. He asked why I wasn't working and Mum said I had girl's problems. Dad was drinking again, although I don't think he'd ever really stopped. He'd already got the sack from a labouring job, then he started to badger Stan down the docks for work but Stan wasn't having any of it. Then he got a job as a coal man. Came in every night black as the ace of spades, with pink holes for eyes, wearing that black leather vest. Pissed off he was, dirty work he said. Honest work, Mum said. He'd find out about me sooner or later. Mum kept shooing me off when he was around but he'd find out soon enough. There wasn't anywhere to hide in that damn small flat.

The baby. I didn't want to think about it, didn't know what I was gonna do. Mum asked me about it every day: who was the boy? How did I feel? It wasn't a baby to me, just an uncomfortable bump that made me walk funny. Mum wanted me to keep it and get married. That was the last of my options. It would be the end for me. What else was there? I just studied my books and tried not to think about it.

Dad was already sitting in his chair reading his racing pages when Mum and Babs got home from work and Mikey was back from school. We were all waiting for our tea. Mum rolled up her sleeves and started on the spuds. Babs moped about, she was pining for Jim. They had met up a couple of times at a dance in Grays, but she said his dad was sending him away for the rest of his sixth form. Jim told her his dad had beaten him for writing messages in the factory. I didn't like to say anything about that. Serves him right anyway.

There wasn't anywhere quiet to talk to Babs in that bedsitter, there wasn't even enough room for us all to sleep. When Dad turned up he chucked us kids out the bed so from then Babs slept on the settee, I was on a mattress on the sitting-room floor and Mikey slept on the floor in the bedroom.

'Jeanie, get the plates out will you, love?'

I tutted, she could see I was looking at my books, why couldn't Mikey do it for once? Dad glanced over his paper and stuck out his leg to kick me with his toe. My books slipped on to the floor when I got up. I bent down to get them and I didn't mean to, but I winced with pain because my belly was so tight and underneath it felt weird, and I knew I straightened up like an old lady but I couldn't help it. I only had my nightie on, and when I held my books against me I suppose they sort of sat on top of my big belly and made it stand out. Out the corner of my eye I saw Dad scrunch his paper into the side of his chair and lean forwards to look at me. I turned away from him to go and put my books down somewhere but all of a sudden he grabbed my arm really roughly and pulled me round to face him.

He got up out of his chair and knocked my books away out of my hands. I wobbled on the spot, scared stiff. Mum heard the books smack on the ground and looked up from the stove. Everyone stood stock still. Dad straightened my nightie down at the front, I looked down and my belly was gigantic.

'Look at me,' he said.

As soon as my eyes met his, he knew for sure. There was only a second. His right hand was the size of a dinner plate. It hit me round the side of my face and the force knocked me backwards. I fell into the sideboard and on to my knees on the floor. Mum leapt forwards, screamed *No* but he just pulled me up to standing.

'You little whore.' He hardly raised his voice,

314

seemed to relish saying the words. 'Whose is it? Tell me, I'll make sure he does the right thing.'

He stood there waiting for an answer. He'd belt me again if I didn't say anything.

'James Monday,' I said.

'What? No it's not, you liar.' It was Babs shouting. Mrs No-Teeth banged on her ceiling and we all shut up for a minute.

'James Monday, the boss's son, eh? Well, I never,' said Dad, stepping backwards. He sort of chuckled and rolled a cigarette, thought about it a bit.

Maybe I should have left it at that but I didn't want him to think there was anything in it for him. 'No, it wasn't James Monday, you bloody drunken fool, I'm never telling you who it is.'

He jerked like someone had slapped him.

'What the—' He dropped his half-rolled fag and came at me, punched me in the chest so hard that I blacked out. I must have fallen down but all I remember was his fist hitting my chest bone like a steam express. When I came round Mum was leaning over me.

'You all right, love?' she said, peering into my face. I didn't know why *she* was crying. 'He's gone out.'

I nodded. It felt like a ton of bricks had fallen on me. The first thing I could think was wasn't the fire in the grate big, it was blazing away like we were rich or something. The second thing I thought was I wonder if Dad had done me a favour. I put my hand up my nightie and brought it out, but there wasn't any blood and I didn't feel any pain in my belly so I guess the hiding he'd given me hadn't really helped.

Mum got me up on to the settee and put the kettle on. I stared into the fire, I hated him so much I couldn't even say. But I wouldn't let him bother me, what could he do to me now? I noticed something in the flames and peered closer, got off the settee and over by the fireplace. There was something green burning in there, looked like green cardboard, and then I saw a stack of white paper burning up, curling away all black and charred, and I grabbed the coal shovel and got it under a big lump, pushed it up and over the grate on to the hearth where it thumped down in a rush of orange sparks. My college books. He had burned my books.

'Jeanie? Where you going?'

Flo banged the teapot down when Jeanie pulled on her coat and went for the door. 'Come back, love,' she called down the stairs, but her voice broke. Where was she going? Fred bashing her like that when she was in the family way.

'Jean?' she called down the stairs again but the front door slammed. Flo let out a loud howl of anguish. 'Oh, god!'

'Oh just leave her, the vicious little bitch,' said Babs, still resenting Jeanie for pinning her pregnancy on Jim. 'He should send her off to Runwell like he said he would.'

'Oh god, Babs, she might do anything. And someone might see she's showing. Sort that out.' She gestured towards the smouldering book that Jeanie had turned out of the fire on to the hearth. 'Dump the tealeaves on it.'

Flo grabbed her coat and stumbled down the stairs. Her heel caught the doorstep and her foot buckled sideways. Jeanie was down the end of the street going into the phone box and Flo started to sprint, trying to ignore the pain of her twisted ankle. As she reached the public booth Jeanie was pushing her pennies into the slot and when she wrenched open the door, Jeanie was talking to the operator. Flo tore the phone receiver out of Jeanie's hand and rattled it down on to the cradle hook.

'What you doing, Jeanie? You scared the life out of me.'

Jeanie turned on Flo, looked like she was going to open her mouth to speak, then didn't. She pushed Flo out of the phone box so she could get through, and walked back down the road towards the flat. Flo stared after her, wondered who she'd been trying to call. She was angry and up to no good, that was certain. On top of the little metal shelf that held the phone book, Flo saw a slip of paper. Jeanie's handwriting. *Ministry of Labour and National Service.*

Flo stared at it for a minute. Ministry of Labour and National Service. She gave a little gasp and her heart pulsed a thick beat. 'Jesus Christ,' she said under her breath. 'She was going to shop him.'

She held on to the door of the phone box to steady herself, tried to think of any other reason Jeanie would have written that down but she couldn't. Jeanie was going to shop Fred for dodging National Service. She would report her own father to the authorities? They'd make him sign

317

up, do his service, he was terrified of that, he wouldn't do it, he'd likely get banged up in prison. Thank God she had got to the phone box in time. It didn't bear thinking about.

She let the door of the phone booth go and scuffed her way back down the road. Her legs were heavy and the road seemed to stretch away for ever. A single seagull rose into the air with a screech and dove down again at the rooftops. Up in the air and back down. The other houses in the street, the neighbours, the rumble of a ship's horn in the docks, nothing else featured. She was on a long road in her own little pocket of foul air where everything went bad. She scrunched up the slip of paper so tight her knuckles went white.

Fred still hadn't come home when Flo crawled into bed that night. She was careful not to wake Mikey, asleep on the floor, and the girls in the sitting room. Babs was asleep but Jeanie lay there with her eyes open. And Flo couldn't sleep either. Mikey's soft breathing would normally have soothed her. But not tonight. She kept re-living the moment when Fred had punched Jeanie in the chest. A pregnant girl, punched her so hard that she blacked out. She couldn't shake it out of her thoughts. Of course he'd gone out after that, to find solace in a glass of wallop somewhere because he knew he'd done wrong, lost his temper again. She knew that most men give their wives a swipe now and then, the man of the house and all that, and Fred had given the kids an occasional slap when they'd been playing up. But a full force punch in the chest? He was sober too. What did that mean? That it wasn't the drink making him hit them, it was just him.

Flo's mind flitted back to the young wives club and Tabby, who had got divorced. That wasn't something people down the docks did. When you got married it was for life, for better or for worse. For worse in her case. And if it wasn't going too well you just got on with it, that was life. But she'd always thought it was the drink that made him violent, that if he could just stop the drinking they'd be all right.

She wanted to kill him sometimes. Of course she did. When she did the washing up she'd hold the big kitchen knife and run her fingers over the blade in the water, imagine herself pushing it into his back one day. She'd do it when the kids were out. She'd get the knife sharpened first, so it would go in smoothly, like cutting soft butter. The fantasy helped sometimes. Then he'd come in and demand his dinner or demand his rights in bed and she knew she'd never do it, she'd always just soldier on, for the family. Her old mum's words haunted her, *Stay together, that's top priority.* She and Fred had been together a long time. They had a bond and that wasn't something you just picked up or put back down, it was something physical, a padding around the heart. To pull away from that takes guts, you have to cut it out of yourself or you can't carry on. But to stay with it takes more than guts. It takes a special kind of resolve, a selfless determination. Not just anyone can see through a marriage like that.

She tensed at the sound of the key in the lock of the street door and heavy footsteps on the stairs, the flat door opening. Flo's thoughts shattered and fell in pieces. She turned over in bed, faced the wall, drew her knees up to her chest and shut her eyes tight. Fred's shoes scraped over the floor in the other room, she could feel his bulk approach, he was in the bedroom, she heard the zip of his fly, he took his clothes off and dropped them on to the floor. The stench of beer and fags as he knelt on his side of the bed and leant over her. She kept her eyes closed.

'You awake?' his voice rasped. She didn't answer. Maybe he'd roll over and drop off. She hoped he wouldn't climb on top of her. She had endured it enough times but tonight she didn't think she could bear it. The bed bounced and creaked as he shifted position. She felt him up against her back. He reached down under the covers, pulled her nightie up and her knickers down. He shook her arm to wake her but she kept still. It wasn't the first time he'd done it when he thought she was asleep. To him she was a thing to use when he wanted. He would take his marital rights and not hear a word against it, otherwise he'd raise his hand to her. There was no love in it, no pleasure for her, it was a disgusting, humiliating job. Part of being a wife.

Lying on his side he got into her from behind, pulled her hips up and backwards to get her right, and he pounded away, grunting, the bed springs creaking in time. Flo started to cry, the tears ran and she couldn't stop them. She scrunched up her face and kept quiet, didn't want Mikey to wake up. Every time it happened, the new pain just piled on to the old. Not just the physical pain, where it still hurt from the abortion, but all the times she had just gone along with the rough treatment, the lack of love. He had kicked the life out of her – you don't treat someone you love like that.

He reached his limit and rolled away – left her knickers down with the wet seeping out on to her leg. She could hardly breathe, tried to calm down so he wouldn't hear the sobs that choked her. Once he started to snore, she wiped her face on her nightie and slipped out of bed, pulled the enamel bowl off the wash stand on to the floor, poured in some water from the jug and squatted over it to sluice him out of her.

In the dark she lay there, staring up at the ceiling, listened to the loud tick of the wall clock in the other room. She hated him sometimes, yes, of course. But in some twisted way they needed each other, she didn't know if it was some kind of sick love or what it could be called. In any case, he stamped all over any chance they had of making things better, like he didn't even care. And he'd been sober when he hit Jeanie, it didn't make sense. The pressure around her eyes from crying was terrible, like her face would blow apart.

She couldn't help him, he wasn't interested in her help, he never was. It was like a sudden punch to the stomach to realise it. All the years she had felt so sorry for him, his mum and dad. But she had lost her dad too. A month after Fred's mum had walked into that pub, Flo's dad had died in service. One day she was waiting for his next letter and the next she was told he'd never be coming back. Flo remembered how she couldn't understand that he didn't exist any more. Her mum had said she'd see him in heaven and she'd grown to rely on that idea, especially as she couldn't talk to Fred about it, what with his mum gone just a month before and how he was waiting for his dad to come home. She had suppressed her grief, pushed it away to deal with later. A sob escaped her lips. She'd never been allowed to grieve for her father, she'd given herself over to Fred and he didn't give a damn. She was going round in circles, her kindness was only helping him carry on doing the same thing. It was hopeless to imagine anything else.

She'd rather be dead than spend the rest of her days like this. It was a despair she hadn't fully considered before and it frightened her, like she was trapped inside that clicking press at the factory, the vice coming down, the knives cutting her into pieces. But the thought of not having to worry any more, not having to stay strong for the children. The children. Just the thought of leaving them sparked something within her. Something else elbowed forward through these dark thoughts, a clarity offered itself gently to her. She *could* give up, let him win. Or she could make a decision to find something of herself deep down, something that flickered in the dead fire, the half-burned coals damp and black. There, underneath, a tiny ember still alight. She could make a decision to blow on it, see if it glowed. Carl. She needed to talk to Carl.

The following night Flo waited for Fred to eat his tea. She stood at the window, stared down into the street. Arthur over the road was on his knees with his little Terry, making a go-cart together out of an old pram chassis and an apple box. Little Terry's face was bright and interested, Arthur frowned with concentration as he tied on some wire. When the steering rope was nailed into place, father and son looked at each other for a moment, both smiled. Flo let the net curtain drop back. Fred had never played with Mikey like that. Not in Tilbury and not at Monday's. Living somewhere else didn't change things. Her problems just followed her around. She watched Fred shovel his food in, then stand up and go out to the pub without saying goodbye.

'I'm going out for a bit, love, keep an eye on Mikey.'

Babs frowned. 'Where you going?'

'Just got to pop out, won't be long.'

It was cold out. The wind off the river rushed between the houses, it picked up Flo's coat collar and dashed the brown autumn leaves against her shins. She was glad she had a scarf around her hair, anyway she'd need to keep her head down at Monday's; people didn't forget the shame of others in a hurry. The train journey seemed to take for ever.

When she stepped down on to the platform she felt a sting of disgrace as she remembered leaving with the kids in the summer, watching everyone else go off on holiday. She could smell leather in the air and she realised how much she had missed the place. It was late, around nine, dark enough to scuttle along the main road unseen. She came into the quadrangle with the factory buildings looming up on the right side. The silhouetted poplar trees swayed in the wind, their leaves had dropped for the winter, but they stood tall and stayed strong. She headed for the college building. The full-time students lived on the top floor and she hoped she'd be able to see Carl. She didn't know what to say to him but clung to her conviction that he had his head on his shoulders. She trusted him, he was something real and true.

Standing at the door to the college, she remembered Carl talking about the formidable Mrs Brown, the college warden, who ran a tight ship. Her hand shook as she rang the bell. She'd just ask to see Carl, she'd say it was important.

After a while the door opened and there stood Carl himself. Framed by the dim hall light behind him, in his shirtsleeves and slacks, his pipe in his teeth and a lopsided grin like nothing could surprise him.

'Well, hello, Mrs Blundell.'

Flo could have cried. She wanted to but swallowed hard.

'Hello, Carl, how are you then?'

'Well, apart from losing my partner in crime and having to suffer this dull college with a bunch of upstarts, I'm pretty good. How's your good self?'

She nodded, in lieu of speaking. Pressed her lips together and frowned, tried to stay calm.

'Like that is it?' He said it softly, with so much sympathy it was too much for her. She dropped her chin to her chest and screwed up her eyes, the tears squeezing out on to her cheeks. 'Come on,' he said. 'You're lucky, the formidable Mrs Brown has gone off on a coach trip to quick-step around Streatham Locarno, so I can let you in without being strung up and having my breakfast liberties threatened.'

He held the door for her as she came into the tiled hallway.

'My room's up here,' he said, gesturing towards the stairs. 'Otherwise it's the common room but there are a couple of lads playing cards in there, so we might not be able to talk...?'

Flo hesitated then followed him up the stairs, hoping no one would see.

'So, Supermac got another term, then?' he said over his shoulder. 'People evidently like buying things – maybe they think the union bosses are fat enough, huh?'

She didn't like to say she hadn't voted. It was the last thing on her mind.

'Welcome to my little palace.' He held the door for her. It was a small room with a single bed, a desk and a wardrobe, spick and span, with a little wireless and a pile of books on the desk. Carl drew out the desk chair for her and perched on the bed himself. It was quiet. Flo shuffled in her seat, looked around at the empty walls.

'We're not allowed to put pictures up. It's like a school dorm, but mustn't grumble, I suppose.' He smiled and relit his pipe. She took off her headscarf and lit a cigarette, crossed her legs, didn't know what to say.

'What's up then, little lady?'

'I dunno, I'm sorry, maybe I shouldn't have come. Things are a bit...'

He waited.

'Fred found us and he's working, but drinking, and Jean's in the family way.' She looked at her lap, she hadn't meant to tell him about Jeanie.

'I'm really sorry to hear that, Flo.'

'And, I dunno, I know I wasn't much good at it and that's probably why Mr Monday let me in in the first place but I miss being in the college.'

'Hang on, not from where I'm sitting, you were pretty super on the training course, I thought you had real potential.'

'Did you?'

'Of course, and it was a real shame that you had to leave after all your hard work.'

Flo bit her lip. 'But there's no worrying about it now, the Mondays don't want us here, Fred made sure of that.'

'Yes, that Fred of yours, he's a real character, that's for sure. The Mondays certainly don't want *him* back after what he did.' Carl puffed on the pipe and held Flo's gaze. 'But I'm not so sure they wouldn't consider having *you* back.'

Flo's heart rippled in her chest. 'What?'

He shrugged. 'You don't have to live on the estate to work here. No harm in asking, is there? What have you got to lose?'

'Nothing.'

'What was that club you went to, with Mrs Monday?'

'The young wives club?'

'Yes, that's it, I reckon you should appeal to them. Didn't they have something to do with why you were at the college anyway?'

Flo nodded. 'They were the ones who put me up to it. But I already asked Maggie, after the fire, and she more or less told me to get lost.'

Carl nodded and sucked his pipe, looked into

the bowl and relit it. 'Well, some time has passed, why don't you give it a try?'

'Do you really think so, Carl?'

'Yes, I *really* think so,' he said, laughing at her. 'And I've got something here for you.'

Flo frowned as he got off the bed and opened the wardrobe door, rummaged in a cubby hole. He held something out to her. She took Mikey's football cards from his hand, disbelieving, fanned them out with her thumb, all signed.

'I talked to one of the West Ham lads, got him to take the other cards back to the club to get all of them signed, and he posted them back to me. Pretty decent of him really.'

'Thanks, Carl,' she whispered. 'I don't know what to say.'

'Say you'll go to that club of yours and give it a try. You're a great lady, Flo Blundell, I hate to see you down on your luck.'

Flo bit her lip and nodded, gripped the football cards until the edges scored her palm, needing to feel the pain that made it all real.

18

'No one'll want you now, used goods you are.'

Dad shovelled barley stew into his gob, using a slice of bread for a spade.

'Fred, that's not nice.' Mum was being brave for once, talking back to him.

'Opening her legs at fifteen's not nice. Look at

the state of her, having a kid and no husband, what a fucking disgrace.' He didn't seem to notice that the stew dripped down his shirt off his chin. I would have got up but I was starving, I couldn't get enough food.

'I was fifteen, Fred, remember?'

'And if she does find a boy she won't be able to get married in white. Didn't think about that, did you, when you let him have his way? Who was it then, tell me, I'd love to have a little word with him.'

He could hit me again if he wanted, I wouldn't tell him about Skylon. Dad would make him marry me and I didn't want that, why would I? They were all staring at me, I didn't care, let them. The stew tasted so good, I finished mine and got hold of the pot, scraped out some more.

'Oh look, and she'll be like the back end of a bus with all the food she's putting away.'

Every day they were on at me. I'd learned to switch off from it.

'A fallen woman in the family, bloody lovely that is. You're not keeping it without getting married, my girl. You can go to a mothers' home and give it away.'

'Fred, no.' Mum's face went white. She got up to clear the plates away.

'And don't let me see you going out of this flat, not unless it's for the right reason, you hear me?'

I nodded. If I didn't nod he'd have lost his temper. Drunken pig. I didn't tell him I was think-ing about what to do. I was over seven months gone, too late to get rid of it. Maybe I should have risked that after all. If I had the baby I couldn't stay with the family without getting married, like Dad said. I could have it and leave, but unmarried mothers couldn't get housed so where would I live? What did I want with a baby anyway? I couldn't even think of it like that, even though it was moving inside of me, waking me up in the night, bloody uncomfortable.

'When we getting a Christmas tree, Dad?' Mikey brought his paper chains to the table, started gluing them together with flour paste.

'I dunno. We'll see.'

Someone knocked on the street door and we heard Mrs No-Teeth answer it, then light footsteps coming up. It was that old midwife, I bet. Interfering as usual.

'Midwife,' she called out as she opened the door and walked straight in. All done up in her starched uniform ready to come prodding and poking around. Dad saw her and got up to go, it wasn't done for men to be around.

'The Sally Army band are out, lovely Christmas carols,' she said, coughing into a hankie. 'Oh but the blasted fog.'

'They better not come knocking here,' said Dad on his way out.

The midwife ignored him. 'How you been then, my dear?'

I shrugged and looked at the enormous mole on her chin. 'Let's have a look at you then.'

We went through into the bedroom. I laid down and she got out her ear trumpet thing and listened for a heartbeat. I couldn't think of a little person in there with a heart, it just wasn't real.

'Go and get me a sample then, dear, if you still

329

won't come down to clinic.' She raised her eyebrows at me. I took the little cup she gave me, went down to the freezing back garden to the khazi and tried to aim into it, even though I couldn't see down there any more. It was dark in there too. I felt blind for the pieces of newspaper hanging from a string off the wall, imagined old Mrs No-Teeth cutting out those squares thinking how clever she was to save money.

I shut the bedroom door when I came back with the piss pot, Mum was trying to poke her nose in. The midwife tested it with a little burner and nodded her approval.

'All ready for Baby then? You'll need a little crib, won't you, dear, and some little clothes?'

'Maybe I won't.'

She spun round on her toe and cursed when she burnt her finger on the test tube. It was the first time I'd spoken to her.

'I wanted to ask you about them homes for mothers.'

She stood very still and fixed her face in the right way before she spoke with a funny high-pitched voice.

'Mother and baby home, dear?'

'Yes, that's right.'

'You don't want to keep Baby, dear?'

'Nope I don't. What do I want with a baby?'

I had to get rid of it somehow, didn't I? I was going to college to get my A levels, I wanted to be a doctor. Giving it away was all I could do.

'Well, have you thought about how you'll feel when you've seen your baby? It's often very difficult for a first-time mother to imagine how she'll feel.'

'No, I know how I'll feel. I don't want it.'

'I'll need to speak to your mother.'

'No. It's up to me. I don't want you talking to them.'

'Well, you'll have to talk to your parents about it, you're a minor and they need to know, then I'll talk to them once you have.'

I shrugged. I weren't gonna tell them, was I? Mum'd go mad.

'Just tell me where to go and I'll talk to them about it.'

She nodded and pressed her lips together, turned to her bag and wrote something down on a bit of paper for me.

'All right then, love, how you feeling?' Flo sat in the armchair knitting, tried again to talk to Jeanie, but there was no answer.

'Want me to set your hair for you, Jeanie?' Even Babs was being nice. But Jeanie didn't respond, she wouldn't talk to anyone, she just got bigger and bigger and no one knew what she was thinking, how she felt about the baby, nothing.

'Look, love.' Flo held up half of a tiny white cardigan. 'White, so's it can be for a boy or a girl, see? Then, when we know which, I'll make some blue or pink too. I'll love it, I will, making things for the new baby, it'll be lovely, won't it?'

Flo didn't know if it'd be lovely, but she wanted to try to draw Jeanie out. It wasn't healthy, bottling everything up like that.

'It'll be such a precious little thing, you'll see, we'll all chip in to help, won't we, Babs?'

'Yeah, course.' Babs frowned. Flo could tell she was worried about her sister.

Mikey burst in through the door of the flat.

'Mum, it's the telephone for you.' He collapsed on to the settee, gasping for breath. Flo jumped up, threw her knitting down in the seat behind her and ran out in her slippers, down the stairs and up the street. Four people were queuing for the public telephone, they gave Flo impatient looks, one of them mumbled *Get a move on.* She pulled open the heavy iron door and reached for the receiver.

'Hello?'

'Flo? It's Lil.'

'Oh, Lil. Lovely to hear you.'

'Look, the pips are gonna go soon. Carl said for me to call and tell you it's the young wives club on tonight, it's at Maggie's as usual.'

'Oh, right, thanks, love, I'll' – the pips started – 'I might see you there, love.' There was a click on the line and the phone went dead. Flo replaced the receiver and stared at the black Bakelite phone for a few seconds until the next person in the queue tapped on the window with a penny.

Flo was on pins the rest of the day. Carl had fixed it up for her, the least she could do was go. But to face the women in the club after what Fred had done, the thought of it made her stomach churn. And the last time she'd seen Maggie was so awful, what if she didn't even let her in? She had to chance it. If Carl thought it was worth trying then she'd try.

At teatime the fog came down thicker than ever. Flo peered out of the window wondering if it was a sign she shouldn't go. Fred hadn't come in yet, he was still out with the coal truck. Either that or out drinking – he'd drink himself to death.

'I've left your dad's tea in the oven, love.'

Babs jerked up her head. 'Why, where you going, Mum?'

'Never you mind, I'm off out for a bit, I won't be long. You stay in with your brother, you hear?'

'When we getting a Christmas tree, Mum?'

'Oh, Mikey, I dunno, ask your dad to get one from the woods.'

Flo tied a scarf around her hair and pulled on her coat with the rabbit fur collar. She'd treated herself when she was at Monday's and now it just served to remind her of what she had lost. It was getting really cold out. Lucky it wasn't snowing otherwise the train wouldn't run. It had been a few weeks since she'd seen Carl, but she'd thought about what he'd said, wondered whether he meant it, that she'd done well at the college.

She hurried along Calcutta Road on to Station Road, ducked aside when she saw the coal truck up ahead. Fred must have been making the last of his deliveries. It was difficult to tell the coal-men apart, covered in soot and built like brick shithouses, wearing flat caps and black leather waistcoats. She saw the profile of his face in the light of the street lamp, a sack on his shoulder, he bent down to lift the coal cover by a front door, nudged the sack forwards, the black lumps tumbling out and hitting the chute with a deep rumble. Flo tutted. A decent day's work didn't mean anything to Fred. He'd soon make trouble, get fired and that would be that.

On the steam train to Monday station, she wondered whether there was any chance that Maggie would be pleased to see her. Perhaps it had been wishful thinking on Flo's part that she thought they were friends. With a stab of resentment Flo wondered whether Maggie had been playing with her all along. The train pulled in, the fog wasn't as bad there but it was raining. Flo ducked her head, felt it soak through on to her shoulders. Looking down at her wet shoes and clutching her coat about her, she picked up the pace and half ran, half walked. No one was about. All tucked up in their lovely houses, nice and warm with the central heating and indoor bathroom. The lights of the hotel shone in the puddles at the side of the road and Flo turned left, along the poplar-lined avenue to the Monday Mansion. She remembered the first time she'd knocked on that door.

Flo wiped under her eyes with her finger, gave the maid her wet coat and scarf. When she stepped into the sitting-room doorway, the murmur of voices ceased and the women turned to look. There was a huge tree in the corner, heavy with glass baubles and velvet ribbons and candles everywhere. A Christmas party. Flo felt like turning on her heel and running away.

The usual faces: Tabby at the cocktail cabinet, Doreen and Alice, Dot, Liz and Carol, and Maggie perched on the side of the chaise, cigarette and drink in hand. She kept her composure but Flo could tell Lil hadn't mentioned that she might turn up.

'Flo, darling. What a lovely surprise. Come in,

come in, oh, look at you, soaked to the bone. Tabby, dear, whip something warming up for Flo at once.'

With Maggie's consent, everyone else chipped in.

'Oh, it's super to see you, Flo, how are you?' said Doreen, a little line of worry around her eyes.

Flo caught sight of Lil, on a settee between Doreen and Dot. She looked drawn and unwell.

'Blimey, Lil, you've had the baby.' With a start Flo realised she hadn't thought about Lil's baby, only her own. 'What is it, boy or girl? Sorry, love, I've been so caught up in everything I haven't had a chance to see you.'

'I'm all right thanks, Flo.'

Something wasn't right. Flo moved closer to Lil, Dot moved aside so she could sit down.

'And the baby?'

Lil worked hard to stay composed, the muscles in her face clenched as she chewed the inside of her cheeks.

'Not so good, love.'

'Why?'

'Crippled.' Lil whispered the word and looked at her hands twisting in her lap.

Flo put her own hands over Lil's.

'I'm sorry, Lil, I really am. Can I come and see you soon?'

Lil nodded and lit a cigarette, avoiding Flo's eyes.

Tabby strode over and handed Flo a drink.

'So how have you been, darling?' she said.

'Oh, all right.' Flo glanced at Lil and gulped her drink. 'Well, not brilliant. My Fred's found work but we're struggling a bit, Jean's not well...'

There was a silence. 'That's why I came. It's not that I haven't got work in Tilbury, I have. But I miss it here, my job and my training in the college. I loved working here and I miss it.'

The women looked at Maggie.

'Yes, that's why it's such a shame that your husband behaved so awfully, darling, spoiling your chances as well as his own.'

'Yeah, I know, he ruined it all for us, he loses his temper and it's not really anyone's fault, it's not my fault and it's not really his fault, it's just the way he's made.'

'Well, I can highly recommend divorce, Flo,' said Tabby, smiling around at everyone. But no one got the joke, it was in poor taste.

'It was you lot who put me up to the college in the first place, don't you think I deserve another chance? I didn't do anything wrong after all.'

Flo looked at Alice, who she expected might say something in her defence, but Alice just gave her a meek smile. It was like they were all waiting for something.

'Yes, Flo, we did encourage you to aim high here, and that's why working for Monday Leather is such a privilege.' Maggie lit a cigarette. She looked splendid in a cream silk skirt and blouse. 'All of our workers are supported and encouraged to do well, they are given the best benefits one can expect. And for all of that, we expect a high level of commitment in return. It stands to reason, does it not?'

Maggie looked at the other women, there was a general murmur of consent. Flo clutched her bag

336

to her and sat upright.

'Your husband's behaviour was *extraordinary* and almost jeopardised a very special and important relationship we have built with West Ham United football club. Do not underestimate the importance of a relationship like that, Flo. It takes years to build and gives our workers something to look forward to.'

Flo nodded, hoping Maggie would be able to forgive her all of that, she herself had forgiven Maggie's betrayal after all.

'But, Flo, it's not just your husband's behaviour that has brought shame on the company.'

Flo frowned and met Maggie's eyes.

'We have been under investigation by the police. We have had the local newspaper here asking questions. Do you know why?'

Flo shook her head.

'Your daughter, Jean, had been very busy causing trouble for us in the box-making department, did you know that?'

'What you talking about?' Flo looked at Lil, who gave a small smile of sympathy. This is what they'd all been talking about then.

'Well, I'll tell you, Flo. The police came here, *here*, asking to speak to Mr Monday and myself about our son James. They accused him of sending out messages in the shoeboxes, messages that said he and the other workers here are kept as ... I can hardly bear to say it ... *slaves*.'

'What?' Flo laughed, she couldn't help it, it was ridiculous.

'You may laugh, Flo, but the police had a duty to search the factory, to question our workers, to question *my son*. It was humiliating beyond words.'

'But why did James do it?'

'*James?* It wasn't my James, heaven help us, it was your Jean, writing falsehoods and sending them out in the shoe-boxes. One of her co-workers had seen her do it.'

'Oh, shit.'

'Yes, quite.'

Flo cast around for something to say. 'I don't know what she was playing at, Mags, I'm really sorry, she can't have realised the trouble she was causing.'

'Oh dear, I think I have a headache coming on. Ladies, would you mind if we said goodbye for today?'

There was a collective murmured *No, of course* and a shuffling of handbags and ashtrays as the women got up to leave the party prematurely. Maggie left the room, leaving them to be shown out by the maid. Flo watched her leave, annoyed at having been dismissed, again. She mouthed *Sorry* and smiled awkwardly at anyone who caught her eye and went out to wait on the drive in the dark rain for Lil.

'Fancy a quick cuppa?'

'That'd be lovely, Lil.' Flo gave her a smile of gratitude, eternally grateful for Lil's loyalty.

They walked off arm in arm against the weather, past the hotel and turned right into one of the residential streets, Queen Elizabeth Avenue.

'So you got a house, then? That's good.'

Lil looked sheepish. 'Yes, love, sorry, Flo, it's your old house. They gave it to us when you left, seeing as I was expecting and all.'

Flo bit her lip and nodded, fished in her bag for her pack of cigarettes, then decided against trying to light one in the rain.

Sure enough, Lil turned into the garden gate of number thirty-eight.

'Looks like you've had a go at the garden then?' said Flo, making light. The garden looked a lot tidier than when they were there. She glanced left to Mr Ductle's next door. The burnt topiary cockerel had been cut down.

The hallway had been newly papered with big lime green and grey daisies, not Flo's taste, and Lil's furniture in the sitting room changed the look of the place, which made it a little easier for Flo to be in there. They had their Christmas decorations up, sprigs of holly and mistletoe and a little tree in the corner with balls of cotton wool for snow. Bowls of chestnuts and marshmallows sat on the sideboard and Ted was in his armchair smoking a pipe and watching television.

'Hello, Ted, how are you, love?'

He jumped in his seat. 'Flo? Well I never.' His face clouded over, he resumed puffing on his pipe and let his gaze wander back to the small screen.

'Come on, love, let me show you the baby.' Lil led Flo up the stairs. In the front bedroom there was a little white crib next to Lil and Ted's bed. The women tiptoed over and peered inside. A tiny pink face stuck out of the white blankets.

'Ah, adorable, boy or girl?'

Lil's face was set in a frown. 'Girl.'

'What did you call her then?'

'Karen.'

'Ah, lovely.'

The baby stirred in her sleep, seemed to sense her mother and opened her eyes. Lil reached into the crib to lift her out bundled in a blanket. She perched on the bed with the baby in her lap and started to unwrap the swaddling.

Lil gave Flo an uneasy glance. Flo tried to smile and watched while the blanket was pulled away from the baby's little white sleeveless vest and nappy. She had no arms, just two little stumps below her shoulders. Flo gasped.

'When I had her, the midwife did that, made the same sound you just made. She took her away from me, over to the chest of drawers to check her over, tutting and clucking she was, then she brought her back and showed me. My heart sank, Flo, I couldn't believe it, that my baby could be so crippled, so ... spoilt. Me and Ted'd waited so long for her, years we've waited, we just wanted her to be perfect. I couldn't look at her at first. Then the midwife put her on me, made me take her.'

Lil lifted the baby away from the blanket and held her up against her chest, the baby nuzzled under her chin.

'She opened her eyes for the first time then and looked at me. She slipped straight into my heart, Flo, my little angel, and the love I felt was ... well, you know.'

Lil smiled, the most peaceful happy smile. Flo nodded and put her arm around her friend's shoulders, pressed her lips tight together and tried not to cry.

'She's perfect to me, Flo.'

'She's beautiful, Lil, really beautiful.'

Flo readied herself when Lil held the baby out to

her. She remembered holding Mikey, such an age ago, that perfect weight in her arms, as natural as anything, as if a woman would die if she never held her own baby. Flo *would* have been holding her own baby by then if she hadn't let the old missioner take it away. It was too much. Flo passed Karen back and Lil settled her into the crib, rocked her for a while and the women went down to the kitchen for a cup of tea.

Flo couldn't help but look at the Frigidaire while Lil boiled the kettle. There it was, in the corner, like a piece of white magic.

'I'm glad you're here, Lil, I'd rather you than anyone else.'

'Thanks, love, it is lovely.'

Flo wanted to tell Lil about Jeanie but stopped herself – all of Fred's talk about it shaming the family.

'So, what we gonna do about you then? Where you working?'

'Cleaning down Tilbury hotel. It's nothing like here though, Lil, I really miss it.'

'And Fred?'

'He's a coal man now but God knows how long it'll last, and we're staying in a tiny bedsitter and can't afford anything better yet, and Jeanie's not well, it's been hard ... sorry, love.'

Flo groped in her bag for her handkerchief.

'I wish you could get back in at Monday's, you'd be better off here.'

'Well, I tried, didn't I?' sniffed Flo, 'but Maggie's having none of it, she's really turned against me.'

'Yeah, she's a fickle one all right, you were her golden girl, weren't you? All that stuff with Fred and Jeanie, though, god, you've really got the odds against you.'

Both women sipped their tea.

'But, you know what?' Lil put her cup down on the saucer. 'You and Maggie were good friends, she had a real soft spot for you, I reckon you should go and see her on your own. You know what she's like when she's queening it over the club, she'd never want to lose face then.'

'I dunno, Lil. You reckon?'

'Yeah, I do. You know, why don't you go over there now? She'll be on her own and a bit tipsy, I bet she's thinking about you. Have a little chat, just the two of you, what have you got to lose?'

'Yeah, not a lot.' Flo didn't know whether to laugh or cry.

19

Maggie looked the picture of elegance, if not a little odd, lounging on the chaise. In one hand she held a whisky glass, with the other she stroked the fur coat that was draped around her shoulders. It was the coat that Flo had ordered on the telephone from Selfridges for Maggie's birthday, that she had taken delivery of in her office, had lifted out of the box with a gasp. A Norman Hartnell car coat, in blue fox, the most extravagant item Flo had ever touched.

'Hello again, Maggie. Happy Christmas.'

'Here's Flo,' Maggie slurred, wiped her mouth

with the side of her hand holding the glass. 'Come back to see Maggie, have you?'

As she spoke her head wobbled on her neck.

'Come and sit with Mags, I've been thinking about you, Flo.' She leant forward to pat the space on the chaise next to her legs.

Flo perched on the edge of the seat. Maggie scooted forwards to put her arm around Flo's shoulder.

'Can I get you a drink?' she said it right into Flo's face. The stench of alcohol got into Flo's mouth and down her throat. 'Sod Tabby's bloody cocktails. I prefer a drop of Scotch.' She held up her glass to show Flo, her eyebrows raised comically high. 'Single malt?'

Flo shrugged and gave a tiny nod. Maggie made a minimal effort to get up, and stopped when she realised her legs were penned in.

'Be a darling, would you?' She wriggled back into the fur and watched Flo pour her drink at the cocktail cabinet and resume her seat.

'So you came back to see me.' Maggie smiled into Flo's face. 'I miss you, Flo, miss our talks.'

'I miss you too, Mags, but I can't help wonder...'

Maggie's eyes searched hers, her head gave a tiny shake of anticipation.

'I can't help but wonder if you were ever really that bothered with me...'

Maggie pulled back in exaggerated shock.

'...if you ever believed I could do what you challenged me to do.'

'What on earth do you mean? Of course I believed in you, I bent over backwards for you, Flo.'

'Yeah and you chucked me aside just as quickly

as you took me in. It's almost like you were playing with me, Maggie. Or was it just the thought of my Babs and your James being together that you didn't like?' Flo stared hard with her eyebrows raised.

Maggie's smile vanished. 'I fail to see what that has to do with anything.'

'It wouldn't surprise me if getting me into that college was just a bit of a laugh for you and the others.'

Maggie bristled. 'I think you should leave, I'm tired.'

'Oh, that chestnut again?' Hot anger pumped through Flo, Maggie thought she was just an inconvenience, she could flick her hand and Flo would go away. 'Poor Queen Maggie is tired, after all her lounging around and drinking and playing games.'

'Well, if you don't like it, just get out.'

'Why don't you be honest with me? Don't I deserve that, or am I beneath you or something?'

'Don't be ridiculous.' Maggie gave a cruel laugh. 'I mean, it's not as if I bet against you or anything.' Her eyes sparkled, watching for Flo's reaction.

'You what?'

'Like I said, it was Tabby who bet you couldn't do it, not me, I bet *for* you. You see? I believed in you all along.'

'I might have known.' Flo snorted her derision. 'Who do you think you are, treating people like that? I'm just as much of a person as you are, Mags, for all your money and posh voice.' She thought for a second and laughed, relished saying it. 'You must be bored out of your mind.'

The look of outrage on Maggie's face.

'Who the hell...' She drew back her hand and aimed her palm at Flo's face but Flo grabbed her wrist before the slap was delivered. She held it there for a second, felt the bone and sinew beneath Maggie's skin, looked straight at the woman who could do so much for her but who sat there mad with drink and misplaced resentment. Maggie's face was loaded with spite, she wasn't accustomed to being spoken to in that manner but Flo wasn't going to be dismissed again.

Maggie yanked her arm away and slipped sideways, the glass in her other hand spilling whisky on to her cream silk skirt.

'Argh,' Maggie screeched, flapping at her skirt, but her eyes darted towards Flo. She was glad of the diversion and ready to play out the drama of it. They both jumped up off the seat, the fur coat falling from Maggie's shoulders. 'Bloody hell, look at it, ruined.' She shook the front of her skirt, pale brown and dripping. 'How dare you come here to judge me.' Her face coloured with anger. 'Get out, go on, get out.'

Flo stood her ground.

'You and your family, causing trouble. I wish none of you had ever come here.'

'You don't mean that.'

'Oh, don't I?' Maggie unzipped her skirt and let it fall to the ground. She bent to retrieve her fur and swung it back on to her shoulders. Wearing just the coat over her slip she wobbled in her heels over to the cocktail cabinet and poured herself another whisky, knocked it back in one, dabbed her mouth with her fingertips and stared at Flo.

Flo stared back at the woman she had thought was her friend. She looked like any pathetic drunk. It was in Flo's best interest to smooth things over with her, but as well as that, Flo still felt an affection for this woman. She was endearing in some way, she was *interesting* and Flo related to her despite their different backgrounds.

'I could forgive you all of that, Mags, I care about you. I also care about my *job*.'

Maggie calmed down a little, shook her head and mouthed something Flo couldn't hear, talking to herself. She rummaged on the top of the cabinet, found a pack of cigarettes and lit one.

'Oh, you and that bloody job. You're like a dog with a rag.' She seemed suddenly drained of energy, she sighed and sat down on one of the chairs, peered at Flo with her head tilted back.

Flo took her cue and sat down too. A minute or two passed in silence and the moment of animosity weakened with the time. The quiet sorted things out for them, acknowledged and underlined their argument. They wouldn't have been able to carry on without it having happened.

Maggie wagged her finger. 'You have courage, Flo, coming back here, I admire you for that. A lesser woman would have run away with her tail between her legs.'

'Well, I want to try and prove you right, Mags. I don't know if I'm any good at it but I need to try. I need to do it for the family.' She paused, not knowing how much to say. 'For me and the kids.'

'Oh? And what about that ruinous husband of yours?'

'I miss you, Mags, and I miss the company. I

346

worked hard and it's not fair that I've been tarred with Fred's brush.'

'Well, that's the way things are, I'm afraid.'

'He knocks me about, you know.'

Maggie's cigarette stopped midway to her mouth.

'And the kids.'

A tiny frown appeared on Maggie's brow.

'He drinks and spends our food money on booze, and he comes home and forces me in bed.'

Flo said it looking directly at Maggie, without flinching, just a statement of fact.

'I've had enough of him, Mags. I've lost myself in his never-ending shit and I want to get myself back.'

Maggie let out a chuckle, which formed into a laugh, her shoulders shaking. 'My husband told me about your sordid little soirée with him.'

'What?'

Maggie studied Flo's face and made a judgement. 'Ha, the bastard, I should have guessed he was lying.'

'What are you talking about?'

'Your husband must really have humiliated him out on that football pitch.'

'He said I...?'

'Yes, are you surprised? I'm not. My husband spends a fortune on prostitutes, and I'm convinced he keeps a flat in town for his various tarts.'

Flo gasped and couldn't help but laugh.

'He knows I'm trapped here, away from society. He has an irritating amount of power over me. He keeps me as a trophy. There's no love, Flo, that went long ago.'

The two women considered one another. Flo saw a reflection of herself in Maggie. She'd never imagined they were the same in so many ways. Both trapped, unhappy, duty-bound to their husbands. Maggie put on a good show, Flo would give her that. A bloody good show. Who would have thought?

'The only nice thing he has done for me in a long time is find this beautiful object.' Maggie stroked the coat and smiled. 'He hunted for it personally in London – it's a *Hartnell*.'

Flo wasn't surprised Mr Monday had lied about buying the coat himself, but she was surprised that Maggie would consider it equal to his treatment of her. Then again, wasn't it the same as Flo's sympathy for Fred? Misguided and self-destructive.

The front door banged. Flo glimpsed the maid trotting to see. Mr Monday, wearing an immaculate tuxedo, filled the sitting-room doorway.

'Well, the Christmas party was a riot,' he bellowed. 'And what do we have here?' He saw Flo and raised his eyebrows. 'A surprise Christmas package? Did Santa drop down the chimney to deliver you?' He roared with laughter, his face shining and red. 'That disastrous husband of yours isn't here, I trust?' He looked around with mock fear, laughing again.

The women stared at him.

'Get me a Scotch, Mags, would you?'

Maggie got up, touched the back of the chair for support and poured him a whisky. He made no attempt to go and get it, but watched her walk unsteadily across the floor to deliver it to him.

'Just how much have you had to drink, my

dear? You've forgotten to put your skirt on.' At that, he snorted and laughed so hard he bent forwards.

'I spilt my drink,' said Maggie, waiting for him to stop. He stood serious for a second, nodding his head slightly as he considered them.

'So, just popped in to say hi?' he asked Flo. He went to the cabinet, took out a cigar, trimmed and lit it.

'Flo would like her job back.' Maggie said it without expression but a bombshell exploded in Flo's gut. Her head jerked from Maggie to Mr Monday and back again.

Mr Monday coughed on his cigar smoke. 'You must be out of your mind. The trouble that family has caused us.'

Maggie stood up in her fur and slip, she held up her chin and tottered over to her husband. She went right up as if to kiss him, pressed herself against his chest and leant in to sniff his neck. She stayed there, then drew back to look up into his face. His eyes were heavy with guilt. Flo strained to hear what Maggie said.

'Did you enjoy the Christmas party, my darling? Did you have your fill?'

His face twitched with indignation. Maggie stepped back, satisfied she had established her side of the bargain.

'Flo has worked hard for this company. She is a loyal worker with great potential and ambition. Letting a woman into the college is progressive and modern, it looks good for us. I think you were right to give her that chance and it's not fair she's tarred with the same brush as her ruinous husband, who we most definitely do not want back here in any shape or form.'

Grateful for Maggie's surprising testimony and impressed with her sudden composure, Flo walked over to join her. She stood next to Maggie, linked arms, felt the luxurious softness of the fur coat against her skin. Maggie turned to smile at her gesture of solidarity but Flo looked Mr Monday in the eye and with her other hand slowly and deliberately stroked Maggie's sleeve.

Mr Monday took an angry puff at his cigar, stared hard at his wife, at Flo's hand on the fur coat. Flo watched him, he was tired and full of drink, he was faced with two women, one knew of his adultery, the other knew of his lies. They were both offering their respective silence. It was a matter of priority, he didn't have a leg to stand on.

'Yes, all right,' he snapped and jabbed his finger at the women. 'But not Fred, understand?' and he strode out of the room.

Flo's very soul leapt up through her body, through the ceiling and into the heavens. She watched Mr Monday leave and stared at the doorway after he'd gone. She wanted to jump up and down, laugh and clap her hands but her brain couldn't take it all in. The thought that she had betrayed her friend momentarily crossed her mind, but she dismissed the thought – her betrayal had been a silent one, it had spared Maggie's dignity, unlike Maggie's recent abandonment of her.

'Celebratory drink?'

Flo turned to watch Maggie at the cocktail cabinet. 'God, yes. Thanks, Mags, thanks a million, I won't let you down.'

'I know you won't. You're a strong lady, Flo, I admire you, I really do.' Maggie tapped her glass against Flo's. 'Now for the sixty-four-thousand-dollar question,' she said. 'Will you leave him?'

Flo paused, her drink halfway to her lips. Her chest tightened with pain.

'Yes, Mags, I will. And will you?'

Maggie nestled her cheek into the fox fur on her shoulder and smiled.

'Oh, I don't know, Flo, I really don't.'

The midwife said they send girls away from their home town because the parents don't want the neighbours to hear about it. December, and I was nearly eight months gone. The train went extra slow because there was still a pea-souper out there. I twisted the metal Woolworths wedding ring on my finger and wished I'd thought to bring some food. I was already hungry and needed a wee. My canvas bag was on the seat opposite. I hadn't brought much, nothing fitted me anyway. I had two college books that Dad hadn't burned. I just wanted to get there and get it over with.

Dad's smoke smelled so nice, I tried to take little sips of the air when he puffed it out. His big legs took up his own seat and some of mine, and I needed all the room I could get. After weeks of telling me to go to a mother's home, he couldn't hide his shock when I'd told him that morning that I would, that he had to take me because I was underage. For a start I hadn't spoken to him properly for a long time. For another thing, maybe he thought I'd want to keep the baby. He was wrong. I agreed with him. The best thing to do was give it up. I gave him the telephone number – Barking 2371 – and he went to the phone box straight away to tell them we were coming. Mum and Babs were at work and Mikey was at school. There was no sense telling Mum, it was up to me, it was my life.

Dad made me wear his pea coat so no one would see my belly. He peered around the carriage and leant sideways to whisper,

'Make sure you're married next time, hear?'

I glanced at him and nodded.

'But don't tell your husband about this, mind you, or he'll think you're funny in the head.'

I looked at my lap.

'I done the decent thing when me and your mum were fifteen, your lad should've too. Just give me his name and I'll do the rest, it's not too late.'

I shook my head without looking at him. He shifted in his seat and clenched his fists.

'You should of tried leeches.' He said it like it was something I'd do, put leeches up myself. 'I told your mother to do that last time but she wouldn't.'

I jerked up my head. 'Last time?'

'No matter,' he mumbled.

What happened to Mum? She must have been expecting and got rid of it somehow. I imagined Mum and Dad doing what me and Skylon did. I heard them sometimes when I couldn't sleep, the bed creaking. Anyway, if she'd gotten rid of hers, she couldn't say anything about me getting rid of mine.

'This'll do the trick anyway,' he said. 'Enough now.'

I looked out the window but couldn't see anything except my own face staring back at me, scared witless. The train stopped but the smog was too thick to tell if we were at the station or not. Soon a guard came along the platform, banging on the doors. Stepping out, it was worse than at home, because it was nearer to London, the smog was yellowy grey and got right in your lungs, made you cough and choke. It was the same station I used for college but Dad didn't know that.

'Number ten bus down Langton Road,' he said, peering into the gloom outside the station. I waddled down the steps and over the road to the bus stop. At least no one from college would see me in that weather.

On the bus, Dad made me climb up the stairs so he could smoke, that was a job when you're eight months gone. 'Here's your stop.'

The conductor gave me a right look, knew where we were headed. The house was big and set back from the road. We walked down the drive and saw a sign near the front porch. *Barking Home for Unmarried Mothers.*

'Looks like a bleeding workhouse, don't it?' Dad looked nervous too when he rang the bell.

A woman in a nurse's uniform answered the door. Looked like she smelled something bad when she laid eyes on me. She raised her eyebrows at Dad.

'Blundell,' he said.

The place smelled of damp and disinfectant, it was old with high ceilings in the hallway and a big curved wooden staircase. There was a fancy nativity scene on a side cabinet. We followed the nurse down a corridor into an office where she waved us into chairs in front of a huge desk. Her seat gave a big sigh when she sat down, our chairs were wooden.

'I'm Matron Lisset. I'm in charge here. Your name please?'

'Jean Blundell.'

'Age?'

'Sixteen.'

'Are you in education or employment?'

I hesitated. Dad couldn't know I was at college, he'd go mad. I shook my head.

'Baby's father's name?'

Dad elbowed me. I shook my head again. The matron eyed me.

'Do you not know the father's name?'

I shook my head and looked at my lap, slipped off the wedding ring that Dad had got me for the journey and put it in the coat pocket.

'She won't tell us.' Dad said it and sucked in his breath, straightening his back to fit all the anger in his body.

'Father's employment?'

I chewed my lip and kept quiet.

'Is the father coloured?'

I looked up at her then and frowned. Shook my head. She made a note in her records and explained to Dad.

'Coloured babies are incredibly difficult to place for adoption.'

'First pregnancy?' She asked Dad that one. He nodded.

'Venereal disease?'

'No,' I said. She gave a smirk like she was pleased she'd got me talking.

'You'll be tested for syphilis in any case, and so will the baby in due course.'

She put down her pen and glared at us for a few seconds until we were twitching in our seats.

'This is a Church of England home for un-married mothers. For the rehabilitation of fallen women. You will stay here until you give birth to your child, then until your child is six weeks old. I take it you wish to have the baby adopted?'

'Yes,' said Dad.

She looked at me and I nodded too.

'Good. You have sinned. It would be selfish to keep an illegitimate child. It will be better off with a proper family, a married couple.'

She waited a minute before she continued.

'We worship the Lord here every morning with church on Sundays. During your confinement you will atone for your sins. Every woman has daily duties to fulfil. You will also give the home your government maternity allowance to help pay for your keep.'

She looked at us as if waiting for questions.

'As you are underage, would Mr Blundell and yourself sign this admission form to indicate that you agree to abide by the rules of the home.'

'Why do I have to stay for six weeks then?' I blurted it out even though she was scary. She sighed through her nose.

'Legal consent for the adoption cannot be given until the infant is six weeks old.' She paused. 'And, it is usually sufficient time to establish whether the infant is deficient in some way, in which case it would be impossible to place for adoption.'

I signed the paper.

'Will you be collecting your daughter at the end of her confinement?'

Dad pursed his lips and shook his head without looking at me.

'Then would you complete this form now. It is the consent to adoption. Miss Blundell will sign it at the six-week mark before she leaves.'

Dad signed the form without looking at it properly. 'Your daughter will need some money to pay for sundries such as nappies for the baby and wool for knitting a layette.'

Dad frowned and rummaged in his pocket, gave me a five-pound note. I took it, surprised that he'd given me so much.

The matron stood up. 'You may bid your father goodbye.'

My stomach flipped and the blood seemed to drain out of my body. I tried to stand up but sat back down quick, I felt like I was gonna faint.

'All right, then. Behave yourself,' he said, standing up and taking his tobacco tin out of his pocket.

Then he was gone.

'Well, did she say anything? Try and think.' Flo peered into Babs's face, waiting for some clue as to why Jeanie was missing. She hadn't come home the night before.

'No, I dunno, you know what she's like, she doesn't even talk to me much nowadays.'

There were tears in Babs's eyes. Flo bit her

fingernail and looked around the room.

'Well, I don't know what to do, she's nearly eight months gone, she shouldn't be out on her own. And it's nearly Christmas.'

'Where is she?' Babs burst into tears. 'What if she gets hurt, or tries to get rid of the baby?'

'She's gone *somewhere*, hasn't she? Driven off by your father no doubt, him slating her all these weeks. I could kill him.'

They heard the street door open and Fred's footsteps on the stairs.

'Oh, talk of the bloody devil.' Flo stood up from the table to face the door.

Fred came in dragging his feet, his head hung down, his fringe in his eyes.

'Where you been then? Out drinking? Jeanie's missing.'

He looked at them with glazed eyes. 'Don't question me, woman.'

Anger bubbled up inside Flo, he was so pissed he could hardly speak.

'I said, *Jeanie's missing*, didn't you hear? Do you know where she's gone or not?'

His body went rigid. Flo never got away with talking to him like that.

'I said, don't question me.' He took her by the shoulders and shoved her aside as though she was just in his way. The force knocked her off her feet on to the floor by the fire. A couple of inches closer and she would have knocked her head on the ceramic surround.

Babs gasped. 'Mum?'

'And you get out, go on OUT.'

Babs yelped and ran for the door.

On the ground, Flo's arm burst into pain. The thought that it might be broken flickered into her thoughts and away again. All she wanted was an answer to her question about Jeanie. He took a step closer to her while she was down, brought his foot back and aimed his boot into her back. A rush of rage overcame her. The coal scuttle and rack of fireplace tools were by her head. She pulled the rack over on its side, grabbed the wrought-iron poker and swung it with all her might on to his leg. It caught his shin bone. He roared and hopped backwards, fell across the armchair and collapsed into the corner, his limbs giving way to the drink.

Flo pushed herself to her feet with her good arm, held the poker aloft and stood over him. She was furious, she wanted an answer to her question.

'You bitch.' Strands of saliva flicked from his mouth. He glanced from her face to the poker, looked as if he'd swing out his legs to bring her down. She clutched the poker even tighter, readied herself.

'Now answer my question. Where's my Jeanie? Where's she gone?'

Fred's face crumpled into wretchedness.

'I don't know where she is.'

Flo dropped her arm; he was too drunk to be lying to her. She threw the poker on to the settee but stood her ground.

'Well, where is she then? She could be in all sorts of trouble. All that stuff you've been spouting, telling her to get rid of the baby.'

'But we don't want a bastard shaming the family.' Fred sat up and wiped his nose on his shirt cuff.

'Why not? We've already got one of those, haven't we?' Flo glared at him. 'What's wrong with you, scaring her like that? Why do you always have to muck things up, Fred? That poor fella next door at Monday's, whatshisname.'

'Percy Thrower?'

'You're laughing already? Mr Ductle, setting fire to his bloody garden, what kind of maniac does that? And that poor West Ham boy. You're out of control, Fred, you're a liability.'

He put his head down, his voice broke as he spoke. 'I dunno, Flo, I can't get back in the docks, Stan won't have me. It's my blood, I'm lost anywhere else.'

'No, Fred, *we're* your blood.' Flo waited, he made no response, it was like talking to a sack of flour. 'You've let us down, Fred.' Flo glared at him. 'I can't help you any more.' She shook her head and swallowed. 'I never could have helped you.'

He stared at his lap, she wanted to slap him for staying quiet.

'And you know what, Fred? My dad died in the war too' – her voice caught in her throat – 'and I still miss him every day, and I know it wasn't the same, but...'

'You don't know what it's like living with those memories.'

'No you're right, I don't, but not everyone who has been through that kind of thing is violent and a drunk. You've got to admit it, Fred.'

Someone banged on the door downstairs and they listened as Mrs Niblett answered it. There were unfamiliar male voices, several people started to come up. Fred swiped his palm over his face and stood to open the bedsitter door.

'Mr Frederick Blundell?'

Flo peered around him, trying to see. There were two policemen and a man in an army uniform.

'Yeah, who's asking?'

'You are under arrest for fraudulent evasion of National Service conscription. You...'

Fred staggered backwards, his face ashen. He stumbled over the settee. Flo darted out of the way.

'No,' he said.

'You must come with us, Mr Blundell,' said one of the policemen, stepping forward into the flat. Fred cast about him, his eyes appealing to Flo for help.

'Get back,' he roared, grabbing the poker from the settee. 'I'm not going with you, get away.'

The three men exchanged a quick glance and rushed forward, they overpowered Fred, took the poker from him and threw it into a corner with a clang. Fred shouted out, twisted to get away. They turned him face down on to the floor, one stood with his boot on Fred's back while another pulled his arms into handcuffs. Fred writhed and cursed. They got him up on his feet and nudged him towards the door.

Flo backed against the wall, her heels shuffling against the skirting board as if she'd go back and back, kicking into the bricks and mortar. Fred whipped around, saw something in her eyes, he opened his mouth, then closed it, and was pushed out of the door and bundled down the stairs.

Dashing to the front window Flo saw the men shove Fred into the back of a police car parked in the street. It drove away, the neighbours and children crowded around, looked after the car and up at Flo at the window. Babs was there too, looking up. Flo craned her neck until the car was out of sight, stayed there in case it came back, until her hands ached from clutching the window frame. She took a deep breath and her stomach untwisted itself, she thought she would float to the ceiling – she put her hands on her head and gaped her disbelief into the room, winced with pain and pulled her arm to her chest.

'What happened?' Babs came back in.

'They took your dad, arrested him.'

'Oh my god, what for?'

'What you crying for? They've taken him to do his National Service, that's all. He should have done it a long time ago.'

'Why, how come?'

Flo shrugged and looked away. 'Dunno.'

But Flo did know. She had kept the piece of paper from the telephone box when she caught Jeanie trying to report Fred. She had run down to the phone box this morning, dialled nought for the operator and asked for the Department of Labour and National Service. Just like that.

'Right, get your coat on, we're going to find that midwife.'

20

'Jeanie? Visitor.'

I dropped a stitch – I wasn't expecting visitors. 'Who is it?'

Pat shrugged. 'Your mum?'

I shuffled to the edge of the bed and pushed myself up. It was Christmas Eve and getting hard to move around, I was like a big hard lump that couldn't bend over. Not that it stopped them making me do hard labour in that god-awful place. The servants' stairs at the back were a death trap when you couldn't see your feet, but the main staircase was only to be used by visitors. When I got down to the rec room I hung back to peer round the doorframe. Yes, it was Mum. Bloody hell. I backed off and went round to Matron's office, tapped on the door.

'Enter.'

'Sorry, Matron, but my mum's here to see me and I don't wanna see her, she'll make me keep the baby and I don't want to, I'm too young and silly to look after it, it's better off with a proper family, like you say.'

All the right things, I hoped. She gave me a curt nod and stood up.

'Can you just tell her I'm all right but tired so I'm having a lie-down. Tell her I'll write to her and that I don't want her to come up here again.'

Matron brushed past me and disappeared into

the rec room. That place, the home, it was a baby farm. She'd rather get her adoption donation than see the baby with its real mother. That's what the other girls reckoned.

After visiting time I went back down. The girls sat around chatting and smoking, and knitting things for their baby boxes.

'Your mum kicked up a right stink earlier, Jeanie.' It was Angie, she'd had her baby a week before and was just out of the lying-in room. 'Shouted at Matron, said she had to let her in to see you.'

'Well, I don't wanna see her.' I should have known Mum wouldn't have gone away without a fuss.

The girls went quiet.

'What was it like then, Angie?' Diane was heavily pregnant like me and trying to look like she wasn't scared.

'You know what, it was all right, I don't even remember it.'

'They drugged you, that's why,' said another girl, Tricia, who had had her baby too. 'That's what happened to me, otherwise I'd remember it, wouldn't I? I woke up in the hospital and they'd taken the baby off to the nursery.'

'Well, mine hurt like hell, but I don't wanna scare you lot, you'll be all right.' Megan smiled at us pregnant ones. We all knitted away, click clack, making a layette for our babies, had to fill up our baby box with clothes and blankets, had to buy three dozen nappies to put in there too. All for when the baby came, and for after, when it was adopted. I'd had to learn how to knit pretty sharpish.

'I feel like I'm getting close to the baby and it hasn't even been born yet,' said Diane, stroking her belly. I knew what she meant, being in the home around all that baby stuff got to you, but you had to be strong and push all that away.

'I can't...' She broke down into sobs. We all looked at each other.

'Keep it then, tell your mum and dad.' It was Pat. Diane smiled through her tears, like for a second she believed it was possible. 'One of the girls changed her mind at the last minute,' said Pat. 'You don't have to sign the form until right at the end.'

'But I know just what they'd say. Go on then, get off and do it by yourself because we're not having the shame on the family.' She put her hands over her face and cried. 'I can't, can I? I've got no choice.'

'No, that's right, we haven't got a choice. They'll put you in the madhouse if you make a fuss,' said Megan. She wasn't smiling any more.

Everyone went quiet. Click, clack.

The next morning was Monday, Christmas Day, it was up at seven as usual, get washed at the sink, go to prayers, have a bit of porridge for breakfast, then start work. I was on floors that day. It was hard enough filling the tin bucket with water and carrying it up those damn back stairs, let alone getting down on my hands and knees at eight months gone to scrub the floors with a brush. My belly hung low. I thought about Mum waiting for me in the rec room the day before. Matron had come up to the dorm after, handed me a letter and

364

a little white cardigan. The letter said she hoped I was all right, that Dad had gone, that she was going back to work at Monday's, that she would write again with a new address. She said her and Babs were worried about me, that they couldn't wait to see me and the baby. She said I wasn't allowed to do anything silly like give the baby up, she'd be really upset if I did that, she said she wanted me to bring the baby home.

I heard a small slosh of water and looked around, thought the bucket had toppled, then realised my dress was wet, and my knickers. My face burned hot, I must have wet myself. Blimey, it wasn't bad enough that I had to go for a wee every five minutes, I was wetting myself too. With a groan I got to my feet and put one hand on the wall, could feel wee running down my leg. I had to get to the dorm quick. A weird pain gripped me from behind, like there were hands squeezing me around my belly from the back. I groaned and faltered. Something was up. I felt panicky, like I needed to get somewhere.

I saw Tricia down the corridor.

'Tricia!' She came running.

'Something's up, I've wet myself and I've got this pain.'

'Your waters have broke, you daft bird, I'll get Matron, wait a minute.'

'But it's not due for another month.' It was too early, it was gonna come out dead. I groaned with the pain, a weird ache that gripped me then let go.

'Just wait a minute,' Trish said and ran off.

Matron came, had a look at me and told Tricia

to get my stuff. They got me down the back stairs and into the hallway to wait for a taxi.

'You'll have to go alone, I don't have the staff to send someone with you. It is Christmas Day, you know.' Matron said it like it was my fault the baby was coming, like it didn't deserve to come on Christmas Day, the day her precious baby Jesus had come. She helped me into the taxi and that was it, I was off to the hospital on my own. I wasn't even due yet, I hadn't finished my baby box or anything. Another pain came, it was all round my back and belly and hurt like hell, I almost couldn't bear it but ground my teeth together. It'd be all right when I got to the hospital.

But when I got there, I had to shuffle in by myself, carrying my bag, try and find out where to go, had to keep stopping because the pain was getting worse, and when I did find the right place it wasn't much better.

'Are you alone?' the nurse asked me.

I nodded. 'Came from the home.'

'The mother and baby home?'

I nodded again, and she pursed her lips, got me along to a bed on a ward. A doctor came to have a look after a while, then they took me off to a dark room and just left me there on my own. I wished Mum was there. The pain got worse and worse, it was like I was in a big vice and the devil was turning it tighter and tighter, and all I could think of was the matron telling me it was penance for my sin. I groaned and just wanted to die. Some people came in, I couldn't make them out, I was half delirious by then, shadowy figures all round the bed, talking to each other but not to me, and I cried out and they told me to be quiet, and then a black mask came down on my face and then nothing.

I woke up in the morning and it hurt like anything down there. My big belly had shrunk down a bit, but was still big so I wondered if the baby was still in there or not. I was in bed on a large ward, beds down each side. Some of the women were holding their babies. A nurse came to have a look at me, peered at the upside-down watch pinned to her bib and took my pulse before she said a word.

'You've been stitched, we had to use forceps, but I shouldn't think you'll feel the stitches when you've been given pills for the afterbirth pain.'

'I need the pills, I can feel it.'

She gave me a look. 'I'll bring Baby for feeding now that you're awake.'

My body jolted with shock and I winced at the pain. She was going to bring the baby. And in a few minutes she was back, carrying a little bundle wrapped in a blanket. She just handed it to me. I looked up at her face, and down at the bundle.

'A boy,' she said.

He was pink and scrunched up, had waxy yellow stuff on his face and in his fair hair. Then he opened his eyes, dark blue they were, and looked at me through little slits and I started to cry. I couldn't stop. The midwife stood by ready to grab the baby because my whole body shook with the force of the sobs that came out of me in waves.

'Now, now, Baby's hungry. Undo your nightdress.'

I couldn't take my eyes off him, he was the most unbelievable thing I had ever seen. A real thing, a tiny person, from me, from inside me. I did what she said, she showed me how to offer him the breast. He wouldn't take it. She rubbed the nipple on his cheek and he turned towards it but wouldn't open his mouth. I looked up at her, distraught, like he would die if he didn't take it. She tried again, put her finger in his mouth, got the nipple in, and he sucked and I felt a tingling in my breast and it was like nothing I could have imagined in the whole world. I was feeding him, with my body. I had grown him, in my body. I lay there with him like that for ages. He stopped feeding and fell asleep nuzzled against my skin. It was like a magic spell.

I stayed in hospital for a day. When it was visiting time and the other women in the ward had their adoring families cooing around them and I was on my own, I didn't care. When the nurses came to attend to me, called me 'Miss' loudly so everyone would know I wasn't married, I didn't care. All I cared about was when they'd bring me the baby so I could feed him.

The next morning they bundled me off in the taxi, me holding the baby in his swaddling. Back at the home, Matron opened the door to me. I gave her a soppy grin and she looked like she wanted to slap my face. In the lying-in room they let me have the baby in a little crib by the bed. Then one of the nurses came and bound my breasts to stop my milk coming. Bound them up tight. I screamed at her that I wanted to feed him myself. She went to fetch the matron who told me off, said how could I have him adopted if he was breast-fed? My chest swelled and burned, I cried out from the pain, and had to feed him with a bottle of formula that they brought to the room while milk seeped through the bandages and soaked my nightie.

I stayed in there for four days, stayed awake to see the new year in. Heard people banging pots and pans out in the street and drunk shouting. 1960 – it wasn't the fifties any more. When my stitches had healed a bit they got me out of the room, took the baby to the nursery with all the other babies and sent me back to work. I had to carry buckets of coal down to the cellar when I was still bleeding from the birth.

'It's not right,' I said to one of the nurses. 'I'll bleed to death.'

'You should have thought about that, shouldn't you?' she said.

From then on I woke up at five thirty in the morning to give the baby his first feed in the nursery.

'Change his nappy, Miss Blundell, and back to work,' the matron would say. I even looked forward to washing his nappies in the laundry room, just to do something for him. Soon it was five weeks left, then four. We'd all count down, then one of the girls would go quiet and cry because it was her last day with her baby, but no one would say anything because that's how it was.

Two weeks left, and I'd knitted so many clothes for him I'd filled up the baby box. I just wanted everything perfect so he wouldn't be without. Matron said we could write a letter for the baby to open when he was grown up. But I couldn't do it. It was like, if I wrote that letter that would mean he was gone, like he was dead, and I couldn't stand it.

One week left and the social worker came. I was called into Matron's office.

'Hello, Jean, I'm the church moral welfare worker. I'm here to talk to you about the baby.'

I couldn't speak.

'I understand your father has given consent for the baby to be adopted?'

I nodded and looked at my lap.

'And you will sign the consent form next week when the time comes to give the baby to the new couple?'

I just sat there.

'Miss Blundell? You do understand that, as a minor, you would need parental consent to be able to keep the baby? And that bringing an illegitimate child up yourself would be, shall we say, less than ideal?'

I nodded.

'To have the baby adopted is the best thing for Baby and the best thing for you, don't you see?'

The social worker and Matron stared at me.

'You'll say goodbye to the baby and give him his things, I'll take him to his new family, then you'll never see the baby again.' She said it breezily, as if she was telling me how to make pancakes. 'Then you can get on with your life as if nothing had ever happened.' She smiled.

'You do understand, Miss Blundell?' Matron glared.

I nodded and they sent me back to work.

'Mikey. Elbows off.'

Flo, Babs and Mikey sat at the table eating their tea. They were back on the Monday estate. Maggie had somehow persuaded Mr Monday to give them a house, what with Fred gone. Fate had it that they were back on their old road, Queen Elizabeth Avenue. Not number thirty-eight, but number seventy-two, just down the road from Lil and Ted. Flo didn't have her Frigidaire and Mikey hated not having a television set but she couldn't get things on hire purchase without a husband's signature.

The main thing was she was back in the college, she had to start another year as she'd missed so much, and they were already talking about the exam at the end when every student had to make a pair of shoes from scratch. Job-wise, she was relieved Mr Monday didn't want her as his secretary; he put her in the offices to work part-time in the typing pool. She'd sit at the desk in a room with seven other typists, young women hoping to snare a professional husband, perhaps take dictation for an up-and-coming manager. Talking was forbidden and the thunderous rattle of tapping keys became a comfort to her, she used it as time to think about the training course.

It was hard to believe that Fred had gone and wouldn't be around to mess things up for them. She was no longer tiptoeing through life for fear of upsetting him. She was going to grab her new freedom and dance around with it, stamp and shout and wave her arms. No more tiptoeing. When she looked back she saw herself stiffen when the door

371

opened, flinch when the bedsprings compressed. She saw herself begging the grocer to give her more credit and patching the patches on Mikey's trousers. It was someone else, not her, it was someone who had learned to live with fear and couldn't see through it. It took some getting used to, being the only one responsible for the house and the kids, but every day she felt stronger. She thought about Jeanie all the time and wrote to her once a week. She told her that Queen Elizabeth was expecting too, told her that bringing the baby home was the right thing to do, told her they would cope together.

One letter had come back. Jeanie said she was all right and didn't feel much like writing or having visitors. She said she'd do the right thing, that it was good that her dad wouldn't be there telling her she was shaming the family when she came home. Flo kept the box room for the baby, had done it up with some lovely wallpaper, and bought a little cot second-hand to surprise Jeanie. And it wouldn't be long. The matron had told Flo the due date. Maggie said Jeanie could live there too as long as she didn't work at the factory. So far Flo had got by with telling neighbours that Jeanie was staying at an aunt's house. Unspoken nods of understanding usually followed, but she didn't talk to anyone about it, even Lil.

'So, you going to the dance tonight?'

Babs frowned and tutted. 'No, I don't feel like it.'

Maggie had allowed them to move back to the estate, had supported Flo in her college course and job, but Maggie's refusal to let Babs see her son was the only thing neither of them discussed. It was too much to admit that even though the Blundells were good enough for the factory, they still weren't good enough for the Mondays. Some things never really change. Flo had asked her about Monday's so-called classless community but Maggie made excuses. Babs was devastated.

The doorbell rang.

'Get that, love, it's probably Doreen with the Pools.'

'I need the bog,' Babs called out and disappeared into the bathroom.

Flo tutted. 'Lazy cow.' She got up from the table chewing her last mouthful of bread and butter and opened the front door. Her legs nearly gave way.

'Jean?'

Jeanie stood on the doorstep with her canvas bag.

'Oh my god, what's happened?' Flo grabbed her daughter in an embrace, tried to feel Jeanie's stomach against her own, looked over Jeanie's shoulder for a pram or something, out to the road to see if there was a car parked there.

'What's happened?' She pulled Jeanie into the house, sat her down on the sofa, knelt in front of her. When Jeanie's face crumpled, Flo panicked, shook her by the shoulders. 'Please Jean, tell me.'

'I left him, Mum.' Jeanie heaved for breath, she could barely speak.

'What? The baby? No. Oh, no.'

'I left him.' Jeanie shook her head, her face pulled and wretched.

'What do you mean, you left him?' It was Babs,

back from the bathroom, she was crying for her sister even before she knew what had happened. At the table, Mikey gawped, a piece of bread halfway to his mouth.

They waited for Jeanie to get the words out, all of them staring at her.

'I had him adopted like they told me to, like Dad told me to.'

'Well sod your dad,' Flo cried. 'Sod him. Let's go, let's go and get the baby, we want it back.'

'We can't.' Jeanie dissolved into tears again. 'He's gone. I signed the paper.'

'But that's not legal, surely?' Flo looked up at Babs who stood over them both, her face sheet white. 'You're not old enough.' Flo searched her daughter's face.

'Dad signed it too.'

Flo let out a wail of despair. It was her grand-child, her blood. Gone.

21

'How you doing, love?'

Mum asked me that every day, and I didn't really mind. A couple of weeks after I got back from the home, I started to feel a bit better, stopped crying all the time. A few weeks had gone by and I don't know why, but I spoke to Mum instead of just nodding.

'I'm all right, thanks.'

Mum stopped still, came and sat down on the

sofa next to me and put her arm around my shoulders. It was nice, I'll admit that. Dad was gone, we weren't always on edge about him coming in pissed, wondering who was gonna get a hiding next.

Mum kissed my head and stayed quiet for a minute. We hadn't talked properly in a long time.

'Have you thought about what you're gonna do now?'

I nodded. I knew what I wanted to do.

'College.'

She drew back to look at my face. 'College eh? What for?'

'To get my A levels.'

'A levels?'

'I need to get them if I want to go university.'

Mum jolted, her mouth opened but she didn't speak at first.

'I didn't know you wanted to go to university.'

'You don't know a lot of things about me.' I stopped, didn't want to have a row.

'Well, tell me then. I don't even know why you haven't been talking to me all this time. It's like you hate me and I don't know what I've done.'

Oh god, she started crying then and so did I.

'You made me go sec mod, that's why.'

'What?'

'I passed my eleven plus, didn't I?'

'What? Yeah, you did, but...'

'But what? That was my ticket to a good school where I could have got all my O levels and A levels, somewhere you learn proper stuff not just childcare and cleaning.'

'But it was better for you and Babs to go to the

375

same school.'

'Better for who? Babs is thick as pig shit.'

Mum sat back, thinking about it for the first time.

'Jeanie, is that why you haven't spoken to your dad and me in all that time?'

I nodded and tried not to cry.

'You ruined my life, made me work in a grocer's and a factory. I wanna learn medicine, I wanna be a doctor.' Mum laughed and then stopped herself.

'A doctor, Jeanie? Love, I don't think you're really–'

'Really what? *You* don't know.'

She just stared at me. I took a deep breath. 'I've been going to a college. Secretly.'

'You what?' She pulled her chin back with a look on her face like I'd murdered someone.

'Started studying for my A levels at a college in Barking, went up there once a week on the train and bus. But had to stop it when ... you know ... and now I'm ready to start it again.'

'Blimey, love, that's bloody sneaky.'

'What was I supposed to do? Roll over and die making boxes in a factory cellar?'

Mum paused and frowned, this was all new, it must have been hard to believe how little she knew me. 'The factory's not so bad, it's all right for me and Babs anyway.'

'Yeah, and you wanna do well, you're studying too, you should know how I feel.'

'Yes, you're right, you are.'

Mum lit a cigarette and stared at me while she smoked.

'I'm sorry, love, I didn't know, and Babs didn't say anything.'

'Well, you know about it now, and you know how much it means to me...'

She frowned and went pale, forgot to blow her smoke out, it curled from her nose in wisps and darted out with her words. 'You mean, the baby. Good god, Jeanie. Is that why, the baby?'

I nodded. 'And don't think I don't know about you getting rid of a baby, Dad told me.'

'That's none of your business,' she snapped, 'what I have to do, what I had to put up with from your dad.'

'Yeah, it is my business, because I had to do the same thing for my own reasons.'

A pause. We looked at each other, and all of a sudden I was grown up and a woman, and Mum knew it.

22

The end-of-year exam wasn't timed but they were expected to get on with it sharpish. Flo tied on a leather apron and stood at the clicking machine. The first time she had been there she'd butchered Ted's thumb. She put it out of her mind and placed the shaped cutting knives on to the leather. The brief: make a pair of men's working shoes, 'Hardies', from the basic material. Cut, close, last, stitch and finish. Flo blew a strand of hair out of her eyes and reached up to pull down the clamp.

It was lovely to get your letter, Carl, sorry it's been a while since I wrote. Thanks for asking after Jeanie. It's funny, you're the only person I've told about it, seeing as you knew Jeanie was expecting and all. I'll be honest, it sickened me to think of her walking away from her baby like that, but it taught me a lot about my daughter, the sacrifice she made. I got her into the local grammar sixth form (I hadn't heard of sixth form before that!). She's been doing her A levels, full time this time, and she cycles there, instead of getting a train and bus all the way to Barking. Remember that funny motorcycle you had? Clapped out old thing, I bet you've got a nice car now?

It sounds brilliant working out there, I still dream of doing that one day. Did I mention I changed my course for home management instead of overseas, so I can be here for Jeanie while she does her college? She wants to go to university and be a doctor, I don't know about that, but I said to Jeanie – life's too short and too hard to not take chances.

I've finished the year at college and guess what? I passed the exams! Even the end bit when we all had to make a pair of men's shoes doing all the operations ourselves. You should've seen me on closing and stitching! That pair of shoes aren't half bad. They're on my mantelpiece at home now, and I can't help but smile every time I look at them. They were my ticket to a management job in the factory. Florence Blundell, Glove Factory Floor Manager, I bet you can't believe it, I can hardly believe it myself. I've got my own office and everything, and I love it, even though I still get gyp about Fred and the football.

Flo glanced up at the pair of men's shoes on the mantelpiece and smiled, thought about Carl working out in Ceylon. If things had happened differently, who knows? But she was still married, after all. She got a letter from Fred, he was banged up in Wandsworth, had refused to do his National Service. More fool him. He'd never shake off his parents' ghosts. He didn't know it was her who had shopped him, and she'd never say. Tabby told Flo she'd get a lawyer for her, see if they could arrange a divorce. Flo hated to think of it and in the back of her mind knew she'd see Fred again one day.

She and Maggie stayed good friends and Maggie said she had great respect for Flo leaving Fred but it never seemed the right time to ask Maggie why she stayed with Mr Monday. Maggie said that Flo looked different, dressed differently, said something about Maslow's hierarchy of needs and Flo's self-esteem. Flo wondered if Maslow ever said how hard it would be, how much a person might lose as well as gain. Flo Blundell's hierarchy of needs – perhaps she was nearly at the top, she'd forgotten what that was called, but it wasn't the star on the Christmas tree, more like the flag on the mountain.

Maggie threw a young wives club party for her. For the first woman manager at the factory. What a night.

When I told Mum I'd got a place at the University of London, she had to sit down. That's when I knew she never really believed I could do it. But she was there for me, I'll give her that. I was the

379

only secondary modern girl to go to university that year. That's quite something.

Poor Babs, she pined for James for ages, talked about how they'd had their wedding all planned out, and the honeymoon in Bournemouth. He was sent away to finish his A levels but I saw him once when I started at the sixth form. Turns out they did really love each other. I couldn't have been more wrong about my own twin sister. She was just a nice girl all along, not some cheap tart like I thought. They wrote to each other for a while then James's letters stopped coming. Babs would be all right, she was courting one of the factory lads now, she'd have her own house and family before long.

I think about my little one every day – I wonder where he is, what he looks like. He didn't deserve being given up like that. The day before he went, Matron called me into her office.

'Tomorrow the new couple shall come for the baby,' she told me.

I bit my lip and nodded but my nose started to run.

'You'd better go and get the baby's box packed up.' She tutted. 'Where's your handkerchief?'

The next day they let me get him ready.

'Come on, James,' I whispered, lifting him out of his cot. They'd probably change his name, I knew that. I bathed him slowly, making it last, washed his little body and dried him in a new fluffy towel and kissed him all over. I dressed him in the clothes I'd knitted and the cardigan Mum had made.

'Come on, Miss Blundell, put him in the cot and go to the dorm.'

I kissed him goodbye and put my face into his neck to breathe in his baby smell. I almost couldn't bear to do it, take my hands off him for the last time. When I put him down into the cot I bent over to tuck him in but Matron pulled my arm.

'Let him go now.'

She said it sternly and gestured to one of the nurses standing by, who pulled me away. They sent me upstairs to the dorm, told the other girls to leave me be. I sat on my bed crying and biting my nails, imagined Matron handing James over to a couple of smiling strangers. I thought about the letter I wrote for him and put into his little box. *I love you,* it said, *and I'm sorry. I'll find you one day, you'll see.*

The publishers hope that this book has given you enjoyable reading. Large Print Books are especially designed to be as easy to see and hold as possible. If you wish a complete list of our books please ask at your local library or write directly to:

Magna Large Print Books
Magna House, Long Preston,
Skipton, North Yorkshire.
BD23 4ND

This Large Print Book for the partially sighted, who cannot read normal print, is published under the auspices of

THE ULVERSCROFT FOUNDATION

THE ULVERSCROFT FOUNDATION

... we hope that you have enjoyed this Large Print Book. Please think for a moment about those people who have worse eyesight problems than you ... and are unable to even read or enjoy Large Print, without great difficulty.

You can help them by sending a donation, large or small to:

**The Ulverscroft Foundation,
1, The Green, Bradgate Road,
Anstey, Leicestershire, LE7 7FU,
England.**
or request a copy of our brochure for more details.

The Foundation will use all your help to assist those people who are handicapped by various sight problems and need special attention.

Thank you very much for your help.